THE CALL TO ARMS—

"The Mist of Melusine"—As York and Lancaster fought the battle that would determine a nation's future, she bargained for her husband's victory with a power that might demand more than she could give....

"Eye of Flame"—From the misuse of power, she had lost everything to the Tatar invaders. Could she now find the courage to set things right?

"Phaistides"—Haunted by her father's restless ghost, would she find the peace they both sought on the battlefield at Troy?

These are just a few of the wondrous women you'll meet in this inspiring and inspired volume—women ready to defend family, homeland, and the goddesses themselves....

WARRIOR ENCHANTRESSES

WARRIOR ENCHANTRESSES

Edited by
Kathleen M. Massie-Ferch
and Martin H. Greenberg

DAW BOOKS, INC.
DONALD A. WOLLHEIM, FOUNDER
375 Hudson Street, New York, NY 10014

ELIZABETH R. WOLLHEIM
SHEILA E. GILBERT
PUBLISHERS

First Printing, April 1996
1 2 3 4 5 6 7 8 9

ACKNOWLEDGMENTS

CONTENTS

INTRODUCTION

Though all of us know war veterans, few of us have really seen battle. Our experiences are limited to stories told by relatives or friends, or through books and films. Yet it seems that throughout history humans have had an obsession with war. It appears we just can't get along very well with our neighbors. Most wars seem to originate from the basic problem: "*You* have something *I* want." This coveted object might be an essential commodity such as food, water, or mineral resources, or maybe just a simple trinket. Perhaps *I* would trade *you* for it, but *I* have nothing *you* want.

At other times war's triggering event might be lost in a series of apparently disconnected events. Examine the beginnings of World War I and you will understand what I mean.

The amount of time war has occupied humanity throughout history is enormous—if not in active combat, then in the contemplation, planning of strategies, or plotting of revenge. The artifacts of war hold our attention whether it is a Samurai sword or a World War II war bird. Artistic scenes depicting war decorate all forms of objects from ancient Egyptian pottery to medieval tapestries to modern abstract canvases. And we cannot leave out the time consumed by grieving and the picking up of the pieces afterward. Few cultures were spared this activity. Sometimes it seems so much time was spent in the pursuit of war that I wonder how anything else was ever accomplished.

Many advances were achieved as a result of war. The nomads needed to cross the Eurasian Steppe and thus developed the stirrup. The Romans needed to move troops and so they built highways across the landscape. Who among us does not find castles intriguing? Yet castles were built to protect the land's people from invaders or those seeking revenge.

So men, usually young men, go tramping off to war. A few cultures allowed their women to fight; most did not. Much of my adolescence was influenced by war—in particular the Vietnam War and the fighting in Northern Ireland. The battles were brought right into my living room each night. The tally of dead and wounded, displayed in black and white, increased each week. I remember cousins going off to war. I can still see the tears of aunts (mothers), uncles (fathers) and cousins (wives and sisters). The women I knew stayed behind. And that is perhaps one of the most difficult aspects of war—staying home.

So why *Warrior Enchantresses*? Because those who were left behind—name a war, any war—often seemed the most desperate. If the war was lost, women became part of the spoils to be divided up. The women had vital interests in who won, but often had little or no say in how that victory was obtained. Over the course of history it is not unreasonable to believe a few strong women got involved, and refused to just go along. Some women had no choice; they were thrust into power by war's constant companion: death. Other women claimed they answered God's call, again name the god or goddess. The deity's name may change, but the concept reaches through time and across many cultures. Still other women truly chose to take up weapons. Thus women such as Boudicca and

Joan of Arc come down to us from the pages of the past. To me this seemed fertile ground for storytelling.

During the period of the Old Kingdom of Ancient Egypt (4000–3300 BCE) there was no regular or standing army. If soldiers were needed they were called up by their local governor to serve the Pharaoh. But by the time of the New Kingdom (1700–1100 BCE) soldiering was an honorable profession. Of course, by this time Egypt had been invaded a number of times and even occupied by foreign governments. Which Pharaoh wouldn't want to keep an army at the ready? Apparently being a soldier was very attractive. From the New Kingdom a text has survived that discusses how to convince an unwilling student to become a scribe. This lesson was probably repeatedly copied by the student. The purpose was twofold: to teach the students their hieroglyphs and to convince them of their chosen career. Many professions are listed such as sentry, baker, and pot maker. And for each career one or two lines is given on why to avoid this profession. But for the soldier the text goes on for several long paragraphs telling how awful the soldier's life will be and that the soldier will suffer in death as in life. *Never* choose the life of a solider is the emphatic lesson!

In this collection of stories, we have reached back through time and sampled the lives of women who made choices. These are stories woven around anger and fear; love and hate; and death and survival. You will find tales of quiet heroism and tales of power for power's sake. You will not find stories about Amazons clad in leather or bronze bikinis out of some comic strip. But rather you will find tales about women who faced their challenges and dealt with them their own way. Often the only way their culture would allow.

The other aspect of the title is Enchantresses. Magic or enchantment was as much a part of daily life, for many cultures, as obtaining food. Magic was vital to making the rains or floods come on time, or keeping them at bay until after the harvest. A forest fire might be evil magic sent as a punishment or be part of war. If you believed that the specific prayers said each morning by the priests or priestesses brought the sun back, would you fail to say those prayers each day? Would you take the chance?

In our Western culture, most people believe there is only one god; a god who is all powerful. *We* do not believe that this great power has any connection to magic whatsoever; it just is. Other cultures, past or present, might view this belief with amusement. Because *we* believe something is holy, does that make it free of sorcery or magic? And, conversely, because something involves enchantment, is it automatically unholy or evil? Perhaps not. As a famous physicist once said, it all depends on your frame of reference.

A delicate blend of history and enchantment is addressed in each story presented in this anthology. These stories are not meant to replace history books, but to breathe life into past cultures and historic women who refused to be left behind, who chose to take up a weapon and fight for their beliefs and way of life. But remember, there are as many different weapons from which to choose as there are women who choose.

I would like to thank Marty Greenberg for taking on this project and for his advice. And I thank my husband and friend, Thomas Ferch, for doing all that yard work by himself so I could put this anthology together, and for being there.

—Kathleen M. Massie-Ferch
August 1995

THE WORLD WELL LOST
by Tanith Lee

There are some battles in which the participant's actions
defy logic, either in historic times or modern. No matter how
we study the battle or search the subject's psychology, their
rationale defies us. These actions are usually blamed on
misinformation or treachery. But what if these actions are
deliberate? How does that change our view of these
people?

The following story is about the events leading up to one
of the more puzzling defeats in history—a tale nearly every
American knows—and it is by the award-winning author,
Tanith Lee, who is best known for her wonderful adult and
juvenile heroic fantasy stories. She has published over forty
novels and several short story collections. Her short fiction
appears in numerous anthologies including *Ancient Enchantresses* and *Sisters in Fantasy*.

The world was flat, and the sun had fallen behind
it, into earth and sea, leaving only a strand of coral
red. High above, the supernatural sow had birthed the
stars, which glided one by one into the evening sky
and lay there glittering. Below, was the city, fabulous
with less than three hundred years of youth. And upon
a height of that city, a woman, who stood as if all
things, city, sky, stars, world, hung loosely from her
slender hands inside a silver net.

More than a month ago, the star, Sothis, had
brought the Nights of Tears, and the River had risen.

From inland now came the swampy reek of fertility
occasioned by water, and mingled with the open fragrance of the sea. While out of the city of Alexandria,
the smokes of fires and lamps, the cloy of spices and
fried fish, the blue aroma of the lotus, the smell of
human life ascended. Standing away from shore, the
Pharos craned in the sea, and its beacon light blazed up.
The windows of the city, too, were revealing their amber
eyes, and at the land's edge, on the great temple-tomb of
Alexandros, who had conquered the world, the yellow
watch fire perched like a soul upon a white brow.

She looked at these things, the woman, slowly, as if
she had newly entered Alexandria. Even she looked
into the sky as if never before had she seen the stars.

A man, a servant, had come up the stair and crossed
the palace roof. He bowed to the woman in the Greek
manner. In Greek, the speech of the palace, he said,
"Queen, the magus is waiting below."

"Yes," she said. She glanced at him. And the servant went away.

A lamp upon the wall had caught her now. She was
not young, nearing her fortieth year, but she was royal,
the daughter of a line of famous kings, as her name
itself displayed: Kleopatra. Alexandros himself had
probably been her distant partial kin, and his beauty
was legendary, as hers also had become.

Her hair was long, black, and curling, her eyes of a
darkness some declared to be blue, as had been the
eyes of Queen Tiy, though Kleopatra was a Greek,
and if any Egyptian blood had twined with her own,
it was in secret.

Yet Greek Alexandros had fallen deeply in love
with the East, and Kleopatra, descendant of his half
brother, Ptolemais, perhaps was in love, too, with the
land of Khem. Though her clothing was in the Greek
style, yet it had the filmy simplicity of Egypt, and the
jewels that burned on her arms had once graced the

arms of Pharaohs' wives. Around her forehead was a
golden snake, the Creature of the Black Land's spirit,
and under her throat lay a scarab of emerald, the most
potent amulet in Khemic magic.

From some distance across the courts of the palace
there came a burst of male laughter. Kleopatra inclined her head. Her eyes were opaque and unread-
able. She might have been attending—briefly—to the
noise of unknown strangers. But she knew very well
where the sound originated, the first of many outcries,
at the supper party of her lover. There in a frescoed
room, he and his officers reclined on their couches,
and Egyptian girls danced bare-breasted as flowers.
The red Roman wine would flow and the brown Egyptian beer. They would eat, and tell each other, hearts
growing high, how they would defeat their enemies
and straddle the earth, as it had always been their
destiny to do. And perhaps, tonight, he would come
to her bed, Kleopatra's lover. And though the un-
guents of slaves might linger on him, she would give
him her body, and hold him in her arms. And if he
woke to evil dreams, she would console him. She
would praise his valor and his warrior skills, remind
him how she had loved him at sight when he had first
visited Khem, a soldier with the forces of Rome, and
had not even seen her. He would sleep against her,
and as the dawn came up over the city and the water,
she would see the lines of gray in his bright hair.
Drunk, he might snore a little. Yet, smoothed by
sleep, he was like a boy, more like a boy than she had
seen him in his youth. Although she had borne him
a son and a daughter, Antonius was now her child.
Incestuous as the rulers of Old Egypt, they lay together in their bed of love. She was his mother. She
held him protectively and fast as only the nurses had
held the two sons of her flesh.

Had Julius been this way also? Julius, who had been

a Caesar, the only king the Romans would acknowledge—and in the end, not even that. Julius had
seemed like a father to her—if again, an incestuous
father, as Antonius was her incestuous son. But ulti-
mately Julius, too, had been reduced. Unnerved,
afraid when shut into the country of the mind—
thought, or dream. Despite being more clever than
Antonius, and probably more brave, he, too, had lain
tremulously upon her breast. He, too, had grown up
to be her child. And his son, the small son of Julius,
had in comparison seemed so bold as he stood, the
gilded wooden sword upraised, his head thrown back,
defiant, eager. But the very young are often courageous. They do not know yet what there is to fear, or
how it will feel, the sword entering the heart. Julius
had learned, the shadow and the reality. And Antonius? Must he learn the truth of this lesson?

Kleopatra looked once more across the heights of
the city, its Grecian places. She saw the library which,
through Julius' fault, had burned, where now Antonius' gift of some two hundred thousand scrolls had
made token amends. An irony, for Julius Caesar had
been a great reader, had even written some history
himself, and Antonius did not much care for books.

Kleopatra turned toward the stair.

She, the mother, old, for there were crones in the
streets of her city who were only four or five years her
senior, was yet brave as any warrior child. However, a
child who knew of pain and danger, who knew how
the sword might hurt. Her bravery did not come from
ignorance, but from pride. And now, in the lamplight
as she passed, her dark eyes flashed as had the light
of the lighthouse, the Pharos, a wonder of the world.
And there *was* blue in them.

They said she had been brought to Caesar, smug-
gled into his presence rolled in a carpet, but this story

was not true. It was an invention of the city, which set great store by storytellers. The effect was anyway the same, for when he saw her face, with its long lioness' nose, its large eyes, and her body, boyish then and very slim, Caesar had taken the side of Kleopatra.

True, however, was the tale of the fabulous ship, by means of which she had gone to seek Antonius later, after his demand that she come to him, and her countering announcement that she would not leave the ground of Egypt. Of course, the ship was made of Egyptian materials, it was Egypt still. She duly refused to leave it, and seduced by its sails and veils of Tyrian purple and scarlet, its breathings of myrrh, and the sight of half-naked girls above the richly golden-plated oars, Antonius had walked down, barbered and handsome, laughing and gracious, to Kleopatra's supper. She received him dressed as Aphrodite, the love goddess of Greece, her hair loose and thick with flowers, her gown transparent. Alexandria said she doctored his wine that night with aphrodisiacs, but she needed nothing but her own tawny skin, the scent of her hair, her eyes, and lips. Just like Julius Caesar, Marcus Antonius would have been happy enough to have cast her out, or killed her. Instead he, too, sank beneath her spell. To men she could do this. She could bring them low, both in her bed and in her power. And now it seemed to her that by conquering them, she took away their might. She left them hollow. After this, they died.

She had descended seven groups of stairs, and was now in the red-dark under her palace. Lamps on bronze chains hung glowing down the walls, and pausing, she heard the lap of water. Cisterns ran beneath Alexandria, enough to sustain the city against a year of siege. She heard their music.

Rome, that enormous giant birthed by a she-wolf, threatened Egypt now, again. And the enemy, Octavianus, was drawing closer by the day, like old age. He longed to murder Antonius, for several personal festering reasons. And Kleopatra also he would be rid of. She had come this way before. Yet the magus, divining the nature of the new male enemy, Octavianus, had told her this was a man of stone. She could not move him as a woman. Instead, she must meet him as a warrior. She and Antonius together. Destroy Octavianus, and their world, the world of Egypt, and perhaps of love, would go on.

Kleopatra thought of the song the girl had fluted to her lyre on the hot terrace, at noon. It was an Egyptian song. *O, my Brother, when I see you, it is like sunlight falling on my garden. O, my Brother, how long before I am one with you?*

There had been the smell of the crimson roses the Persians had brought into Egypt. But Kleopatra had thought of the gathering of their two fleets, the Roman ships of Antonius, her lord, her "Brother," and her own fleet, Eastern vessels trimmed with blue and gold. She would sail with him, aboard her own flagship. She would wear the war-crown of the Pharaohs. And in the prow, incense would burn, to Roman Mars and Egyptian Mut.

Over and over she had said to Antonius, "I love you." It was like the refrain of the song the girl had sung.

I love him. We must be strong. And we must win.

But *she* must be strong, she the warrior, for both.

And tonight, as Antonius lay eating and drinking, and the dancing girls rippled before him, she, Kleopatra, had come down into the secret cistern, the empty cistern that had no water.

The wall was a blank of granite. This she touched with her finger, and a slab slid up. The chamber beyond was wide and rounded, massed with shadows, at the center of which rested, like a gem upon a black lake, the altar fire.

Behind her, the slab slipped down.

Like two beings of the Afterlife, the True Life, two girls came to Kleopatra. They were her handmaidens, the Greek, Kharmion, and the Persian, Irash. She knew them very well, yet now they seemed changed, and pale with awe. They undid the clasps of her dress, loosed the girdle, and stepped back, as the garment fell, leaving her naked in the shining darkness.

Before they had entered her service they had been trained, these two young women, in different ways, Kharmion with strictures and rewards, and Irash cruelly with the whip. Now they were perfect servants, who believed that they loved her, Kleopatra the Queen, because she was beautiful and powerful and did not hurt them, and because, through her, their lives had become better. Was love only ever this?

Kharmion, the more free, drew breath to whisper, and Kleopatra turned to her, and frowned. Kharmion bit back her lips. There must obtain, at first, silence. For this was to be *heka,* the magic of Khem.

And now her women drew away, and naked, clothed in her ornaments and her body, Kleopatra stepped forward toward the blacker darkness and the jewel of light. Despite her years and though she had borne three children, she was lovely and moved with composite grace. Life had been cruel, yet honorably so. It had not given her disease or obesity, it had only robbed her of some nameless thing that might be fulfillment.

She reached the altar, a table of smoothest stone, reflective, like water. And beyond the flame that burned there, she saw the three priests who were eunuchs, in their white kilts, and before them, the magus, naked as she was, a thin tall man with a shaven head.

"Who is here?" said the magician. He spoke in

Egyptian, a tongue that, of all the Ptolemies, Kleopatra had learned early and fluently.

"Kleopatra."

"And who is Kleopatra?"

"Of the line of Alexandros. Queen of Khem by the grace of all the gods."

"What then does the Queen wish?"

"Victory over enemies, for herself and for her lord, Marcus Antonius, known also here by the name Helios, the sun."

"Have you observed the rituals, O Queen?"

"I have."

"From this moment, to the dying of the fire, all that is said is real."

The magus lifted his head. He stretched out his hand, and in it appeared a black serpent, twisting and hissing, which slowly straightened out into a long stiff stick of ebony, the wand of magic.

Kleopatra said, "I entreat the Godhead, in Its manifestation as Isis, Queen of Heaven and Earth, and Aphrodite of the Greeks."

The magus said, "And I invoke the Lord Ousir, King of the Western Lands, and Re, who is Life, and Sutekh, Prince of the Delta, the Mouths of Ocean."

The wand took on a flame at its tip and the fire on the alter burned very red.

One of the eunuchs approached, carrying a white kid. It had been garlanded, and drugged with a sweet wine, so it was lifted onto the altar without protest. The man held it gently, soothing it, and cut the vein in its throat. The kid seemed to feel nothing, and fell asleep, after which it was laid down, and its blood ran out in scarlet ink.

The magus lifted his arms, on the underside of which were peculiar marks normally hidden. He spoke in silence to the gods.

Kleopatra stood waiting, patient, poised, her eyes

wide and bright in the firelight. Ousir was Osiris, and
Re was Jupiter-Amon, and Sutekh was Typhon or Set,
in whose earthly province Alexandria stood. As a
Queen, she had a right to gods. She did not fear them,
nor anything that was to come. Only human things
had ever made her afraid, and this she had never
shown, and now scarcely acknowledged.

A cloud formed above the flames and the blood. It
was rosy, somber. Lightning wove in and out of it.

Kleopatra raised her hands, the palms outward, and
she spoke the words of the magic prayer which she
had learned, while bathing and fasting for three days—
telling Antonius all the time that she menstruated and
must be private, which was of course a falsehood.

Between death and death, between life and life,
Here upon the river of the world,
I am.

She heard her own voice, the words clear as pieces
of crystal, and on her wrists smoldered the corals and
pearls and turquoise and the rich blue faience work,
as if on the wrists of a doll.

She thought, *Am I so small, then, floating between*
earth and heaven, adrift upon my life? What need in
that case to trouble or to fight? What need to ask for
anything. Let me be still. Let me glide quietly down the
stream toward the sea of Night.

But her voice went on.

"Great Isis, who is Eset, the Star standing upon the
boat of the moon. Great Ousir-Osiris, who is the
Green Reed sprung from the black soil. Hear me. Oh,
hear me now."

Beyond the naked magus and his three assistants,
Kleopatra dimly saw, perhaps fashioned only from the
smoke, seven veiled women, each crowned with the

crescent moon, with aprons of stars—the Fates of Egypt.

She had known her fate since childhood, but had forgotten it. She could not die, Kleopatra, so they had told her, the gods. Yet she herself had killed, in order to be safe, and not only in war. Her sister, her brother. . . . Was not death always the price of death?

The magus cast powder into the altar fire, and the flames opened and spread wide. Kleopatra looked down, as if from the height of a mountain, and beheld a dark blue sea, and here ships lay, small as shards of wood, but large in numbers, winged with their sails like insects. Some were on fire, sinking. She saw the glitter of their tiny oars and beaked rams, the shooting stars that burst from their ballistas. It was the battle to come.

And still she spoke the prayer, she spoke it above the battle, and from her mouth now the magus plucked the words, which sparkled and took form in the dark and luminous air: A golden fish—the destroying sword, the silver birds of victory.

Like a feather in her brain Kleopatra heard the supernatural reply. It was delivered, ironically, in Greek. *Take what you wish. It shall be yours.*

Kleopatra stepped back. She said, "I will have made a temple, a temple of this victory. *Qenu*—the Victorious Prize. It shall rival the Pharos, and the tomb of my Ancestor. It, too, shall be a wonder of the world." She spoke in Egyptian, politely.

She touched the green emerald amulet on her breast and it was scalding hot, possibly had even scorched her.

The vision faded in the fire, and instead, across the upper atmosphere a huge shrouded form seemed to move, and she heard the sistrum, the holy belled instrument of Isis and Hathor.

"I, a Queen, shall be your slave in Eternity," she said.

But she did not mean it, nor did she expect the gods of Egypt to think that she did. It was her courtesy.

The magus laid down the ebony wand, which, meeting the altar, became again a black snake. Kleopatra reached out, and lifting the snake, put it against her breast. It quested, as she remembered her children had done, although she had not given them her milk, that had come from the breasts of their nurses. Then the snake lapsed, and was only a length of black Persian silk.

The fire had gone out. The chamber was hugely still and terribly hot. Sweat laved the body of the Queen, and fell in big droplets like rare rain from the body of the magus. Kleopatra felt a dullness and a deep weakness, like the curious empty despair that had followed the birth of Antonius' two children. But now she had birthed the spell. It had worked through her. It existed, shimmering on the tablet of Destiny, as the words had done in the dark. *Victory.*

Kharmion came and drew a robe across Kleopatra's shoulders. But Irash hung back a little, fearful, pleased with fear, not wanting to be part of it, only to admire.

She lay looking at a Shesp, or Sphinx, of silver, the more precious metal, that crouched on a stand of alabaster beside her couch. The sphinxes of Egypt were not riddle-makers, dangerous teases, nor were they women, like the sphinxes of the Greeks.

Kleopatra lay supine, her hair spread round her and down across the silks, her ankles were together, her arms at her sides. She might lie this way in death, but that was far off.

She had bathed, been oiled and perfumed, been dressed in the byssos of Egypt. She had eaten some fruit and bread, and drunk a little of the pink wine of the South. Somewhere music played, very softly. She felt her city sleeping, breathing. How still, this night. Despite the preparation for war, no agitation. Even the elephants stabled below were mute.

The inert quiet of achievement was on her. She had done all she could. The gods had blessed her, listened, and would aid her. The rest was simple, a show of bellicosity, of royalty. And that more subtle thing, the murmur to her lover, Antonius, to reassure him. All would be well.

How empty she felt—again, how like the days after her labor. Her body freed of children, toil and pain over. Everything done. And—what now?

For a moment she slept, or lost her consciousness, for a moment she swung from the stars. And then, opening her eyes, she saw the lamps had burned very low, and she knew that he had come into her rooms, unchallenged, naturally, for he was her husband and her king.

Turning her head upon the cushion, she looked out into the brighter room, beyond the curtain, and seemed to see him there. Antonius.

How handsome he had been. And if some of that blaze had lessened, so it must, with the years. Yet she could recall how she had looked into his eyes there on that ship that was Egypt, at Tarshish, she dressed as Aphrodite, and he beautiful as Roman Mars, with his golden hair and tanned body, his aroma of masculine health and strength. Looking into those eyes of Antonius, she had seen her own reflection. Had there been more? Surely there had been more.

How still the night, how strange . . . not a sound. Even the music faded away, even the faint audible flutter of the lamp-flames lost. But now, she could detect the notes of water, as if in the cistern—it must be some trick of the ears, as sometimes she might think she heard the sea in this room, although she had not heard the sea from her palace since her thirtieth year.

She called his name. "Antonius."

He shadow-passed across the curtain, and for a second she smiled, quite tenderly, as if it had been her child. And then she sat upright and reached for the little knife that waited inside her jeweled belt. For it was not Antonius. Too tall, too large—too different.

"I am here, my love," said Kleopatra, winningly, waiting now, like the knife, to kill. She had experienced this minute often in her youth, the assassin, the imposter, the poisoned cup, the snake in the basket of figs.

The curtain billowed and an enormous light poured through. It was like a sunrise flowering from the center of midnight. Her grip on the dagger faltered. And then, he was seated by her, there on the couch. She let the dagger go. She could do nothing.

Kleopatra, Queen of Egypt, goddess on earth. She knew this was no man. Nothing human. This was a god.

She said, in an Egyptian which, she assumed, was now not old enough, "Shall I obeise myself, my lord? Or do you see, I have already done so."

She had said something like this to Julius Caesar: *Shall I bow to you, or can you see the homage in my eyes?* That had been a lie. But this—was not a lie.

He spoke very softly. Why not, when, if he wished, his voice could shake down the whole of Alexandria?

"You need do nothing, Kleopatra. You need only be."

So she lay there, and looked up at him.

It was true, he had the form of a man. He would be capable of any form. Had he done this from kindness? But he was taller than any man she had seen, and built to a greater scale. He was the color of alabaster, white—yet a living, glowing white, like a lamp with fire inside it. And then, again, she knew he could be black as ebony. His hair was very long, thick as the hair in a king's ceremonial wig, the bronzy red of polished copper. His eyes—there could be no mistake—were blue as the Nile in sunlight, or the farther sea. She had heard of his coloring. She knew him.

Foolishly, however, as if she had not lived to maturity and grown wise, she tried to compare him with men. Although his beauty was like agony, she tried to think that he was only beautiful. And the scent of him she compared to perfumes and to wine. Then, because she had never been a fool, she threw all that away.

"Have I angered you?" she said. She knew she had not. He would not have come to her in this guise if she had. He had put on his best—but no, of course not. The god Zeus had come to Semele in his best— and it had been so wonderful she had flared up in flame and died. This was not, unbearably, the best at all. Simply what she could withstand.

And he smiled, for, obviously, he knew what she thought.

"Sutekh," she said, giving him properly his Khemic name. "Prince of the Delta. God, Essence of God."

"I have seen you," he said. He leaned toward her, and at his nearness, her blood flamed if not her flesh. She trembled as if she had only been thirteen. She longed for him to touch her, but she was not thirteen, and she guessed that he would not.

"You will see all things and everyone," said Kleopatra.

"But you," he said. "There is not often one like you."

He breathed on her then. In this breath were spring and summer, stars and flames, and the desert. She could have lived on his breath. She wished she might lie on the red land of the desert, and taste his breath that was the desert wind.

"No," he said, "better than that. You can come to me, if you want."

"How could I want anything else?"

"You have asked for life. For yourself and for your lord, the Roman man."

Kleopatra pared her mind of thought. She lay looking up into his eyes, which were now the blue of all evenings, and starred.

"Do you deny me victory?" she asked.

"You can have this life, if you wish," said Sutekh, Set, Master of the Delta, brother of Osiris, murderer and hunter, the red-haired god. "You were promised success and may have it. You, and your Antonius. Win there in the sea, at that place called Actium. And come home to Egypt with your lord, and rule from Alexandria all the world. And he will love you till death."

"For that I asked," she said.

"Or," said Sutekh, and now he lowered his eyes, charmingly, sly, like a mortal, perhaps he had learned the fascination of the gesture, "or you can be mine."

"Your slave," she said, "which would be great honor."

"My wife," said the god. "I will make you my Nephthys."

He spoke—in Greek—of his goddess-sister.

"She was faithless to you," said Kleopatra sharply, recklessly.

"So she was, but with gods, these things . . . are otherwise. Know this, she is an enchantress, as you are."

"Why such glory for me?"

"There is seldom one like you."

The notes of water from the cisterns had faded, and again, after nine years, Kleopatra heard the thrumming of the sea.

She said, "I must believe this a game."

But looking up at him, she saw to his golden heart, he was a god, transparent to her as she to him. He need hide nothing.

She considered for an instant that it might be some ploy, even some *heka* spell sent against *her,* or some malediction of the Romans. Then she said, "If I remain loyal to my human lover, you will punish me and make me die."

"No, I shall only lose interest in you."

Kleopatra closed her eyes. She knew the worth of her vulnerability. She knew that even he—evidently— was not immune to it.

He said, "Go with Antonius to fight. You have asked for victory and can have it. Only, Greek Kleopatra, watch him in the battle. Look at him. See how he is. You can live long with him, you can grow old with him. If you wish. Or come to me, in Eternity."

"I must stay with him," she said. She looked at Set. "Of course."

"But if you change your mind," he said, "you must give me a sign."

"What sign?"

"A vital one. A sign that the world will remember."

He put out his hand, then, slowly. On his fingers were rings such as ancient Pharaohs had worn. Perhaps those had been a copy of these. They gleamed like the eyes of snakes and lions. He placed his palm under her throat, where the amulet of emerald had been. Her soul rose through her body, and for a moment she was in the air, winged, knowing how it would be, to be his, and a goddess.

"Kleopatra, you need not even take your life. I can draw you out, your gorgeous soul, and leave your pretty body behind you, your pretty, pretty body, which is nothing to your exquisite soul. No knife, no poison. It will be easy."

"But the sign," she said again.

"In the midst of that battle," the god said. "Abandon *him*."

"But he is a child," she said.

"All you have had are children," said the god.

He had lifted off his hand. But she seemed still to lie up in the sky. His eyes were blue stars. He, her husband. *Greater* than she. She could be lost in him. *Found* in him.

As if through a spangled golden mist she saw the Greek girl called Little Delight—Kharmion—standing at the end of the couch. Then the goldenness melted. No one, nothing was there, but for the mortal girl, the lamplight, the night.

"He will not be coming to you, Queen," said Kharmion. She spoke of Antonius, doubtless drunk, as before, and in other arms.

Kleopatra rose and left the couch. She went to one of the wide window places, and here she remained, staring out across her city to the sea.

Kharmion, like a ghost, moved softly through the rooms, and stole away.

What now? Well, it had only been a dream.

Kleopatra smiled again, now not knowing that she did so. Dreams, she could still recollect, were sometimes better than life.

She had struggled all her days in her bright mail against the onslaught of everything. But in the battle she might lay down her blade. Yes, she would look at him, her Antonius, as she rode her ship, and he rode his, commander and lord. She would look at him and see, whether or not he was worth her further and exhausting effort, her warrior's sword, her enchantress' spells. Or if Set, eternity or oblivion, fulfillment or silence, immortal love—or utter death—was better.

AUÔUR THE DEEPMINDED
by Andre Norton

Here follows the true adventures of an Icelandic sorceress' search. This courageous woman appears in many sagas, but was never given her own story until now. Many places in Iceland are named for her and her search, though little is known about her outside her chosen homeland. There are many quiet heroines like Auôur in history. They do what needs to be done. So often historic accounts focus on the glitz. Remembering the less flashy people brings us closer to reality and our past.

Andre Norton is an award-winning author who has written over one hundred novels and countless short stories, both in science fiction and fantasy. She edited the popular *Cat-fantastic* anthologies with Martin H. Greenberg. Her short stories appear in numerous anthologies including *Ancient Enchantresses, Sisters in Fantasy,* and *Grails: Quests, Visitations and Other Occurrences.*

Outside the wind was dank with what seemed an ever-present rain. Auôur did not try to pull the folds of her heavy cloak any tighter about her—the thick wool seemed to seep up the damp even though she had not been any closer to the day without than this narrow window. There was a hoarse call from behind her; it sounded twice before it drew her attention.

Three ravens bobbed and sidled along their home perch, and seeing that they now had her attention, their harsh voices rose to a scream. She turned to face them squarely, holding out the scarred wooden bowl into which they dipped bills in turn, small drops of blood flung aside by the jerking of the strips of raw mutton she provided. Odin's birds—and these were hatchlings of hatchlings of hatchlings—going far back in the past to when her father, Ketill Flatnose, had beached his longboat on the shore of the Irish and set out to reap the harvests and riches of those unfortunate enough to lie in the pathway of his force.

But he had been a prudent man, as well as a fine wielder of a battle ax, and in the end he had made a truce with one of his own countrymen who had done very well for himself—Olafur—so mighty a warlord that he had named himself king.

She had been twelve years old that summer, though sturdy enough that she had taken to far faring as well as any lad eager to win his war name. So she had made no complaint when her father sealed his bargain by giving her as wife to Olafur. She had a man to whom people pointed in pride and he was lucky in his riving until at last his enemies (and those were of his own kind) cut him down. She had been in the great hall with her lusty babe of a son, Thorstein, on her knee when they brought her the news.

Only she had already known that ill hung over them, for it was born in her mother's clan to foreknow and sometimes even farknow.

Thorstein. Now she twirled the bowl so that the last greedy raven could strip it bare. Thorstein. Though she was his mother, she had always known there was a lack in him. He was not quite the bearsacker he wished—to rush into battle uncaring for anything but bringing death to the enemy. Though he had sworn blood oaths against those he held his father's death givers and made them good. She had warnings that he could not hold the land his father had taken, nor survive the bloody path he followed.

But she had done her duty. He had been handfasted at fourteen to Heild, who came from proper stock and at least he had not been backward in bed. Five daughters he had sired between raidings and at last a son. Then his last Viking raid had taken him to the land of the Scots and he had returned full of tales of rich land to bundle them all off across the sea, only to himself die before the second snow encased the wild land.

Now— Auôur turned once more to the window slit. Now it was she who must uphold the honor of the house, but she was sick of constant fighting and only four months ago she had learned that MacMann planned to wipe them out.

How many fighting men would answer *her* war horn? She smiled grimly. More thralls (who must not be allowed weapons) than men who could swing them to a good purpose. Still there was a sureness in her that their line would not end here. Ah, no! Had she not sacrificed the fine horse which was part of Thorstein's last looting? Its smoking blood surely had drawn Odin's one all-knowing eye.

And to Freya she had also given her finest treasures, those broad gold bands of bracelets which Olafur had made her as first morning gifts. No, she was as certain that the gods would favor her plan as she was that she lived, breathed, and stood where she did at that moment.

The messages from overseas—the new lands waiting for any bold enough to claim them. With no ancient blood feuds to cut down family lines. Two of her brothers had ventured there and prospered—could she do less?

Yet the going, as she well knew, would not be easy. It must be done with secrecy since MacMann would be watching. From this vantage point she could see the screen of forest within which her thralls labored under the watchful and knowledgeable eye of Thorfin Shipmaker. A ship grew into shape there among the very trees from which it was being wrought.

There was a stir behind her and one of the ravens screeched.

"Maudlen? What is it?" She was always able to recognize the step of any of the household.

"Janor sends a message—MacMann rides!"

Almost Auôur held her breath. "How does he ride?" She schooled her voice to be even.

"Toward the Demon's Hill." There was breathless fear in her eldest granddaughter's voice.

Auôur swung around. "So. Send me the Saxon wench!"

"You would—" The fear in Maudlen's voice was ever stronger.

"What matters with you, girl? This is none of your concern. Get me Wulfra."

When the old thrall sidled around the edge of the doorway, her eyes were downcast, but Auôur knew well what red lights held in their depths.

"MacMann goes to the demons."

"So, mistress?" There was a shadow of insolence in the other's answer.

"So, MacMann is of the new faith and yet he seeks the demons. Think you what would he do with your old bones if he took us. Have you such a liking for fire to curl in you?"

"You have powers, mistress."

"I have powers, yes—it is in the blood of my mother's line. But power joined to power is even greater. Serve me well, Wulfra. You will no longer be a thrall, but have a snug seat by the fire and a girl to wait on you."

Now those eyes with their red sparks caught hers. And suddenly the thrall nodded.

"Truth you speak. What is in your mind, mistress?"

Auôur drew a deep breath. "Three days we need and then, even though it be a time of storms, we shall take to the sea. Already they load the carts to go by night and provision the ship."

Wulfra had gone to stand before the ravens, her gray head on one side. Her lips moved and uttered a cry so like those of an angry bird that Auôur could tell no difference.

The largest of the ravens bent forward on his perch so that his sharp bill struck at the old woman. Then he took wing, went out of the window, and was gone.

Wulfra now made a sound like a snicker. "A hard ride for MacMann, mistress. He'll not forget it for a time."

From the watchers who had ringed the holding came the news. A bird out of nowhere—one of Odin's own sacred flock—had flung him to the ground and those who followed him had borne him, cursing loudly, away.

Two mornings later Auôur went through the deserted great hall. Yes, they had carefully followed instructions and taken the carved pillars of the high seat. If all went as she hoped, those would be her guide to a new life. She was tired of living always with death near beside her—a new land where there was freedom for the just—

The ship was crowded. They had had to leave behind the sadly needed sheep and cattle. But they were free and driving down the bay when the steerman, Halgar Cunnersson, pointed out moving dots on the shore. MacMann had no ship in these waters, he had not thought of their escaping so.

Within two days they had near doubled their company—taking over a well-set fishing boat—the men manning her letting fall their few weapons when they saw the determination of the Northmen and one of the ravens flew down to their mast to sign it so as Odin's gift. They were returned to their duties under guard, and Auôur was pleased that her *Storm Beaker* was the less crowded.

It was long, that voyage, and they weathered seas which would have turned their ships end for end had not Freya, the ever merciful, answered to the pleas of those two aboard who were of the power. Auôur the Deepminded they had called her from childhood, and now she was to prove that as she never had been before.

First they raised the Orkneys and were guested by a lord of kin to Olafur. However, still in Auôur was the need to go on. But she made a good marriage for Maudlen, who was ever sick on the sea, and took on supplies.

Beyond were seas even less known, yet there were isles to be found—the Faroes—and once again they sheltered for some months, working on their ships. Here the second of her granddaughters was hand-fasted to a man of good name and well-worked land. But Auôur and Wulfra went to the highest point of the land, circled about by the ravens. And those flew seaward for a space, so she knew her farseeing was right—she had not yet discovered what she would have.

Only, once more asea, they found bitter going. Twice at a distance they saw mountains of ice move on the waters as if those were also ships. And each third day Auôur sent forth the ravens, but always they returned. Sometimes she moved along the crowded ship to lay hand on the carven supports of the high seat and wondered if they would ever be loosed into the sea to guide them to land. She called her grandson to her—he was still only a lad with not even full strength in his sword arm—but he listened as she spoke and nodded, understanding well that full duty must be paid to the gods.

Then at last there came a morning when the rime of frost lay like a blanket over the ships. And the ravens went forth—not together but singly in slightly different directions. That one who had been the centermost of the three did not return. There were cries of excitement then and two of the younger and more agile men made their way to the bow of the *Storm Beaker* and there detached the carefully wrought serpent head, for all knew that if a ship approached land in peace, not for raiding, such a menacing promise must not arouse the demons of the country ahead who should be offered due rights.

On the ship went with the oarsmen at labor now and then out of the sea arose a dark hump of shadow, while out of the sky dropped Odin's bird to perch with his mates.

Once more Auôur pushed to the side of the high chair posts, and with her she brought Thorgimmur, her grandson, her hand upon his shoulder. She gave him a nudge forward so that he could reach the salt encrusted ropes which held them safe. He struggled with the knots until, though his fingers were bleeding, he had accomplished the task. But he had not the strength to hurl them overboard as the ritual demanded and two of the oarsmen sent them into the sea, but not before the boy had laid the hand of possession upon them.

So did they come at last into the harbor of this strange land which had pulled Auôur's farsight for so long. Here they would set up their hall and prosper, that the blood of two strong lines would know many years.

Though her brethren sent for her and offered land and shelter, she took only the latter until she could set out once more, with some of her household. Inward they roved, ever marveling at a land walled with ice and yet offering springs of hot water, sea worn heights, and cliffs above fields of black lava.

In the end Auôur found her homestead, striking the end of her staff into a patch of soil. Within a year there came from her younger brother a party of thralls carrying with them the wave-beaten pillars of the high seat, and she knew then that the gods had served her well.

OF THE DEATHS OF KINGS
by Melanie Rawn

Some of our earliest tales have been preserved in the classical myths. Myths tell us about the *old ways,* and are generally grounded in some historic event. Yet there comes a time when the old ways flow into new. This change can be sudden, due to conquest or natural disaster. But when the change is slow, and we suddenly find ourselves drowning in a world no longer under our control, how do we stay afloat? How do we salvage as much of the past as we dare? And do we dare? Or do we just accept the future?

This next story spins together several tales from classical Greek mythology and leaves us with a fresh look at the distant past. Melanie Rawn is a gifted writer who has enchanted fantasy readers with her *Dragon Prince* and *Dragon Star* trilogies. She has also written a *Quantum Leap* novel, *Knights of the Morningstar*. Her latest series begins with *Exiles I: The Ruins of Ambrai*. She has a fantasy collaboration, *The Golden Key,* with Jennifer Roberson and Kate Elliott. Melanie also has short stories in *Ancient Enchantresses* and *Return to Avalon*.

In the last generation before the River Skamandros flowed crimson with the blood of Achilles son of Thetis and Hektor son of Hekuba, there dwelled along the shores of the Myrtoan Sea the Lady Elatë, her daughter Kainis, and their clan of the greater clan of the Lapithai. Kainis was bright and beautiful of face, and swift and strong of limb, and the joy of her mother and her people from Mount Ossa to Mount Pelion.

This land, called Magnesia, stretched along the sea like the arms of a priestess praising the Great Goddess, and the people led their lives according to the rituals of the sea. They harvested the sea as other folk harvested the land, and sailed their trim boats in trade and friendship to the near islands of Skiathos and Ikos, and to other places. They lived and they died to the rhythm of the storms and calms of the sea, and with every changing of the Great Year, the sea roared like a bull to signal that their king's fate was at hand.

Now, in some places the fate of the king was to be taken to the high cliffs where the rocks and the deep water waited for him below. In others, the king was taken to the rocky beach and put into a boat and pushed into the lapping waves. In still others, the king rode in his chariot along the shore, pulled by fine thundering horses, until the wax linchpin melted and the harness came asunder and the chariot crashed and he died, far behind the free-running horses.

But along the shores of the Myrtoan Sea, at the changing of the Great Year the king was given fine clothes and a feast, and at the end of this, with wine singing in his head, he lay upon a bed made of lovely shells and purple cloth, and was covered as he slept with offerings of the needles and branches and logs of the fir tree, and in this way he gently died. And when he was dead, he was burned so that his blood and flesh turned to ash that spread with the wind across land and sea, impregnating each with the next harvests. A sand-colored cuckoo carried his soul to the Great Lady, and in the next year every child born was carefully watched for signs of future kingship, for it is well-known that the cuckoo is the bird that lays its eggs in the nests of other birds, for them to raise up into the rainbird sacred to the Great Lady.

It so happened that one day in late winter that was the last of a Great Year, while the Lady Elatë was still living and thus was the Goddess on the land beside the Myrtoan Sea, the priestly youth chosen as her next king wondered why he should serve an older woman when the daughter was so young and appealing. Surely, he reasoned, youth should mate with youth, be honored with youth, and rule with youth. And so on the night in spring when the old king was dead and the new king would have gone to the Lady Elatë, he went instead to her daughter Kainis.

Strong and nimble as she was from the hunt, she was no match for the stealth of his approach and the suddenness of his seizing. Kainis was taken and violated and when he was finished, the young priest stood up from her bed and righted his rich ceremonial clothing.

"I have heard," he said, "that in other places, it is the king who chooses his queen, and that the sacred marriage is forever, not only for the Great Year."

Kainis, drawing her torn nightclothes and her long black hair around her in her tumbled bed, stared at him in silent loathing.

"Further," he went on, "that it is a marriage not of the queen-as-Goddess with the king-as-Her-Son, but of the Great Lady and the Father of Gods Himself."

"You see yourself as Zeus?" Kainis exclaimed.

"Of course not!" He sat on an ivory tripod stool, elbows on knees, as if he were a schoolmate discussing philosophy rather than the man who had just raped her. "I am a priest of Poseidon Earthshaker. We along the Myrtoan shore are sea-folk, and it is His part I humbly take as His Son, just as you are the Daughter of the Goddess."

"And so?" she asked, knowing what he would say but wishing to hear the blasphemy from his own lips.

Schoolmaster now, not fellow student, he answered,

smiling: "If I play the part of the God's Son in our marriage, then surely I cannot be given in death to the Goddess as a mere son of hers must be."

"And so?" she asked once again. There was more; she had heard it before and scorned it before, but now it sat in her bedchamber, all blithe confident arrogance.

"It follows, naturally, that my sons, as sons of Poseidon, must be kings."

"To rule after you," Kainis murmured. "I see."

Taking this for agreement, he rose and stepped toward her across the sea-blue, sea-green tiles of the floor.

Kainis lifted one hand in a warding. "You speak Achaioi sacrilege, and you have done Achaioi profanation. You deserve to die for what you have spoken and done. But you are the king. For another eight turnings of the sun-wheel, you are the king. Therefore I cannot kill you. But neither will you be *my* king. You are my mother's, and you will go to her now and say nothing of what you have done here tonight."

He laughed. "And how will you stop me from speaking? Once word of this is known, she will have to relinquish her position to you. She is old; you are young. *I* am young. The people need youth to lead them. Youth and strength we both have aplenty. It is right and fitting that we should rule, Kainis."

"You will have your kingship and your Great Year, but you will never again have me. Go to my mother, perform your sacred duty to her. But know this: no man will ever again do to me what you just did."

Now he frowned. "You will take up the place of the Goddess, and I will do as I please."

"No," replied Kainis, and reached for her hunting knife. The youth stood back from her, for there was that in her eyes that made him fear that she meant to kill him after all.

"Leave me," she commanded. "Say nothing—or, if you speak, spend your kingship wondering what form of accident will befall you at any moment of the day or night."

"Kainis—! You would not dare defile the sacred king—"

"As *you* would not dare defile *me?*"

She ran her thumb delicately along the edge of her knife, smearing a thin line of blood to stain its sharp shining bronze. The young priest saw the blood on the blade, and on her thumb, and on the tumbled linen of her bed, and he fled her room, bare feet slapping on the sea-blue, sea-green tiles.

Kainis did not watch him go. After a time, rising and dressing herself in seemly clothes, she crept from her mother's palace and walked with long strides to the shore. She waded deep into the sea, to wash herself in waters claimed these several years past by Poseidon—waters long ago named Myrtoan, which means the waters of the Goddess. Raising her hands and her knife high toward the moon, she breathed a prayer of anger and sorrow and fear and, finally, supplication.

When a cloud shadowed the shining face of the moon, she had her answer.

Standing waist-deep in the waves, with the bloodied blade she slowly hacked off her long black hair. In those curling tresses was power, and she felt it drain from her body with every stroke of the knife. Woman's power—which had not prevented a man who believed himself the son of a god from raping her. But she would never suffer such violation again.

She watched in the darkness as her thick black locks floated out to sea, and to the shadowed moon she whispered. "My mother has no daughter. I am not Kainis. She is no more."

And, so saying, she covered her face with her hands

as the clouds had covered the face of the moon, and wept.

Thus did the young woman Kainis become the young man Kainios. When she was seen the next day, her black hair shorn like a man's, her lithe body dressed in men's clothing, all the people cried aloud in wonderment. To those bold enough to dare question, she explained that Poseidon, in the fashion of the Achaioi gods, had come to her the night before and ravished her, and then in apology (which was more than Zeus or Apollo was ever reported to have done) offered her any love-gift she pleased.

"It pleased me," said Kainios, "to become a man. And so I bathed last night in the sea, and emerged as you see me now."

Some few were skeptical enough to whisper that if Kainis had truly become Kainios, everyone would know the truth or falsity of it the first time she stood to relieve herself. But those who revered Poseidon cuffed these people on the head, and within the day the priests of the god were warning against such disbelief, calling it sacrilege. Kainis had become Kainios, and no one was to question the marvel wrought by the god.

But to Elatë, in private, Kainios said, "It is true I was raped last night. In my despair I lamented my womanhood that allowed this to happen. The Great Lady gave me a sign by darkening Her shining face. Thus I choose to live henceforth not as a woman, but as a man."

"But who has done this to you?" cried the heartsick mother. "Who dared touch you?"

"He claimed himself a son of Poseidon, acting in the god's stead."

"Tell me his name!"

"I cannot. Believe me, Mother, I truly cannot."

And no matter how her mother commanded and pleaded, Kainios would not give the name, for she could not allow her mother to kill the sacred king before his time came to die.

At last the Lady Elatë believed that she would never learn the name, and began to weep. "But what of my daughter? What of her?"

"You have no daughter. You now have a son—to rule after you, as will be the case from now on in every land."

"Not this land!" cried Elatë.

Kainios took her mother's hands in her own. "You have heard the tales from all over, how the gods of men make them arrogant and bold, and demand war as proof of worth. It has been increasingly thus for generations. Few are the places now that adhere truly to the old ways. As a woman, as a queen, under the new ways I would not rule as you rule. I would be subject to a king, who would call himself the son of a god. Our marriage would be sacred only because he with his godly lineage made it so. This is the future, Mother, this is how things will be. And I cannot bear to live that way."

"And so now I have a son, not a daughter," said the Lady Elatë. "Who will rule as a king."

"Who must prove himself as a warrior, in the new ways, before he can become a king. You named me well, Mother," Kainios added, "for I am to walk a path that is new. Thus it is that I must leave you, and our home, and win myself renown in the only way men understand and respect. When I have done so, I will return and become king."

Elatë turned away from Kainios, fists raised to the sky. After a moment she swung back around and embraced Kainios, whispering, "Do this. Become a man, and a king. If you have to, make for yourself a beard, as they say the queens of Aigyptos do when they rule alone. But you must do one thing for me, Kai–Kai-nios—" When her tongue stumbled slightly over the new name, she spoke it again more firmly. "Kainios. You must give me another daughter to replace Kainis. Your own daughter. While you fight beside the men, I will teach her all the old ways *and* the new, so that she will take her rightful place without having to take a king who will give our land to his sons. Do this, Kainios. For the one who was the mother of Kainis."

"And is yet the mother of Kainios," she whispered. "for I am still and always will be your child. You shall have *my* child, Mother, and within the year."

The Lady Elatë caught her breath, and Kainios nod-ded confirmation to the question in her mother's eyes, for she knew, as a woman always knows from the cycle of the moon that is the cycle of her bleeding, that the previous night must bear fruit.

So Kainios left her mother's palace by the shores of the Goddess' own sea, and the tale of the transformation preceded her wherever she went. She was accorded that wonderment and respect given those touched by a god. Her secret was kept—for the one time that a man attempted to ravish her and prove her still female, she killed him with a single thrust of her knife in his very loins. She hefted his body over her shoulder, still bleeding, and dumped him onto the steps of a Temple of Poseidon, where the priests gladly burned him as a heretic where he lay, without so much as touching his corpse lest they defile their god-consecrated hands.

The young woman Kainis had been an accomplished hunter with knife and spear. It was no difficult thing to turn those skills to the killing of men instead of animals. The young man Kainios thus waged war with great success for five moons. Then, one night in Thes-salia, because her growing belly would soon betray her, she vanished from her host's palace without word to anyone. From Thessalia she went to a tiny village on a tiny island far from her home, and there lived quietly as a woman, awaiting the birth.

During this time she lived also in great turmoil of spirit. Her body was a woman's body, not a man's. Below her heart was the firm swell of a child, and in her heart was eager tenderness for it. When she bathed in the river with the other women, she saw that she was like them in the making of their flesh. When she sat with them, spinning and weaving, while others of them sang verses and played the lyre, and discussing the cares of the village and the larger world, she knew she was like them in the manner of their thought and feeling. When she participated in the festivals and the rituals, dancing lightly despite her bulk, she felt again the woman's power that had come back to her along with the growing of her hair and the growing of the child in her womb. And when her time came and she labored in birthing, she cried out in pain and triumph as women had always done.

And yet within her was the surety that she could not live as a woman in this new world where to be a woman was to submit to a man, to all men. She had taken the Great Lady's shadowing of her moon-face to mean that she must shadow her own womanhood, and live now as a man. But during the months of bearing and birthing and nursing, Kainios became Kainis again. She cherished this time, for she knew she would never know again what it was to live as a woman.

The child was a daughter, and Kainis named her Koronis. The villagers shook their heads when they heard her name her child, for the black-winged crow is the bird of the Great Lady as Giver of Death. Kainios merely shrugged, for the crow is also the bird that brings the future—death being the future of all living things.

When Koronis was old enough to travel, and Kainis

had shed the soft curves of motherhood, one night she vanished from the village after leaving costly presents behind her in thanks. Once again she cut off her long hair, and donned men's clothing, and took up her spear and bow and sword.

She returned to the Lady Elatë's palace and presented her daughter to the people. No one enquired after the woman who had birthed Koronis. They were all too awestruck that a man who had been born a woman had sired a child, and Koronis was viewed as the daughter of the god's living miracle that was Kainios.

But some wise people were torn, as all lands were torn in those generations. A king could protect them and their crops and herds from the ravages of their neighbors, a thing that had rarely been necessary before; but only a queen could protect them and their crops and herds from the ravages of drought and flood, a thing that was eternally necessary. The warrior king gave security against other men; the sacred queen gave security against famine. Which was the more important? Which should be done the greater honor? By which ways should the people live? No one could decide—for what good if the Great Lady gave of Her bounty in plentiful crops, but there was no son of a god bearing spear and sword to drive off those who would plunder or burn that bounty?

The Lady Elatë, hearing of the people's distress as she always heard of everything, spoke a few words in useful places. Soon it was being said, with great relief, that in Kainios the people had their warrior, and in Elatë—and, in time, Koronis—they had their queen. So the trouble in their minds was resolved for the immediate future.

"And quite the warrior Kainios has become," said Elatë, dandling little Koronis on her knees. "Did you know that he's been as far as the Argolid in his slaughters? And this only in the last six months!"

"But I've been nowhere," Kainios responded in confusion. "Not since my fifth moon of bearing!"

"Does that matter to a clever singer who knows a good story when he hears it?" her mother asked dryly. "Oh yes, you've been all over, sword flashing and spear flying and knife glinting and bowstring singing. The priests of Poseidon think you the most wonderful thing since the discovery of fish in the sea!"

Kainios looked at her mother, stricken. "So . . . so even if I wanted to. . . ."

"Just so, my child. Even if you bared your breasts in public, walked stark naked from Ilium to Ithaka, or brought a child into the world with a thousand priests watching, you could not resume a woman's life now."

After a grim and rebellious moment, Kainios bent her head. "So be it."

Leaving her daughter behind in Elatë's care, she rode out once more to other countries, and the renown of Kainios grew from simple song to epic poetry on the lips of the bards.

One summer's day she had just finished butchering a clan of cattle thieves when, during the feast given by the grateful clan she had served, she heard about the Kalydonian Boar.

This monstrous animal—sworn to be five times the size of any other boar, with tusks as thick as gateposts and twice as long as two javelins laid end-to-end—had been slaughtering people and cattle in the lands of King Oeneos of Kalydon. All the bravest fighters of all lands were invited to hunt down the great beast, with the promise that whoever killed it would be entitled to the pelt and tusks.

When Kainios heard this, she nodded slowly, and

from the set expression on her face everyone at the feast knew—or thought they knew—what was in the great warrior's mind. Mighty Kainios would join in this hunt, and win the pelt and tusks, to the greater glory of his name. But what Kainios was really thinking was this: that the boar, with its curving half-moon tusks, was sacred to the Great Lady, a holy beast on whose blood the most solemn oaths were sworn. That men should hunt it down and kill it was, to Kainios, a sacrilege. Therefore she determined that she would be the one to sacrifice the sacred boar to the Great Lady, in thanks for showing her the new path she must take in this new age of men and war.

Accordingly, she traveled to Kalydon. There she found herself in company with the greatest warriors of the age. Young Kastor and Polydeukes of Sparte; boastful Idas and his brother Lynkeos of Messene; mighty Theseos of Athens and his cherished friend Peirithoüs of Larissa, who was Kainios' own kinsman; Iason of Iolkos and his cousin Admetos of Pherai; javelin-skilled Nestor of Pylos; strong Peleos, his brother Telamon of Salamis, and Eurytion of Phthia, Peleos' father-in-law; Alkmene's mortal son Iphikles of Thebai; Argive warrior and seer Amphiaraos; and Ankaios and Kepheos of Arkadia. King Oeneos lavishly feasted the company for nine days, while singers praised their individual deeds and told the tales of their valor, Kainios not least among them.

Kainios listened unblushing to her own story of rape and transformation and warlike accomplishments, drinking thoughtfully from a silver horn of wine. After the singer was finished, and the usual praise was given both to him and to Kainios, another singer took his place. This was an older woman from Arkadia, and she sang in a rich pure voice a tale that set all the men to nodding agreement but set a burning into Kainios' cheeks that her own story had been unable to do.

The tale was of King Iasos of Tegea, who longed for a son. Queen Klymene, barren for many years, finally conceived. But the child was born a girl, and Iasos was so cruelly disappointed that he exposed her on the Parthenian Hill near Kalydon. Klymene never conceived again.

The child did not die. A clan of hunters in the wild mountains found her and raised her to womanhood—strong of bow-arm, fleet of foot, and beautiful as the moonrise. Her name was Atalante, the unswaying, the impassible one, and when she was old enough she went to the sacred precincts of Delphi, there to enquire of the Sibyl her lineage and her fate.

The Sibyl, enthroned on her ragged rock and wreathed in laurel leaves, answered her petition by telling her that a King's son she was to have been, but a Queen's daughter she had been born. "Look to Tegea," said the Sibyl, "but look to a husband, for marriage will be your doom."

Atalante thus discovered that her father was King Iasos and her mother was Queen Klymene, and her excitement was great as she rode from Delphi to Tegea to claim her rightful place. But although Klymene welcomed her lost daughter with open arms and joyous tears, Iasos, still hoping for a son to follow him with warlike strength, would not acknowledge Atalante. "Come back," he said, "when you have found a husband to take my place when I am dead. Only then will I recognize you as my heir, and your husband with you."

Not even Atalante's telling of the Sibyl's warning would sway her father. In truth, the stricture against marriage suited her well, for her spirit and body were dedicated to Artemis, and like the Goddess she had vowed to remain forever virgin, her maidenhood unpierced. So she rode away again, through the land of Tegea, to roam the forested hills with her bow.

The woman finished her song to jeers of disapproval from the warriors—excepting Kainios, who, though a fine companion at the table or in the fray, was known to keep his thoughts and opinions to himself. No one minded this; what counted was a man's prowess and piety, and if he chose not to advertise either, that was his business.

"A foul song!" cried one of the warriors.

"Virginity is holy and proper in a goddess, but an unnatural state in a woman," proclaimed another.

"What use," exclaimed a third, "is a beautiful girl—and a daughter of a king as well!—if she doesn't marry and bear strong sons?"

Thus they began to wager among themselves, even those who were married, as to which of them had the better chance of ending the stubborn girl's virgin state.

"Polydeukes—he's the prettiest!"

"Ah, but Iphikles has almost as many muscles as his brother—and this huntress is doubtless very strong—"

"Who's the richest of us? Women want wealth enough to buy fine woolens and gold baubles!"

"The prize goes to me, then," said Theseos of Athens, with a wry grin. "For not only am I at least passingly pretty—graying hair does distinguish a man, you know!—I have a muscle or three left and plenty of money. But I have another asset, well-proven, to most generously assist the lady in losing her virginity—and most sweetly reconcile her to its loss!"

Roars of laughter greeted this sally, and when it had died down, Kainios spoke for the first time. "And you, Amphiaraos? Accomplished not only in war but in sight, what see you for this Atalante?"

Amphiaraos the Doubly-Cursed pursed his lips, closed his eyes, and after a moment of silence in the hall shook his head. "I dislike to say it, noble Kainios."

"Say! Say!" the others cried.

But he would not, and when further pressed, eyed them all with a narrow glance of dark eyes and told them. "Not while the lady herself is within this hall."

The only women present, to their knowledge, were the serving maids. The company erupted in shouts and demands to know where this Atalante might be hiding herself. From the group of Arkadians who had followed Ankaios and Kepheos to Kalydon there rose a tall, proud, clean-limbed youth who shook back curls the color of chestnut bark and proclaimed, "I am Atalante, and I hide nothing that you are not too blind to see!"

In the ensuing tumult Ankaios and Kepheos surged to their feet, flinging down their horns of wine and howling their outrage. King Oeneos looked about him in alarm as the two Arkadians declared their absolute refusal to hunt in company with a woman. Theseos grinned to himself and winked at his friend Peirithoüs, sharing the joke of the girl's successful imposture. Kainios was seen to hide laughter behind his hand.

Atalante, however, was furious. "Not hunt with me? You who were raised under the roofs of great halls and palaces, you played at hunting for sport! What do you know about the ways of boar and hind and wolf? I spent the years of my childhood in the wild, with no roof but the treetops and no hall but the forest, and hunted for *food!*"

Ankaios threw the half-eaten leg of a guinea fowl at her feet. As the dogs scrambled and snarled over it, he cried, "Hunt that, with the other bitches! But not the boar, not with the likes of us!"

The hall was silent. The insult was twofold, as all present knew: not only the words but the thing Ankaios flung so contemptuously at Atalante's feet. Those dedicated to Artemis were forbidden to touch guinea fowl, a bird as sacred to Her as the peacock is to Hera.

King Oeneos' son, Meleagros, a well-made youth with a smoldering gaze, rose at his father's side. Into the hush he said, "My royal father has told me to say this: that if objections to Lady Atalante's presence on this hunt are not withdrawn, there will be no hunt at all."

The bellows of protest shook the rafters. Peirithoüs got to his feet as soon as Meleagros sat down, and shouted, "Reconcile yourselves, friends Ankaios and Kepheos! There is room here for all! We hunt tomorrow!"

Lounging at his side, Theseos called out, "And by the look of this maiden, we had all best go to our beds and sleep, or we might as well turn around and go home to tend our glens and gardens!"

Everyone burst our laughing again, and the meal ended in high good humor, for Theseos had punned not only on Peirithoüs's name—he who turns around—but those of Ankaios, man of the glen, and Kepheos, gardener. The two warriors so named and so used for the entertainment of their fellows left unhappily and with a grudge burning in their hearts.

But Kainios saw something else. As the company broke up, Meleagros, who was married to the daughter of Idas of Messene, stared after Atalante with his smoldering dark eyes; and as Kainios passed him on the way to the sleeping quarters, she heard him murmur, "Ah, how happy the man whom she marries!"

Kainios did not go immediately to her bed that night. She stayed awake, sharpening her spear, until all the night-sounds were quiet. Then she rose and glided through the palace to the rooms given over to the Arkadians. Knowing that Atalante would no longer be with the men in their common chamber—and knowing as well that the girl's fury would not allow her to sleep at all this night—she waited outside in the palace gardens. Surely as sunrise, Atalante

eventually stole forth, and in the dimness she saw
Kainios.

"Have you come to steal the march on Theseos?"
she hissed.

Kainios smiled at her, and, undoing the ties of her
clothes, showed her that she, too, was a woman. Atalante's lovely lips parted in wonder, and her fine
brown eyes grew big as hen's eggs. And then she
giggled.

Kainios, who'd thought this proud, angry girl had no
sense of humor, grinned back. Together they walked
through the gardens, and sat in a secluded place beneath a tree heavy with apples.

"Well met, Atalante," Kainios said. "Though I
nearly killed myself trying not to laugh when you revealed yourself to those idiots!"

"I could have killed every one of *them!* You in-
cluded! Except for my swinish countrymen, you were
all laughing at me!"

"Nothing of the kind! My kinsman Peirithoüs and
his friend Theseos were laughing at the joke you
played on everyone, including them."

"Yes, it was a very good joke." Atalante was mollified. "But it's nothing compared to what *you're* doing.
How did you ever think of it? Will you ever let on
who you truly are?"

So Kainios told her the tale of the rape and the
transformation, and all laughter left them as the moon
climbed high in the sky over Kalydon.

"Your story I know," Kainios finished. "And I
knew the instant I heard the singer that I wanted to
meet you. For you alone—except for my mother—can
know my truth and understand."

"The singer was my warning," said Atalante. "It
wasn't supposed to happen the way it did tonight, but
I could hardly think for rage!" She clasped Kainios'
war-roughened hands with her own that were callused

from bow and spear in the hunt. "I am so sorry for what happened to you, Kainis—oh, I'll remember to call you by your man's name around others, never fear. But here, when we are alone, we are two women who share a secret and a purpose."

"My secret," Kainios said. "But what purpose?"

"Never to marry," Atalante said fiercely. "Never to submit. Never to be taken and tamed into those pale, pretty, prating creatures these barbarians call 'women'—good only for spreading their thighs for a man to enter and a baby to come out!"

Kainios said thoughtfully, "But there is more to it than that. Our personal troubles are part of a larger whole, Atalante. You are the daughter of a queen. You have a duty to her, to your people, and, most of all, to the Great Lady."

"I serve Her the way I know best." She paused, gesturing at the apple trees around them. "Do you know what happens in Tegea when the time comes for the sacred marriage with a new king?"

Kainios shook her head.

"At each turning of the Great Year," Atalante said, "those who would be king run a footrace with the queen. Along the way, three golden apples must be snatched up from their plinths and carried to the finish ahead of the queen."

"One apple for the Maiden, one for the Mother, and one for the Crone," Kainios said.

"There used to be thirteen, but some have been stolen or lost over the years, and now we have only seven left. They came from Kretia a very long time ago, a gift from Konossos itself. They're gold through and through, and very heavy, so even the swiftest young man is weighed down by them. And they're awkward as well. The first unbalances the runner. The second makes things easier because there's one in each hand. But the third—! Not only does he have to run his heart out to stay ahead of the queen, but he's juggling three apples that are smooth to begin with and grow more slippery with his sweat and weigh as much as a newborn baby!" Atalante giggled again. "Oh, Kainis, you should see them sometimes! It's the funniest thing in the world!"

"I can imagine," said Kainios. "What happens next?"

"Well, when the queen is young and quick-footed, it's a real contest—unless she favors a certain man and allows him to win. She's done this with my father three times now. Yes, I know what you're thinking— that my father is still alive, and still king. But in Tegea, as in all Arkadia, we offer the Great Lady a surrogate pleasing to her—in Tegea, a boar." And her expression became grim.

"I have heard," Kainios said carefully, "that this done, with much honor and reverence, in many lands."

"In Tegea, it was my mother's doing," Atalante said in curt tones. "She loves my father, you see."

"Such loving is the Lady's gift," replied a woman who had never known the Goddess' bounty in such things.

"And it also could be the reason Klymene bore only one child. Me." Atalante raked both hands back through her curls. "My father has adopted the ways of the Achaioi, and my mother's love for him allows it, and the only reason he cannot have his son rule after him is that he has no son. He has only me. And I will prove to him that I am as worthy to be his son as I am to be my mother's daughter."

Kainios considered Atalante's words, and nodded. "It is why I pose as a manly warrior, to prove the same things to the priests and the people in my own country."

"I am so glad you're here!" Atalante exclaimed. "No one else understands!"

"When the time comes for you to become queen—"

"I will never let *any* man win the race!" the girl replied fiercely. "And if by some horrid mischance one of them outdistances me, I'll choke him on the golden apples he carries!" After a moment she calmed, and went on, "But aside from my personal vow, there is the Sibyl's warning. Marriage will be my doom."

"But your duty to your country is to take a king, that your line should continue."

"Duty? What about you? Look at you—dressed as a man, warring like a man—"

"I have a daughter, born of that rape. Her name is Koronis. She will rule after me."

"All very well. But I have no intention of being raped!"

"May the Great Lady protect you from it," Kainios said.

It was growing very late, and they decided to go back indoors. Just at the threshold of the palace, Kainios chuckled softly and whispered to Atalante, "Why not share my room tonight? Think of their faces when the servants report that we slept in the same bed!"

Atalante nearly choked on repressed mirth, but then shook her head. "Though it would enhance your reputation as a man, it would do nothing for mine as a virgin! No, though I thank you for the laughter this idea brought me, Kainis. Sleep you well, and tomorrow stay far from me, for I don't want to give your game away by laughing aloud during the hunt!"

And so the next dawn the hunt began. All the warriors and their followers armed themselves with bow, arrow, knife, boar-spear, and javelin as their skills demanded, and organized themselves into the form of a crescent-moon, and went to hunt down the Kalydonian Boar.

Atalante positioned herself on the extreme right flank, as far from Ankaios and Kepheos as she could get. Kainios, seeing this, and seeing, too, that there was a look in some warriors' eyes that boded ill for her new friend, placed herself near enough to warn if necessary but not near enough to be seen.

Her caution proved justified. As the company moved forward through the dense woods, the dogs crying out with frustration at the lack of the boar's scent, two Kentauroi who had come to Kalydon with their cousin Peirithoüs shadowed Atalante from behind. Hylaios and Rhaikos were their names, and they were strong and wild-haired and silently laughing as they stalked Atalante with their intent obvious in their eyes. Kainios in turn stalked them, hoping that a warning would not be necessary. Kentauroi on foot were not in their natural element; horsemen all, they were deadly enough when mounted but probably unskilled in the subtleties necessary to a hunt on foot. But Kainios was wrong. Hylaios and Rhaikos advanced with the stealth of sheer cunning. If Atalante did not hear them, her shame would be great at her failure. Kainios knew enough of her by now to understand that Atalante would not accept that the huntress unused to being hunted would not be alert for such things. It would be no excuse, and her pride would be sorely wounded.

And so, just as the Kentauroi were about to seize upon her friend, Kainios cupped her hands to her lips and made the cry of the guinea fowl sacred to Artemis. Atalante whirled and with movements too swift for the mortal eye to follow nocked and drew two arrows. These found the throat of Hylaios and the heart of Rhaikos, and they died.

Kainios, melting back into the forest, watched Atalante retrieve her arrows from the dead Kentauroi and wipe the blood on the grass. With a final contemptuous glance for those who would have raped her, Atalante strode through the forest and went to hunt at Meleagros' side. Kainios, seeing this, realized her own mistake: for Meleagros' name meant guinea fowl, and Atalante had drawn the obvious conclusion. The Great Lady had saved her from rape with the cry of that bird. She would be safe with Meleagros. But Kainios, watching the young man's eyes like banked black-and-red coals of a fire, was not so certain.

At length the dogs belled in triumph. The warriors centered upon the watercourse, wild with willow trees, where the boar had been flushed from cover, and chased it up the hill to a rocky defile where it was cornered.

At sight of the monster, all the warriors, with all their experience of ferocity and all their valor in battle, blanched. Massive in body, it had hooves as wide as offering plates and glaring crimson-rimmed eyes and tusks that could sink into the ribs of a full-grown bull and come out the other side.

Valiant Iphikles, recovering his color and his tongue before the others, muttered. "Look at this beast! Not a scar on its hide!"

Theseos leaned on his spear and drawled, "It will make a nice addition to my hall."

Peirithoüs gave his friend a sidelong look. "Every other creature in Kalydon has too much respect for this boar to challenge it—and it may very well be that we are all utter fools for doing so."

"Granted," Theseos agreed pleasantly. "Iphikles, too bad your brother is busy with another of his little projects! We could use the noble Herakles about now!"

The boar scraped at the grassy ground, tearing up clods of earth. Whining and growling, cornered by the rocks at its back and the contracting crescent of hunters, it suddenly charged. Two of Idas' men were killed

immediately by gigantic tusks that went into them like
knives into apples. A single toss of the boar's huge
head flung them behind onto the rocks. Next a young
warrior in Iphikles' train moved in with arrogance
gleaming in his eyes. He was hamstrung, and collapsed
screaming onto the ground. Iphikles swung him over
a shoulder and bore him off to be tended by others.

Next came Nestor, who approached warily with his
javelin. The boar lunged, head down and tusks slick
with blood. Nestor watched the beast run at him, swift
as a horse across a pasture, and prudently used his
javelin to vault himself into the branches of a tree. No
one laughed; there was death already in the air, and
more death to come.

Iason and others flung their own javelins, but did
not hit the boar; only Iphikles, returning to the fray,
was able to graze the mighty shoulder, but even he did
not draw blood from that thick, tough, unscarred hide.

Telamon and Peleos went in with boar-spears. But
Telamon tripped over a tree root and fell. The boar,
glee in its red eyes, thundered for him. Peleos yanked
his brother to his feet, screaming at him to get up and
run. Telamon's foot and ankle had been twisted and
he could not gain his feet. The boar, jaws agape in a
kind of grin, was nearly upon them.

With breathtaking suddenness an arrow sprouted
behind the boar's ear. It squealed and broke off its
charge. Snorting, shaking his head, it tried to dislodge
the bolt. Then it began running in a small, tight, frantic
circle, as if its tormentor was behind it.

Atalante lowered her bow and, without so much as
a glance at the men, declared, "Mine. I drew first
blood, the beast is mine."

"That pinprick?" sneered Ankaios. "That's no way
to kill a boar! See, he's already thrown off your frail
little arrow! Observe and learn, woman!" And with
this he rushed in and swung his battle-ax at the boar

as, bleeding but freed of the shaft, it charged once more.

Ankaios was skilled with the ax, and quick, but not skilled or quick enough. In less time than it took to draw two breaths, he lay on the ground—castrated and disemboweled. He looked up with an expression of simple bewilderment, one hand trying to hold his entrails within his body, the other still holding his clean-bladed ax. A breath later he was dead.

Telamon still sprawled on the ground nearby, unable to rise even with his brother Peleos tugging desperately at his arms. But the boar only trotted back toward the rocks and turned, its eyes now daring the other hunters to come and be finished as it had finished Ankaios.

The company froze in horror. The boar surveyed them disdainfully, then dug up the earth again with its hooves in preparation for another attack. Peleos shouted for a weapon, any weapon, with which to defend his helpless brother. Eurytion, his father-in-law, tossed a javelin into Peleos' outstretched hand, crying, "Here, my son! Kill the monster!"

The boar rushed forward. Suddenly all was frenzy and confusion. Theseos flung his own javelin, but it flew wide. Amphiaraos shot one arrow, then another, and the second hit the boar in the left eye, blinding it. It screamed again, but did not break off or swerve from its charge on Telamon and Peleos. Warriors ran in behind the boar, letting fly arrows and thrusting with spears, yet still it would not turn aside. Peleos, on the ground, could not fling the javelin; neither could he plant it angled in the ground like a boar-spear to impale the beast in its charge, for the shaft was slim and far too long, and would break against the animal's tough, muscular chest ere it thrust home to the heart.

Kainios, who had used up all her arrows and was

readying her sword, gasped as she saw Peleos rear up in desperation and throw the javelin. A hopeless effort—and a tragic one, for the javelin embedded itself deep in the belly of Eurytion, his father-in-law and his king.

Abruptly, and insanely, Meleagros broke from the milling crowd of warriors with sword in hand. As the boar ran past, he sliced its right flank. The animal whirled in pain. Meleagros drove the sword deep under the left shoulder blade to the boar's heart. The monster fell over, twitched, and was dead.

There was a shocked, thunderous silence—but for the labored breaths of dying Eurytion, transfixed by the javelin he had thrown to Peleos. Swallowing hard, Kainios went to help Telamon to his feet so that Peleos could go to his king. As she approached, however, she heard Telamon mutter to his brother: "A javelin!" And Peleos responded in a fierce whisper, "When he had both sword and boar-spear to hand—a javelin!"

Kainios nearly strangled on a gasp of horrified comprehension. Eurytion had *wanted* Peleos to die beneath the boat's hooves and tusks—and Peleos, knowing it, had killed Eurytion for it. There would be a new king in Phthia now.

Kainios could have wept at this travesty and desecration. The old king did not spill the blood of the new; neither did the new king murder the old. Both sacred, both with their parts to play in the eternal drama of life and death and life, they had abandoned their ritual places, flouted the meaning and the duty and the law.

But there would be no more of the law. No more meaning. The only duty these men felt was to their own everlasting fame. Why else had Theseos destroyed the last Minos? Why else had Iason sailed his *Argo* to seize the hallowed Golden Fleece? Why else did all these men seek greedily after battle and plunder, if not to make their names live forever?

What had any of them done except destroy the old ways? Fabled Konossos lay in earthshaken ruin. The shrines and sacred gold-glittering springs of the Fleece had been defiled and abandoned. Men became kings not for the Great Year but for a lifetime, and sacrificed not themselves for the good of the land but surrogates and animals—and now each other.

Kainios stared down at the boar lying dead on the blood-soaked ground. She had thought to offer it to the Great Lady, as was fitting and proper. But this day stank, and of worse things than blood. Meleagros wanted the boar dead so he could impress Atalante; Atalante wanted it dead to prove her worth to her father; all the others wanted it dead for their own glory.

Dead the mighty boar was, its once-unmarked hide scored with wounds and prickled with arrows. Kainios gazed upon it, and felt sick. She turned, ignoring everyone, and made her slow, weary way back to King Oeneos' palace.

Kainios almost did not go to the feast that night. A strange celebration it would be, she told herself, with so many deaths, including that of a king—and a way of reverence. But she bathed and dressed herself, and walked into the hall, and sat with her kinsman Peirithoüs, but ate little and drank nothing.

Peleos and Telamon had departed, taking with them King Eurytion's body to Phthia. What they would say about the death was anyone's guess, though everyone was whispering about events of some years earlier, when the brothers had—perhaps accidentally, perhaps not—killed their younger brother, Phokos, during an athletic contest. Each had been purified of suspected fratricide, while claiming all along it had been mis-

chance and no fault of theirs. But everyone knew that
Peleos' part in the death of his father's favorite son
had been as muddy as his name. Perhaps the javelin
had been Eurytion's instrument of vengeance for the
death of Phokos. No one would ever know now.

Meleagros, as killer of the Kalydonian Boar, had
flayed the hide and removed its tusks. These were on
display: the hide brushed and readied for tanning, the
tusks scoured of blood and polished white as alabaster.
As the surviving hunters partook of the beast's tough
flesh, Meleagros was presented, all ceremoniously,
with the shoulder cut.

This, along with the hide and the tusks, he presented formally to Atalante.

"You drew first blood," he told her, his voice firm
and steady in the startled stillness of the hall. "Had
we left the beast alone, it would have succumbed to
your arrow."

Plexippos, Meleagros' uncle, sprang to his feet. "No!
You won the pelt yourself! If you refuse to take it,
then by rights it ought to go to the most honorable
person present at the hunt!"

"Namely, Plexippos," murmured Theseos, and Kainios heard him, and felt the first smile of the day tug
at the corners of her mouth. But it was a sour smile,
for if Plexippos so insisted, he would be calling on
ancient Mother Right: he was the brother of Meleagros' mother, Althaia. Whereas in many places—
including Kalydon nowadays—he would have only
small status as the brother of the queen, in some others he would be honored second only to his sister's
king.

Others had heard Theseos' words as well, and repeated them, and Plexippos turned crimson with anger
at being mocked. Because he could not now in good
countenance put himself forth as the most worthy to
receive the boar's hide and tusks and the shoulder cut,

he said, "In any case, it was great Iphikles who drew first blood." With a scornful look for Atalante, he added, "The womb-brother of Herakles, not some mere girl!"

Meleagros, exhausted from the hunt and the killing and the flaying and the tension—and unwise with wine and his emotions for Atalante—drew himself stiffly up. "Uncle," he said, his smoldering dark eyes igniting at last to flame, "you insult this lady, whose arrow *did* draw first blood and *would* have killed boar. Does any man here deny it?"

Such was the expression in his eyes that no man dared.

Except Plexippos. "*I* deny it!"

"Then *I* deny *you*," said Meleagros, and sliced off a great hunk of shoulder meat and placed it on Atalante's plate.

She was too stunned to move. Kainios bit her lips together over a silent chant: *Eat, eat!* For if Atalante did not, she would humiliate Meleagros in front of everyone—and any chance to sanctify this boar to the Great Lady would be lost.

Atalante's wide brown eyes sought Kainios. As if in a trance, the girl picked a slice of meat and placed it in her mouth.

Plexippos let out a cry of incoherent fury and stormed from the hall, and his followers went with him.

"There's war in this," Theseos sighed. "Peirithoüs, what will you wager that within the year, Meleagros meets his mother's brother on the battlefield and slaughters him?"

"Only a fool would hazard such a gamble," said the warrior and seer Amphiaraos.

"You know, then?" asked Peirithoüs.

"One need not be a seer to see this."

"There's irony in it," Theseos remarked. "Meleagros will violate his own mother's bloodline in order to honor the Great Mother in the form of this girl.''

"Irony, or fatal contradiction?" Amphiaraos asked sadly.

"Both. One wonders which of the charming Ladies will drive him mad trying to reconcile the two—Alekto the Unresting or Tisiphone the Avenger."

The others who had heard made signs of warding against Those Who Were Not Named, the terrible ones who punished those who sinned against the Mother Right. Kainios did not join them. She was too sickened by the truth of the men's words, and wondered in bleak misery why they could speak of and understand the sacredness of the old ways and yet work so hard to obliterate them.

"I would wager," said Amphiaraos at last, "on the Lady Althaia."

In the end, it did come to pass as the seer had said. Meleagros met Plexippos in battle, and Plexippos was slain. And before the spring came again, justice was exacted: the youth with eyes like burning coals was burned to death by his own mother.

As for Atalante, grateful as she was to Meleagros for upholding her right and honoring her as he had, she could never have accepted him even as a lover.

"I am dedicated to Artemis," she told Kainios many days later, on the night before all the remaining hunters departed Kalydon. "If there was ever a clearer sign that he is not meant for me, it is beyond my understanding! Even swallowing the piece of boar meat given me by his hand was the hardest thing I've ever done."

"I understand," said Kainios.

"But did I tell you?" Atalante went on, eagerness shining now in her eyes. "My father has already heard of the boar, and he sent me word himself of his delight at my success! I'm to be welcomed as his daughter,

and will enjoy all honors and when my mother dies—
may it not be for fifty years!—I will inherit both as
daughter *and* son!"

"I am happy for you, my friend," said Kainios, hiding her own sorrow and misgivings, and wished Atalante well before setting off for her own country.

The Lady Elatë welcomed her with joyous tears.
Little Koronis—not so little now, for it had been some
years since Kainios had left home—shied back from
this strange man who wanted to cover her face in
happy kisses. It was many days before the child would
accept her presence, and many more before she became used to it. Kainios hid her pain, and was patient,
and eventually Koronis treated her with affection. But
Elatë was the child's mother now, and Kainios knew
it.

She was feasted and celebrated, and made to tell
the tale of the Kalydonian Boar many times. She did
not tell the truth, but it would not have mattered over-
much if she had; no singer ever let the truth get in
the way of a good story, as Kainios' own tale proved.

The spear she had herself used in the hunt, clotted
at its tip with dried blood, she set up in the center
of the marketplace. In solemn ceremony she led a
procession to consecrate the spear, which suited the
priests of Poseidon; they took it to be a substitute
for their god's holy trident. Those who honored Zeus
argued incessantly with the Earthshaker's followers,
saying that the spear was more like unto the lightning
bolt hurled by the Father of the Gods. Kainios kept
her peace, for it mattered little to her whether Poseidon or Zeus claimed the spear. She knew to whom she
had dedicated it, and to whom the offerings of flowers
and votary statues were left. And at each new moon,
when the last crescent had faded into darkness, she left
her own offering of a burning branch of fir in honor
of the Great Lady, and the boar with its crescent-

curved tusks, and the sacred king she both was and was not.

Kainios now ruled the Lady Elatë's lands. Because Koronis had taken her heart and her time, Elatë was glad to give up her duties. It was an unusual situation they found themselves in: a queen who no longer ruled, a king who had been her daughter, and neither husband nor wife in view—for the young man who was Koronis' father had drowned in a storm while fishing. Yet their circumstances were no more strange in these strange days than, for instance, Atalante's— she who had been welcomed by her father and named as his heir.

A year passed, and another, and at length Kainios received an invitation to Peirithoüs' wedding in Larissa at the mouth of the River Peneios. His intended bride was Hippodameia, daughter of Boutes of many herds.

"Who else is coming to the marriage rites?" Kainios asked idly of the messenger, who let out a quiet sigh.

"The usual, Lord—kings and princes and warriors, most notably Theseos of Athens, my master's beloved friend. And . . . the Kentauroi."

Kainios blinked her astonishment. "Has my kinsman run mad? Unwashed, uncivilized, untamed Kentauroi at his wedding?"

The messenger gave the shrug all servants give when their masters behave in inexplicable ways. "He wishes peace among all the sons of Ixion, Lord."

Kainios dismissed him to a meal and a warm bath, and sat for a long time contemplating the view from the palace windows. Below her, the sea lapped daintily at the rocky shore where, nearly eight years ago now, she had waded into the waves a woman and emerged a man. Excepting her mother and Atalante, no one knew the truth; and by now she had lived so long as a man that she had forgotten what it was like to live as a woman. Her body was lean and hard and power-ful, and her skin was darkly tanned, and her hands were callused and scarred, and not even her people recalled now that once she had been not Kainios but Kainis. She was just twenty-three years old.

So Peirithoüs was getting married, mused Kainios—and to one of those pale, pretty, prattling creatures Atalante has scorned. Kainios had heard of Hippoda-meia: a useless little thing noted for her beauty and her laughter and nothing else. Her grand name of "horse tamer" was a joke, for she was terrified of any animal larger than a cat.

Kainios foresaw nothing more dire than a few bor-ing days in Larissa, listening to the men's boasts and coarse jests. Still, better that than the same time spent in company with Hippodameia and her ladies, who were doubtless as lackwit as she. Kainios was tempted to decline on the excuse of pressing duties or illness or some other pretext, but the promised presence of Kentauroi at the wedding decided her otherwise. She had an intense interest in them, as anyone of Lapith blood must, for the dissension between the tribes had been going on for many years.

Both the Lapithai and the Kentauroi were de-scended from Ixion and had devotion to horses in common. The main royal line of the Lapithai, of which Kainios' line was an offshoot, came from Ixion's union with Dia, sky-eyed daughter of Eioneos. The Ken-tauroi claimed even grander descent: from a cloud, no less, sent by Zeus. Their proud lineage was based on nothing more substantial than their ancestress' name: Nephele, which means cloud. But because Ixion had fathered both lines, the Kentauroi believed themselves entitled to a slice of Larissa—and, in the year when Kainios was bearing and birthing and nursing Koronis, had gone to war with Peirithoüs to seize it.

Peace had been reached on some grounds with

which Kainios was not familiar; it was before her greatness as a warrior, and in any case Peirithoüs was closemouthed with everyone except Theseos. The presence of the Kentauroi Hylaios and Rhaikos at the hunt for the Kalydonian Boar surprised Kainios at the time, but she merely assumed that the peace was holding well. This invitation to the wedding of the Lapith King of Larissa was either a masterstroke of diplomacy or a cover for some deep dealings—and, having met and observed Peirithoüs' friend Theseos, she firmly suspected the latter.

Kainios had another reason for attending. The spring would see the ending of another Great Year, when the blood of the king—or the king's surrogate, or an animal sacrifice—would be shed to sanctify the land, and a new king be chosen to become the husband of the queen. But Kainios was not a true king. The Lady Elatë had relinquished her queenship. Koronis, the next true queen, was a child of not yet eight years, too young for the sacred marriage. Kainios could find no solution, except to depart from the palace and attend Peirithoüs' wedding to Hippodameia, and hope that something would occur to her.

On arriving at her kinsman's palace in Larissa, Kainios found that the bride was as useless and foolish as rumor portrayed her. That night during a family feast, for sheer curiosity at what Hippodameia would do—and perhaps to remind her kinfolk of their shared history—Kainios paid a singer to tell the tale of Ixion.

The song of the oak-king who was the thunder god was one of the bloodiest in all the world. He married Dia, the rain-making moon, and was then scourged so his blood would flow upon the earth. Then his limbs were spread and nails were driven into his hands and feet, securing him to a tree. Beheaded and emasculated, his blood flowed in rivers. He was roasted on an oak fire, and his kinsmen completed the sacrament by reverently eating him.

To Kainios' surprise, Hippodameia lasted until the end of the song, whereupon she fainted.

Peirithoüs' sister Theisadië shot the singer a glance filled with daggers, and leaped up to help her brother carry his swooning bride from the hall. The singer in his turn cast a look of reproach at Kainios—who buried her nose in a horn of wine and ignored him.

"The days of our barbarism," Theseos remarked with a sigh. "We have progressed somewhat, I think, from killing the king to killing his substitute to killing an animal most pleasing to the Great Lady of Death and Rebirth."

As Kainis, she would have protested the words. As Kainios, however, she mused for a long time on the advantages of newer ways.

"An amazing tale to sing to a son of Ixion before his wedding day, though," Theseos went on. Then he grinned and rose. "Please be so gracious as to excuse me. I'd best go reassure Peirithoüs that we have no trees ready for him, nor nails, nor cookpot!"

Kainios sought to restore the mood by asking who else would attend the wedding. "For I have only just arrived, and came straight to the hall from a bath, and we are kinsfolk here tonight with no foreign guests."

She learned from Boutes, father of Hippodameia, that so many kings and princes were due on the morrow that there wasn't room enough in Peirithoüs' palace for them.

"Most of our companions from the hunt for the Kalydonian Boar, I should think," said Kainios. "Perhaps Atalante as well? I heard she had married, and borne a son."

"As the Fates would have it, she will not be here," Boutes replied. "The lady is dead, her husband with her."

Kainios exclaimed in shock and sorrow. Boutes, who had spent his youth with only his cattle for an audience, now had every ear in Peirithoüs' hall, and told the tale with a kind of smug sadness. And in his voice Kainios suddenly heard the voices of the priests of Zeus, and she was hard put to hide her tremors of foreboding.

Atalante's mother, Klymene, died (said Boutes), and Atalante became queen, for she and her father had been reconciled—and her father reconciled to his sonless state. Because she now required a husband, the race was held. Having eyed Melanion, son of Amphidamas the Arkadian, and liking what she saw, Atalante allowed him to seize three golden apples and cross the line ahead of her. They were married, and lived very happily together, and she gave birth to a son she called Parthenopaios, for the hill upon which her father had exposed her as a child.

One day in the winter just past, as she and Melanion were returning from a hunt, a storm opened the clouds. Lashed by fierce wind and rain, separated from their companions, the couple took shelter in a cave. As a natural result of their love for each other and the excitement of a dangerous, successful hunt, they made love while the thunder crashed across the sky and echoed through the cavern.

The next morning dawned fair and soft for a winter's day. What had been unseen in darkness was now revealed by sunlight: the cave was a shrine of Zeus Thunderer, who had made his displeasure at their lovemaking known the previous night—a warning unheeded.

The priests came, and accused Atalante and Melanion of profaning the sanctuary. The pair added to their sacrilege by asserting that they had done nothing wrong by consummating their sacred marriage in a place ever sacred to the Goddess, as all caves were.

They clung to this defiance even as the priests killed them. For, whereas it had been true that caves were places of the Mother, mighty Zeus had been hidden in a cave on Kretia during his holy infancy, and thus all such places were now sacred to him.

Thus Atalante and Melanion were slain, and their bodies thrown out onto the hillside. Rather than give them decent rites, the priests covered them with lion skins so that the carrion-eaters—those birds and beasts who were the Goddess' servants in death— would be too frightened to approach, and their bodies would rot into dust, unhonored.

"Iasos," concluded Boutes, "will raise young Parthenopaios, this son of a pierced maidenhead, to be king after him. Thus everything has been settled for the best in all ways."

"The best!" Kainios could not help but exclaim, filled with horror at the fate of her friend.

"Of a certainty, good Kainios! Atalante is rightly punished for her unwomanly conduct, but by the god's mercy she leaves a boy-child of Iasos' blood behind to become king. The golden apples, by the way—the seven left of the original thirteen—have been dedicated to Father Zeus. But I have heard tell that the priestesses of Aphrodite have claimed at least one."

Theseos, who had returned during the latter portion of the tale, arched a brow. "Ah, but I am curious, friend Boutes. Who did the punishing? Zeus, for violating his holy precincts? Artemis, for Atalante's abandonment of virginity? Or perhaps beauteous Aphrodite, for the girl's remaining a virgin so long? I find these theological matters fascinating, and would have your learned opinion on whose was the punishing of the girl."

"Does it matter?" Kainios muttered. "She is dead."

"Does it *matter?*" Boutes half-rose from his seat, then settled back down again, unwilling to cause dissension with Peirithoüs' kinsman on the eve of the wedding. In milder tones he went on, "It is possible, of course, that Great Zeus and His Daughter the Huntress acted together in this, well-satisfied that each could take appropriate revenge for profanation of their separate precepts. And that Aphrodite only later claimed her due."

"I wonder whose idea it was," murmured Theseos, "or if Artemis was just waiting for her chance to complain to her papa."

Boutes stiffened once more, then excused himself to inquire after his daughter. Theseos surveyed the depleted family gathering and sighed.

"Interesting man. He has a look about him as if, were his skull to be cracked open, moths would fly out. Yet he speaks like a priest—or like a man who has memorized the long words of priests without knowing precisely what they mean."

"Do you?" Kainios asked bluntly.

"I flatter myself that I am not stupid," Theseos responded quietly.

And, recalling the man's youth—even if only half the deeds ascribed to him were in fact his own—Kainios at last understood the King of Athens. He had seen, as she had seen, the ways of the future.

Chosen for the Great Year's tribute from Athens, the past had tried to claim him at Konossos; he had destroyed Konossos, and taken the past with him in the form of his first wife, Ariadne, Minos' daughter. But her he abandoned on an island as she celebrated the ancient rites, knowing she would insist upon the old ways when they reached his home.

Some said it was carelessness, others that it was a deliberate thing, when on his return to Athens Theseos neglected to change black sails to white. Seeing the color of death, his father plunged from a cliff— some said from despair at losing his son, some said from duty. Whichever, the old king died, and Theseos

became the new king. He captured and wed proud
Hippolyta of the Amazones against her will; she bore
him a son and then died. His third wife, Ariadne's
sister Phaedra, and the pious son of Hippolyta attempted to assert the old ways by deposing Theseos.
He had her hanged and his son trampled by horses.
It was said that, sending Hippolytos to his death, Theseos told him in cynical tones, "You wished to restore
the old way of kingship. Hereby I give you your wish."

Thus had Theseos become and remained King of
Athens. He understood the old ways, and that they
were giving way to the new. And because the new
ensured his survival, he embraced them—and killed
whomever he must.

Yet Kainios could not hate or despise him for it.
Lacking the murders, it was only what she herself had
done. What she was unsure of was whether he had
done it because he believed, or because he wished
to live.

Alone in her bed that night, Kainios struggled anew
with her conflict that was the same conflict in the
hearts of all the people—and yet was uniquely personal. The old ways taught that the marriage of the
queen and king was the marriage of the eternal female
and male: virility mated with fecundity to provide for
the health of the land and people. The king was the
son of the Goddess in all Her many Names, wedded
to the queen who was Her personification among the
people. As the Maiden, she wed him; as the Mother,
she gave him birth in new form; as the Crone, she was
his death.

Now people were saying that the king was not the
son of the Mother at all, but of Poseidon, or Zeus, or
Apollo, and not by the Goddess but by a mortal
woman. As the son of a god, the king could not be
killed; the breath swelling his lungs and the life lighting his eyes belonged not to the Mother who had

borne him but to the father who had begotten him. He was sacred not for being Her son and her lover who renewed her and the land and his own life in the life she bore, but for being the offspring of a god.

Thus he could not die.

But if he did not die, he could not be reborn. The king *must* die, Kainios told herself, turning restlessly in her bed. Upon his willing shoulder as he went to his death rested all the evils and ills and crimes of the preceding Great Year. Had not the father of Theseos died, after which Athens rose in new strength under the rule of her new King? From death emerged new life. In dying, the grain seeded next year's harvest. In dying, the clouds watered the land. In dying, the kine fed the people. Tampering with these truths in their ceaseless cycle was too terrible to contemplate.

And still . . . for many years now, in many lands, the king's substitute reigned for a day and then died in his place, whereupon the king emerged from death to rule another Great Year. In many others, the sacrifice was of a bull, a stag, a boar, a ram, a bear.

And these lands, the lands of Athens and the Argolid and Boeotia and Arkadia and Lakonia and Elis and Thessalia—these lands *thrived*.

Kainios sat up in bed, clenching her fists on her knees. Whence did such blessings come? From the Goddess, satisfied with the spilled blood of Her sacred animals in place of Her sacred sons? Or was it as the Achaioi avowed, that it was the power of Poseidon or Zeus or Apollo that spread protection across the land?

Who *had* punished poor Atalante and her husband Melanion? Artemis, because Atalante was no longer virgin? Zeus, for violating his sacred place? Aphrodite, for Atalante's long scorn of marriage?

Kainios trembled even to be thinking these things. Yet had she not known from the moment she walked into the sea—eight years ago tomorrow night—that the old ways were dying? Had she not chosen to become a man, live as a man, pretend to have begotten a daughter, denied her own motherhood? Had she not warred and killed and lifted silver horns of wine in the halls of other men, *as* a man?

Was she not king of her people?

The king must die.

"I am a woman," she whispered. "I am Kainis, daughter of Elate*, daughter of the fir trees and the seacoast and the Great Lady who is the Mother of us all."

As a woman, she could not be a king. But as king, she could not be a woman.

And she realized in grief and humility and with shame for her presumption that, on that night eight years ago, by drawing the clouds to shadow Her face in the moon, the Lady was not agreeing to her transformation. The Lady had known what was in Kainis' heart, and had covered Her shining face in sorrow at losing a daughter.

Kainios no longer knew what she was. She had abandoned womanhood to become warrior and king. Watching the encroachment of the new ways, she had neither honestly embraced them nor honestly held fast to the old. She had tried to find her own new path, denying the gods and the Goddess their due.

She could not be a woman in these new times, submissive and silent, foolish and fainting like Hippodameia. Her pride would not allow it.

Neither could she be a man, a king claiming a god as his father, and fathering sons to come after him. Her woman's body would not allow it.

She could not be a queen of the old ways, ruling her lands and taking her kings and mothering a generation of daughters and sons to do the Goddess' work. Her own lie of transformation—and the priests who believed and fostered that lie—would not allow it.

Neither could she be a sacred king, dying for the good of the land and the people, or even selecting a substitute of male flesh, human or animal, to blood the earth in her place. Her woman's blood would not allow it.

She felt the hardness of shoulders that had borne the weight of sword and spear and quiver, and of thighs that had encircled the ribs of horses. She felt the softness of small breasts that had borne the weight of her daughter's sleeping head, and of the moist hollow that had once, only once, encircled a man's thrusting flesh. She was Kainios, but she was also Kainis.

Kainis had died, and been reborn as Kainios. The old ways died, and were reborn as the new.

And she wondered very suddenly if Theseos, King of Athens, ever felt as alone as she did right now.

Boutes had been correct: more celebrants came to Peirithoüs' palace than it could contain. So it was that Nestor of Pylos and Kainios of Magnesia and other kings and princes of Thessalia, together with Peirithoüs' cousins the Kentauroi, were seated apart from the main celebration in a vast cave near the palace.

Kainios, remembering her friend Atalante, entered this cave unwillingly, and sat as close to its wide, tree-shaded mouth as she could. She accepted a platter of food and a silver horn of wine, and tried to join in the talk and laughter all around her.

The Kentauroi were served their preferred drink of sour mare's milk—a potent fermentation used in Kainios' land for some feasts but more usually given to children to strengthen their bones. Smelling the familiar drink, she smiled in memory; on returning to the Lady Elatë's palace with her infant daughter, she'd watched laughing as Koronis' little face screwed up in dislike at her first taste of "Lapithai wine."

It appeared the Kentauroi were no more disposed

to drink it today than Koronis had been. Despite Peirithoüs' gracious offering of their traditional drink, they
demanded to be served the same wine that everyone
else was drinking.

"Are we barbarians?" roared their leader, a woolly-
haired blusterer named Eurytos. He was half again
the size of most Kentauroi, who were generally small
and dark and compact of form. "Are we not good
enough to fill the hundred horns of the bulls we ourselves have slain with the civilized wine of these swag-
gering flint-chippers?" Striding to the huge amphorae
of wine, he lifted one in his arms and lugged it to the
back of the cave, shouting for his fellows to come and
drink their fill.

Kainios shrugged at their rejection of Peirithoüs'
thoughtfulness, and hoped they knew at least enough
about wine to mix it with water before they drank.
But Euryton's references in his speech did not bode
well. When Kentauroi, which meant "war-band of a
hundred" or "those who spear bulls," depending on
what part of the country one came from, threw the
two meanings of Lapithai—"swaggerer" and "flint-
chipper"—in their cousins' faces, they were already
primed for a fight.

The celebration progressed, with the usual ribald
jests and unsolicited obscene advice for tonight's first
consummation. Kainios, long used to contributing a
share to such revelry, made her token responses and
longed to be gone from the place. She had good reason that day to cherish her reputation for quietness
and self-containment, unusual in a warrior but toler-
ated because of her amazing circumstances. She knew
it was said that some of Kainis lingered in Kainios,
for the man was as modest as a maid. She looked out
at the trees and the clear blue sky and the field below
where Peirithoüs and Hippodameia drank from the
same gold cup and ate from the same gold platter,

with Theseos in his royal lion-skin leaning across his
friend to tease a deeper blush into the bride's already
pink cheeks.

Kainios asked herself if she would like to be a bride.
She had to answer *No*. But neither would she be Theseos—thrice-married murderous king, whom she still
could not find it in herself to hate. Yet, if neither bride
nor king, what was left for her?

The Kentauroi were becoming very drunk. Unused
to wine, and swilling it as if it were water, they began
singing lewd and riotous songs at the top of their con-
siderable lungs. Kainios watched as Peirithoüs, Hippodameia, and Theseos climbed the short hill to the
cave, and hoped the Kentauroi would settle into more
seemly behavior. In their present state, they would
terrify timid Hippodameia to death.

The bride was escorted into the cavern to greet the
guests. Kainios bowed and handed over her gift of
matching copper armbands, one for Peirithoüs and
one for Hippodameia, made in the twisting shape of
snakes. She had been unable to resist this invocation
of the Goddess—copper being Her sacred metal that
warded off pain in the joints, and snakes being her
chthonic emblem. Theseos, who at Konossos had had
extensive experience of snakes, understood the meaning of the gift; Peirithoüs and Hippodameia did not.

They moved on toward the back of the cave, where
the Kentauroi still bellowed out indecent songs. Kainios stood up, ready to assist in calming them if necessary. So she saw the whole thing from the beginning.

Eurytos, sighting the bride, let out a roar and leaped
from his stool. The table overturned as he vaulted it,
plates and cups and food and wine flying everywhere.
Hippodameia's screams echoed shrilly within the cavern as Eurytos, drunk and once again singing, seized
her by the hair and dragged her into a rocky recess.
His fellow Kentauroi cheered him on while following

his example by grabbing the young Lapithai serving women.

Peirithoüs and Theseos yelled for their men and attacked the Kentauroi with anything that came to hand. Kainios, struggling through the frightened crowd, was deafened by the women's shrieks and the clash and clatter of everything from stools and plates to eating knives. She cracked the skull of one Kentauroi with a small clay amphora, and kneed another in the groin as he lifted his tunic to rape a terrified Lapithai girl.

Fighting her way through to her kinsman, she saw Peirithoüs yank Eurytos up from the floor by the hair and, using a carving knife, lop off both his ears and his nose. Together he and Theseos hoisted the would-be ravisher and shoved through the crowd, throwing Eurytos out of the cavern to roll bleeding and broken down the hill toward the rest of the horrified guests.

With the routing of their leader, the Kentauroi should have yielded. They did not. And as Kainios fought the oddest battle of her life—a battle of planks for cudgels and women's hairpins for swords—she wondered suddenly if the drunkenness that precipitated the fight had been Peirithoüs' intention.

His men arrived with swords, and after that the outcome was inevitable. Kentauroi died beneath Lapithai blades, and those few who retained enough wits to realize they were doomed if they stayed, fled.

At the battle's end, Kainios looked around the blood-soaked cavern with its strewn bodies and huddled women and chaos of tables and stools and the remains of the feast, and knew that, intentionally or not, Peirithoüs had a war on his hands that would settle once and for all which of the sons of Ixion ruled Larissa.

She spied Theseos over to her left, beyond an overturned table, cleaning his sword on a woman's torn and discarded scarf. Picking her way toward him, she felt her heel descend on something soft and hotly moist. She glanced down; it was one of Euryton's ears.

"Ah, you found Peirithoüs' third souvenir," said Theseos. He bent down and retrieved the disgusting flesh from the ground, wrapping it in the gore-smeared scarf. "Not a bad day's work, for a wedding."

And by this Kainios knew that it *had* been planned—though undoubtedly without anticipating the threat to Hippodameia. All at once she knew a very good reason why the king must die: if he was not killed, he spent his time killing others.

"I count sixty-two dead and twenty-nine who will be by tomorrow," Theseos went on. "That leaves nine who escaped. Someone ought to go after them and kill them before they reach home and raise an army." He glanced over at Peirithoüs, cradling the unconscious but unhurt Hippodameia in his arms. "*He* obviously cannot. Good Kainios, these drunken Kentauroi are your kinsmen as well, are they not?"

Kainios shrugged. "Tomorrow will be soon enough to do it," she said, sick unto her soul of the killing and the treachery and the ways of the Achaioi. "As you say, they are drunk—on fear as well as wine. They'll pass out before they reach the river road home."

"Wisely said, but more wisely done today, I think."

The implication was clear. As a warrior, as Peirithoüs' kinsman, she had no choice but to finish his vengeance for the insult done to his bride. And Theseos knew it.

"Very well," Kainios said shortly. "I will go to them myself."

She commanded her horse be brought around, and leaped upon it with a sword in her hand and a bow and quiver strapped to her back, and rode away without even changing her bloodied clothing. The Kentauroi could not have gotten far. As unaccustomed as they were to wine, they were even more unused to traveling afoot. Nine of them, without horses; she should have no trouble killing them. And then she would go home, and have no more to do with the wars and ways of men, and take back her womanhood, and rule her land in peace, and raise her little daughter, and—

They were waiting for her above the river, hidden among the fir trees in the last of the day's sunlight. Drunk as they were, frightened by the day's disaster, still they were the more furious at the killing of Eurytos. And so they waited for her, and fell upon her, and dragged her from her horse.

As she toppled to the ground, and saw that they were armed with branches broken from fir trees, she knew that she would never see her home or her mother or her daughter again. And Kainis almost smiled as—perhaps to herself, perhaps to the Goddess, and perhaps to Theseos of Athens—she murmured, "The king must die."

They beat her about the head and chest with branches of fir, and drove her broken body into the soft damp earth beside the river. And as they struck her body, her own blood joined that of their fellows on her clothes. And her clothes were torn away, and they saw that it was not Kainios they battered but Kainis, and Kainis was dead.

They piled the branches of the fir tree atop her, but did not set fire to the green growth for fear that the smoke would bring others down upon them. And then they fled.

The next morning, Peirithoüs and Theseos rode out to find Kainios. On the banks of the River Peneios they discovered the mound of fir branches instead. And within it, Kainis.

Theseos gazed down at the crushed and shattered

body for a long while. He gazed at the strong lean shoulders that were twisted and broken, and the small soft breasts that were bruised and bloody. He ordered that the branches be made into a litter to carry her back to her mother's country, and then he walked along the river for a while, thinking his own thoughts.

At length Peirithoüs joined him. "I didn't know about him."

"That he was she, or that he and she would die?"

"Either. Both."

"I did."

Peirithoüs arched a brow in imitation of his friend's gesture. "How could you?"

"How could a woman become a man—even with the help of a god?"

"My wife's father, to say nothing of the priests, would slay you for that blasphemy."

"They would try." Theseos shrugged.

After a time, Peirithoüs said, "Claim what you will, Theseos, but I do not believe you knew that he—I mean to say 'she'—would die here."

"Peirithoüs, I love you well, but at times the obvious escapes you. Kainis was a woman who became a king, and for that she deserved to die. I rather think, however, that she herself would say that she was a woman who became a king, and the king must die."

"Not the King of Larissa," said Peirithoüs firmly. "Nor the King of Athens either."

"One day, dear companion. One day." He paused, glancing back over his shoulder. The litter was nearly complete, and Kainis' body lay on the riverbank. "I wonder where the bird flew."

"Bird?"

"A cuckoo, I think, if I recall her country's beliefs. The bird that was her soul."

"Back to Magnesia, I hope—where her people will

rally to my call and march with me to finish off the Kentauroi."

"Their king is dead," said Theseos, very softly.

Peirithoüs was silent for a time. Then he said hesitantly, "Should we tell them? That she was ever a woman, never a man?"

"Will the priests allow even the first word of it to pass your lips? She was transformed again by Poseidon. The king died, and the woman returned, and her soul flew off on sand-colored wings. . . ." Theseos filled his lungs with the clean, soft spring air. "She was brave, Peirithoüs. Braver than you or I."

Peirithoüs stared. "She was a woman pretending to be a man. She must pretend to be brave, or be discovered!"

"That is not what I meant, but no matter." Clapping his friend on the shoulder, he said, "Come, let us return to your palace. Your lady wife will be anxious for your presence."

"You should marry again. You need an heir."

"I have had three wives, that is enough—unless some charming daughter of an immortal offers me marriage."

"A human woman is enough for me. These daughters of gods and goddesses are too proud and headstrong for my tastes."

"Then you've had no trouble taming your little tamer-of-horses?"

"Tame she already is—and a fertile mare she'll prove, I've no doubt." They walked beside the riverbank, and along the way Peirithoüs lost his smile, eyeing his friend sidelong. "Theseos, which of the gods or goddesses do you believe responsible for this?"

Theseos glanced once more at Kainis, now resting on the litter of fir branches. "I believe in this matter as I believe in all matters."

"Which is?" Peirithoüs asked impatiently.

"Why, the only way a man of sense and wit, who wishes to survive in these times, *can* believe."

"Riddles," said Peirithoüs severely, "are for Sphinxes. Tell me straightly. In which deities do you believe?"

"All," replied the King of Athens, "and none." When Peirithoüs looked askance at him, he shrugged once more. "Belief is a dangerous thing. Perhaps even more dangerous than unbelief."

"So you attempt all at once—?"

"My friend, there is no other way to be a king, alive, and forty-seven years old all at once."

Peirithoüs surprised him then, with a smile as cynical as his own was wont to be. "Honor where honor is due?"

And, this time not looking at the body of Kainis, Theseos nodded. "Or, at the very least, where it is the most useful. Come, Peirithoüs. Your lady queen awaits."

THE WARRIOR
AND THE DRAGON'S SON
by Josepha Sherman

The antagonist of this next story is modeled after the eleventh-century Polovetsian Khan, Tugorkan, who is often depicted in Russian folklore as a monstrous figure of sorcery—either a dragon or a dragon's son. The Polovesti were a group of nomadic tribes that often caused trouble for medieval Russians.

Josepha Sherman is renowned as both a fantasy writer and folklorist. She combines both of these skills for her story in this collection. Her latest novels include *The Shattered Oath* and the folklore title, *Once upon a Galaxy,* from August House. She has sold more than 125 short stories, many of which have appeared in various DAW anthologies and a variety of magazines. And she sold a script for the late, lamented TV series, *Adventures of the Galaxy Rangers*.

It was not easy, Elena Nestrovna thought, pacing the length of the city's wooden walls, the still unfamiliar weight of her long skirt tangling her legs, it was not easy at all being both a *bogatyr,* a knightly warrior, and a wife.

Particularly not now. Akh, yes, Alexei was her love, he would always be her love. Their marriage was a good, strong, happy thing, with him even willing to accept without a qualm that his wife was better with a sword than he, and she willing to trade the wandering way for a settled life. But there were times—by God, there were times!—when he infuriated her.

He just will not see danger until it slaps him in the face!

Alexei's kingdom might be small, but it lay just at the verge of forest and the open steppes of the East, which made it a tempting target for nomadic raiders. He was, after all, a prince. And riding out on a hunt with not even his full *druzhina,* his bodyguard, but just a token group of men, was as good as shouting, *"Here I am! Come and get me!"*

Elena snorted. Alexei had waved that threat away with a casual hand, as though she were a gray-haired nanny offering boring axioms rather than his wife, yes, and every bit as young as he, and more experienced in battle. "There have always been raiders, love." His light voice had been maddening. "Eastern bandits, no more."

"Bandits," Elena muttered, then shook her head in sudden impatience, so fiercely that blonde braids flew about her shoulders. Akh, yes, for now the nomads were little more than mere bandits, but if a tribe such as those war-loving Polevetsi ever found themselves a war leader who could unite them—

A war leader . . . or perhaps a shaman? Elena stopped short, wondering why that, of all things, should enter her mind. She shivered, remembering other days in her young life, battles that had, for all she was a good Christian woman, not always been with the sword. She had never told Alexei of them, of course. Magic was forbidden, everyone knew it.

Yet everyone knew just as surely that the Old Ways still lived in the forest, the earth. And there were some who could, while not being sorcerers, talk to certain Others. . . .

And, of course, the tribes, being pagan, were under

no restraint at all. There had been stories lately of one Tugarin, who was indeed of those raiding Polev-etsi tribes, or at least one of them in name. For he was also known as the Dragon's Son, and rumor had it that he was tall as a mountain and rode a winged, demonic steed. Mere pagan boasting? Or . . . could there be some narrow thread of truth behind it?

I am a prince's wife now. A respectable, civilized, Christian woman. I must not think of anything else.

But then she lost those prim, proper thoughts, snap-ping out a warrior's sharp oath at the sight of Alexei's hunting party returning—or rather, the sad, bedrag-gled, bloodstained remnants of that party.

"Alexei," Elena breathed, then gathered up the cursedly cumbersome skirt and ran, dimly aware that what seemed like half the city was following her but seeing only the men who had failed Alexei. "Where is he?" she shouted as savagely as any battle cry. "Where is my husband?"

Far too worn for shame, almost too worn for speech, the men told her, "Tugarin. The Dragon's Son has him."

"How is this?" Elena barely kept herself from screaming it. "Did no one even raise a spear to Tu-garin? Shoot so much as a single arrow?"

Not a head roused at that. "He is no mere man," came the weary reply. "Too tall, too strong. Spears the Dragon's Son snapped in one hand as though they were mere straws, and arrows did him no harm at all. He snatched up Prince Alexei as lightly as a man snatches up a child and—and flew off on a great-winged beast."

"And you did *nothing?*"

"Princess Elena, we tried. As God is our witness, we tried to defend our prince. But the Dragon's Son smashed us into the ground, leaving only these few of us alive to tell the tale."

"But Alexei is still alive? My husband is alive?"

"When last we saw him, yes, Prince Alexei was alive and unharmed."

"But Tugarin said nothing?" Elena prodded. "No boasting? No demands for ransom?"

"He said not a word." The men exchanged uneasy glances. "And his eyes . . . were not those of a sane man."

Or a human man? Larger than the norm, riding a winged steed. . . . An ugly thought slipped its way into Elena's mind and refused to be banished. "Tugarin was alone? No sign of other tribesmen?"

"There was not the slightest trace of others."

The thought roused itself in all its ugliness: Tugarin, the Dragon's Son, with his more than human strength and eerie mount, could only be the shaman of his tribe. And as such, akh, what magical power he would gain by sacrificing the land's rightful ruler!

Elena fought down her shudder; she would not show weakness, not now. She must be *bogatyr,* not woman. But . . . magic, she thought. Magic prying itself into her life yet again.

"I will go after Tugarin," she said after a moment. "I, alone."

That brought about the storm of arguments she'd expected. Elena waited till it had died down a bit, then snapped, "It will be done," and watched them all belatedly remember that she was, after all, their prince's wife. In his absence, like it or not, her word was law. "It must be alone," she added more softly, taking pity on them a bit. "An army would cause Tugarin to slay him. This is our only hope."

This is Alexei's only hope.

Even so, even after the men had sworn not to follow her, Elena stole out from the city at night in her *bogatyr*'s armor, sword a familiar weight at her side, her horse's hoofs wrapped with cloth to make no sound, leave no trace. Her night sight had always been keener than the norm; it was not at all difficult to find her way deep into open, uncultivated land.

For a long time Elena sat her horse under the moonless, star-filled night, trying to calm her thoughts, trying to steel herself for what she was about to do. It was no sin, surely. The good Lord took care of heavenly matters, but didn't that mean the matters of the earth belonged to another Power?

And for every moment she sat dithering, Alexei was suffering who knew what. With a muttered oath, Elena sprang from her horse, letting the reins trail. Nothing to tie them to; she'd just have to trust in the animal's good training not to run off.

She knelt, palm to bare earth, trying not to notice the damp chill of the soil. "All right," Elena said without preamble. "I never was much good with flowery words; You know that. I'm here, my cause is just, and I and the land both need Your help."

Silence.

"Are you here?"

Silence. Elena sighed. You didn't beg or implore such a Power as this; you didn't show weakness to the heart of earth's life.

"Mati-Syra-Zemlya, Warm Mother Earth, I've served you as truly as I have the Sky Lord. And You know as well as I what's going to happen if some foreign shaman gets a chance to sacrifice the rightful ruler to who knows what Darkness. So enough hiding. Are you here?"

"Troublesome girl."

Elena straightened with a startled gasp, going back on her rump then scrambling to her knees. She never could predict what would materialize. What had formed this time was nothing beautiful or glamorous; she evidently wasn't important enough for that. The

. . . woman . . . was barely that, squat and short, her skin the exact color of the dark soil, her eyes hard and glittering as jet. She smelled of musky earth and woman both, and Elena, who knew she harbored no hidden desires for her own gender, still found herself, as always, filled with sudden heat.

"What would you, troublesome girl?"

Elena knew better than to try meeting the so-much-more-than-human stare of those jet-hard eyes. "Help against the invader. He is Tugarin Dragon's Son, and if what I've heard of his power is true, I can only fight him with your aid."

The woman-shape gave the softest of dark chuckles. "At least you don't ask Me to do your job for you. So. I don't like his foreign spells in this land either."

She tossed a handful of soil over Elena, making the startled woman cough.

"You have the earth's aid. Use it well."

She was gone so suddenly Elena was left wondering, as always, if the apparition really had been Warm Mother Earth at all. If not, though, who? Or what?

Deciding she really didn't want the answer to that, the *bogatyr* got to her feet and retrieved her trembling horse, soothing him as best she could with soft words. Of course Warm Mother Earth—or Whatever—hadn't spelled out what form Her aid would take; that would have been too humanly helpful.

"As long as it lets me save Alexei," Elena told the horse, and rode on. As she'd been hoping, one gift she'd just been granted was a clear *feel* for Tugarin's trail, an odd, shivery sense of *alien* and *wrongness* sharp as a knife.

There. She knew it with a sudden chill certainty. That was he, that eerie bulk outlined against the night. That could only be the Dragon's Son himself—

It was. The wind shifted, blowing toward her, and her horse shuddered and bolted as the reek of man-sweat and horse-sweat and . . . something else, a dry, alien scent—dragon?—hit them. Just as horrified, Elena let the animal run, trying to muster her thoughts. No use now in trying to approach by stealth; best to get a safe distance away before trying anything else.

At last, feeling the horse beginning to tire, Elena reined it in and dismounted, stroking the sweaty neck. "God, horse, I'm with you. I don't want to go back there either." But . . . Alexei. Elena sighed. "You're not going to do me any good," she told the horse, "not if that creature's scent terrorizes you like this."

Well now, she never had thought the traditional reckless charge made much sense. *Next plan,* Elena thought and waited uneasily till the first faint gray light of dawn. It was going to be a dark, dull day, judging from the heavy clouds rolling in: rainy, too. Not that it mattered right now. Rummaging about in her saddlebags, she found the worn, much-patched clothing she'd packed in there. The loose blouse and skirt, the common costume of a peasant woman, covered her *bogatyr* armor nicely. Tying a scarf about her head, hiding her sword under a faded shawl and—she hoped—hiding her fear behind a mask of stolid calm, Elena started the slow journey on foot, back toward Tugarin.

He was awake and aware by now, sitting at his ease before a small fire over which was cooking what Elena really hoped was only squirrel. There was not the slightest sign of any other nomads; plainly the man was so confident of his powers that he'd come alone into enemy territory. (But the tribe would follow, yes, once he'd slain Alexei and opened the path to—No!) Elena's breath caught in her throat at the sight of his demonic, bat-winged steed (that was *grazing?* Would a demon-steed *graze?*). But then her heart gave a great leap at the sight of a huddled figure behind Tu-

garin. It was lying limp and battered, but it was unde-
niably a living, breathing Alexei.

But one didn't ignore the foe, even for an instant.
He was still sitting as peacefully as an innocent soul,
as yet unaware of her presence, and Elena took advantage of those precious few moments to study him. Tugarin's hair was dark, sleekly oiled, and neatly braided,
the braids studded with bits of bone she hoped but
doubted were only animal. Bone necklaces hung from
about his thick neck, too: he was definitely a shaman
of his people. His face, though, was narrower than the
Polovetsi norm, sharper of feature. And there really
was something other than human glittering in those
black eyes.

Then all at once Tugarin saw her and rose—and
kept right on rising. Elena swallowed hard at the terri-
fying height of him: Whatever had sired him, she decided then and there, had most definitely not been
human. Dragon's Son, indeed.

*And only quick trickery is going to get me out of
this mess.*

"Who are you?" Tugarin shouted, his voice heavy
with its Polovetsian accent.

"Forgive me for disturbing you." Elena forced her
voice into an old woman's quaver.

"You do disturb me, old one. Who are you?"

"Akh, akh, forgive me. My ears are none too sharp.
What did you say?"

"Who are you?"

"Sorry, I can't quite make out what. . . ."

She hobbled a shaky step forward, another, hand to
ear. With a coldly superior laugh, Tugarin strode forward, bending down over her. "I said, old fool," he
mocked, *"who are you?"*

"Your enemy," Elena told him. And with as swift
a move as ever she'd done on the battlefield, she
whipped out her sword. But no, no, either he was

wearing scaly armor or that eerie substance seen under his tunic really was his skin. Elena hastily reversed the sword, smacking him instead with all her *bogatyr*'s tried-in-battle strength right between the eyes. There was a satisfying *crack,* and Tugarin sagged to the ground.

But I haven't hurt him, not really. He's just stunned for the moment.

A flash of memory, the men saying: "Spears the Dragon's Son snapped in one hand as though they were mere straws, and arrows did him no harm at all."

Wonderful. Then a sword blade probably wasn't going to do any good, either. Their best chance, hers and Alexei's, was to just get out of here, worry about Tugarin after. Elena hurried to her husband, shaking him. "Alexei!" she whispered, then, more frantically, "Alexei!"

Groaning, he opened his eyes, their blue gaze so soft and unfocused it sent a pang through her, an unexpected memory of their nights together. "Elena . . . what . . . where. . . ."

"No time! Hurry, love, we've got to get out of here, *now*."

He was plainly still dazed, whether from wounds or magic, Elena couldn't tell. They stumbled away together, she half supporting him. God, they were never going to get far enough away in time! But then the first drops of rain hit her head, and Elena glanced up with a sudden sharp twinge of hope, thinking, *Yes. Maybe.*

"Come on," she muttered, as much to Mati-Syra-Zemlya and all the forces of nature as to Alexei. "Grant me this. Rain, curse you, rain!"

And—yes! Here it came, nice, heavy torrents, turning the world to water, turning the earth to mud. Alexei flinched in her arms, swearing, but Elena told him, "No, love, this rain's our friend, not our foe."

"You were right, dammit. I never should have gone out with so small a group."

"Never mind that now."

"Right. I only hope," he added, glancing up, "that we live long enough for me to properly apologize to you. Here comes Tugarin on that cursed demon-steed."

But the steed was struggling in the air, and Elena gave a sharp bark of a laugh. "Its wings are water-logged! The rain did its work."

The creature was definitely unable to stay airborne. With a scream, it fell to earth. "Mud!" Elena shrieked. "Let there be mud!"

And mud there was, a great, heavy wave of it, en-gulfing the squirming beast. The beast whose wings were fading, its demon-shape fading, leaving nothing but a normal, earthly horse scrambling to its feet, en-chantment broken, shaking the mud from its coat then racing away.

Of course Tugarin hadn't been hurt by anything as small as a fall from the sky. He sprang to his feet, staring, and the fury in his eyes was far more fierce than the storm. "A clever disguise," he snarled at Elena, and she realized she'd lost both shawl and scarf in the escape. Quickly she squirmed out of blouse and skirt, now a true *bogatyr,* retorting, "It served its purpose."

Beside her, Alexei had drawn the only weapon left to him, a small belt-knife presumably overlooked by his captor.

Or, more likely, Tugarin left it to him in contempt, knowing it couldn't hurt him. Any more than can my sword. Warm Mother Earth, what are we to do?

Warm Mother Earth, indeed! What was it Mati-Syra-Zemlya had said? *"I don't like his foreign spells in this land either."* "Then give me a weapon," Elena muttered, then froze. Yes? Yes! Surely the spike of rock hadn't been visible a moment ago, but who cared? She dropped her sword and snatched up the rock, hefting it in a hand. Not bad, not bad at all. Now, if only it worked.

If it doesn't, I won't care. Won't care about anything anymore.

Here came Tugarin, and sorcery was beginning to swirl about him. "For you, Mother Earth!" Elena screamed, and threw the rock.

It did what swords could not. The bone of the earth pierced the Dragon's Son through. He crumpled to his knees, gasping, choking, then fell headlong.

"Is he . . . ?" Alexei breathed.

"I . . . hope so."

They stood frozen in terrified suspense.

If he starts moving, Elena thought, *what do we do then?*

But the gigantic form was all at once growing hazy, fading . . . fading. . . .

It was gone, and Elena let out her breath in a soft sigh. "She *really* didn't want him here."

" 'She,' " Alexei echoed. "No. Never mind. I don't want to know. I'm a good Christian prince and I'm not supposed to know about such things. And, of course, my wife doesn't know about such things either."

"Of course not," Elena agreed. But she was grinning, seeing the hint of humor in his blue eyes—eyes that, most reassuringly, no longer looked at all dazed.

"Then nothing happened," he told her. "We're in agreement on that."

"Nothing at all. Except that we're both getting soaked to the skin. For no reason at all. Come, love, we've a long, wet walk ahead of us."

But Alexei hesitated. "Do you think he's dead?" he wondered softly. "Really dead?"

Elena sighed. "Who knows? We may still get unwelcome Polovetsi 'visitors.' "

"Those, at least, I can handle with sword or bow."

"But," Elena added with a start, "at least Tugarin won't be coming back to bother us."

Alexei raised a brow. "How can you be so sure?"

"Akh, I can. Believe me."

For, just for a moment, a woman's face, heavy-featured and dark, had appeared in the earth.

And one jet-hard eye had most definitely winked.

EARTHEN MOUND
by Diana L. Paxson

In many cultures war is an accepted, even expected, part of life. And as such, war usually has rules. This is perhaps one of the most dangerous forms of warfare because war takes on a life, a personality of its own. The truly hideous aspects of war are hidden and people complacently let it survive too long. But what happens when warfare breaks the rules? Can war survive? This next story has the feel of a folktale in the making and grew out of the author's interest in African myth and religion. This story also has its roots based on a report from 1917 when, after a disturbance, a Nana priestess and her niece were arrested and then thrown into a British jail. The two women later mysteriously disappeared from the jail, leaving behind puzzled jailers.

Diana L. Paxson is a fantasy writer who has published over four dozen short stories and seventeen novels, most of them historicals. Her novels include the fantasy series *Chronicles of Westria,* as well as *The White Raven* and *The Serpent's Tooth.* Her most recent book, *The Lord of Horses,* concludes the *Wodan's Children* trilogy. Diana also plays and composes music for the Celtic harp.

This was in very ancient times, before Dako became king over the Fon and built Dahomey upon the belly of Da. The kings of Adja made war, and the kings of Abomé fought, and all the others, and when they were not fighting each other, they made raids against the Mahi, who lived on the savannah north of the coastal plain. The kings of Teju-Ade were the most warlike of all.

They say that in those days there was a shrine in the Mahi country at Dassa-Zoumé on the hillside above the town. It belonged to Nana Bukúu, oldest of all the *vodun,* which is what the people of Dahomey call their gods. It was in the dry season, when the wind scours the red earth from the plain and dust covers everything like the powdered camwood bark that reddens Bukúu's staff, that war came to the Mahi land.

Naé Tetilidga the priestess sat before her house on the highest terrace of the Grove of Bukúu, waiting for Hweno to bring water so they could cook their evening meal. At that time Dassa-Zoumé was not a large town, and the deities who were worshiped inside its gates received most of the offerings. Bukúu was an "outside" goddess, too dangerous, according to the old tales, to be contained within walls, though she had done nothing to deserve this reputation within living memory. Her shrine was small, with only the one priestess to serve it, and the young woman Hweno whom the goddess had "named" when she was a child and who was bound for eight years to serve the shrine.

Tetilidga sat on her carved stool with knees spread wide and hands on her thighs, for though she was past the age of childbearing, she was a big woman still. Sometimes at this hour a cool breeze would reach Bukúu's hill from the far-distant sea. But on this day the air was still. Sometimes, when she sat here, it seemed to her that the shrine had departed entirely from the world. Or perhaps it was only she who had separated herself from ordinary existence when she dedicated her life to the shrine. But she was content to have it so. The peace of this place had become precious to her as the seasons rolled on.

The light of the setting sun shone red through the

leaves. Beyond her house, with the second room in which they kept the *ileesin* staff and the other sacred regalia, there was only the shrine itself on the brow of the hill. A narrow pathway wound down the hill to the terrace of the initiates where Hweno's hut stood, then continued to the wide court where the people gathered at feast days of the *vodun*. Below the hills, the bush fell away in long swales of grass and brushland, barely glimpsed between the trees of the Grove.

Beyond them smoke rose in many separate columns like the ghosts of trees, spreading out to haze the air. It was true then. The men of Teju-Ade had come against them, and were burning the outlying villages.

Ahlihan, the crown bird who in season cries "War! War!", called harshly, then was still. The priestess waited for the soft brush of Hweno's footsteps on the path. If the people took refuge on the hill as they had before when war came, they must be fed. She and the girl would need to count over the nets full of cassavas and yams, the earthenware jars of palm oil and dried meat in the storesheds. The shrine was not rich, but Tetilidga had taken good care of the offerings.

From below came a murmur of voices, a man's laughter, and then, shrill in the stillness, a scream. Tetilidga surged to her feet, the stool clattering over behind her. As she reached the lowest court, she saw men fleeing. Hweno lay curled on the ground, her waistcloth crumpled nearby and blood on her thighs.

The priestess squatted, pressed her fingers against the girl's neck to feel the pulse. At the touch, Hweno's dark lashes quivered. Her skin was ashy with shock, the tripled tribal marks on brow and cheeks stood out strongly.

"I told them . . . I told them I belonged to the *vodun*, that we do not do such things here. If I held the *ileesin*, they would not have dared. But they forced me!" The girl began to sob aloud and Tetilidga gathered her against her broad bosom. "I have three years left before I can marry. Will Nana kill me?" Hweno gulped and clutched at the older woman's arms. She was a big, strong girl, her features too large for perfect beauty, but blessed with the pointed breasts and smooth brown skin.

"The *vodun* will not hate you. Are we not taught that she herself was once raped by Gu? She has no love for the lord of war. You must be purified, but I will speak for you. We will make an offering." Tetilidga patted the trembling back, blinking away her own tears. She had been widowed young. Hweno was like the daughter she had never had.

"Who was it, child, do you know?"

"Soldiers. . . ." whispered Hweno, her eyes black with fear. "They said they were scouting. They were men of Teju-Ade."

Night came suddenly, as if an indigo cloth had been drawn across the sky. Tetilidga lit several of the seed-pods of the oil palm tree and set them on the smoothed clay of the dais. As they burned, the oily husks cast an uncertain illumination over the trunk of the baobab tree, and the conical hood of straw, like the thatched roof of a roundhouse in miniature, sitting there. Hweno stepped back as Tetilidga lifted the hood and set it aside.

Long ago, when the priestess had first been brought to the shrine, she had been surprised to see that the *kata* beneath the straw was only a mound of clay studded with potsherds, dusted with the powdered red bark of the camwood tree. Then she had learned to sense the presence of the *vodun* within, and grown afraid. Now she faced the *kata* with a peculiar doubled awareness of its inner and outer natures, as she had learned to see other things, like fire or water, whose familiar and friendly appearance veiled an awesome power.

> "Mound of earth called *kata*,
>   Blood of life, blood of death on your garments,
>   You kill without using a knife.
>   *Pele, Nana, pele,*
>   Go gently. . . ."

Tetilidga caught one of the gray pigeons that fluttered about the shrine, rubbed it vigorously all over Hweno's body to absorb the evil as she murmured prayers. Then, with a deft twist she beheaded it. Warm blood splattered; she held the bird over the mound and a brighter red moistened the clay. She waited until she could no longer feel the fluttering heartbeat beneath her hand.

She blinked, dizzied by a rush of energy unexpected in its power. The *vodun* was awake, and angry.

"Nana, Honored One, hear me!" murmured the priestess. "Gu walks, and no one can stop him. There are bad men in the country. They have hurt your child, Hweno. It was not her fault—she did not mean to break your law. Now she has been purified. Forgive her, my mother. Make her whole!"

She gestured, and Hweno came forward with a vessel of water and sprinkled it on the mound.

"The eye of death is not to be regarded." The priestess slipped into the cadence of the praise-poem once more. "Be cool to us. Let your silent waters be peaceful. Nana, bring us luck!" She sat back on her heels, hands open upon her knees.

For a moment she was confused by the swirl of sensations—the smell of blood, the whisper of wind in the baobab's leaves, then came the familiar shift in awareness, as if she were sinking into the soil. But Nana Bukúu was not the earth, though she was a connection to it. Now her presence rode like a dark bird on the night wind, ancient beyond understanding, not angry so much as out of patience with those who had broken her peace.

"Help us," whispered Tetilidga. "Help us to help your people. *Okiti kata*—earthmound called *kata, pele, Nana, pele!*"

As the dry season advanced, the king of Dassa-Zoumé retreated behind his mud walls, waiting with his queens around him, while the Teju-Ade ranged over the countryside. Refugees began to come to the shrine—young men wounded in the fighting, co-wives who had lost their husband, children whose parents were gone. Tetilidga and Hweno fed them and bound up their wounds, sending those who could still fight back to the king, nursing those who could not until they healed or died.

The pure waters of the spring, which had never failed, continued to flow. But as the season continued, drought swept the plain with a scorching wind, and dust lifted in choking swirls from the parched grass. It was fever weather, when Sakpata walked, and the spotted sickness spread where his broom swept the ground. They heard there was disease in the enemy army, but no one fell ill at the shrine.

"Omo-Olu, the Child of the Lord, punishes those who torment us," said the people, who did not voice Sakpata's true name. "Nana Bukúu is his mother. He will not touch those under her protection."

"If we are worthy—" said Hweno, looking up at the dust-gray sky. Since the rape, the spirit seemed to have gone out of her. She moved like an old woman, and Tetilidga would have worried about her if she had had the time. "If we deserve to be saved."

* * *

Naé Tetilidga sat up suddenly on her sleeping mat. The interior of her house was dim, but she had left the woven cloth that covered the door pulled up to let in the air, and the opening showed a dim rectangle of sky. Then the crown bird called once more, its cry shocking in the stillness. It must have been that which had awakened her. The priestess took a deep breath of the cool, predawn air and paused, frowning.

She set one hand on the wooden headrest and pushed herself to her feet, wound the figured cloth around her waist and tucked it in, and stepped outside. With every moment the sky was growing brighter. But the wind, that at this hour should have borne nothing more than the sweet scent of dry grass dampened by the dew, smelled wrong. Smoke . . . surely she should be familiar with that reek by now. She moved around the hut and looked out through the trees.

Dassa-Zoumé was burning. Clouds of black smoke billowed upward to stain the pale sky. The king of Teju-Ade must have decided to move before Sakpata struck down any more of his army, and made a dawn rush against the town. Tetilidga sighed. The fall of a city was always a terrible thing, but now that the invaders had achieved their goal, perhaps they would go home.

She heard a step. Hweno, her eyes rounding with horror, joined her. One by one others woke and came in silence to watch as their city burned.

It was not until evening that they began to learn just how evil the fall of Dassa-Zoumé had been. Traditionally, such attacks were destructive, but not deadly. Part of the wealth of a city was in its people, and an attacker strove to capture the defenders rather than to kill them. Those who were marched off to slavery with other tribes would not be treated badly, and some might earn back their freedom. To take a town without bloodshed was considered a greater victory.

But the men of Teju-Ade, maddened, perhaps, by fever, had slaughtered every man, woman, and child they found.

By evening, the refugees gathered at the shrine had become a babbling mob. Hweno, silent among the many, stood with staring eyes.

"Naé Tetilidga, you must speak to the *vodun*! Our enemies are possessed by an evil spirit. Who knows what they will do?"

The priestess looked from one face to another, and presently her silence began to calm them. She understood them better than they knew. Surely something uncanny was at work to make the men of Teju-Ade act in a way so contrary to law and custom. She had been safe here on her hill for too long. She would not have believed there was anything that could shake her, but when she thought of their foes, she too felt fear.

But Nana Bukúu was older than everything. Nothing that happened beneath the sky-realm could surprise *her*. Tetilidga realized that just now she needed the comfort of that ancient, patient presence as much as anyone here. She went up alone to the shrine, leaving the weeping people behind her, and sat down on the dais. A warm wind rustled in the treetops, but she found herself shivering.

"Old One—" she whispered, "where are you? Dassa-Zoumé was your city. How could you allow this thing to be?"

The straw that covered the *kata* quivered in the wind's passing, but that was not an answer. Tetilidga stared into the darkness, trying to remember if she had failed in any of the required salutations or offerings. It had been a long time since the first ecstasy of her union with the goddess, but when she prayed, there had always been *something*.

Was it because of Hweno? The rape had not been

the girl's fault. Surely the *vodun*'s anger should fall on the men who had attacked her. And in any case, the killing had begun long before.

"Nana, I have tried to serve you. Is there something else you want from us here?"

The only answer was that heavy silence. Tetilidga sighed. She had performed all the regular rituals. She would offer her own life in expiation, but she doubted it would make any difference. She was not important enough, either to arouse Nana's wrath or to appease her. Perhaps the king had somehow offended. Some might say it was her responsibility to know such things and admonish him, but why should he listen to her? At that moment it seemed to her that if she walked out onto the plain to be killed, it would make no difference to anyone.

She shook herself, knowing that despair would be self-indulgence. Nana Bukúu must speak to them. Because of the fighting, that year there had been no festival. It had been too long since the goddess had been offered the opportunity to walk in human flesh and speak to her people directly. It would not be easy to bear the full power of that spirit, Tetilidga thought grimly, for after so long, and in such a time, the *vodun* was bound to be angry. At least, she thought as she turned to go, the people could hear the goddess in that way even when they could not hear Nana's voice in their hearts.

When Tetilidga came down the hill, it was late. The lower terrace was mounded with sleepers wrapped in their cloths. Hweno was nowhere to be seen. Weariness weighted Tetilidga's bones, but she found that sleep would not come. In the hour before dawn, when the air was almost cool, she rose from her sleeping mat, wrapped her cloth loosely around her, and stepped out of her hut.

From below she could hear snoring. But from somewhere nearer came the sound of weeping. The priestess frowned and picked her way through the shadows beneath the trees.

Something moved. Tetilidga recognized Hweno and let out her breath in a long sigh. Then she stilled once more. Was that a snake the girl was carrying? Bukúu's python lived by the sacred spring. But this was longer, thinner—it was a rope, one end already tied to a branch, the other curved back into a noose, and the girl was knotting it.

Among her people suicide was the greatest of shames. Horror held the priestess still, and in that moment, the power of the *vodun* shocked through her. She raised her hand, and Hweno gasped as the rope took on a life of its own and whipped away.

"You shall not!" The words came from Tetilidga's throat in a harsh whisper, Bukúu's voice, not her own.

"I failed you!" Hweno dropped to her knees, sobbing. "I cannot forget what was done to me— I am not fit to be your priestess."

"To cut off your own life would deny you rebirth, and in this life or another, your life belongs to me!"

Tetilidga clung to a tree trunk as the power went out of her. She knew the *vodun* could move objects without touching them, even transport the body she was wearing from one place to another. But there had never been a reason for the priestess to use that magic before. Clearly she was not the only one whom this night had tempted to despair. But neither she nor Hweno could be allowed to give way.

"Nana!" cried the girl, peering upward. She sat back, weeping, as she realized the *vodun* had gone.

"Nana Bukúu needs you—" said the priestess in her own voice. "*I* need you. We'll make the offerings tomorrow and she will come. Then you can ask her what you will!"

*   *   *

The black she-goat lifted its head, the tassels of colored yarn that hung from its horns swinging gently as it surveyed the crowd with intelligent yellow eyes. A few petals drifted from its wreath of flowers. Its brushed coat gleamed in the sun. Tetilidga nodded, and two of the men grasped its legs and lifted it. The wreath fell off, but the animal did not struggle. It was a good sign. Grunting, the men swung the goat to each direction in turn. Then they set it down again before the shrine.

Leafy branches had been gathered and laid beneath Bukúu's mound. The she-goat shook its head and began to nibble at the leaves. The people watched, murmuring in approval.

"The *vodun* accepts the offering," said Tetilidga. The men dragged forward the great wide-mouthed basin filled with water from the sacred spring. A few drops splashed onto the thirsty earth, then the waters stilled. The she-goat cocked its head, seemed, for a moment, to regard its own reflection in the water, then began to drink.

The priestess moved swiftly forward, straddling the bony flanks, grasped the curving horns and pressed the head beneath the surface of the water. The goat jerked and heaved, hooves scrabbling in the dust, but Tetilidga's weight bore it downward. She could feel the convulsive inhalation as the goat breathed in the water at last, and the sudden relaxation that followed.

She held the animal as consciousness departed, then spirit, and finally, with the last involuntary twitches, the life of the body, until what she held was only meat. She got to her feet, leaving the carcass beside the shrine.

She nodded to Hweno to sing. The younger woman looked back at her and swallowed as if her throat had gone dry. *She is afraid!* thought Tetilidga. And indeed, if the *vodun* was truly angry, who could say what she might do? But they could not stop now. She glared at Hweno, and though the girl's skin had gone gray, after a moment she opened her mouth and began the song.

"Mound of earth called *kata,*
  leopard who consumes her prey raw,
  your silent waters kill,
  you destroy an animal without using a knife. . . ."

Tetilidga poured red palm oil over the mound. Through a sudden ringing in her ears she heard Hweno chanting the praise poem. One by one the worshipers crept forward, set a flower, a piece of cloth, a cowrie shell, or a string of beads upon the body of the goat, bent to kiss the earth, and backed away.

"Honored One, come to us," they muttered above the rising beat of the drums. "Old Wise One, hear! Nana, Nana Bukúu we need your help! Hear us, hear!"

Tetilidga blinked, seeing in one moment the people, the treetops, Hweno's fearful gaze, and in the next a white darkness that whirled around her as she began to fall inward and away.

Pele, Nana, pele . . .

Sight was gone, but she could still hear the drumming, the calling, Hweno's voice faltering in the song. Then came another voice, cold and still, from within.

"You have done well, but I will do better. Now see my mercy—to her, and to you. . . ."

Tetilidga's body convulsed as the goddess left her. She groaned and opened her eyes just in time to see Hweno fall. A murmur of awe swept the crowd and the drums fell silent. The priestess straightened, and the people who had been supporting her let go. Still dizzied, she staggered to the younger woman, who lay crumpled in a fetal curl on the ground.

Sometimes the *vodun* came with violence, forcing

the spirit to yield. But Bukúu had entered the younger priestess like rising water, between one breath and another, between the words of the song.

"Nana!" Tetilidga called softly, not touching her. "Nana Bukúu, I call you, come fully into this body and let us honor you!"

A serpentine shudder ran through the girl's form. Then, slowly, she began to uncoil. She grunted, heaved onto knees and forearms, her back the curve of the *kata* mound. Tetilidga motioned to the men to bring Bukúu's carved stool.

"Ashé, Mother. Here is your seat of honor. Will you let me help you to sit?"

"This body is young. It moves well—" came the harsh reply. Suddenly she heaved up onto her haunches.

"Be gentle to your horse, mother. She loves you, and she was afraid. Keep Hweno's spirit safely. Show her your love!"

Tetilidga held out her hands, and with another heave, the *vodun* rose to her feet, bent like an old woman, but massive as a mountain, dense as stone. The head turned. Black eyes glinted between narrowed lids at once implacable and amused.

Tetilidga flinched. It had been a long time since she had assisted the priestess who had trained her when she tranced. *Is this how I look,* she wondered, *when She is in me?*

Nana Bukúu looked at her and cackled softly. "You don't trust me?" Tetilidga bowed her head. In a lifetime of service to the shrine she had come to understand that one could depend on the gods to act according to their natures. But their purposes were not always those of men.

A woman edged forward with an indigo cloth of state, dappled with paler patterns, and the *vodun* let the priestess wrap it around her. With a sigh she lowered herself to the carven stool and held out her hand.

For a moment Tetilidga did not understand. Then her glance fell on the *ileesin,* still swathed in its wrappings beside the shrine. Swiftly she released it, and kneeling, offered it to the *vodun,* balanced across the palms of her hands. The leather that wrapped it was dyed a deep indigo, but the palm fibers that formed the loop had been colored with a paste of red camwood. The cowries that adorned it gleamed in the bright sun.

As Bukúu grasped the *ileesin,* the men who stood nearest flinched, and she laughed. Once the staff was consecrated, it must not be touched by a male, and any woman who bore it must take care lest her words become a spell. When the *vodun* held it, then, how much greater its power.

"Ashé, Nana," a warrior who had been speared in the leg cast down his crutch and stretched himself in the dust before her. "We know your power. Point your *ileesin* at our enemies!"

"Enemies?" Bukúu raised one eyebrow. It was wonderful how Hweno's young face could look so ancient. Maybe, thought Tetilidga, it was the eyes. "I see no enemies here. Foolish child, do you truly wish to see me as I am when I go to war?"

"The men of Teju-Ade burned your city!" exclaimed the warrior, pressing his forehead against the earth.

"They kill everyone!" "They destroy the land!" the people cried.

"They attacked the priestess," said Tetilidga, "whose body you wear."

The *vodun* looked at her. "She will survive it, as earth endures the planting stick. I remember before the city was made, before the rivers cut their channels to the sea. This land has seen many changes, but the earth remains."

Tetilidga nodded, wondering if she should offer the goddess some palm wine. Then the wounded warrior sat up suddenly. "Someone comes!"

At the same moment there came a shout from the men they had left on watch below. People looked round fearfully, but they were already at the top of the hill. There was nowhere else to go.

"It is the warriors of Teju-Ade," they cried. "They have come to kill us, too!"

The men who could walk began to gather, muttering angrily. "Not without a fight—"

Some of the younger women handed their babies to the others and stepped forward. "The king of Abomé has women warriors. We will fight, too!"

"Wait!" Slowly, but with inexorable power, Nana Bukúu got to her feet. "Now I see an enemy. You follow me!"

The people looked uncertainly at Tetilidga, who nodded, and fell in behind the *vodun* as she began to stump down the hill. She envied Hweno, who would know nothing of all this until it was done. She understood now why Bukúu had chosen her. Hweno's younger body was better able to bear this load of power. The people would accept Tetilidga's authority, whereas if the girl had been left in charge of the people, she would have panicked by now. Behind them, the people were picking up stones to throw and branches of trees. And they were singing—

> "Yeyi mi, okiti kata,
>   Da ogun meji!
>   Mother mine, from mound of earth,
>   She splits war in two."

Still singing, they approached the gates. A score of enemy warriors capered before it, drumming on their shields with their spears. Two of the guards lay dead;

another curled against a tree, holding his gut and moaning.

"Ho—" cried one of the attackers, brandishing his spear drunkenly. "Now they send the old mothers against us!"

"The mothers come against you indeed!" said Tetilidga, intentionally using the word for old women who work magic. "Cannot you hear them flying through the air? Go home, sons of Gu. There is nothing for you here!"

"There is food—" The man grimaced.

What was wrong with him? Tetilidga shaded her eyes with her hand, trying to decide if the discolorations on his face were tribal scars. The leader took a step forward, and the others came after him.

"Wait . . ." said Nana Bukúu. Her voice was soft, but several of the enemy paused, eyes widening.

"Believe her!" cried Tetilidga. "Don't you see what she is? Don't you know what she can do?"

"You are old, and your *vodun* is old. I fear no one but my king—" The leader lifted his spear.

Use your powers, Nana, thought the priestess. *Snatch the weapons from their hands!*

But the *vodun* lifted the *ileesin,* her action mirroring that of her enemy. As its looped end pointed at his body, he paused. For a moment no one moved. Then they could see that his belly was swelling in an obscene parody of pregnancy. He gasped, doubling over, and the spear slipped from his hand. The man behind him cast his own weapon. A gesture from the goddess deflected it in midair. The others did not wait to see if the magic would work on them as well. They ran.

Trembling with reaction, Tetilidga watched them go. Behind her, men and women who had been braced to fight and die hugged each other or sank laughing to the ground.

"They have gone! Now we are saved!" the people

cried. One woman began to kick the body of the man the *vodun* had struck down.

"Leave him—" Bukúu spoke, and the murmur of rejoicing died. "Do you blame the spear or the man who throws it? You bend the sword, or break the spear to keep it from doing harm. But the sons of Gu will make more. This man was only a weapon, and now he is broken. It is his master you should blame."

"We have suffered," said the woman who had attacked the fallen man. "And the king of Teju-Ade is not here. I cannot make him pay for the death of my son."

"I can," said Nana Bukúu.

Beneath the trees the air was close and still, but suddenly Tetilidga felt cold. *Perhaps it is the fever*, she told herself, but she knew it was not.

"The mothers fly through the air like birds. You yourself said so—" The face of the goddess seemed to crease into a thousand wrinkles when she smiled. "I will break his city as he broke mine."

Her gaze went inward and she held the *ileesin* against her breast.

"What do you mean?" cried Tetilidga, starting toward her. She believed the *vodun* had great powers. She had herself seen them hold burning coals and close up wounds and other marvelous things while wearing the flesh of their priests at the festivals. Yet to travel as Bukúu proposed was no mere triumph over the body, but a magic that went beyond the boundaries of the world. Could the body of Hweno endure it? She reached out as the *vodun* began to turn.

Tetilidga's fingers closed on the cloth of ceremony. She tried to grab the arm beneath it and found herself running. Trees, people, sky blurred around her. A hard hand seized hers, and the world disappeared.

It was like falling upward, like the moment before

self-awareness vanished in trance. There was no time, only a blur of sensation that ended abruptly as something hard came up to smack her and she fell. For a moment Tetilidga could not breathe. Then she sat up, gasping.

The blue-clad figure of the *vodun* stood a few paces away, feet planted firmly on the ground. She was gazing at the city that stood on a rise a short distance away, its mud walls gleaming in the sun. Teju-Ade was a great city, wearing its defenses with pride. She could see the roofs of many fine dwellings above the wall. Its king was right to feel secure. But Tetilidga no longer dared call anything impossible. She could only struggle to her feet and wonder what Bukúu was going to do now.

"Come—" The voice of the *vodun* drew her forward. "How shall we break this city of our enemy?"

Tetilidga stared at her in astonishment. All that happened here now would be by the will of Bukúu. She herself had abandoned all pretense of being able to control the situation some time ago. But the goddess continued to look out at her from Hweno's dark eyes, and she felt her heart moved as it had not been since all things were possible and she was young.

They had been seen. Men appeared at the gate of the city, gesturing.

"If you point at them with the *ileesin*, they will die," said the priestess.

"Do you wish them to die?"

Tetilidga stared. It was for killing that they blamed the conqueror of Dassa-Zoumé.

"I wish that the breaking of Teju-Ade will become legend, so that men will never again doubt your power," she answered at last.

Nana Bukúu smiled. "Set your hands over mine." She raised the *ileesin,* directing it not toward the men, but at the walls. "Let my earthen mound arise," said Bukúu. With the *ileesin* she drew a sign in the hot air.

Tetilidga felt the earth move beneath her feet as if it trembled at the passage of many men. Above the walls the air shimmered. Behind them the rooftops were rising. She took an involuntary step backward as the walls of houses cracked and crashed down one after another as the circle of destruction radiated outward from the center of the town. Now the walls themselves were beginning to quiver. The ground they encircled continued to heave upward, and with a groan of almost human pain the defenses of Teju-Ade disintegrated into their component particles and fell.

But there was no longer anything for them to protect. A great plume of dust rose upward, and as the wind began to carry it away the priestess saw, where the city of Teju-Ade had been, a great, rubble-covered mound.

"Now do you believe?" asked the *vodun*. Tetilidga bent down and pressed her forehead against the living earth, and felt the hand of her goddess rest in blessing upon her hair.

That is how Nana Bukúu punished the city of Teju-Ade.

"Ashé, Bukúu, ashé!" the people sang when their goddess returned to them and Tetilidga told what she had seen.

> "Outside ruler of the town!
> *Ileesian* kills all ill,
> You split war in two!"

Hweno lay as one dead for a night and a day after the *vodun* left her, and when she woke could remember nothing. But her heart was comforted, and after Naé Tetilidga passed to the ancestors, she became the guardian of the shrine.

After that, the fame of Nana Bukúu spread from Siare in Togo, to Ife in the Yoruba lands. She became the patroness of Ketu. The kings of Asante, Gonja, and Dagomba sent gifts to her altar. She went with the people of Dahomey who were carried off to the New World, where her priestesses are few, but highly respected. People make pilgrimage to her shrine in Dassa-Zoumé to this day.

This is *hwenoho,* an old-time story, not just a tale. Good.

THE GINSENG POTION
by William F. Wu

This next story grew from a Chinese folk ballad first set down around 500 A.D. Though it describes the realistic events from roughly a century earlier. Given the cool climate of northeast China and the folklore about the magical properties of the ginseng plant, the author presents us with a believable account of one warrior who must masquerade as another.

William F. Wu has a PhD in American Culture and did his undergraduate work in East Asian Studies. He has published many short stories and thirteen novels, including a six-book young adult series, *Isaac Asimov's Robots In Time*. Bill, a multiple-award nominee, had his short story "Wong's Lost and Found Emporium" made into an episode of the *Twilight Zone* television series in 1985. His short stories can be found in many places including the anthologies *Ancient Enchantresses* and *Star Wars: Tales from Jabba's Palace*, and the magazine, *Realms of Fantasy*.

A.D. 398

Hua Mulan stood sentry duty on the night watch. A half moon rose over Mount Tianshou and shone gently down through the chilly mountain air. Rainwater still dripped from the trees overhead, but the sky had cleared.

The army of General Li, led in the name of the Khan, had camped on the north bank of the Yellow River the night before. Today they had ridden east and north behind a thunderstorm that had drenched the mountains and brightened the sky with crashes of lightning. Tonight, for the first time, the army camped within the Kingdom of Yen, its tents lined up and down the forested slopes of the Black Hills among the sweet scents of spring.

"Are you finished?" Mulan asked roughly, in the Toba language.

"The drum is ready," said Gao Liang, Mulan's sentry partner. Like Mulan, he was a young, untried soldier on his first campaign. He yawned in the moonlight as he gave a final tug to the tightened drumskin across their squad's cauldron, which doubled as a sentry drum.

Mulan picked up the drumstick and pounded out the watch, sending the loud, metallic thrum across the camp. In response, fires were banked and torches snuffed. Men began to retire to their tents.

"The sound is good," said Mulan, tossing the drumstick down.

"I have orders." Sergeant Huang, a short, stocky man with a trailing black mustache, strode up to them. As usual, he carried a small horsewhip in one hand. "Our squad rides at first light."

"Will we meet the enemy?" Mulan asked.

"Possibly. A patrol just returned. They found the campfires of the Yen host on the far side of Mount Tianshou. The enemy has not located us."

Mulan nodded with approval.

"Another patrol stands night watch over them now. At first light, our squad rides out to relieve them. The army will follow."

"At first light?" Gao stared at the sergeant. "The rest of the squad will be ready. The two of us won't get any rest."

"We ride at first light." Sergeant Huang turned and

marched away to his tent, idly toying with the horse-whip in the moonlight.

Gao turned away and furtively slipped a hand under his loosened shirt of armor, rattling the small metal plates tied together by leather thongs. Every night, he drank wine from a small earthen flask he refilled from a cask tied to his saddle. He would sleep tonight, even on sentry duty.

"Aren't you going to offer me a swig?" Mulan prodded.

Embarrassed, Gao held out the flask. Mulan took a quick drink and handed it back. The wine was not as important as telling him his drinking was no secret.

Mulan looked away from him out into the darkness. Twinkling in the moonlight, a narrow stream flowed fast but quietly down the slope into the camp here, swollen by the recent storm and the spring thaw from the mountain crests. It provided water for both the soldiers and their mounts.

At this hour, even the horses were quiet.

Soon the half moon had risen higher, and Gao dozed quietly against a tree trunk. Mulan eyed Gao to see if he would waken. He did not.

Mulan glanced at the rows of tents in the moonlight. The army slept, except for the other sentries out of sight around the camp. Mulan crept forward on the damp ground by the stream, away from the sentry post.

On silent footsteps, Mulan slipped among the dense trees, ducking under dripping branches. A short distance up the slope from the picket line, the trees opened on a small, rocky clearing by the stream bank. Mulan walked into the middle of the clearing and looked up gratefully at the moon, which shone down brightly on this spot.

A wild hare stared for a moment, its nose twitching, before springing away into the darkness.

Letting out a deep breath, Mulan pulled off the conical leather helmet that every soldier of the Khan wore, and dropped both sword belt and scabbard to the ground. Then, with fingers stiff from the cold, Mulan untied the laces holding closed the heavy shirt of body armor.

Mulan set the helmet and armor next to the sword belt. That left a tunic of rough cloth and leather leggings and boots. Stretching wearily, and running a hand through hair matted with sweat, Mulan sat down on a smooth rock next to the stream. The water would be very cold, but a quick wash would be very welcome now, while the camp slept.

Mulan began to pull off the tunic.

"This is a cold night for a swim." A man's voice, dry with age, spoke Chinese from among the trees.

Startled, Mulan let the tunic fall again and responded in Chinese, a hand on the cold sword. "Who's there "

An old man in a white robe walked out of the trees, a gnarled wooden staff in one hand. He was short and bald, with a prominent forehead. A white beard trailed from his face. In his other hand, he carried a peach.

"Who are you?" Mulan relaxed slightly but still held the sword.

"Merely a hermit." Moonlight shimmered on his gown and bald pate.

"You may be trapped between warring armies before long. This is no place for a hermit." Mulan stood.

"I will not linger. I came to find a spring that feeds this stream. Earlier today, lightning struck the spring."

"If you need water, the stream runs clear and fresh now. The mud stirred up by the rain has settled."

"The water is good—but it is cold for a swim, young mistress."

Mulan stiffened proudly. "I am Hua Mulan, a soldier of the Khan."

"Hua Mulan." The hermit smiled gently. "Mulan—the magnolia tree. It is beautiful, especially when it blooms this time of year."

Mulan nodded toward the peach in his hand, hoping to change the subject. "Where do you get a ripe peach in the springtime?"

"From the south, where peach trees grow." The hermit held up the peach in the moonlight and gazed at it. "I have known men named for the magnolia, soldier Hua. If you are a man, then go ahead with your bath."

Mulan scowled. "If you seek a spring, then go on with your search."

The hermit lowered the peach and looked at Mulan's clothing. "Man or woman, why does a soldier with a Chinese name wear the armor and leggings of a nomad?"

"My father is a man of the Toba tribe. His father moved south of the Great Wall to live in the small kingdom of the Western Yen. Many Toba have done so. My father took a Chinese name and a Chinese wife."

"Your mother is Chinese, then."

"She is."

"That is why you speak Chinese. Do you speak Toba, as well?"

"Yes. General Li, who leads us, is also a Toba with a Chinese name."

"That is the way of life here in the north, now. Many kingdoms quarrel over the remains of the fallen Han Empire. Tell me whose armies would fight in these mountains."

"Two years ago our Khan, Toba Guei, overthrew the Western Yen. He called up a battle roll this spring and declared himself Emperor of the Wei Dynasty in

his capital Ping Chen, just south of the Great Wall.
Then he sent our army to conquer the remaining
Kingdom of Yen, to the east."

"So what is Toba Guei's title now? Is he the Khan
of the Toba or the Emperor of Wei?"

"When I speak Toba, he is the Khan. When I speak
Chinese, he is the Emperor."

"He has large ambitions, to call himself Emperor."

"I have seen the map of Yen. Their kingdom is
not large."

"It would only stretch from here to the Eastern Sea,
north of the Yellow River," said the hermit. "I have
just been south of the Yellow River and they do not
rule there. This Kingdom of Yen is not much larger
than the little kingdom your emperor rules now."

Mulan shrugged, shivering now in the chilly air.
"Are you going upstream for that spring or not?"

"In truth, young mistress, I came down to this camp
in search of a virtuous individual who would benefit
from this spring. Put on your clothes and come with
me."

"I tell you I am a soldier of the Khan."

The hermit did not answer. He turned and plodded
up the stream bank, leaning on his staff. His white
gown rippled and flowed in the moonlight.

Mulan hesitated. If Sergeant Huang found his sentry
here, the need for a latrine could explain it. Going
farther could be called desertion.

The camp still slept, and Sergeant Huang slept with
it. Gao would not waken. Fascinated by the odd old
man, Mulan snatched up the helmet, sword belt, and
shirt of armor and hurried after him.

The hermit moved with apparent care and delibera-
tion, yet he did not hesitate or slip as he worked his
way up the rocks and tree roots by the stream bank.
He wove among the trees without effort. Mulan hus-

tled to keep up with him, putting the helmet back on and buckling the sword belt.

The moon had begun to fall by the time the hermit stopped. Mulan came up next to him in another clearing, narrower than the last. Here, on their side of the stream, a small spring sent shining water to the surface, which splashed among the rocks to the main stream several paces away. Lush, green plants stood tall around the spring.

"Lightning struck here." The hermit reached between the tall plants with the end of his staff to touch the springwater. "The fire essence fused with the water essence, creating earth essence around it."

"What has this to do with me?" Mulan spoke over the splashing of water against the rocks.

"Tell me what you hear."

"Water."

"Listen again. Tell me what you hear."

"Splashing."

The hermit looked sternly into Mulan's eyes. "Listen."

For the first time, then, Mulan heard a very faint voice, nearly drowned out by the rush of the water.

"A man's voice?" Mulan leaned down close the ground. "I cannot understand what he is saying."

"You hear it."

"Yes. He's calling ... for help, I think."

The hermit held out a small white vial.

Mulan accepted the little container, which fit entirely in one palm. Cold to the touch, it had been carved smoothly out of white jade. Mulan pulled out the wooden stopper and found the stone vial empty.

"Gently break the branches of these ginseng plants," said the hermit, touching them with the end of his staff. "Squeeze the juice from them into the white jade vessel. Take all you can, but do not dig up the plants. They will grow and heal."

"I know the ginseng root makes medicinal tea, but what of the juice?"

"Touch a drop to your tongue and you will be invisible for the length of a day or the length of a night."

"Ginseng will not do that. It is prized, but too common for that to be true. Many people would be invisible if the juice would make them so."

"You misunderstand, young mistress." The hermit smiled indulgently, the moonlight shining on his bald head. "Only where lightning has touched pure water does the earth essence impart such power to the plants. Only the virtuous can hear the voice of the earth spirit calling. Very few spots like this exist, and most people would drink from this spring without hearing the earth spirit's cry."

"And you just happened to find me near here?" Suspicious, Mulan studied the old man's face.

"It was not a matter of chance. Mulan, I came for you."

"Why?"

"When the Khan called up his battle roll, it did not list your name."

"No."

"Your father was called for the levy and you answered. Why?"

"My family needs my father. I have no elder brother, only an elder sister and a younger brother, still a child. We could send no one else to answer the battle roll. I had no man courting me. I—" Mulan stopped abruptly, realizing that she had admitted at last that she was a woman. Embarrassed, she knew she could not take it back. "I bought a fine horse, and a blanket, saddle, bridle, and whip in the village markets. My mother fears horses, but I am a daughter of the Toba. I can ride."

"And ride you shall, daughter of the Toba. But first

take the earth essence through the blood of the ginseng. Treasure it, for it is rare."

"How did you know about me? Who are you?"

"I am just a hermit."

Mulan did not know what to make of that answer. "Why have you brought me here?"

"To help you live long. That is my duty, soldier of the Khan. I want you to ride well and do your duty and return home to your family."

"How will this help me?"

"You will find a way to use it. Now take the essence and return to your post, before the moon falls any lower."

Mulan knelt by the spring and broke a branch on a ginseng plant. She squeezed the fluid into the jar of white jade. Slowly and patiently, moving from one plant to another, she filled the tiny container with the essence of earth from the ginseng plants by the spring in the moonlight.

A.D. 403

Hidden in a stand of trees, Hua Mulan stood in her stirrups to look down a mountain slope in the afternoon sunlight. She held a lance in one hand and wore her sword at her belt. A small bow and quiver of arrows hung on her saddle. Her white jade vial lay in a saddlebag.

"That is not the main army I expected to find here," said Mulan, lowering into her saddle again. "They are merely a patrol, similar to ours." Mulan pointed with her lance down the mountain to seven enemy riders in the distance, watering their mounts at a lazy river dwindling in the dryness of late summer. She and Gao Liang had remained among these trees long enough for the birds overhead to settle quietly on the branches, disguising their presence from the enemy.

"I suppose they are scouting in advance of the van,"

said Gao. "We will find their host coming up behind them."

"Maybe." Mulan, now a sergeant who led a squad of riders on reconnaissance patrols, frowned as she watched the enemy.

A veteran of five years' campaigning, she had learned that the soldiers of Yen were similar to her own comrades. They, too, wore conical leather helmets, armor shirts of small metal plates, and leggings; they fought with bows and swords and lances. Just as her Toba tribe had moved from their home on the Gobi Desert to live in a fragment of the late Han Empire, the people in the Kingdom of Yen had been nomads who had lived in the Gobi before moving south of the Great Wall. Like the Toba, their soldiers lived in the saddle and rode quickly through the mountains to meet the maneuvers of the Toba invaders.

"Shall I alert the rest of our squad?" Gao asked. "We can circle behind this enemy patrol and take them captive."

"The enemy is too far and our squad is no larger than theirs. I expect they would escape us, and report our presence to their superiors. I prefer that they not know we have seen them."

"You would let them go?"

"I have a greater fear than these few, Gao. General Li has led the army here to engage the host of Yen. Meanwhile, Toba Guei leads another column to the north of us to circle behind their army."

"What is wrong with that? The Khan will take them by surprise."

"Where is their army?"

"Where is it? It follows this advance patrol, of course."

"Does it, Gao? What if the Yen host has turned

north to catch the Khan by surprise while we sit here idly waiting?"

"Then we should advise General Li to advance quickly and attack the Yen from behind while he chases Toba Guei."

"What if I'm wrong about that? What if General Li advances into an ambush by the host of Yen waiting for him in these hills, maybe down this river valley?"

"We're merely guessing." Gao shrugged. "If we take this patrol captive, we can make them tell us where their army lies."

"If we reveal our presence and even one of them escapes, their immediate superiors will know our patrol is observing this valley—whether their patrol comes from the host of Yen or is merely a small troop left here to distract us. I repeat, I don't want them to know we're here."

"All right." Gao pulled out his wine flask and tipped it.

"Aren't you going to offer me a swig?" Mulan asked, annoyed.

Gao handed her the flask.

Mulan took a drink and handed it back. "Take the squad back to our camp. Tell Captain Huang I became separated from you."

"Again?" Gao frowned. "Last time you gave me this order, he told us not to return without you again unless you were captured or killed."

"We have only done this four times in five years."

"I am the one he chastises."

"Yet he has promoted both of us following his own promotions, ever since he was our sergeant. Return our squad to camp, Gao."

"Yes, sir." Gao turned his mount and rode back through the trees.

Mulan watched the enemy riders mount. From the river, they rode up the far slope of the hills and vanished from sight in the forest. However, a small flight of birds lifted from the branches, startled by their passing. As more birds fluttered out of the trees, they told her which way the enemy patrol moved. She would not dare cross the open riverbed until dark, but for now she would pace them on this side of the river.

Turning her own mount, she spurred him lightly and rode among the trees at a walk.

The hillsides threw deep shadows across the river valley long before the red sun fully set. Mulan saw the tiny, flickering flame of the enemy campfire up the shadowed far slope, barely visible in the dense forest. She forded her horse across the shallow river at a quiet walk, aware that she moved in shadows too dark for the enemy to see her.

On the opposite bank, Mulan dismounted and drank, grateful for the water after the hot summer day. Then she unsaddled and unbridled her mount. As darkness fell, broken slightly by a crescent moon, her horse rolled in the grass along the riverbed, grazed at the edge of the forest, and watered at the river.

Smiling to herself, Mulan recalled the first time she had tasted the ginseng juice before approaching an enemy campfire. The potion turned her invisible, but had no effect on her clothing, armor, and weapons. Upon seeing her accoutrements walk toward them of their own accord in ghostly fashion, the enemy had fled from her in terror. However, tonight she wanted to infiltrate the enemy camp unnoticed, so she had to undress.

Mulan leaned her lance against a tree and sat down on a large rock. She took off her helmet, armor, and boots, laying them by the rock. Her sword belt, tunic, and leggings followed; soon she was nude. Then, having given her mount as much of a rest as she could afford, she saddled and bridled him again. She tied his reins to a tree near the rock and took her little white jade vial from the saddlebag.

Carefully, she pulled out the wooden stopper. She placed her tongue on the opening as she had four times before, and tilted it up; as soon as she tasted the tingling, slightly bitter juice, she withdrew the vial and sealed it again. By the time she had placed it back in the saddlebag, she could no longer see her own hands in the moonlight.

The grass felt cool on her bare feet as she began the long hike up the forested hillside. She walked slowly, feeling for each footstep to make it silent as well as firm. With her hands high, she moved small branches away from her face so she could pass; she ducked under the larger ones.

Mulan realized that her own army camped far to the rear. Otherwise, she would have heard the sentries drumming the watch about this time. Captain Huang was probably shouting at Gao again, but if Mulan returned with vital information, Captain Huang would forget his anger and pass it up the line of command.

In any case, Gao would drown his annoyance in the cask of wine he had looted from an enemy town last month.

The sentry drums of Yen also lay beyond her hearing.

The air grew cooler with night. She also felt the chill of the higher altitude. Hoping the night would not become too cold, she wrapped her arms around herself and pushed her way through more branches.

When Mulan saw that she drew near the small campfire, she slowed her movements. She would be in no direct personal danger as long as the ginseng worked on her, but she had another concern now. If the enemy riders heard sounds that alarmed them, they would not simply relax and make ordinary conversation as she hoped.

Overhead, the crescent moon already had moved high. She had only a portion of the night remaining in which to use its light. Taking even greater care to avoid stepping on dry twigs and dead leaves, she slipped among the underbrush and low tree branches to the edge of the firelight.

All seven Yen soldiers sat on rocks or fallen logs around the fire. Their horses, unsaddled and hobbled, grazed on the far side of the little camp. Several wooden spits still stood over the fire, but the men were eating now. They tossed the bones of hares aside as they finished with them, and drank out of skins and flasks at their sides.

Mulan listened as they spoke of shooting the hares earlier that day, joking about the archery skills of those who had missed. Their language was the same as the Toba except for a slight accent. From their casual manner and easy laughter, she knew they had not heard her approach and she suspected they were drinking either koumiss or wine.

"Which way do we ride tomorrow, Sergeant?" A young man, his face flushed with drink, shoved his leather helmet back on his head.

"Overeager." The sergeant laughed good-naturedly, revealing several broken teeth. "The young are always overeager on their first patrol."

The other men around the fire grinned at their youngest comrade.

"We will follow the river, unless we see some sign of the Toba," said the sergeant, tossing his last bone aside.

Mulan found a soft patch of grass and stepped carefully up near the sergeant. The warmth of the fire reached her here. She squatted, slightly behind the soldiers.

"This is exciting," said the young soldier.

"Sergeant, it's a little strange we haven't met the Toba all day," said a third soldier.

"We heard no sentry drums from their main camp tonight," said the sergeant, wiping his mouth on his sleeve. He picked up a skin and drank from it. "That means their army lies too far ahead. We'll probably see some of their patrols tomorrow."

Mulan wanted to know the location of their host and what its intentions were now. She could only wait patiently. The firelight flickered over her body, helping fight the chill.

"Then the challenge begins," said another soldier grimly. "Our horses better get their rest tonight."

"I'll be ready," said the young soldier. "I have a fast horse."

"Don't get overconfident," said the sergeant gruffly. "If we do our job, we'll have the eye of the entire Toba host."

Mulan watched him intently, her heart pounding.

"Speed won't be enough," said the grim soldier. "Toba horses are as good as ours. We'll get away because we know these hills and they don't."

The six veteran soldiers all nodded.

Mulan ached with tension as she waited.

"How will we know when Toba Guei has been defeated?" The young soldier looked from one comrade to another.

Mulan held her breath, looking at the other soldiers.

"How will we know?" The sergeant frowned, staring stonily into the firelight. "Riders will reach us with word of the host. Until they do, we must keep the Toba patrols busy. They must believe that our host advances behind us up the river valley, so that the Toba general remains cautious and holds his current position. If General Li learns that our army has turned north to ambush Toba Guei, he will march down the river valley and take our army from behind."

That told Mulan what she had come to hear. She stood up, tingling with excitement. Anxious to report back, she turned her bare feet to step back into the trees, away from the warmth of the fire.

Her foot snapped on a twig.

"What was that?" The sergeant leaped to his feet, whirling, his hand on his dagger.

Mulan held her position, her heart racing.

The other Yen soldiers stood, grabbing their swords and daggers as they looked around in alarm.

"Spread out," ordered the sergeant, striding toward Mulan.

Mulan tried to step out of his way, but the sergeant bumped into her, knocking her to the ground.

Startled, the sergeant stumbled, slashing the air with his daggar.

Mulan got to her feet and snatched up a lance that was leaning against a tree.

"Look out!" The sergeant stared at the lance, apparently lifting of its own accord.

Mulan shrieked as loud as she could and threw the lance at him.

He flung himself to one side, and the lance thunked into a tree trunk.

"Demons!" One soldier shouted.

Mulan jumped forward over a fallen log and grabbed a burning stick from the fire. She heaved it at another soldier and picked up another. As the soldiers stared, she swung it over her head.

"Ghosts! Run!" The young soldier turned and fled into the darkness.

All the other soldiers panicked and ran into the shadows except the sergeant. Standing up and backing away warily, he eyed the flaming stick as it whirled in the air. He grimaced, showing his broken teeth.

"Beware," Mulan intoned in a low, growling voice. "You cannot defeat the riders of Toba. Flee!"

At her words, even the grizzled sergeant spun and ran from the camp.

Dropping the stick back into the fire, Mulan entered in the chill of the forest and hurried back down the slope.

By the time Mulan stepped out of the forest onto the open riverbank, her body shivered uncontrollably with the cold. However, the night air down in the river valley was warmer than the enemy's campsite except when a gust of breeze off the water struck her. For a moment she wished she could take a quick swim in the river despite the chill, now that she had a rare moment alone without even the men of her own squad around. The crescent moon had fallen too low, however; she needed every moment of moonlight to ride back to camp.

With hands stiff from the cold, Mulan dressed as quickly as she could. Fully armored, with her sword belt buckled and her lance in hand, she swung up into the saddle. Aware that she still presented a ghostly visage, invisible in her clothing and armor, she judged that the potion would wear off before she reached her distant camp. If it did not, she would linger outside the ring of sentries until she could see her own hands again.

Mulan spurred her mount into a canter through the moonlight.

A.D. 410

At dusk on a warm, summer evening, Mulan rode with Gao down the narrow, winding road that led to her village. Behind them, the other members of their squad laughed and joked as they drove a line of slow, heavy wagons drawn by oxen, with their war mounts tied to the rear. On their right, peasants trudged wearily out of rows of wheat and sorghum, their long-handled tools over their shoulders; to the left, horses grazed quietly in a pasture, glancing up as they passed. In the west, the red sunset glowed over rolling hills.

"Does your family know you are coming?" Gao pulled off his helmet and wiped sweat on his sleeve.

"I sent a courier from the court of the emperor to tell them." Mulan's casual tone belied her excitement. "When I left home, I didn't know I would be gone for twelve years. How much farther is your village?"

"Another two days' ride," said Gao. "The rest of the squad has to go even farther." He slipped out his flask and took a drink.

"Aren't you going to offer me a swig?" Mulan teased. His reluctance to share his wine had become a private joke between them.

Gao held out the flask. "Your family will be very proud to learn of your promotions—to say nothing of the emperor's generosity."

Mulan accepted the flask and sipped the wine. She felt a little embarrassed by her success. The white jade vial had given her an advantage no one else had. She had used it judiciously, but only a drop or two of the ginseng fluid remained in the bottom of the vial.

On the night Mulan had learned where the army of Yen had gone, she had reported to Captain Huang as soon as she returned to her camp at sunrise. As a result, General Li had ordered a forced march that caught the enemy from behind just as Toba Guei engaged them in the front. The battle had broken and dispersed the host of Yen.

That had not ended the war, however. In the five years following that battle, the scattered remnants of the enemy had fought a long, dogged series of defensive raids and retreats from their towns and villages across the forested hills. Mulan and her reconnaissance patrol had pursued the enemy and engaged them when possible. More often, they simply learned where the enemy had fled so their columns could track them down.

General Li himself fell in a minor action with the enemy. After ten years of campaigning, and the death of General Li in battle, the soldiers who had been called up in the original levy were ordered out of the field. The Wei Emperor called up a new battle roll to replace them and appointed another general to lead the final assaults on Yen.

"Did you write to your family of the emperor's largesse?" Gao asked.

"No. I want to surprise them. So I only told them I was coming home soon, and that I would have my mess-mates with me."

"They will be deeply gratified." Gao sipped his wine again.

Mulan peered into the distance. Under the darkening sky, the small, wooden dwellings of her village appeared around the next bend in the road. She felt her heart pounding.

At the end of their campaign, Mulan and her comrades had not been released to go home. Summoned to Ping Chen, they served in the capital of Toba Guei for two years, honored for their campaign service by easy garrison duty. During those two years, the army then in the field completed the conquest of Yen, extending the land of Wei to the eastern sea. Now, at last, Mulan and her squad had been freed from service.

Before leaving Ping Chen, Mulan had been summoned before Toba Guei himself, who remained both the Khan of the Toba and Emperor of the Wei Dynasty. In the Hall of Light, he had promoted her to the twelfth rank and awarded her one hundred thousand copper coins. He had even offered her a position at court, but she had modestly declined, requesting permission to return home. Now the coppers filled the chests hauled in the wagons creaking behind them, along with the personal belongings of the squad. Her greatest accomplishment had been reporting the location of the Yen host at its most vulnerable moment.

Children playing near the stream that flowed by the village saw Mulan and her squad first. Shouting, they ran inside the nearest house. Peasants walking out of the nearest fields dropped their tools and came running. Pigs and goats in their pens at the edge of the village looked up; wild hares held in small wooden cages twitched their ears curiously.

When Mulan saw her mother and father walk out of the house leaning on each other, thin and frail, she spurred her mount into a canter. She crossed the little bridge over the stream at the edge of the village and reined up sharply. She jumped from her saddle and ran to her mother and father to embrace them both, her vision blurred with tears.

Crowding around them, other villagers called out excited greetings.

"Say nothing about me yet," Mulan whispered to her mother in Chinese.

Her mother, weeping quietly, nodded.

"Look," said her father, wiping away his own tears. He turned Mulan by the shoulder and pointed toward the pens, where a boy nearly grown ran with a large knife. "There is your Didi, barely more than a baby when you left home. I have ordered a family feast for your return."

"Make it a feast for the entire village." Mulan spoke in Toba out of deference to her father. "Our family will not lack for money ever again."

Her father stared at her in surprise.

"I will explain later." Mulan looked round. "Where is Dajie?"

"Your older sister went to change her clothes when she saw you."

"I must join her." Mulan turned to Gao, who had led the wagons up behind her at a walk. "Gao, have the squad unload the wagons into the house and the barn." She paused to make hasty introductions, then ran inside the front door of her old home, her boots thumping.

Mulan found her elder sister just coming out of her room and threw her arms around her. Her sister, dressed in a fine silk gown and wearing her makeup, also burst into tears. At first they embraced without words.

"I can hardly believe you're really home," her sister said finally, pulling back to look at Mulan in her helmet and armor.

"I have years and years of stories to tell everyone," said Mulan. "First, will you help me?"

"Help you how?"

Mulan smiled playfully. "I haven't worn a woman's gown since I left."

Her sister took her hand. "Your trunk with all your clothes has not been touched. Mother would not allow it. Come on."

In her old room, Mulan sat down on the bed and pulled off her sword belt, armor, and boots. Her sister hurried out to bring water from the well so she could wash in her room. As Mulan undressed, she heard Gao out in front, asking her father exactly where to place the chests.

Mulan shook out her best gown, which was modest but clean and festive. She washed in a basin, dressed, and let her sister powder her face and set her hair in cloudlike swirls with combs. Last, she tied the white jade vial to her sash. By the time she was ready, darkness had fallen outside, broken now by roaring fires built in front of the village.

Together, Mulan and her sister walked to the front door. The villagers drank as they talked to Gao and

the other soldiers around the fires, watching the pigs
and goats roasting over them. Two wild hares in their
basket sat near the fires, quivering their noses. Mulan
stopped in the doorway, where the firelight flickered
and flowed over her.

Gao saw her and bowed politely, holding his flask
of wine.

Mulan smiled graciously and walked up to him, her
gown swaying.

Gao and the other soldiers in their squad turned
toward her, waiting to be introduced. Around them,
her mother and father watched with amusement, and
the other villagers grinned and nudged each other.
The young children looked puzzled.

"Good evening," Gao said awkwardly.

"What's wrong, Gao?" Mulan spoke in her most
commanding soldier's tone. "Aren't you going to offer
me a swig of your wine?"

Gao's jaw dropped and the villagers roared with
laughter. The other soldiers also stared in surprise.
Gao looked carefully at her, speechless.

Mulan laughed and took the flask from his hand.
Still watching him, she took a quick drink from it and
returned it. Then she stepped back.

"We rode together for ten years," Gao whispered.
"And we spent two more years on garrison duty. I
never knew."

Mulan pointed to the pair of hares in the wooden
cage. "Can you tell which one is male and which
female?"

"No, not from here."

"I thought not." Mulan laughed lightly. "Don't be
embarrassed, Gao—nor the rest of you. I kept my
secret from everyone. And I am proud to have served
with you all."

The villagers cheered, still laughing at the soldiers'
shock. All the villagers but those who were too young

had seen Mulan answer the battle roll in her father's name. Gao still eyed her in puzzlement.

"Come, Gao" said Mulan, still enjoying his discomfort. "Help me open one of the chests and show my father and mother what I have brought."

Gao nodded, grinning reluctantly.

Mulan took her father and mother by the arm and led them inside.

The feast lasted long into the warm, summer night. The entire village celebrated Mulan's return, and her mother and father wept at the sight of the chests full of coppers. Gradually the fires burned low. The villagers returned to their homes. Gao and the rest of the squad retired to the barn.

Mulan bid everyone good night, including her mother and father. Last of all, her elder sister went to bed. Mulan stood by the fire alone as others slept, as she had so often done on sentry watch through the years.

By the glowing red coals of one fire, the two hares still sat in their wooden cage. The pigs and goats had provided enough of a feast; no one had bothered to butcher the hares. Mulan walked to the cage and opened it. The hares stared at her cautiously, then sprang away into the darkness.

Mulan listened to the silence around her for a moment. Satisfied that everyone slept, she walked from the light of the dying coals to the stream at the edge of the village. She sat down on a rock by the gently flowing water and loosened her sash in the light of a half moon.

"This is a cold night for a swim." A man's voice, dry with age, spoke from the trees growing by the stream.

Startled, Mulan leaped to her feet, clutching her robe closed.

The old hermit walked out of the shadows, leaning

on the gnarled wooden staff he held in one hand. The moonlight shone on his prominent, bald forehead and shimmered on his white gown. The white beard still trailed from his face. In his other hand, he carried a fresh peach.

"Welcome to my village," said Mulan, bowing.

"Good evening, soldier of the Khan," said the hermit. "You are well."

"Very well, thanks to your aid. I am deeply grateful."

"Only the virtuous can hear the voice of the earth essence." The hermit studied her in the moonlight. "You have come home to take care of your family and your village, when you might have earned more honors and wealth in the court of the emperor. You remain a daughter of virtue."

Mulan bowed deeply.

"Yet you still wish to take a swim in the moonlight?"

"I do." Mulan laughed lightly. "For twelve years, I have remained fully dressed in front of everyone, no matter how hot the summer. When my squad bathed and swam in a river, I remained dressed by the bank, pretending to take sentry watch. When they stripped to the waist to cut firewood or pitch camp, I stayed dressed to work with them. In sharing a tent with Gao, I never undressed completely, and only prepared for sleep after dark. When I could spare a few drops of the ginseng potion, I could sometimes sneak out of camp at night for a quick bath—but I feared to waste it and worried that Gao would wake up and find me gone. Yes, I want to take a swim in the moonlight."

The hermit looked at the white jade vial tied to her sash. "You have a portion of the potion left?"

"Only a few drops." Mulan untied the vial and held it out. "I don't need it any longer. Treasure it, you said, for it is rare."

The hermit accepted the vial. "I will find another who needs it. Thank you for your generosity, Hua Mulan—soldier named after the magnolia tree."

Mulan bowed again.

With a calm nod, the hermit turned and slipped away into the night.

Mulan slid the gown from her shoulders and let it drop. She shed her undergarments and pulled the combs from her hair. Slipping off her shoes, she stepped into the cool, rippling stream. She reclined in the soft, shallow streambed, letting the water flow over her and across her body.

In the sky above her, the half moon shone down on Hua Mulan, former soldier of the Khan.

THE MIST OF MELUSINE
by Rosemary Hawley Jarman

Magic! Enchantment! To some these words bring terror to others sheer wonder. Many religious groups typically view magic as a threat, even though their most sacred traditions usually hinge on some aspect of magic or suspension of rational thought. This fear brought us the Salem witch trials and the Inquisition, both tragic periods in our history. The following story is set in England which was no stranger to this fear, yet the British Isles have a rich history steeped in enchantment and magic.

Rosemary Hawley Jarman is a renowned English writer who specializes in the rulers of fifteenth-century England. Her historical novels include *We Speak No Treason, The King's Grey Mare* (which recounts the life of Elizabeth Woodville) and *Crown in Candlelight*. She has also published a number of short stories and a nonfiction book, *Crispin's Day*.

It is midnight, the dawn of Easter Day. At last I am alone; I have dismissed my women of the bedchamber. The wetnurse has taken my newborn son, who sleeps, into the next room. Everyone was loath to leave me as I am still weak from childbed, but I am not one who is disobeyed. I commanded them, telling them that I shall spend the night in prayer.

I spoke the truth, but if any knew to whom I intend to pray and have prayed to during these many years of trial and triumph, I should, Queen or no Queen, doting husband or no, be dragged to the stake of burning within a very short time indeed.

In this room at Baynards Castle on the Thames, a
great log fire burns in the hearth. I have only to feel
the heat of its flames to be reminded how secret my
work must be. Next to the big bed with its tapestried
canopy, there is a prie-dieu beneath a Christ with
bloody wounds. A little flame flickers under the crucifix. Kneeling here is where everyone envisages me this
night. Not so. For these my prayers, perhaps the most
important of my life, I shall stay before my own
mirror.

I have opened a small high window with latticed
glass and armorial bearings. Muffled by mist rising
from the Thames comes the sound of church bells. It
is Easter, when He who died on the Tree rose from
the dead to redeem us all. And soon, very soon, something else will rise from the mist and enter this room.
And after all these years I am still afraid of her.

I have prayed using the old words, summoning her.
Now I sit motionless in front of my mirror. It is a
large mirror of highly polished silver. All around the
rim are enameled flowers, the White Rose of York. I
hear a faint whisper of breath from the window, and
steel myself to turn my head a little. She is not here
yet. But she is coming.

The mirror shows me myself. Without delusion I
acknowledge my own beauty, undimmed even after all
my tribulation. I still look young and girlish. The recent birth has colored my cheeks, where the skin is
like satin. My hair, with which Edward the King first
fell in love, is the same color and texture as the pale
cloth-of-gold robe I wear. My hair glides from my high
unlined forehead and covers me in a gleaming fall.
And my eyes are the blue of oceans, my hands like
white fishes. My body is once again slender and supple
as an eel. Water is my element. And water is the
dwelling place of the one for whom I wait, trembling
and in hope.

I am Elizabeth Wydville, Queen to Edward the Fourth of England and of York, that powerful House which has been embroiled in bitter warfare against the equal power of Lancaster these past ten years. It is said that I ensnared King Edward with my beauty and my virtue. I, Elizabeth, a commoner, when he could have had any of the great princesses of Europe. I, Elizabeth, whose family was always loyal to Lancaster!

It was not my beauty or my virtue, although these were tools. It was her. Her will, her direction, her limitless power. She, who came long ago from the deep waters of mystery. Beneath the clangor of the Eastertide bells, I utter her name once more in homage.

Melusine.

Melusine, the witch of Luxembourg, from whom I am descended through my mother.

Again there is that whispered sigh at the window. The fire shudders and suddenly burns less brightly, and the room grows chill.

Today there will be another great battle between York and Lancaster. This is why I need her spirit, her craft. I need her sight beyond the dimensions. If King Edward should be vanquished, I, too, am utterly lost.

Last month Edward came back under cover of darkness from exile in Flanders where he had fled with his men after being ambushed and pursued by the armies of Lancaster in the North. I saw him but briefly where I lay in Sanctuary at Westminster in fear of our enemies with my mother and my daughters and with a prince in my womb. Edward mustered his loyal followers and rode off to join battle again. And the battle will be at a place not far from here; that I know already.

I do not love Edward. He is seven years younger than I and they call him the Rose of Rouen, his birthplace, because of his beauty, his generosity, his courage. I only ever loved once, my first husband, John Grey, who was killed in a battle against my grand enemy. Yet I need the King, oh, how I need him! He is my hope and salvation.

He looked magnificent albeit exhausted by his exile, when last I saw him. Six feet four inches tall, golden-haired, full of renewed zeal and lust to restore York to England's throne. At present, witless King Henry the Sixth of Lancaster occupies that throne, knowing not whether it is day or night. He has been restored to this sorry monarchy by my grand enemy, he whom I pray this night will be finally destroyed.

My grand enemy is Richard, Earl of Warwick. They call him the Kingmaker. It was he who set Edward on the throne before turning against him and joining forces with Lancaster. All my life Warwick has persecuted me, at every turn machinating against me and my family. He stripped me of my home, my beloved manor of Bradgate. He has good reason to hate me, for I spoiled his grand design, and his vengeance was terrible. My dear father and brother who fought for Lancaster he beheaded. With his own hands he held up their bloody heads before the people, then spiked the heads upon the walls of Coventry. And now in this turmoil of changing loyalties he rides against King Edward, whom once he professed to love and honor.

The fire is trembling. The logs seem to have been overcome by damp, for they hiss in displeasure and die. The bells have stopped their clangor. I think it was the bells that kept her away, for I feel her presence strongly now. Mist is beginning to pour copiously through the window.

Ah. She is here. My skin is creeping. I am shivering as if with palsy. I must remember that she loves me. She is not my servant. I am hers. And I am afraid.

My eyes in the mirror are enormous. The blue pu-pils have turned black, enlarged by fear in the candlelight. Mist begins to dance and wreathe around the mirror, laying a film of moisture on the enameled Rose of York. Behind me a shape is forming, so amorphous it is barely more than a scintillating shadow, and the candle flames shudder. I cannot look in the mirror any more. I stare down at my own shivering knees, my small feet in their pearl-trimmed slippers of martens' fur. To stop my hands from trembling I twine my fingers in the girdle at my waist, where at other times hang my keys and my crucifix.

I bow my head low. Now I can feel fingers of mist on the nape of my neck where my fine gilt hair parts itself. If I look up, I shall see her in the mirror. This is where she manifests herself when there is no lake or pond nearby. Her essence is palpable behind me. My flesh prickles with chill.

Still I cannot look up, and I have to find the courage.

For courage all I have to do is fan my anger. I will think again of Warwick the Kingmaker. He who had Edward crowned after two great battles when together they routed the forces of Henry the Sixth and his queen, Margaret of Anjou, and my own House of Lancaster fell. York was supreme for a season. Yet as on the toss of a dice, everything changed. And I was the reason for that!

Warwick's wrath was because of my marriage to Edward, for whom he had great plans for a powerful foreign alliance. He hated it when I raised my family to great estate. He calls me witch under his breath. He calls my mother witch. Yes, my lord of Warwick! My anger casts out fear.

And now he and Edward are to meet in the field. If Warwick wins the day, we are all cast down from our height. We shall be utterly demolished. To think I should wish the House of York, my old enemy, to triumph! But Edward is my doting protector, provider of riches and lands and security for me and for my vast brethren, my children. He is my salvation.

Once more the mist lays a finger on the back of my neck. My shivering becomes an ague. And I hear her voice like the faint rush of seas in a conch shell.

Elizabeth?

Soft it comes, so soft. It is not a human voice. It is like the breeze in midnight trees, like the susurration of stirred water. It is a voice of chaos and dreams. It is like the dreams my mother and I gave to Edward when at Melusine's direction we fed him the magic mushroom to make him pliant, and mine.

Elizabeth?

Very slowly I raise my head. And there she is in the mirror.

She is disembodied, which is as well. I have on occasion seen her body and could not bear it again yet. The face is more than enough. There is a kind of reptilian beauty there. It is a face not to be trusted. It is to be feared and homaged, which I do. I spread my shaking hands outward, palms up, and bow a little. Then I look at her squarely.

The face is triangular. It is almost a child's face. The black eyes are also triangular; they slant upward and gleam. They are soulless, reptile's eyes, and very bright. The red mouth is thin and long. It, too, curves upward in a line which could be a smile. The lips are parted and there is the pointed glimmer of little teeth. Her skin is very white, a dead whiteness like one who has been long in water, with the faintest tinge of green. Her hair is black and long and full, and drapes her like waterweed. The mist swirls about her. I can see the merest outline of a breast, with nothing visible below that. She stands in a cloud, but I can see her little hands with their long curved nails.

The face is interested, pert, curious with an unholy curiosity as to what these foolish humans plan and bungle, or maybe it is all beneath her, for what could they do without her aid? Further exposed, the little teeth are jagged as if filed to points. Yes, she is smiling at me. She is mine for tonight, and for the third time she calls me, in that tiny voice of mist and water.

Elizabeth?

My whole body is now transfixed with fright. I try to answer her and am dumb.

Between the little smiling teeth a tongue tip, almost colorless, shows itself for a second. I know from the past that the tongue is thin and bifurcated, and am swooning, thankful when she puts it away. In the hearth the fire has completely died to black ash. And glancing past Melusine in the mirror, I see that the little flame beneath the Christ has also gone out. His Body hangs there in darkness.

"You called me, child," she says. "And I have come. Have you no greeting for me this time?" Her voice is a little louder now, more mature. Still I cannot utter a word, and she says, sounding amused by my fear: "Must I remind you of our first meeting? You were wary of me then. Yet by the end of our time together, you were mine."

She shakes back her long hair and drops of mist or water fly icily on to my hands. She tilts her head backward, looking down at me with sly amusement from her small slanting eyes in the white wedge of face.

"It is Easter Day," I hear myself whisper, and Melusine laughs out loud. Her amusement is the inhuman patter of a falling fountain.

"I am older than Easter Day," she says. "I am eternal."

Then, without warning, she makes a fast flying gesture with her hands, and summons a whirl of mist into the mirror, blotting out her image and mine. A picture is forming, and she says: "Remember what was. Mark what will be."

It is so cold now in this chamber. Yet in the mirror the sun is shining. I am looking at my home, the manor of Grafton Regis where I spent my earliest days before I came to Court as a waiting-woman to the Lancastrian Queen, Margaret of Anjou. I see the greensward and the slope of pasture leading away from the house down to my favorite place, my bower of solitude beside the lonely lake set in a hollow and screened by thick willow trees. The sun is high, but all the birds are silent. The silver mere stretches like an inland sea, and is fringed with reeds and bulrushes.

And I am there, young in my beauty, in a worn silk dress, my hair loose as befits a maiden. It is strange seeing myself as I once was. I knew discontent then, through the poverty of our estate, and longed for excitement and riches. The water ripples.

She is whispering in my ear, and her whisper is like rain.

"It was I who released you from your boredom. I who sent you out into the world, of jewels and jousts and love."

I bow my head in acknowledgment. And now the sun shines no longer in the mirror; dusk is falling, treacherous, menacing, but I am not alone, my mother is with me.

My mother, Jacquetta, Duchess of Bedford, she is young again, not old and senile as she is today, her mind overset with grief at my father's beheading. She is so beautiful, her hair is minted gold, her eyes cobalt butterflies. She is powerful, laughing, teaching, telling, unafraid as the dusk gathers.

Lovely Jacquetta holds my hand. A weird light is gathering on the lake as if the water has sucked up part of the day.

"Hear me well, sweetheart," she says. "We are descended from Melusine the Fair. She who was so cunning. She enchanted the great lord Raymond of

Poitou. Even on their first meeting he promised her all the land that could be covered by a stag's hide. So she cut the hide into ten thousand strips and gained for herself a county. Raymond never knew he had courted an enchantress."

The light grows in the middle of the lake.

"When she was of this earth," says my mother, "Raymond was besotted with her. But he was foolish. Although she had warned him not to, he sought out her secret. He followed her one night to her lake. He found her in her private place. He saw her as she is, in her true form. He never saw her again. Yet men say that what he had seen that night turned him mad."

The water begins to move as if stirred by a giant spoon. Where the light shines a column of mist arises. And there she is, coming toward us, waist-deep in the water, not swimming or wading, but seeming to go as a swan goes, her nether parts moving underwater, strong yet invisible. She is holding out her white arms. She is pleased to greet me. And the Melusine watching the mirror behind me emits a little hiss of amusement to see herself thus out of time, for Melusine is timeless.

She comes to the edge of the lake and lies half in half out of the water. Prone in the reeds by the lake I raise my face to her and she kisses me on the forehead. Her kiss is like the burn of ice. She speaks my name. My mother makes a little noise of pleasure and reverence. She begins to pray, homaging Melusine, thanking her. The mirror-mist swirls like smoke from a bonfire in the wind. The scene changes.

It is the last day of April. Beltane, one of the great pagan feast days. I am older, a widow, the mother of my husband John's two sons. My mother is older, too, but we are both still lovely. There is moonlight and again we are by the lake at Grafton, for I am home again, dispossessed of my lands by the fiend Warwick.

My mother has made a waxen image of the young King Edward. She has taken blood from where he scratched himself upon my pin while he was trying to ravish me. She has taken a strand of his golden hair from the collar of his velvet cloak. She offers the image to Melusine, who rises quickly from her watery demesne. My mother throws the image over the lake and Melusine laughs, like the cry of a night bird, and catches it easily in her hand. She sinks slowly below the water, crying softly: "Elizabeth! Queen Elizabeth!"

The silver mirror shimmers as if about to turn to water. The Melusine of the past rises again, moves closer. I can barely see her shape through the mist of time. She stretches out her hand. I see that she holds another wax image, not Edward for all that was consummated long ago. This is the effigy I and my mother made of Warwick. A perfect replica. Tall, handsome, with black curly hair. Warwick, so popular with the people of London to whom he threw open his banqueting hall, magnanimous, currying favor for so long. His waxen face is contorted in agony; there is a little iron band round his waist. For some years he has complained of the bloody flux and pains in his belly.

The images are fading away. Again I see Melusine, not of the past but of the present, and now the white mist around her is fading too, revealing more of her shape. Her waist, naked, wasplike, shimmering green-white, slowly emerges. She is no longer smiling as she speaks.

"Your mother is in grave danger," she whispers. "Warwick's witch-finder knows about the images. They will burn her, Elizabeth."

And I cry out *No!* in agony, but my cry emerges as a breath.

Just to remind me, she shows in the mirror Jacquetta my mother, holding the bloody severed head of my father to her breast. The bodice of her dress is soaked with red. Tears furrow her old face.

"Oh, poor Mother," says Melusine, almost in mockery.

"Help us," I whisper, and weep.

And she speaks soothingly, her voice like the lap of water on reeds in summer.

"Have I ever failed you, my love?"

My tears are falling. I reach up behind me to take her hand, and clasp a thing of icy water, but water like iron with the power of oceans in it, out of the deeps of centuries.

She is making more pictures. She shows me the battles of yesterday. Snow is falling over the field of Towton, hindering the forces of Lancaster, and Edward rides in a final triumphant charge, glorious, his enemies falling beneath his steel like harvested corn, his golden hair streaming from beneath his helm, his armor bright with the blood of others.

"I sent the snow," she whispers.

She shows me the battle of Mortimer's Cross. Edward gazes upward, rapt at the good omen in the sky. Three suns have appeared to him, harbinger of glory. She shows me again the rout of Lancaster by the forces of York.

"I sent three suns," she whispers.

The picture comes clearer, homing in on the King's standard. The Sun in Splendor. A golden disk within sharp rays, the banner immense and blazing, borne on the wind of triumph like the sail of a fighting ship.

"See the Sun in Splendor!" Melusine says to me. "The spikes around the Sun. It looks like a star!"

I know from her voice that what she says must be significant, but I do not understand. The bells begin again; they are ringing for Prime, the first office of the day and time is rolling forward; we are truly in Easter

Day. Melusine hears the bells and casts a contemptuous glance toward the source of the sound.

I am weeping more now. She has shown me only the triumphs of the past, almost as if I should be content, and we are in mortal danger. The reversal of all Edward fought for is at hand. And if he should lose, we are damned and doomed. "Melusine!" I cry through the tears. "Show me more than yesterday! Where is Edward? Show me Edward, for the love of heaven. . . ."

She laughs, a spiky cackle like waterbirds disturbed on a pond. "Do not speak to me of heaven, Elizabeth," she says. "You chose your heaven. It is here on earth. You have no gods but me."

I am in fear that I have offended her. Yet she is still mine, for she flicks her fingers of water and rolls away time itself, showing the preparations for what will be today. Edward is in his pavilion. His esquires are arming him.

He wears Nuremburg steel. The cuirass over his breast is richly chased and gleaming, like the pauldrons on his shoulders and the gorget covering his throat. They house his arms in bright brassards and his legs in shining greaves. His feet are armored in sollerets. He holds out his hands for the steel gauntlets. Overall he wears the surcoat of the White Rose of York and the royal arms, for in his mind and in the mind of his followers he is still the rightful King. His chaplain is in attendance. Before Edward dons his helm, he crosses his breast, asks pardon of holy Jesus for doing battle on Easter Day. He listens for the voice of Christ. He invokes Saint Michael and Saint George. He is reassured that the cause is good.

His esquires hand him his weapons, his battle-ax and sword, his spiked mace and his dagger. Outside the pavilion his great warhorse, armored in mail from ears to fetlocks, tosses its head, aroused by the smell of war.

Edward's men are all around him: his loyal brother Richard of Gloucester (another of my enemies for once he loved Warwick like a father), the companions of his exile, Lord Hastings and others, his noble peers of York. They are tense but in good heart. And all this is taking place very near.

"They gather at Barnet," says Melusine, in her voice of water. "Not far away. See the camp of the enemy, Elizabeth. Mark well their standards. See the devices on their banners."

There he is. Warwick. Full of hubris, smiling, arming as they are all arming. His standard, the Bear and Ragged Staff, is planted outside his pavilion. The Earl of Oxford, his chief captain and commander of his secondary force, puts on his helm with its trailing plume. His standard-bearer lifts high Oxford's banner of a Silver Star.

There is low and high ground, a valley and a hill. Upon the scene there is real mist, not only in my mirror. The whole valley is becoming filled with it. It is light at the moment, rising like a thin blanket from a deep marshy hollow. The two camps are separated by its veil.

Melusine leans forward. She presses her hand on my head, like a cap of ice. "See what I am conjuring for you, Elizabeth. Mist. Fog. I command the waters."

"Will it be soon?" I ask her. I am still weeping.

The bells ring out again, this time for Matins. Melusine's mirror-time has joined with real time. The time is now.

"Warwick has fielded fifteen thousand men. Far more than the King," she says. "What will you give me, Elizabeth, to safeguard your destiny?"

I am wild now with despair and fear. If she were solid, I would cling to her, for I am less afraid of her than of what will be. I clasp my hand over the hand of water which is soaking my hair. My tears blur the moil of warriors in the mirror-mist, that true mist that Melusine has sent upon Barnet Field.

"My soul," I whisper, and she laughs, her sea-bird's laugh.

"But I have that already, Queen. I took your soul long ago when I gave you the King, riches, security. Will you give me your newborn son?"

"Yes, yes!" I cry. "He is yours. Melusine, my Melusine, do not fail us now."

"And your son to come, your second prince that will be born?"

"If this is so, yes, both of them," I whisper. "Their souls, my Melusine, their bodies, too. Only save us this day."

I only half believe this pledge that I am making, for I have only one prince, yet if there are more to be born, this can only mean that Edward will live as King and come back to me.

Yet she persists, saying: "Even if their lives are short? Another king will come to praise me, my love, Tudor his name...."

She is teasing me and I am desperate, for the time is racing forward, the mirror shows horsemen advancing through mist. I hear the faint sound of trumpets, distorted by the mirror. I nod my head to whatever she is saying in absolute obedience, and drops of water from her caressing hand spatter my gown like tears.

And once again I whisper: "Help us!"

She is growing taller, longer. I see her white body with its greenish tint as far as her belly. She has no navel. I am again in craven dread of her, and she holds my destiny and that of York, of England. She is smiling broadly now with her little shark's teeth. Any beauty she had has vanished; there is only sorcery enjoying itself.

"Watch, Elizabeth! Now they fight!"

I see the armies mustered. The Duke of Exeter commands Warwick's left wing between the St. Albans road and the treacherous marshy hollow. Lord Montagu holds the center, the Earl of Oxford holds the right wing. Warwick commands the reserve.

The watery grayness thickens around them and a little breeze, far from dispersing it, tosses it around them like spectral dancers.

Edward's forces are deployed in similar fashion. Richard of Gloucester leads his men up the slope and they fall upon the flank of Warwick's force, but the hill is steep and they reel back disadvantaged. The trumpets blare in command. They fight like lions with a desperation that augurs ill for York. The mist lightens a little; I look in panic at Melusine. I see she is laughing like a cat, a humorless yawn of laughter. For Warwick's men have rallied and form a new front to north and south. Reinforcements are coming out of the mist to join them. The Yorkists are outmatched.

I can hear myself screaming, but the scream stays inside my head. We watch closely through the mirror and the mist: the masses of horsemen; footsoldiers; archers; the maimed; the slain; the blood. We hear the faint war cries and the screams of men and horses.

The Earl of Oxford crashes into Hastings' flank. Many of Hastings' men are unhorsed or slain; the survivors begin to retreat, some running, some riding in panic toward the town, and my enemy Warwick at the head of a squadron of fighting men pursues them. Some other Yorkist forces begin to flee, already crying that the day is lost.

"Melusine," I moan. "Save us."

The hand of ice comes again to caress my head. Water runs down my brow into my eyes. "Wait, darling, wait," she says, like the sighing of oceans. "See your great lord!"

Edward is fighting under the swaying pulsing standard of the Sun. He fights like twenty men, laying about him with his battle-ax and sword. His Household battle shoulder to shoulder with him. The clang of steel on armor rings through the mirror. The Duke of Gloucester has reformed his troops. Hastings has gathered the remnants of his army. They fight on in mist.

Yet here is my enemy again, shouting in the harsh voice that once berated me as an upstart—giving new commands to the Earl of Oxford. He will fall upon Edward's company from the rear. And they come, pounding toward the lines of battle, and the moment is now, and my Melusine leans forward over my shoulder.

Her whole body changes, becomes a powerful ether. It swells and swells into a gigantic cloud of white, reaching the ceiling of the chamber. The cloud is directed into the mirror in a poisonous stream which bears the stench of putrid oceans, of the corpses of seamen devoured by a pitiless sea, of rank weed, of stagnant ponds, enough to bring a retching to my throat. It streams through the mirror as if from a funnel. It is more than mist. It is more than fog. It is as if the air were a thick broth of gray water. The cold is unbearable. My flesh crawls and my hair stands erect. The last of the white cloud enters the mirror like smoke bellowed out of a storm wind, and the forces of Warwick, Oxford, Exeter, all my enemy's fighting men so close to triumph are surrounded by its denseness.

There is a tremendous crying. There is a limitless confusion. There comes a scream of *Treason!* The fog shifts to allow a tiny window through which Melusine and I can see what passes.

"Look!" she shrieks in her seabird's voice. "Lancaster is undone! They are fighting one another!"

The Earl of Montagu, bringing reinforcements to strike at Edward's rearguard, has in the fog mistaken the Silver Star of Oxford for the Sun in Splendor. They are killing their own men. And my King and his commanders revive; they lay into the enemy forces with all their royal puissance. And Warwick is in flight!

I am on my knees in front of the mirror, crying to her: "Kill him!" No longer weeping, I am laughing, and she is laughing, that crazed seabird's cackle, and with a flick of her fingers it seems that she sends a galloping knot of Yorkists after the great Earl. Warwick's armor is battered by blows. His face is blood-splashed. There is terror on it. They corner him in a hollow and strike at him. As he falls, he turns and slithers along the muddy ground with a great wound in his belly. The fog kisses his head where his helm has been struck away. I see his agony. Through the fog of Melusine he writhes toward us. He sees us! To my dying day I swear he sees us. His mouth opens in horror. He cries *Mercy!* but one of King Edward's captains strikes the word away. And he is dead. I hear the sounds of a great rout. Then the trumpets, the cheering.

"God bless the House of York!" they are yelling. "Praise to Jesus our Redeemer, who sent this victory!"

Then slowly the whole picture fades and I am left, trembling and laughing and crying, my eyes fixed in gratitude on the strange triangular face and the reptilian eyes on mine in the mirror, and I turn my head to kiss her hand and find my mouth filled with water that tastes of the corpses of the drowned.

Day has come. Outside the sun begins to glint through the dispersing river-mist. She speaks to me once more, and her voice is no longer eldritch, but strong, fathoms deep.

"Remember me, Queen, when I come for my dues."

She stretches up her arms, stretches her body to a height so that she is revealed from the top of her head to where she meets the floor. And she has no legs. I knew this once, but I have tried to forget it. This is the sight that drove Raymond of Poitou insane.

From her waist down she is a serpent, shimmering with moisture, a great barrel of a reptile's body gleaming from the water with little pockets of weed and tiny sea creatures caught among her scales. This is no pretty mermaid. This is a loathsome, noxious serpent through all her legs and womanly parts, a serpent like the form Satan took in the Garden of Eden. She is evil.

And she is my savior, and the savior of the King, the House of York, of England. We are safe once more, for a season.

She is fading in all her repulsive power. She does not like the day. Below the window lies the river and she will enter it as she came, as mist. Mist is clearing from the chamber and she goes with it, leaving me with one last languorous glance almost of lust, certainly of triumph. There is a price to be paid, but it is not yet.

Already the news of our victory is beginning. I can hear across the river a courier shouting in hoarse ecstasy. There is distant cheering, no louder than a gnat's whine. The exaltation will grow, as Edward returns in glory. Edward, the Sun in Splendor, whose standard, through Melusine's mist, so resembled a Star.

My women are tapping at the door. My chaplain is with them, come to give thanks with me on Easter Day. I glance toward the Christ over the prie-dieu. His Body is filmed with a patina of damp, and his wet wounds look new.

GOING BACK TO COLCHIS
by Rebecca Ore

Who are we to cry insanity when someone claims divine inspiration? The difference between insanity and the driving forces of the gods is sometimes small. Histories and mythologies are crowded with interesting people who lived partly in a world other than common reality. This next story is about a woman whose story makes up one of the Greek tragedies; a play that is still performed on modern stages throughout Greece and the world.

Rebecca Ore is an ingenious writer, better known for her science fiction than her fantasy. She has had stories appearing in *Asimov's Science Fiction, Amazing,* and *The New York Review of Science Fiction* magazines. She has also written several novels. Her most recent science fiction book is *Gaia's Toys.* She also has a fantasy out, *Slow Funeral.*

The rowers were the usual arrogant Greek princelets from miniature kingdoms in love with their captain, rowing to obscene chants. Greeks. I never noticed the world was so full of Greeks when I was so boldly young, scheming with Hecate's voice always in my ear, falling in love, killing, falling out of love, killing. Now I was down to two sons, only one with me, and surrounded by Greeks.

It's supposed to be your defeat, Medea, Hecate whispered in my mind. I stared out over the Bosporus, rowed home by princes of kingdoms so tiny that I probably would have walked through scores of them between Argos and Athens. If I had walked away from Argos.

But Hecate sent the car. Pulled by Dragons, I whirled over all their little kingdoms to my new friend, King Aegeus. The blood from the boys hadn't dried on my hands when I landed. But even before Theseus exiled me from Athens, I was beginning to understand that Hecate couldn't defeat the Greeks, no matter what her power in our native country.

I was, after all, half Greek myself.

If I were younger, I'd say my life was over, but I've thought my life was over many times earlier and the gods chose to pull me out and set me back in play. The first time, I was very grateful. Now, I make the sacrifices I should make and don't count on either gods or men.

Theseus warned the rowers about me, but I'm now wrinkled.

How they stink! Wool doesn't wash like linen. The Greeks smell peculiar for all their oil baths. Naked, they might be quite marvelous, but they don't stay naked. Sweaty and clothed, they smell like wet sheep.

Fortunately, they row naked, or I'd be quite overwhelmed by the smell. My son, Medeius, sits with them, chattering in perfect Athenian Greek.

Out beyond the Bosporous is the Black Sea and we're going to the end of that. I'm returning to Colchis, rivers and marshes, the mountains at her back, flax retting in her streams. Linen may not be the Golden Fleece, but all and all, our best export.

The real Golden Fleece was a tiny statue of a ram with its horns entangled in a tree—worth far more as a token than for the gold in it.

I stole the Fleece, betrayed my father, killed my brother, now I'm coming home in defeat.

Once through the straits, the captain, ten years

older than his men, decides we should pull up to shore
for the night and no one disagrees with him. The
Greeks consider age suitable rank. All of an age are
equals until one proves superior to his fellows. But he
can only be so superior, or else his age cohort pulls
him back down.

To me, Greeks seem as mechanical as ants. I'm possessed by Hecate and a mechanical ant.

I walk across the beach and find a branch infested
with ants, pick it up, and throw it in the air. The
Greeks lolling around their campfires look at me,
some nervous as if I'd conjure up an army (remember,
boys, it was dragon's teeth I sowed), the others nervous that they're going to have to deal with a mad-
woman for the length of the Black Sea.

Going back to Colchis, yes. My brother's pieces
must be gone beyond rotting to bone, the very bone
must have dissolved. Even Jason's sons are no more
than bones now. I see my son among the Greeks.
They've made him their pet. The mother contributes
only the womb, the child is the man's seed. Yes, that's
what the Greeks claimed. Aegeus' son, not mine,
among them, going as a Greek to my country.

Medeius, I knew you before you were born. The
earth has her own seeds the sowers don't cast. The
woman shapes her children who drink semen before
milk.

But he looks at me as though I embarrass him, an
old woman posturing on the sand, ants biting her feet.
The sun set dramatically behind the Bosporus, the current roiling through.

The land they know crawls off behind us. Hecate
stirs in my mind, whispering of crones, old women
terrors.

I wobble though as I loosen my muscles and walk
away from the disturbed anthill. One of the young

rowers rises as though to help me, but I stab him off with my eyes.

Medeius fears me, and trusts the Greeks to protect him. Why not? I didn't let the squalls of Jason's youngest brats stop me. The oldest boy, all of nine, picked up a pike and fended me away, slashing at my breasts, but I said, "Now, come, I won't hurt you. After all, I'm your mother. The gods drove me mad, but I'm all right now." Lulled by a mother's promises, he ignored the knife I held in front of me. Stupid like his father.

So, I saved them from being bastards, the whining kin of people who have power. I walk toward my tent, hips swaying in the old dance, but I have no partner. The captain says something to his crew and laughs. I ask Hecate to tell me more about crones' powers.

The boy must learn to kill for you, Hecate's voice tells me. *Your uncle, Perses, has the throne now. Did you kill so many to put your father's brother on the throne?*

No. So, my son, on this long voyage, we must learn to trust one another. I am your mother who gathered semen to build you, to feed you in my womb. I want you on the throne, not Perses.

I roll up in linen and stare at the stars, then roll onto my side, away from the men, and sleep.

"Medeius," I whisper in my son's ear. He starts, comes out of sleep onto an elbow to stare at me. "We've got to make plans."

"Mother, aren't you too old for plans?"

"Medeius, your uncle will kill you."

"I'm not going back as heir."

"Oh, Medeius, you can't help but go back as heir." Hecate sang in my mind, the fates behind her spinning, weaving, snipping Perses' shroud. On the other side, my Greek side, geometric form contested with rounded marble humans.

"If I get to be king," Medeius said, "what do you want out of it?"

"Oh, Medeius," I said, making sure to sound hurt, but I had the boy thinking about the fun kings had. If we laid over a year or two in the western end of the Black Sea, he might be grown enough to take Perses without magical aid.

But that would be boring.

Rowing over gobies, pipefish, and trout that swarmed in Colchean rivers in springtime, rowing over wrecks and bones of former men whose past lay traps for the living, rowing over the whistling dolphins and Hecate's voice thinking in my right ear, we moved toward Colchis, with her back to mountains where Prometheus lay chained, his immortal innards exposed by eagle beak, swallowed, regrown.

The fire Prometheus stole for us warmed me on the night beaches. *Medeius, your mother only wishes you the best,* I thought at him, hoping Hecate would send the words to his ear in her own voice. I could not precisely seduce my son. If I pushed him to seize the throne, he'd recoil, side with his uncle, slit my throat in broadest daylight when Hecate couldn't help. *Ah, Medeius, your mother did it all for you.*

Please, Hecate, win me my son back. I bend to the beach and pick up pebbles, shift them in my hand. Medeius glances over the fire at me. I push tears into my eyes, turn my eyes down to watch the stones clinking against each other in my hands. *Medeius, I, Hecate, will make certain your victory.* Only I'm the one thinking this and I hope Hecate doesn't think I commit sacrilege with my mind's voice.

I speak through you, the goddess tells me. I relax, keeping the tears in my eyes, watching the stones bruise each other and my hand. I squeeze them tightly and drop them, then go to sleep where Hecate waits for me with fully developed battle plans that Apollo burns with daylight.

The boat rows on. The land we pass turns wetter; leaking springs drain into the sea. The waves hiss, "Colchis, Colchis."

Ten days later, Medeius says, "How can I, a boy, take your father's brother off the throne?"

"Aren't these your father's men?" I said. "Perhaps they'll support you." I didn't feel he wanted me to offer him magic yet.

"Were you mad when you killed my half brothers?"

"How could they be your half brothers when the male seed is responsible for all the child's growth?" I said. "When their father turned them into bastards, they had to die as is the custom."

"Whose custom?" Medeius asked. "Not the Greeks'."

I hated Jason's brood from my belly, but I couldn't say that. "The gods drove me mad," I said.

Medeius said, "How can I be sure that won't happen again?"

"They were gods who hated Jason's gods," I said, trying to be careful not to blame my claimed madness on Greek gods. "They have no power in Colchis. Hecate will protect us."

"Hecate's a woman's goddess."

I rolled in my blankets and said, "She works quite well in Colchis."

Medeius sits by the captain, in the bow of the rowed boat. He's talking to him, men secrets, but when my son looks at me, I know they're talking about my uncle, what reception we can expect from him, what he might do to Medeius, for Medeius.

Apollo blocks Hecate. The sun beats the waves, sending off light splinters. We row along the shore, off far enough to miss the wave bouncing against the

land. The Greek captain looks at me, then, and half
closes his eyes like a cat looking at the big food
person.

In the bow of the ship, I ignore them, my awning
cooling me as the rowers sweat through the waves.
Below me, hissing in the water, is the face of a falcon
with a solid bronze beak fit for ramming.

At noon, we swing into shore. I move back so the
crew can beach the boat properly. The captain says to
me, "Why are you trying to scare your son? You're
the only one who won't be welcome in Colchis."

I said, "He's my son in Colchis. Our lines go
through the mother."

"And you with a Greek father should know who
makes babies," the captain kinglet said. "Look, you
old bitch, don't upset the boy."

"I'm sure Perses will see him as a guest," I said,
smiling. At night, when Apollo doesn't guard our
thoughts, we all must discuss this further.

Another night by a driftwood fire. My body seems
to be shriveling the closer we get to Colchis. Dried by
salt and sun, an old pickled woman, that's what I've
become. Perhaps Hecate will embody and seduce the
captain kinglet. We may have need of fighting men to
put my son on the throne in Colchis. Hecate says, *The
captain is Apollo's man. He takes his women by daylight so he can inspect them closely for witch marks.*

What about boys? I think back.

Would you offer him your son? Hecate asks.

I look across the fire and see Medeius and the captain laughing together over vinegarish wine. *Oh, I
probably couldn't stop it if the captain has made my
son his boy. Apollo's man is more believable than I
am. I expect to die in chains.*

Medea, I will be with you in Colchis.

I wondered if perhaps I'd been following the wrong

goddess. Initiates in the Mysteries hear at the end, "Orpheus is a dark god," when it's too late to walk away. Dead children litter the lands, sons that don't trust me, my husband warned out of my bed by a puny Greek bastard.

No, no, be angry. Rise in your wrath as the dragons did.

I rose and went to my son among the Greeks. "If we get a favorable reception, then all my fears are those of a foolish old woman," I said. The captain's teeth gleamed at me. "But we should go in with caution."

Medeius said, "My great-uncle will welcome me. I do not seek the throne. I offer him an alliance with my father." He looked back at the captain.

So, I'm a vessel for alliances? I thought, becoming angry enough to feel Hecate gripping my feet through the sand I stood on. I said, "I hope you are right, but the gods can stir up trouble for their own entertainment."

"The gods have nothing to do with it," the captain said.

"I hope for my son's sake that you do not find you're wrong," I said, Hecate whispering in my mind plans I wasn't quite ready to hear.

So we came up, rowing, to the Rioni Delta. A swarm of mosquitoes like miniature Furies flew out of the swamps to greet us. I remembered now that I'd forgotten them, the swamp miasmas, the biting insects, wormy water. Perhaps these were murdered children's Furies.

My son was slapping at them, too. I relaxed. They'd bitten me before I was a child slayer.

The captain said, "Do your people have quays?"

Before I could answer, two coast guard ships came rowing down the main channel at us. I looked around and saw another blocking us. The captain said, "Ship from Athens, returning the Lady Medea to Colchis."

One of the other ships' captains said, "The runner arrived a week ago."

I said to our captain, "I hope you haven't brought Medeius to harm."

Our captain didn't look quite so cocksure now. We pivoted toward the main channel and rowed into the quays by the palace. I'd also forgotten how wooden the palace really was. Somehow, in memory, I'd turned it into stone. But this was a wooded land. The palace burned smudge against the biting insects.

My uncle didn't meet us at the quay. Household guards led the Greeks one way; my son and me another. I felt for Hecate's presence. Some metal I had never felt or smelled before tainted the air.

We were led into a stone room with a door bound in a gray metal pitted with red flakes, not lead. I couldn't cut it with my nails. The guards closed in behind me. I said to Medeius, "Well, my son, you didn't have a chance to explain how you didn't trust me." In the room, I saw two Greek chairs and three slits between stones below the roof timbers showing light, but no clear view. Over the roof timbers, tiles. If I stood on Medeius's shoulders, I could see through the slits, even reach the ceiling.

"Sorry, Mother. We should have listened to you. You knew the politics of Colchis better than we did." The house guards closed the door and barred it on the outside.

"I made the politics of Colchis," I said. What was this metal binding the door? Jason had told me Chalybes worked in strange metal, harder to work and edge than bronze.

Hecate climbed through the floor into my mind. *A dangerous metal, though it does but adorn the door now.*

I asked, *Will you bring us the Greeks in armor to help free me?*

Medeius' face glowed. The goddess spoke to him, not to me. He said, "Mother, we will be freed. I am the foundation of empires."

And he and this metal will feed me many corpses. Hecate said. *Metals and stone are mind-binding, this one more than any other I have seen before.*

Are you seeing those corpses, Hecate?

I see the iron edge coming down from the Hittites, a dagger in an Egyptian tomb. Leagues from here, the blades cut, chatter through the bronze swords.

The future, Hecate?

She would not answer. Or could she? What if I was bound to a goddess with limit. As time-bound as I was, Hecate had only seen the corpses dying now, her promise to Medeius a lie.

Medeius said, "My line will live forever."

Nothing is forever. Hecate of lies. I remembered what she'd promised me when I was young, hot, and killing. *Hecate, what can you do for us next?* The far future was not yet. In this now, we had to get out of the stone cell. I lost my faith in the infinite wisdom of my goddess, but she still connected us through all this time.

The Greeks will lie and rescue you from guilt. You had warned them this could hurt Medeius.

Supposition, not farseeing into that future forming beyond mortal ken. Medeius said, "We didn't think you were right, Mother, but if you were right...."

"Hush," I said to interrupt him. Even stones have flaws that let sound escape into my uncle's ears. He owed me. He was an old man and could step down for my son whose blood was an alliance with Athens.

But I want you to kill him, Hecate said.

Soon, three guards came in with bowls of wheat gruel flavored with sesame. Two women followed them with fresh robes for both of us. The oldest guard said, "Your uncle, Medea, wants to welcome you. We were uncertain about your intentions."

"I always follow the gods of my ancestors," I said.

Medeius stripped like a Greek in front of both the men and women. One of the women blushed, the other averted her head and looked at me. I said, "Conceal me," and changed into flax clothes behind my wool Greek dress. Ah, flax, cool over the insect bites. The women squinched their faces and held the wool with their fingertips. I, too, had sweated on the journey, had too few clothes, no fresh water and women to beat them clean.

Maybe we should just accept my uncle's hospitality? *No,* Hecate said.

My son frowned at the unaccustomed feel against him, then said, "We go to the king dressed like this?"

"It's summer outside. You'll sweat like a pig," the head guard told him. "We thought you'd appreciate a cool room."

I said, "Stone without views to the outside makes a room feel confining." The guards smiled as though they were embarrassed to have to lie. Medeius sat down on one of the chairs and ate his gruel. Everyone waited for him to finish.

We were led into the throne room where curly-bearded Uncle Perses sat on a throne carved and inlaid with ivory and ebony. His men blew brass horns to welcome us. "Ah, niece," he said. "And my grand-nephew. By Aegeus?"

I said, "I killed all Jason's. I begged you to rescue me."

"Sort of," Perses said. "But you killed your half brother and helped Jason kill your father."

Knowing he didn't believe any of this but expected me to lie, I said, "But I was under a spell. The dragon's teeth, Mars."

"Oh, Medea."

"I didn't have ships or men. I was a lone woman in Greece. Now, I am an old woman." *Don't press your luck,* Hecate whispered in my mind.

"Your son, his comrades say, can bring me an Athenian princess."

I gasped. That bastard Aegeus remarried so quickly? "She will be a very young girl," I said.

"A man's children are all his," Perses said.

"So any of your sons can inherit," I said. Some stirred in the crowd around the throne. So Perses had no sons. *Hecate, why kill?*

I need. Remember your illusions, sleight of hand, the poisoner's arts.

Medeius said, "Mother, we're among friends here." His Greek comrades looked at me again with that wary caution of liars looking at another deceiver.

I said, "We are grateful for your shelter," and bowed as though I meant it. Perses looked at the Greeks, then back at me. No trust there at all. I wondered how many women he sowed his seed in. I had to stop any sons.

Perses said, "Medea, you're almost as old as I am, worn from childbearing to a greater decrepitude. Take your last days in ease."

"My uncle king, you're most generous," I said. Hecate cackled. I was once a virgin with tricks, then a woman who killed children, and now I was the Crone. Behind me, behind Hecate, women began to spin the thread for Perses' shroud, of linen weighted with skulls, the warp his guts. *Snip, snip, life threads. Don't remind Medea of her age.*

Perses said, "Medeius, my grandnephew, we'll show you to different rooms, send you serving women. Medea." He nodded to his people.

Two women took my arms while the guard formed

around me with their bronze pikes. "So, you don't
trust me," I said.

"No," Perses said.

I laughed once, then went back to my stone room.
Come, concealing night. I felt the stones as high as I
could reach, searched for fingerholds above my head,
imagined the feel there, there, to the tiles. Then I sat
down on the floor and pulled my hair through my
fingers as though I were mad until the light faded.

Very good, Medea.

The crone climbed up the rocks, her nails breaking.
I felt like I was floating off my left shoulder, then over
my head. Up, up, to the tiles. I pushed. They slid
away, with noise. *Hecate, silence the night.* My fingers
moved. I put one foot in the light slot, eased the tiles
away, slow *screech* of tile against tile. Finally, I could
push my head out, half expecting to have it lopped
off. The stone cell was against a hill. I saw small people coming toward me, ducked down.

One whispered, "Lady Medea," and I was surrounded by small people with curly hair, dark skins,
my mother's people, the country's first inhabitants,
touching me as though I were a goddess who could
bring them luck.

After my mother's people pulled me out, I went
down on one knee and bowed to my goddess. *Hecate,
I am sorry I doubted you.* Then we scurried down to
the river where a punt waited. They wrapped me in a
reed cloak. One small man in the stern poled me into
the marshes.

I was rescued, but what good was this? *Wait.* The
small dark man took me to a platform temple built
over the marsh. I prayed in the dark while he took
the boat off again. He came back with a black chicken
and a knife chipped from god glass, obsidian. I cut the

bird's throat to Hecate. The man handed me a barely glowing brand for the fire. I asked, "Is it safe?"

"Here, yes. No one see here, but to bring fire, it had to be hidden."

I blew the altar fire into flames and felt the insects flee, some dancing into the flames, their own self-sacrifices. *Hecate, feed at my altar. Hecate, lead me in your will.*

The man said, "Lady, we are your knives, pikes, and swords. We would lay down our lives if you would but put your mother's people back on the throne."

I'm half Greek. My son is only one quarter these people. *Lie. Like a Greek.* "My black and glittering knife, I accept your aid." I didn't know if the lies were my own or if Hecate whispered the thoughts to me.

Hecate said, *Their weapons can be defeated by the gray metal from the Chalybians.* So, first defeat my uncle, put my son on the throne, then defeat these people with Chalybean steel. Steel, the knife in Egypt, the voyage back. Iron a strange ornamental thing that developed its own patterns—who'd have thought it could turn weapon.

My dark knife-bearer bowed and said, "Colchis will never forget you, Lady."

We gathered in the night with weapons of stone and bronze. Then I realized I could please everyone, Hecate, too. I said, "Bring me a princess of the old blood, of my mother's people."

My weapons-men muttered to each other and replied, "Lady, we would keep the royal women out of harm until you've made it safe for your mother's people."

So, we all were playing a game here. We hid in the marshes the next day. Messengers from the city said that Medeius was now in the stone cell with heaps of stone over the tile. Other messengers said he was killed, to be killed, feasting with the king, in hiding,

leading the Greeks who'd brought him in a fight
against my uncle. I suspected Perses would think Medeius had something to do with my disappearance.
Medeius would suspect Perses of having done away
with me by night, not so convinced of Hecate's
powers.

I sent my black knife out to check after he'd rested.
He came back by dusk and said, "Lady, Perses keeps
your son at his side, the Greeks away."

Surrounded by guards, of course. I said, "Hecate
and the old gods will be with us at night. Blacken your
glittering weapons and this night, our gods will expel
Apollo and Athena."

"All Greek gods," said a voice from the back.

I almost said, *More important, I think, to control
things Greek than to destroy them.* No, say rather,
"The powers will be ours, Colcheans."

As serving people, my weapons-men had many sta-
tions in the city. I said, "Tomorrow. When the moon
hides and the dark is total, then."

Most faded into the marshes like Hecate's imagina-
tion. We slept through Apollo's search. The moon was
in the back of the sky by nightfall, waning. In dark
reed boats, we poled back into the city, creeping at
river's edge, disguised as servants, beggars, anonymous
people the Greeks kept as concubines. I would have
turned into Jason's concubine. Flax rotted under us,
the mosquitoes chased us, my blood especially valu-
able cased in thinner skin.

Here. We crept through the mud. My black knife
slit a guard's throat. I pushed my hand into the slit,
calling *Hecate, Hecate, be with me tonight and you'll
drink.*

We slid through the shadows, bronze weapons
pitched, the black stone glass ones rubbed with fat
and sand to kill the glitters. My body seemed to shift

through all my ages: crone, virgin, mother, virgin, crone.

We came up the palace steps. Inside, servants who'd never seemed other than dumb and compliant slit throats. Hecate whirled through us. I ran into the room where my son sat with his uncle and cried, "I've brought you your bride's people." My clothes were gray-black, sumac bitten into linen, flying around me like a shroud.

My small black knife put his stone blade into my uncle. He said, "Fool," shook the small Colchean off, smashed the blade. But others swarmed him like ants.

My uncle's guard looked to Medeius. He backed away from me, his mother, and they surrounded him. One blew a brass horn. I stopped, flat bare feet against the wooden floor.

Medeius said, "Well, Mother, you've put me on the throne, have you?"

I saw my small people die on strange gray blades, their bronze cut, their stone weapons shattered. *Hecate, so soon.*

You have betrayed them. I don't care the nation of the blood I drink. But they will never forgive you. I looked at my son. He smiled at me, then more house guards, large Greeks and the minor princes from the rowing ship rushed in.

Medeius said, "Mother, the Kindly Ones alone keep you alive tonight."

I said, "My lord, your mother wishes ..." I looked down at the small bodies. Like ants. "... wishes you to know I love you above all my children." Children come through the mother line, the males giving sperm like rain to nourish them. Colchean or Greek, I felt the Furies put me under their protection. "I say I did this all for you. My uncle is dead."

The Furies began to rip my back, but I lived like Prometheus in a land that fell apart around me.

AMAZON GOLD
by Steven Rogers

This next story takes place in the sixteenth century when
Spain was hungry for gold and land and sought both in
South America. One seeker was Francisco de Orellana who
made two trips to the new world. On his second journey to
the Americas Orellana brought four hundred conquistadors
and his wife, Ana. Why he brought Ana to America is as
much a mystery as why he married her, a penniless woman,
against the wishes of king, church, and a number of well-
dowried noblemen's daughters.

Steven Rogers has several short stories appearing in a
variety of publications, his latest is in *Worlds of Fantasy
and Horror* magazine, as well as a story in *Ancient Enchantresses*. He is working on a young adult fantasy novel.

A na dreamed. A tall, light-skinned woman with a
jaguar's head appeared at the edge of the jungle
and stood along the riverbank singing, shaking a spear
adorned with feathers of oily purple and vermilion.
Her variegated plumes suddenly blossomed, trans-
forming into birds who burst into the sky and began
circling the brigantine—fiery orange-blue macaws,
saffron-billed toucans, emerald jacamars, and black
New World eagles with wings as wide as the ship's
mainsail.

A bird's cry woke Ana. Was the cry real or imagined? She knew in her bones the meaning, even before
her feet touched the damp cabin floor. They'd sailed

beyond an invisible boundary, Ana and a crew of fifty-one men with armor, crossbows, and black powder arquebuses.

She pulled on a yellowed linen dress, scrubbed clean with rainwater the night before. The cloth, still damp, smelled musty. Its coolness gladdened her, for the day would soon swelter, as did each day on this darkly green sea her husband named the Orellana River. Most of the others still called it the Marañón, and the captain had suggested more than once that it should be named the Amazon after those whose land and storied riches they sought. On shore, beyond the sound of the flapping sails, monkeys howled in their trees.

The half-light of false dawn made the cabin's doorway visible. She climbed up the narrow stairs to the brigantine's deck, where she heard her husband's raspy voice barking orders to Captain Peñalosa.

How much strength the tropics had stolen from that once lyrical tenor! Her husband stood at the weathered rail looking toward the distant north shore of the river, waiting for the sun to rise and burn away the white mists.

"Francisco," she called to him.

"Ah, Ana. *Muy bonita.*" He greeted her as he did each morning, with a delighted smile, as though she were a child and not his wife. "Smell the orchids," he said as she neared. "They layer the walls of trees. Perhaps the sweetness of their scent will cure my fever."

"I hope so," she told him. "I've dreamed of an Amazon."

He reached out, gripping her shoulders with scarred, palsied hands, heavy with gold and decreed power. When she'd met him, back in Seville, his hands had possessed the strength of bulls.

"When?" he asked her, his dark gaze intent.

"Just this hour."

"Then at last we can be sure we ride the main channel, free of Portuguese claim," Francisco said. "I must find the flag." His eyes shone with something other than fever for the first time in a fortnight as he stepped away. "Holy Father of all we hold dear, help me wake these tired fellows!" he muttered. Then he began shouting.

"Arise, my sore *compañeros*! Clear your sleepy, cobwebbed minds. Stretch those arms worn hard as cordwood. Take up the oars, for your fortunes await at last. Arise!"

A dozen muted groans answered from the shadows of the brigantine's aft, where the bulk of the men slept, or suffered in sleeplessness. Ana watched as her husband climbed the foredeck with renewed vigor. He spoke to Captain Peñalosa. She couldn't hear Francisco's low tones, but she watched his arms waving a fluttering pantomime of pulling ropes. He puffed his cheeks in an exaggerated blow, then rolled his arms and leaned outward with an imaginary wind that blew toward shore.

Captain Peñalosa bore the sudden onslaught of enthusiasm with studied patience. Long-suffering Peñalosa, who always followed orders though it had cost him four galleons and left him in command of only this small river-going ship.

Though the captain looked unimpressed, the men began to grin and nod. They'd all heard the tales a hundred times, after all. Who among them hadn't hung on Francisco's every word each night as he told of the suffering that Pizarro's conquistadores endured to gain their reward of gold and jewels after taming the Incas? Even the least of Amazon hovels was said to hold enough wealth to put any Inca to shame!

Ana read their minds without the benefit of her gypsy heritage. Their tribulations neared an end! Francisco de Orellana, who'd been one of Pizarro's lieuten-

ants, stood now in their midst in a fever of excitement
such as they hadn't seen in months on this humid
river. Orellana, their leader, their Adelantado, stood
ready to lead them at last to glory! She wondered how
her husband inspired such euphoria. It was as if he
blew gold dust into the men's hearts with every puff
of his breath. Except, perhaps, for Peñalosa.

"To shore!" came the weary-sounding order from
the captain a few minutes later, when Francisco had
found his flag. "To shore!"

Men scurried across the deck, some donning armor
while others gladly took up weighty, long-shanked
oars. For five days their landings had ended in battles
with natives, each time a different tribe, each tribe
more fierce than the last. Ana turned and gripped the
weathered rail as the ship lurched to one side and
began to cut a frothy swath toward shore. She scanned
the riverbank as it grew from shadow to solid. As the
mist retreated, Ana worried. They should wait just a
little while for the morning sun to top the wall of trees
ahead. The northern shore was no place to be while
darkness still hung over the jungle.

She felt a touch on her hair, and a furl of cool silk
fell over her left shoulder.

"The flag of Spain." Francisco leaned its short pole
between them, letting it catch the first hint of morning
breeze over the bow of the ship. "I want you to join
us. I think we'll need your *gitano* magic, my love. I
plan to plant the flag in high ground and proclaim the
land for Spain. Then we must locate an Amazon city
and bring away at least a little treasure, for this journey hasn't gone well. What we garner must be the
seed to fund another."

His expression took on a grim cast as he continued.
"We may need to travel less than a league, or more
than a half-day's journey inland. You should wear the

armor and the leggings I made for you," he said. "And
bring your knives. You may need them."

"Husband," Ana asked, "what of our greater plan?
As much as we've dreamed of ruling a land away from
Spain, I think everyone on the ship knows too many
have perished, and we are too few."

Francisco de Orellana, duly appointed Governor
and Captain-General of New Andalusia, Adelantado
of a force to rival Pizarro's, sent to carve a kingdom
from the vast wilds around the river Marañón, could
only shrug, the energy draining from his bearded gaze.
"With more than a score of our surviving men weak
with fever, what else can I do? One fast raid, for supplies and whatever treasure might convince the King
to finance another expedition. Then we'll return to the
sea, and hope that another time comes when we can
build our city in this land I claim today."

His mind was made up. As always, Ana's role would
be to take care of her husband as best she could. She
nodded solemnly, then made her way toward their tiny
cabin to retrieve her armor. Despite the danger of this
landing, despite the trials ahead, she felt hope. For
the first time Francisco admitted they wouldn't be
staying to found his city of destiny. The fever hadn't
yet claimed all his good sense, as she'd feared more
than once in the past few weeks.

She tarried with her breastplate and her leggings
until the proper dawn lit the sky. When she next came
on deck, they were floating only a short row from the
northern shore.

The Marañón flowed so wide here it seemed they
rode some freshwater sea—the south shore remained
out of sight over the horizon. As they neared the
bank, the jungle loomed as thick in this place as anywhere they'd seen, growing in most places right up to
the river's edge and seemingly beyond. Clumps of
giant water lilies with leaves like great fans rested ma-

jestically wherever the current slowed. Even the backs of the shield-sized, swimming turtles looked darker than those Ana had seen when the green water first spread over the Atlantic blue, more than four hundred leagues back.

Above, gnarled trees four times as tall as a galleon's mast towered over them, their matted tops darkening the newly lit sky overhead. Long vines fell like the snakes they sometimes were, downward into the water, while huge tree roots reached upward. Now and again a dark tail swirled in the water almost under the ship—Ana felt sure if she were belowdeck, she'd hear the sounds of heavy bodies thumping against the hull, those of the manatees, or of crocodiles, much more dangerous. Overhead countless birds, long-tailed explosions of endless bright colors, flitted among the dark greenery, their songs at once beautiful and eerie.

Ana searched the shore as they passed ever nearer into the humid darkness. She looked for movement, but saw none. A thousand natives might pace them among the trees. She only hoped they didn't, and ached to put her feet on soil so she might divine where their nearest enemy waited.

They came alongside a short, flat bank carpeted with moss. Beyond it, the land rose steeply. There might be no better landing site for many leagues. She went to where Francisco stood along the rail.

"What do you think, my love?" he asked her. "Shall we let these skinny fellows set their feet upon the ground of New Andalusia?"

"I think you should, my husband," she answered, her voice as light as she could make it, to match his own. "If we wait much longer, the ground may think your men are aught but birds, and not proper Spanish soldiers."

He smiled and waved them ashore. When the ship's bow groaned to a halt, Ana saw the men stiffen, watching the jungle carefully, ready to duck arrows or loose their own. The landing proceeded without event. Seventeen conquistadores preceded Ana, Francisco, and the captain onto the mossy ground. The battle-hardened, armored men ran immediately to the edge of the tall ferns and lianas bordering their little landing, bows and arquebuses held ready. They spread themselves into a protective half-circle, none more than a few yards from the next, and they watched for movement. They knew the jungle, now.

"We have found a good harbor," Francisco proclaimed, letting the flag lean back on his shoulder. "Captain, call down a few more men off the brigantine, and have them unleash their machetes on the wall of ferns and twiny bushes ahead. When you break through to the sunless, treacherous ground that spreads its vines and shields the jungle's fallen logs beneath these palms, you may fall back to the ship and wait for our return."

The captain nodded and called out to the nearly two-score men who hadn't yet debarked. Only six found the strength to join him, leaving over thirty would-be glory and treasure seekers on the ship, too weakened by fever and dysentery even to lend aid.

"Ana," Francisco rested a hand on her shoulder. "I married you for your fine spirit and your youthful beauty. But I brought you on this journey because of your *gitano* skills. Will this place do, and can you perform your augury with the men so near?"

There was a time not long before when she would not. Back when agents of Friar Torres sailed with them, he who'd been an Inquisitor, she'd show no glimpse of power. Not even for Francisco, who'd known since their wedding night, when he wakened to the glow of tiny creatures dancing around their heads.

But those men had been lost at sea with their second galleon, and during the ensuing months others she

could never trust had died or been left behind. Now
there was only Francisco, Peñalosa, and this handful
of men she'd suffered with.

She scanned the faces of those who made furtive
glances toward her from their newly established posts,
reading each one with all the skill she'd gleaned from
years of watching her mother and her aunts tell fortunes of rough men, men such as these, back in Seville.
Some of her *gitano* ways were indeed magic, while
some were tricks and intuitions that only looked like
magic. She didn't know which her faculty for judging
men's trustworthiness was, but she nodded her affir-
mation. She believed none among the group at hand
would accuse her of witchery, should they ever return
to Spain.

"Good," Francisco said. "This land has its Amazons, but we have my gypsy wife."

She rolled her eyes. The Governor and Captain-
General of New Andalusia grinned and plunked down
on the ground like a schoolboy.

Ana pulled her dagger from her belt and peeled
back a patch of moss no wider than the length of her
forearm. She drew a circle in the exposed soil. When
she finished, she sniffed the southern breeze. The natives burned *heve* tree sticks in their cook fires, over
which they commonly cooked fish. One such tree over-
hung their beachhead only a few yards back, so she
went for it, breaking off two dozen twigs, each smaller
than her littlest finger. These she stacked in the center
of her circle. Dipping into her bag of runes, she selected enough tiny obsidian pebbles to build a border
around the twigs. A silver scale from a man-sized *pira-
rucu* fish the natives relished and often carried around
on their backs brought the spell near completion. She
put it on the twigs to symbolize the fish.

"Work your magic, Ana" Francisco said. "The

guards haven't signaled. We aren't in danger, at least for this moment."

Ana lowered her face toward the ground. From the south, gently, she breathed the ancient words her grandmother had taught her onto the twigs. She hoped to pull the smallest of creatures from their instinctual wanderings and put them to mimicking the doings of men.

As Peñalosa and his six jungle cutters gathered round, their hacking done, a thumbnail-sized brown beetle wandered across the moss and up to the disturbed space delineating the outer circle. Soon a second beetle appeared, then a third. They crossed inward together, moving straight, as though they'd found a purpose. Before another moment passed a dozen meandered in, then more, until more than a hundred milled inside the ring of sandy soil Ana had cleared with her blade. Among them there was a single beetle, larger than the others, with a shiny golden back and fierce-looking red mandibles.

"Look, some of them gather around the twigs and pause to rest, facing inward. The rest crowd together, but none walk within your smaller circle of stones," a conquistador named Tierno observed.

"Of course not," Ana answered. "Who would walk through a cook fire?"

A party of two-score beetles assembled. Led by the golden-back, they crept away from the larger group. They moved toward the river, moving quickly at first, as though making up for lost time. When they reached a place about halfway between Ana's circle and the water they slowed, but continued on.

Francisco watched intently. "We are informed our closest opportunity is an inland village of over five score," he said. "A large war party has somehow learned of us, or perhaps they merely assembled to hunt between their village and the river. Either way, a threat is revealed. Peñalosa, do you remember what the natives downriver told us of a vassal-settlement of the Amazons along a small tributary?"

"They said we might find a small city about an hour's walk inland from the big river," Peñalosa said.

"Yes," grinned Vibero, the best of their arquebusers, whose place in their line of guards put him nearby. "They also told how the natives drape whole trees in chains of gold, just to watch the glint of sunlight while they rest and drink the wine they named *chicha* in the shade below."

"And even that spectacle pales beside *El Dorado*, the great city of the Amazons," added Ruiz, one of the captain's machete men.

"Enough!" Francisco ordered. "This smaller city will have to do, for now, and we have to get there first. With the warriors but halfway here, we'll have time to plant our flag in the highest ground we can find in the first league inland. Then we'll circle around our enemies and strike the city, bringing away what we can for the glory of Spain. After that, my wife will perform her augury again. We'll circle the warriors once more and return to the ship. With the care of good Christian men we'll avoid having to slay too many of those poor, heathen women and their minions."

Those within earshot nodded, their faces grave. It had been part of their charter from King Philip to treat the natives as gently as they might, only taking what they felt was necessary, and inflicting as little harm as possible. Ana had seen, though, that battle, the prospect of treasure, or even simple power over others drained most men of all their good intentions. Even men of the cloth, supposedly far more saintly than these.

"I think you should be about it then, lord," Captain Peñalosa said. "We'll hold the ship here until your return."

"I agree," Francisco said, slowly rising to stand, using the flag stick as a walking staff. "Ana, do you think that large beetle represents an Amazon?"

Ana shrugged. "Back in Spain this spell calls only ants," she said. "Different kinds of ants represent different kinds of people. I can only guess the larger beetle reveals a stronger race. And I dreamed of an Amazon with a jaguar's head of striking golden color."

"Stay close beside me, my love," Francisco said. "We may need another spell sooner than I've planned."

Ana nodded and fell in beside him as he called his seventeen hale conquistadores together. She mustn't argue with her husband, though there was little magic she could call forth beyond what she had just done. Still, she was healthier than most—and she had her knives.

The path Peñalosa and his *compañeros* had made was narrow and opened into hot darkness, like the entrance to some huge cave. Ana could hardly believe that the growth atop the huge trees could be so thickly layered, while upon the ground only moss and tangled roots grew. When the roots were kicked, lizards scurried forth, and when roots moved without kicking, they were most often snakes.

As they penetrated inward, they found it so gloomy it seemed for a while they would need lamps, but gradually their eyes became accustomed, and the terrain became visible through the gray-green gloom. The ground rose steadily. When they'd traveled a league, climbing constantly over the rotting corpses of once-mighty trees, swatting every biting bug the Earth ever spawned, Francisco said he was ready to plant the flag.

The men spread out once more, this time to gather stones in addition to keeping watch. Ana wiped sweat from her eyes and started preparing a second circle, while Francisco planted his flag as deep into the ground as his tired body would push it—then his men heaped stones around it to keep it in its place. She paused to stand beside her husband while he made his proclamation.

"Tierno, and Griego and Celiz, stand guard," Francisco ordered. "We should have circled well west of our enemy, but who knows what sorcery they possess?" Without further preamble he took a wide stance and lifted his arms. "I proclaim this land for Philip, King of Spain," he said simply. "We name everything west to Peru New Andalusia, to whence we will return as soon as we gather more provisions and men. I'll scribe this event in my log when we return to the ship. Now, let us bow our heads in prayer, except for you guards, who have my leave and the Lord's, I'm sure, to keep a careful watch. God also willing, we'll be long gone before you might see anything threatening. If you others would—"

A pan flute trilled somewhere in the murk ahead. A hail of darts and arrows suddenly rained among them. A host of naked natives with spears began melting out of the forest ahead.

Most of the men dove for cover. Ana instinctively sought to move in front of Francisco, shielding him from harm.

"Get down!" Francisco pulled her to the ground. She restrained herself from rising above a kneeling position, realizing she mustn't distract him, despite her fear for his safety. The outcome of this battle would hinge on his wits. To one side a shout went up.

"To arms! *Amigos,* to arms!" Griego, one of their would-be watchmen, cried out. Reaching toward his legs he sank into the undergrowth until only his helmed head showed. He looked toward Ana, his mouth twisted in a grimace of pain. Their eyes met. "Just a graze, Doña," he grunted.

Fine, brave one, Ana thought. *No poison on the tip, I pray.* The conquistadores returned fire. A full half-dozen arquebuses roared and belched blue smoke, startling the natives. These had not battled Spaniards before, Ana realized. Three fell to the conquistadores' volley while three dozen others closed in, carrying spears or clubs with sharp protrusions. Spanish steel rang, and harsh cries resounded.

One warrior broke through the protective half-circle the men had formed once more around Ana and Francisco. Ana caught the fleeting impression of a well-muscled, barrel-chested man, his dark, grimacing face painted with white lines. He stood no taller than four feet, but his spear's wicked point looked deadly. He cried out as he ran, drawing back his weapon, about to throw. Francisco drew his sword. Before he could move forward on his fever-weakened legs Ana drew the dagger from her right hip and hurled it through the air.

The blade flew true, taking the running native in the chest. He fell roughly to the ground and writhed among the bloodstained undergrowth, his death no easy thing. Ana swallowed a sudden urge to bolt forward and see if she could help him.

"By God, *muchacha*!" Francisco cried. "We'll make a conquistador of you!"

But she felt no joy.

The attack continued. Francisco had told her of battles past wherein he and his men triumphed when outnumbered one hundred to one. By contrast, this seemed an almost even contest. As another hail of arrows began, Ana scurried a few feet back and ducked down behind a huge tree stump. She looked out along the ragged line the Spaniards now formed, and saw that two more conquistadores had fallen.

Moments later a few of the natives began to retreat, fighting fiercely one moment, and melting into the tangled forest underbrush the next. Only one arrow flew toward them at a time now, but together those arrows made a steady stream, as if a single tireless archer had replaced all the ineffective native warriors. Each brightly plumed shaft seemed to seek out flesh among the folds of metal armor that had served the Spaniards so well in the New World up to this time. It occurred to Ana this foe's archery skills exceeded her own mastery with knives—an adeptness aided in no small part by her magic.

Tierno, who fought almost next to Francisco, fell with a choking cry. An arrow had taken him in the throat. Francisco hurriedly helped him behind the log where Ana hid, but to no avail. He was dead.

Her husband collapsed nearly on top of her. Ana feared an unseen arrow, but his panting breath told her he lived, and when he turned and put his back to the tree, she realized he was exhausted.

"Can you tell me how the battle fares?" he asked. He stared at the air before him. His fever and his sweat had left him nearly blind.

"Nearly all the natives who charged are gone," Ana answered. "Ten of them will feed this jungle's voracious worms. Francisco, all our men have been forced to the ground behind clusters of roots, or stumps like ours here. We've lost five . . . no, six, with Tierno, and two others are hurt. All to arrows, I think."

Francisco turned and gazed outward, wiping the sweat from his eyes with one weary hand. The flutes played on somewhere in the darkness.

"They will attack again," Francisco said.

He called out, loud enough for the others to hear. "Stay down, *amigos*. It's not the charging warriors who exacted this toll, but a small number of archers in the trees somewhere to our front. Perhaps just one archer, but with an eye and a hand the likes of which I've never seen."

He turned back around, pushing himself a little away from their fallen *compañero*. "Ana, I think our plans to take the city are ruined. We'll have to be pleased to come away with our lives. Do you have a spell that might lend us aid?"

"No, Francisco," she admitted. "I have nothing for peril such as this."

He nodded, his face grave, then turned once more to shout to the men. "Someone must try to draw this archer's fire toward the middle of our line, while exposing himself as little as possible. When the arrows fly, we'll see where our enemy is, and our arquebusers must be ready."

A little muttering answered him. Ana heard rattling and the click of metal on metal as their four remaining arquebusers struck tinders and loaded their weapons. Before a moment passed a tense voice rose from a tangle of roots to one side.

"Adelantado, I will try to match this cur's skill." Ana recognized the voice as a conquistador named Aguila.

"Fine, brave *amigo*," Francisco replied, loud enough so all would hear. "Whenever you are ready." A look of terrible worry crossed his face, though.

Aguila stood, a scarce few yards from where Ana and Francisco watched. He pulled back his bowstring quickly, hoping, no doubt, that speed would aid him. He'd barely begun to scan the terrain ahead when an arrow sliced his forward hand. As he cursed and dropped his bow a second shaft pierced his right eye. He cried out in pain and fell back behind the wide log he'd used as cover. Several of the men scurried to aid him, careful not to expose themselves.

"Return fire," Francisco cried. For a breath of time nothing happened. Ana feared no one had seen from whence the arrow came. Then she caught a glimpse of something—a movement in the green half-light, well ahead of them but not too far above, where a mat of twisted foliage hung down from the trees. She thought at first some deft-climbing animal with golden fur watched their battle. One of the arquebusers saw it, too, for he rose and fired, followed closely by his fellows.

"Perhaps you got one," Francisco said after the explosions ceased to echo. Blue-black smoke hung over their heads as the pan flutes continued to fill the forest with their haunting music.

Without further discussion a young conquistador named Ortez tried to determine if their shooting had been worth the effort, although Ana thought an unkind observer might say he simply bolted, hoping to escape. Before he ran three yards an arrow cut him down from behind. The shot came from the very place in the trees where Ana had seen movement, upon which the men had loosed their volley.

"It is as our Adelantado surmised, no troop of warriors, but a single demon," Griego, the wounded one, cried. He sounded far away, though none of them hid more than a short distance from the others. "See, the feathers on the arrows of the dead are all from the same crimson bird. A bird of hell! Doom stalks us."

Grunts of agreement rippled along the forest floor. No conquistador moved. At least the natives had made no new charge. Perhaps, Ana thought, they fear their own archer.

Doom, indeed! Griego's still-echoing words caused Ana to wonder why the men of Europe never failed to name those they feared demons, or witches. The best of her own people had been stoned for daring to use the gifts God had given them. Above them, she realized, an Amazon waited—she who had entered Ana's dreams as a human jaguar. Ana feared this archer no less than Griego did his demon. Ana's worry was for her enemy's deadly skill, though. At least her fear knew what it was about.

"When they charge again, we'll be forced to stand

and fight, and the archer will fire," Francisco called forth. "If they injure or slay even a few more of us, we'll not be able to carry our own wounded. Demon or no, one of us must find a way to strike down that archer."

Ana felt glad that her husband's fears were real, too. She reached out and touched his shoulder. "Husband," she said, "I think it must be me."

He turned to her with a dismissive frown. "No," he said simply.

"I've thought of a spell that might aid us. I think it's the only way we might survive this."

As if to lend credence to her words, an arrow thumped into the stump beside them. Could the Amazon have heard their low voices from so far, above the trill of the incessant flutes? Francisco's expression grew suddenly solemn. He began to shake his head, but then he stopped and looked at the ground, plainly reasoning their situation as best he could with his fevered mind. Finally, he looked up at her again. "I counted the risk when I brought you along, you know. It does not mean I do not love you."

She nodded. "I know. I only risk death more quickly, not more surely."

He nodded and sighed, looking even more miserable than before. "You have our attention, my lady."

"I am going to perform magic," Ana called out to the men. "All I ask is that you watch the trees, and shoot any who attack me from the ground. I must approach this archer, who is no demon."

She held her husband's hand for one brief moment. "This will be hardest for you," she said. "This spell isn't all you might hope." In fact, it was all she had.

She closed her eyes and let her body sway, looking inward, calling. They appeared almost at once to her call, and when she opened her eyes, they fluttered in the half-light of the jungle as well, tiny fay creatures who might be mistaken in this place as butterflies, their iridescent blue wings fluttering, circling her hair with fairy fire, called gypsy fire by some who had seen it.

Ana stood up, straightened her shoulders, and walked toward the tree where the archer waited. She kept her arms folded, right over left, to hide the dagger as she drew it from her side, held blade-palmed in her right hand. Francisco cried out behind her. He'd seen her dancers and knew them harmless.

"Don't follow," she called out, without looking back. "Do not distract she who waits above by showing movement. The one who aims a killing arrow at my breast has the instincts of a cat." Ana kept her pace steady, meandering like a bird on soft ground. She held her head high, but not tilted upward. She couldn't risk eye contact. "Gypsy families carry their cats with them, you know. When I was a child, I used to watch them hunt." Her tiny dancers continued their wobbling circle, their glowing paths forming luminescent halos around her head.

One of the native warriors stepped out from behind a tree some distance ahead, looking more astonished than threatening. Ana shuddered as she heard the twang of a bowstring somewhere behind her, and a Spanish arrow sliced into his middle. He clutched it, his surprised awe turning to a grimace, and fell back out of her sight. The pan flutes of their attackers trailed to a confused halt. Her dancers began to buzz.

Just a dozen more steps, Ana decided, letting her magic tell her precisely where she must go. She must trust her inner self, or all was doomed. "The cat, you see, is true to her nature," she said, loud enough so her uncomprehending enemy might hear her seemingly unconcerned tone.

Eight more steps. "She will seldom pounce on prey that walks toward her."

Six more. Her right foot snapped a branch, causing her to wince inwardly.

Five more steps, and four, and three. "As long as she remains fascinated."

One more.

"Unless our paths intersect."

With her last word Ana glanced upward. Overhead, through the low-hanging branches, she saw the tawny gold she sought. She flicked her blade as strongly as she could toward that flash of color. A tiny, high-pitched yelp answered her. Through a gap in the tangle of scalloped leaves and stringy vines overhead, their eyes, at last, met—Amazon pools of green reflecting Ana's dancers. Then the archer plummeted from the tree and struck the ground with a bloody thump.

She was a woman. She wore armor of a sort, but no jewels. Her hair was as golden as a newly minted coin. Her arrows bore red feathers.

Francisco burst forth from his cover, running as best he could to where she stood, holding his sword ready before him. Others of their men ran to the dead and wounded, while still others roared challenges and charged the trees ahead.

The natives had vanished.

Ana shared the relief of the men, yet as they shouted in victory, she couldn't contain her tears. Through a watery blur she watched the green of the Amazon warrior's eyes deepen in death. Ana reached to close them. She would have weighted them with silver if she'd had coins. As she groped blindly for pebbles from her sack, Francisco gently pulled her away, then held her while she wept.

It took some time to prepare the wounded for travel. When they set out at last for the brigantine, Ana leaned on Francisco's shoulder. Those Amazon pools would haunt her for a long time.

* * *

During the journey down the Marañón River to the Atlantic Ocean many of the crew succumbed to fever. On a stormy November afternoon, when they sailed near the ocean and beat their oars against *pororoca* waves as tall as a man, Francisco died as well.

The conquistadores dug the grave of Lord de Orellana, Adelantado of New Andalusia, where an immense palm stood a little out from its fellows along the river's shore. They laid his shrouded remains deep into the ground, so deep that even a great flood would not expose his bones. After prayers were said, Captain Peñalosa leaned over the grave's edge and dropped down a parcel wrapped in a silken Spanish flag. Despite Ana's grief she wondered what it was, for she'd placed every small thing that he'd loved in various pockets of his surcoat.

"His journal of these last weeks," the captain told Ana.

"His writing?" Sudden anger penetrated her grief. "No! That goes back to Spain. He must have his place in history." She knelt, soiling her dress in the wet dirt. The bottom of the grave stood deep in shadow. She would climb in.

As she pushed herself forward, the captain grasped her upper arm and pulled her away from the grave's edge. She spun to face him, her jaw set with anger.

"Doña Ana," he said quickly. "The Adelantado wished for this. He told me so only yesterday."

"But we have no other written record! There must be an account for King Philip—"

"No," Peñalosa said. "The Adelantado needed his journal only as a tool to build support for another journey. Now he's dead, and without him to protect you, that chronicle is dangerous. Within, he named your wonders pious magic. But he doubted, and I agree with him, that Mother Church would see your feats as such. Let him do one last thing to protect you, Doña, as you protected him."

She looked into the captain's eyes, and she knew he spoke the truth. The river of the Amazons split a continent, and Francisco had been the first European to ride it. If that feat didn't ensure fame, what would? *A wife must sometimes be a good widow,* her grandmother had once said. Her words came now, unbidden. When Peñalosa released his grip, Ana made no effort to return to the grave.

A little later they cast off. The sky had cleared. When Ana looked back, she saw the last golden light of dusk. She fancied she heard a jaguar's cry in the distance, answered faintly by the bellow of an unrepentant bull.

QADISHTU
by Laura Resnick and Kathy Chwedyk

At a time when the world was locked in chaotic barbarism, the realm of Sumer emerged between two turbulent rivers, the Tigris and the Euphrates. The people of Sumer made tremendous advances in crop cultivation, herd management, and flood control. The concept that people could control such things on a cultural scale was revolutionary. But these people lived in a harsh world. Even their gods were a hostile bunch. Knowing this, it is not surprising to learn that the people of Sumer gave our world one of the most enduring of myths: Paradise.

Laura Resnick is an award-winning author. Under the name Laura Leone, she wrote a dozen romance novels. In 1993 she won the John W. Campbell Award for best new writer. Her numerous science fiction and fantasy short stories have appeared in many magazines and anthologies. She also has written a nonfiction book about her eight-month camping trip across Africa, *A Blonde in Africa.* Her next fantasy novel, *In Legend Born,* begins a trilogy.

Kathy Chwedyk has published Regency romances under a pseudonym and is a former newspaper editor who is fascinated by ancient history. She is working on a fantasy novel set in Mesopotamia. This is a first-ever collaboration between these two authors.

Sirara watched the old priest examine her son, chanting and mumbling as he searched for signs of the evil spirits which had brought this wasting sickness upon the boy.

"Well?" she prodded, when she could bear the tension no longer. "Can you drive out the demon?"

The priest closed his eyes and placed his hand on the boy's forehead. "Lahar is ill, very ill. . . ."

Sirara's dark eyes narrowed, anger flowing forth to smother her fear. This gnarled, scented old man was her last hope, for all other cures had failed Lahar; he had grown steadily weaker since the last moon and now lay near death.

"You are said to be the wisest healer, the most powerful priest in all of Ur. Can you not cure one small boy who wants to live?" she snapped.

Old Sumugan's kohl-rimmed eyes scorched her for speaking to him so disrespectfully. Sirara stared back, openly challenging him; she was *qadishtu,* a sacred woman of the goddess. As chief priestess of the temple, she consummated the annual ritual marriage with the king to ensure the fertility of the land. A woman of influence and importance, she was wealthy and owned property. A servant and conduit of Inanna, the goddess of love and war, Sirara had no need to bow before this pompous old man.

"An amulet," the magician suggested at last.

"Another one?" Sirara snapped contemptuously. "He already has so many that, when he is better, he can make a fortune by selling the ones the other priests have already brought."

"Then I will fashion a likeness of the demon in clay and—"

"We already have a likeness in clay, as well as one in wax and one in bronze." She plucked one of these from her son's bedside and flung it violently across the room. The old man flinched as she whirled on him and snarled, "Are you no better than the useless tricksters who have already come here?"

"You must not speak that way about—"

"They have *failed,*" she accused. "All of their chanting and amulets and idols...." Her long black hair was uncombed and undressed. Her gown was stained with Lahar's vomit, and she had not bathed for two days. At this moment, no one in the streets would recognize her as high priestess of Inanna's sacred temple. "Day by day, he grows worse. Moment by moment, the demon eats his spirit and his body."

Her throat filled with sorrow, and tears clouded her vision. Four-year-old Lahar was her only child. Though he was born of some forgotten union with a stranger who had paid well to sleep with a *qadishtu* and help ensure the fertility of the land, Sirara loved the boy with all her heart and soul. Loved him so fervently that her spirit would be wounded beyond healing if he should die. The priest, of course, didn't understand. What man could possibly understand what it meant to feel another life blossom within you, to give birth to it, to nurture it and watch it grow? What man could know the pride and pain, the joy and fear of a mother's love?

Sirara was normally a politically astute woman and shrewd diplomat, but with Lahar's life at stake, she couldn't spare the time or energy to massage the pride of Ur's most important priest. So she simply challenged him: "Cure him. Or have you lied about your power the way most men lie about their virility?"

The old man's oiled, gray-streaked locks seemed to quiver with his rage. The gold, lapis-studded pendant on his chest rose and fell with the deep breaths he took in anger. Pride, however, eventually outweighed his fury; he intended to succeed where others had failed.

"I will give a suckling pig to the evil spirits in his stead," he said slowly, stroking his curled beard as he pondered the ceremony. "Let the flesh be as his flesh, and the blood as his blood."

"In the temple?" Sirara asked.

"No. Here. Summon a slave, woman, that I may tell him what will be needed."

Properly clothed in a simple, slim, one-shouldered gown, her hair elaborately dressed as suited her position, and her face modestly veiled, Sirara left the cool, thick-walled confines of her whitewashed house. Lahar's bed was still stained with the blood of the suckling pig, and his skin still stank of it; but he was no better than he had been before the priest had cut the heart out of the pig and laid it upon the boy's heart. Two days after this elaborate ceremony, the old magician had nothing left to offer but useless platitudes as Lahar lay dying. And so Sirara had developed a desperate plan to save her son's life.

This close to the Festival of the New Year, in which she played a crucial role, Sirara would need the king's permission to leave Ur, and so today she sought him out, pushing a path through the bustling streets of the city on her way to the palace. For a hundred years, since the time Utuhegal had driven out the fierce Gutians, Ur had been the greatest and wealthiest city in Sumer. Caravans arrived here from afar, laden with timber, stone, and precious metals. Weavers, fullers, gem-cutters, jewelers, metal workers, perfume-makers, painters, scribes, and merchants filled the narrow streets of the crowded city, trading their work for gold, iron, silver, grain, wool, wine, and oil. There were few earthly desires which could not be satisfied here in Ur.

Sirara passed by the city's great mountain-shaped temple-tower, built by Ur-Nammu, the usurper king who had begun this never-ending age of prosperity for his people. Standing as high as twelve men, the temple was surely evidence of the unconquerable might of this people. Sirara knew that Ibbi-Sin, descended from Ur-Nammu, was afraid, for he was threatened on many sides now; but as she looked up at the sky-reaching temple, she felt the same awe she always had. What did the king of such greatness truly have to fear?

As expected, she was granted immediate audience upon arriving at the palace and asking to see the king. A broad-chested man in his prime, Ibbi-Sin walked with the unconscious arrogance bred by five generations of great kings. His face, however, was lined with worry.

"Was it not enough that Ishbi-Erra, whom I trusted like a brother, betrayed me and made himself master of Isin?" he thundered.

"My lord?" Sirara knew that the betrayal of Ibbi-Sin's most trusted general, as well as the king's loss of influence in Isin, was a serious blow. With the Elamites attacking from the east, and a new people, the Amorites, invading from the great deserts to the west, the loyalty of Ibbi-Sin's men was being tested; and not all of them proved to be honorable.

"*Now* Ishbi-Erra has declared himself king of all Sumer!" Ibbi-Sin raged. "And he is subverting the governors of other cities by means of force or threats!"

"But how can he—" Sirara began.

"I should have killed him when I had the opportunity," Ibbi-Sin muttered, stalking past her.

She followed him out to the main courtyard, where the scent of jasmine perfumed the air and plump concubines stuffed themselves with fresh figs. "You will slay him yet, lord, and all the world will see the sad fate of a man who challenges Ibbi-Sin."

For the first time since her arrival, his face relaxed somewhat. "May Inanna, goddess of love and war, so will it."

"I will make offerings to her in the temple," Sirara promised. "She will be your sword and your shield, and your enemies will be as dust."

He nodded, considering. "It is true, you have influence with Inanna. More than a priestess; almost as a favored sister of the goddess."

"You honor me, lord."

"Even the priests talk about your power."

"If I have been greatly blessed, then it is only that I may serve my king well." She bowed with dignity. "And if I have served you well and found favor in your eyes—"

"You have."

"Then I must request a favor, lord."

"Name it."

"I ask my lord for an immediate escort to Dilmun, for myself and my son."

"Dilmun!" Ibbi-Sin looked as stunned as she had expected. *"Why?"*

"My son is dying. All medicines, spells, priests, chants, and offerings have failed to cure him. Not even Sumugan can save him."

Ibbi-Sin made an awkward half-gesture of comfort. "I'm sorry, Sirara. But if his time has come—"

"He will not journey to the Land of No Return," she said fiercely. "He is only a child, and—"

"Even children must die sometimes."

"And he is *mine.*" She fixed him with the same hard stare she had given the old magician. "If we can reach Dilmun in time. . . ."

"But Dilmun is *days* from here. I don't even know how far! And the journey is dangerous."

"That is why I ask you for an escort, my lord. Half a dozen armed men—"

"To guard a woman and her sick child while my empire falls apart?" he said scornfully. "They have more important things to do."

She stared at him with bitter anger for a moment, for men always thought their power was all that mattered, then lowered her head with a sigh, indicating her acceptance of his decision. She was a wealthy woman, after all; she could hire mercenaries to guard her on her journey. "Very well, lord. We must go, nevertheless."

"No," he said suddenly. "You cannot leave, not with the Festival of the New Year approaching. I need you for that."

"Another priestess can consummate the sacred marriage with you this year," she said.

"No, it must be you. It *must* be the chief priestess. We are beset by enemies on every side." His voice was laced with suppressed fear. "Perhaps we have angered the gods, perhaps our offerings have not been sufficient. We must placate them. Everything must be precise in the rituals this year."

"The other priestesses are trained—"

"I need *your* power. Do you think my coupling with just any woman will give enough strength to the land in these troubled times?"

"My son will die if I don't take him to Dilmun immediately." Her throat felt raw as she saw the uncompromising determination in his expression.

"I forbid you to leave Ur until the Festival is over." There was iron in his voice.

"My lord . . ."

"Upon pain of death, I *forbid* you."

Too proud to weep in front of him, she watched him with hot, dry eyes as he turned away from her. Her vision darkened as she imagined gutting him with her ritual knife. Her chest burned with tautly controlled grief and rage as she heard the silly, idle chatter of his concubines across the courtyard. A moment later, Ibbi-Sin's soft laughter joined in with their squeals of delight over some new jest.

"You will pay." The whispered promise slipped past her trembling lips. "You will pay for my son's life with everything you hold dear, everything you value in this world."

*   *   *

Irsit La Tari they called it; the Land of No Return.
A bleak, barren place where everyone, good or bad,
kind or cruel, went after he had exhaled his last breath
of air. How would Lahar fare there, a young, shy boy,
all alone in the nether world of shadows, demons, and
lost souls?

"To journey on the road from which there is no
way back," Sirara whispered to the scented night as
she watched over Lahar's wasted, shivering body. "To
dwell in the house of dust, bereft of light." She would
bring food and drink to his grave long after his death,
for clay was the only food the gods gave to those who
dwelt in *Irsit La Tari*.

"We *must* go to Dilmun," she moaned, watching
the life seep out of her son. A rich land, the earthly
home of some of the gods, Dilmun was paradise on
earth. It was said that no one ever got ill or grew old
in Dilmun. If she could only get Lahar there before
he died, there was still a chance that he might survive.
Surely the powerful magic of such a city would save
him!

The boy whimpered in his fitful sleep. He had little
time left. The shadow of death was sweeping across
him, moment by moment. Even if they left tonight. . . .

"Even if we left tonight," Sirara murmured, her
heart pounding as she recognized the plan which had
been secretly forming in her mind ever since leaving
Ibbi-Sin's palace this afternoon. *Upon pain of death*,
he had warned her. What did she care? She would
gladly risk her life for Lahar's. Coming to a sudden,
mad decision, she left Lahar's shadowed room and ran
downstairs to wake two of her slaves. They must
hurry; they must be far from the city gates by dawn.

She rode her best mule; the other mule carried supplies on his back and hauled Lahar behind him on the

litter that had once been used to carry Sirara's brother home from battle. Harran, a male slave who had been captured from some distant northern tribe in his childhood, tended the mules and guarded the supplies. Ninmah, an aging female whom Sirara had inherited from her mother, tended to Lahar's comfort. Meanwhile, Sirara focused all her energy on finding Dilmun.

She had asked Inanna for guidance and, in exchange for her offerings, had been shown visions of a vast body of water, a great sea reaching into the desert: The Lower Sea. She knew where it was; to the south, at the mouth of the great river, far beyond the place where the Tigris and Euphrates joined into one. At their current pace, they wouldn't reach for it for four days. And once they arrived, what then? Dilmun, she knew for certain, was not in that exact spot. How far along the shores of the Lower Sea must they travel, and for how long?

She glanced over her shoulder at her unconscious son, her vision blurry with exhaustion. How long did he have?

Sirara's hasty departure having allowed for only two mules, two slaves, minimal supplies, and no extra clothing, her wealth and position were well-concealed beneath her plain traveling cloak. Considering the lack of an escort, as well as the death sentence predicated by her departure from Ur, she had thought it best to appear humble and ordinary. But at sunset, as a wild band of Elamites rode out of the desert, her heart clawed at her chest in fear, and she longed for the banners and symbols that would have warned them to leave her alone.

They rode horses, undignified and unpredictable beasts which no wealthy Sumerian would deign to keep in his mule stables. Whooping and shouting, they descended upon her party like ravening beasts, attacking without mercy or conscience. Sirara had chosen Harran for his bravery, and now it was his undoing; as he attempted to protect her, one of the Elamites ripped his throat open with a heavy sword, slaying him within seconds. Another of these smelly barbarians pulled Sirara off her mule and nearly broke her wrist in punishment as she reached for her knife. Men tore her veil from her face and laughed as she struck out at their groping hands.

"I am *qadishtu*!" she snarled. "You may *not* do this. Inanna herself will eat your entrails for insulting me so!"

The hairy, dust-coated Elamites swarmed over the two mules, investigating the supplies they carried. They ignored Lahar, whimpering feebly on his litter, and struck Ninmah when she got in their way. Three of them bore Sirara roughly to the ground, grinning as she struggled against them.

"I am protected by Ibbi-Sin," she screamed, "the King of Sumer! You will *die* for this! You will—" She lost her voice as one of them struck her across the face. Blood flowed through her mouth and her vision darkened. She fought unconsciousness as the barbarians' hands ripped roughly at her garments. By the time she was able to focus her gaze again, she was surprised to realize they had stopped their attack and were now just . . . staring at her. Or rather, staring at the heavy jewelry she wore beneath her traveling cloak: the rich gold, jewels, and carved seals which marked her position as the most important woman in Ur.

One of the dark-eyed, foul-breathed savages met her gaze at last. She wondered if he was so dazzled by her concealed wealth that he had forgotten his interest in violating her.

"Ibbi-Sin will kill you for this," she promised.

The man stared in evident surprise. "Ibbi-Sin?" he asked at last, his voice openly disbelieving.

"Ibbi-Sin," she repeated firmly, summoning all the arrogance that she could in this humiliating position. "Ibbi-Sin, king of all Sumer, will put your head on a spike and display it at the city gates if you hurt me."

"Ibbi-Sin?" another of the men repeated.

Yet another man shook his head, and several of them began arguing in their thick-tongued language.

Recognizing that she must seize the moment, Sirara snapped, "Let me up, you cud-chewing fools!"

Someone hit her again. She didn't understand what he said to her, but she gathered she was supposed to keep her mouth shut. She lay in silence, fuming with helpless rage while they continued to argue around her. Then, to her surprise, she was hauled roughly to her feet and placed back upon her mule. Ninmah, weeping with terror, was placed behind her. They were surrounded by the Elamites. One of them told her—his gestures making his meaning clear—that he would kill the servant and the child if Sirara tried to escape. Nodding her understanding, she rode into captivity with them.

The Elamite camp was a rough place hidden high in the dry, rocky hills. Sirara wondered how much Ibbi-Sin knew about their presence here. Although these marauding Elamites might not be strong enough to seize her king's mighty walled city without help, there were more of them here than she would have expected to find within a day's hard ride from Ur.

Torches illuminated the dark night, simple tents were pitched in the shadows, and a goat roasted over an open fire pit. Dismounting her mule on legs which shook with exhaustion, Sirara stumbled over to her son. Mercifully, his condition was unchanged; she had feared to find him much worse as a result of this long journey into the hills.

A crowd of fascinated men surrounded her as she

crouched over the boy, pouring the last of her precious water between his cracked lips, drop by drop. She ignored the greedy gazes which roamed from her jeweled collar to her unveiled face, from her round breasts to her broad hips. A dark, begrimed hand reached out to squeeze her bare shoulder, and she struck it away. If they were going to hold her for ransom, then she expected them to return her to Ibbi-Sin undamaged, and her warning glare told them so.

Quivering with fear, Ninmah crouched beside her as she tended to her son. "Mistress," the woman whispered when the crowd around them parted. Sirara didn't look up, so the slave poked her and said more insistently, "Mistress!"

Sirara finally followed the direction of the woman's terrified gaze. The man who approached them was certainly no king, for kings did not hide in secret war camps in foreign lands; but there was no doubt that here was the leader of this pack of beasts. Tall and proud, with a body made strong and scarred by war, he stalked forward into the torchlight, his dark gaze holding hers. His wild mane of hair was uncombed and unoiled, and his face was already lined from too many years spent in the open desert. Like Ibbi-Sin, he was a man in his prime. Unlike her king, however, this man clearly feared nothing and no one.

His gaze flashed from her to one of his men as he listened to the tale of how she had been found and captured. She recognized only the name of her king in the long, hurried speech. Finally, the warrior chief looked at Sirara again. His lips quirked with amusement. And, to her relieved surprise, he spoke to her in slightly accented Sumerian.

"My men say that you are Ibbi-Sin."

She gasped and glanced at her captors in blank surprise. They had thought *she* was the famous ruler of Sumer? No wonder they had seemed so confused. Apparently they had understood nothing but the king's name in all that she had said.

Their chieftain claimed her attention again as he asked with open amusement, for he clearly did not make the same mistake his men had. "Have the Sumerians grown so weak and befuddled they truly let a woman lead them?"

She lifted her chin. "Are the Elamites so ignorant they know nothing of Ibbi-Sin, who rules the greatest empire in the world?"

His expression hardened. "Who are you, woman?"

"Sirara, sacred woman of the goddess, chief priestess of Ur," she replied coldly. "And if I am mistreated, Ibbi-Sin's terrible revenge will be as nothing compared to what Inanna will do to you, barbarian."

With no change in his expression, he seized the sacred seal she wore around her neck, jerked it hard enough to break the slender golden chain, and ground it into the dust beneath his sandaled foot. Appalled by this sacrilege, Sirara jumped to her feet. Someone immediately struck her in the head, and she fell to her knees.

"Your gods have no power over *us*, priestess," the Elamite chief said scornfully.

"Then Inanna will give all her strength to Ibbi-Sin, and he will crush you in battle," she hissed, her head reeling from the blow she had received.

He crouched before her. "And how will he ask Inanna for such power, with his chief priestess lost here in the wilderness?"

Having no immediate answer, Sirara glared at him in mute hatred. She maintained a proud, infuriated silence while he had her stripped of the rest of her gold, silver, and jewels. Then she, Ninmah, and Lahar were taken to a simple tent, given bread and water, and surrounded by guards for the rest of the night.

In the morning, the chieftain sent for Sirara. He

offered her the hospitality of his tent—bread, cheese, dates, wine—and acceded to her request to have something better than last night's fare taken to Nin-mah and Lahar.

"I have been asking myself," he said at last, his powerful body reclining comfortably against his saddle, "why the most powerful woman in Ur was riding alone through the desert, disguised as an ordinary traveler, accompanied by only two defenseless servants and a sickly boy."

She had realized that, unless he was a fool, he would recognize how strange her circumstances were. Since Lahar's life was all that mattered now, she had decided to tell the truth; the boy was no threat to these warriors, after all. Perhaps this hairy chieftain would let her go in exchange for the wealth he had seized from her last night.

"Dilmun," he repeated when she had finished her explanation. He studied her with something akin to pity. She bristled against it.

"It is the earthly home of gods," she insisted. "It is paradise on earth. He *cannot* die in Dilmun. I must reach it while he still lives!"

He considered her passionate plea for a moment before asking, "And why would Ibbi-Sin permit such a valued servant of his to make such a long journey alone? You have not explained that."

"The boy is not his child," she said shortly. "This is not his affair."

He leaned forward and took her chin in his callused hand, forcing her gaze up to his. "That's no answer, and you know it, priestess." He studied her for a moment before saying, "You aren't really the high priestess, are you?"

"Yes, I am!"

"No. You stole those things I took from you last night."

"They are *mine*."

"I don't believe you. You're just a useless woman. Why shouldn't I just give you to my men and let the child die?"

"I am the chief priestess of Ur!" she cried. "You can't—"

"Prove it. Answer my question, woman!"

The grip on her chin was painful now. Her eyes watered. She clenched her teeth and, in remembered hatred, said, "Ibbi-Sin forbade me to leave Ur before the Festival of the New Year."

"Why?" He snapped out the question.

"The waning of his power and the growing strength of his enemies frighten him. I am ... I am a powerful woman. I am gifted by the goddess. He believes the annual ritual marriage won't be as effective with any other priestess."

He released her so suddenly that she fell back against the saddle behind her. Studying her with glittering interest, he concluded, "So you ran away."

"Yes."

"And the festival approaches," he mused. "Ibbi-Sin must be eager to get you back. He must be searching for you even now."

"Probably," she agreed dully.

"You don't sound very hopeful, Sirara."

"He will take me back to Ur." She added with bitterness, "And after the ritual marriage, he will kill me. He swore he would, if I left Ur without his permission."

"Yet you left anyhow."

"Nothing is more important to me than my son's life." There was iron in her voice. "Ibbi-Sin would spend it to protect his position. What do I care how many cities he rules if my son must die as a result?"

"Still ..." The Elamite folded his arms across his

chest and said idly, "He would no doubt pay dearly to get you back."

Her eyes narrowed. "If you ransom me to him, if you send me back to Ur, then I *promise* you that before he kills me, I will ensure that he slaughters every Elamite from here to Susa."

His thick lashes lowered as he asked, "Do you really have that much power, priestess?"

"Ibbi-Sin thinks so," she answered confidently. "So do his priests."

"Yet you cannot save your own son."

Sirara's shoulders slumped. "Inanna is as a queen among the gods. She weaves the great tapestry of Sumer's destiny. She does not intercede in the lives of . . . ordinary children."

"But she will answer your prayers to make Ibbi-Sin victorious in war?" he probed.

"She always has," Sirara said boldly.

He seemed to consider this for a moment, then stretched luxuriantly, his long muscles flexing with ready strength. "Then I see no sense in returning you to your king."

"Then you will let me go on to Dilmun?" she breathed, scarcely daring to hope.

"Well . . ." He scratched his hairy chest and seemed to consider her request. "I have need of the mules, supplies, and gold you brought with you."

"I cannot walk to Dilmun," she said tersely, "carrying my son on my back and begging for food and water every step of the way."

"No, I don't suppose you can," he conceded.

She stared at him for a long moment before finally asking, "What do you want?"

"The same thing Ibbi-Sin wants. To control Ur and rule Sumer." He met her wary gaze. "If you are so powerful, priestess, then surely you can help me take the city."

"I ..." She shook her head in mute refusal.

"Come, Sirara. What do you care? It's not as if you can ever go back." Seeing her expression, he pressed his advantage. "Ibbi-Sin would have let your son die. Indeed, did he not choose to sacrifice your son in order to preserve his *own* power? What loyalty do you owe him now, after such an injury to your progeny?"

"I owe no loyalty to an Elamite barbarian," she pointed out.

He could have snapped her neck with his two strong hands, but he only laughed. "When I take you back to Susa as a war prize," he promised languidly, "you will pay for such insults, priestess."

You will pay. Sirara's memory slipped back to Ibbi-Sin's courtyard, to his careless dismissal of Lahar's life.

"To tell the truth," the chieftain confided, "I think it would be a great pity to see you dragged through the streets of Susa, stripped of your gown and your dignity, while the crowds throw refuse at you."

You will pay for my son's life with everything you hold dear, everything you value in this world.

Sirara remembered her vow, remembered how Ibbi-Sin had turned away from her desperate pleas to make sport with his witless, overfed concubines.

"And as for the boy . . ." The Elamite shook his head. "How can I offer help to the half-dead child of my enemy, if his mother will offer me nothing in exchange?"

"Ibbi-Sin will pay," Sirara murmured to herself.

"What?"

She blinked. "You're right." She held his interested gaze, keeping her own expression carefully controlled. "I owe Ibbi-Sin nothing anymore."

"Then you will help me defeat him?"

"In exchange for my son's safe passage to Dilmun."

"When Ur has fallen," he agreed. "I give you my word."

She stared at him for one long moment, weighing his promise, before saying, "Then let us begin immediately."

Sirara leaned back and felt her unbound hair fall against the naked skin of her back. The seal of her office was raised in her hands, held high above her head as she opened her mind to the goddess.

When the gold seal grew heavy in her hands, she let it fall against her breast. Then she caught the hobbled young kid in her arms, gentling it before she slashed its throat in one quick motion. Ordinarily she would be assisted by four priests and six priestesses, but that was to impress the king and the citizens of Ur rather than the goddess.

The goddess didn't want pageantry; Inanna, the Holy Maiden, wanted to feed upon her priestess' passion and strength. Sirara could feel the blood rush through her veins as she concentrated on her hatred for Ibbi-Sin. She told the goddess of the king's weakness, his cowardice, his unworthiness to be her consort. *May the radiant Inanna,* Sirara prayed, *harden her heart against Ibbi-Sin, the unworthy, and take instead as her husband the Elamite chieftain.* Sirara ran her hands up her rounded hips and cupped her breasts, offering Inanna the use of her own ripe, supple body so that the goddess might take her divine pleasure of this fierce, virile mortal.

O, Goddess: Let Ibbi-Sin be rendered impotent, she prayed. *May the winds of heaven blow his arrow from its mark. May the shaft of his spear splinter and break. May the blade of his knife shatter in its sheath. May his house be violated by strangers, and may his line perish from the earth.*

May you give this proud Elamite, your bridegroom, victory over Ibbi-Sin. Come and take your pleasure of the Elamite; taste of his strength.

Sirara gestured for the barbarian chieftain to set the wood beneath the goat's carcass on fire with a torch. There was nothing mocking in his gaze now. Sirara could feel the Holy Maiden's presence in the air about her; she could feel Inanna's lust for the Elamite. The glitter in the barbarian's eyes told her that he felt it, too.

Sirara took a deep breath and gestured gracefully toward the sun, which was high in the sky. Every eye in the camp focused upward. Utu, the sun-god, was Inanna's brother. If Inanna accepted Sirara's sacrifice, she would send Sirara a sign through him. Sirara bared her teeth in triumph and spared a contemptuous glance for the filthy barbarians, who set up a collective cry of horror.

A moment ago, Utu's golden chariot had been directly overhead. Now it was spinning in dizzying circles as the heavens darkened. The warriors ran, screaming in terror, as Utu threw deadly arrows of fire from the sky and thunder crashed about them. Hard missiles of ice fell upon the camp, sizzling as they struck the hot sand.

Sirara let out a long sigh of relief. The goddess was pleased. Inanna would accept the barbarian chieftain as her consort in the king's place. And surely she would smite Ibbi-Sin's army and burn his city.

The Sacred Marriage Rite was all that remained to seal Ibbi-Sin's doom and that of the royal city.

Sirara lowered her eyes from the sun to look at the Elamite chieftain. He alone had the courage to stand his ground in defiance of the sun-god's demonstration of power. All of his followers had abandoned him.

"Bridegroom, let me caress you." Sirara's eyelids grew heavy as she intoned the words of the ancient ritual. "My precious caress is more savory than honey."

When she reached out for him, the Elamite took her hands in his. There was a look of wonder on his face.

"In the bedchamber, honey filled, let us enjoy your sweet allure. Lion, let me caress you. My precious caress is more savory than honey."

The air about them was dark and soundless. Inanna was eager for her bridegroom.

"Your heart, I know where to gladden your heart. Lion, sleep in our house until dawn," Sirara whispered as she led the Elamite chieftain into his tent.

Naked beneath the sheepskin which they had shared during the chill night, Sirara watched the Elamite rise at dawn and dress for battle. She heard activity outside his tent as the camp stirred and men prepared for war. Their voices were excited, their footsteps light and fast. Whether awed by or contemptuous of her Sumerian magic, each man's spirits now swelled with confidence as he contemplated glory in battle—whether it came by death or by victory.

The Elamites did not dress their hair or polish their shields before battle, and they lacked the ornate metal-studded cloaks of Sumerian warriors. There was no denying their fierceness, though, as they made their own ritual sacrifices and painted each other's faces and bodies with sacred symbols.

Putting on her gown, Sirara followed the Elamite chief out into the crisp morning air, watched him survey his men, and listened without comprehension to his speech, which was received with noisy enthusiasm. The warriors would ride all day and attack at sunset, as Sirara had advised, for she had seen visions that night would fall upon Ur and darkness would cover the land.

The Elamite chief mounted his horse and looked down at Sirara.

"When I return in victory, priestess, I will send you

to Dilmun with food, water, mules, and gold. But without," he added with a quirk to his lips, "your seals of power. I have seen how well you use them, and I would not have you use them against *me*."

"If you destroy Ibbi-Sin and send me to Dilmun in time to save my son," she swore, "then I will never want to use them against you."

Neither of them spoke of what would happen if he did not succeed. Not only did such talk tempt the gods to mischief, but Sirara already knew; she and Lahar would die in pain and humiliation, whether here or in the Elamite capital of Susa. That was the way of the world.

"May Inanna be your sword and your shield," Sirara said in final blessing. "May your enemies flee before you as dust flees before a desert wind."

"May it be so."

Their gaze held a moment longer. Looking up at this fierce, painted, long-haired warrior whom she had held between her thighs only hours ago, Sirara said suddenly, "Before you go, I would like to know. . . ."

"What?"

"What is your name?"

He grinned. "Chedor," he replied. Then, with the blood-chilling war whoop of the Elamites, he rode away.

She fed the glowing brazier tirelessly for two days, peering into her power for some sign of what occurred in Ur while she waited helplessly in these forbidding hills, her son growing weaker, her slave weeping copiously, and her guards watching her every move.

Then, somewhere in the empty hours of the third night, she saw victory in the glowing coals. She saw Ibbi-Sin's symbol tumble from the top of Ur's great temple-tower, saw flames engulf the palace, and saw

Chedor's sword cut a swath through the city and straight to the throne.

"We have won!" she breathed, relief flooding her veins. Chedor would return her mules and her gold and send her to Dilmun. "We have *won*."

And Ibbi-Sin, she thought with bitter joy, would now pay dearly for his injury to her. Revenge tasted cold, and sweeter than she would have expected.

"Mistress," Ninmah cried, shaking her awake hours later. "Mistress!"

"What?" She hauled herself to a sitting position, disoriented, wondering when she had fallen asleep. "Is Chedor back? Has he sent word?"

"Mistress . . ." Ninmah started sobbing. Annoyed by the woman's gibbering, Sirara slapped her.

"What is it?"

"The young master . . ."

Sirara's blood froze as she lurched to her feet. "What?"

"He scarcely breathes, he does not answer, he does not move . . . I think . . . He is . . ."

"*No!*" Sirara flew to her son's side and fell to her knees to examine him. "No, no, no. . . ." She scooped his limp body into her arms and cried, "No! We have *won*. No! Dilmun! You must hold onto life until we reach Dilmun! Answer me! *Lahar!*"

But death had stolen him away while she slept.

Ibbi-Sin no longer looked like a king when a party of Elamites, led by Chedor, brought him back to their camp in the hills. Covered in dust, sweat, and blood, his shoulders were stooped with the weight of his defeat, and his eyes were glazed with the horror of what he had seen. He could not even summon the strength to spit when Sirara stood before him.

She faced the king who had once commanded her

loyalty. He had lain in her arms for the sacred marriage many times. Once, he had even planted his seed in her belly; it had not taken root, though, but bled out of her womb a few months later as she lay in sweat-drenched pain.

She could still summon the strength to spit, and she did so.

"When I return to Ur," she said, her voice raw with pain, "I will make sacrifices daily in the temple to thank Inanna for standing with your enemies and driving you from your throne."

"When you return to Ur ..." Too devastated even for hatred in the face of what his chief priestess had done, Ibbi-Sin's bloody, swollen lips quivered briefly before he said, "You will return to dust and ruin, woman. Houses burned, the temple defiled, the river flowing bitter with blood...."

"You should never have traded my son's life for your throne," she hissed, trying to blot out the image he conjured of her city.

"Ruined, laid waste," he rasped. "Women lying dead in the streets. Babies split in half by the single blow of an Elamite sword." A tear rolled through the filth caked on his cheek. "The great law tablets smashed, fields of crops burned, and men...."

"Stop it," she said suddenly, her heart twisting with horror. "Stop it!"

"And men ... how many men died ... are there any left?" Ibbi-Sin's voice broke.

"*Stop it,*" Sirara snarled. He was her enemy! Her son lay dead because of him! "Tell me no more!"

"Gone ..." he murmured. "All that was Ur, all that made us a people ... destroyed by these barbarians."

She turned and ran away from him, ran back to the body of her son, which still lay in her prison tent. She knelt before Lahar's death-cold form and wept, trying to call up her hatred, trying to summon the taste of revenge.

She had done this. She had crumbled the indestructible might of Ur and tumbled the sky-reaching towers into dust. She had forever ended the great days of her own people. And she had not even saved her son. In the midst of her sobs, she heard someone enter the tent. She looked up and saw Chedor—powerful in his victory, strong where Ibbi-Sin was weak, full of vitality and glory.

"Go away," she cried. "Go! Go away!"

"Ah, Sirara . . ." He knelt beside her and looked at the boy's corpse. "I am sorry. Truly."

"What do you care, slaughterer of children?"

"That is the nature of war," he said quietly. "Did you really think it would be otherwise, priestess of Inanna?"

"I thought . . ."

"Did Inanna show you flowers and mercy when she gave you visions of Ur's conquest? Did you beg her for a bloodless victory when you asked her to destroy Ibbi-Sin?"

She quivered away from the accusation in his voice. Only one thing mattered now: "You let my son die."

"The gods let him die."

"No, *you* did!" She whirled on him, full of hatred. "We'd be in Dilmun now if your savages hadn't captured me, if you hadn't—"

"He'd never have lived to reach Dilmun." Chedor's voice was hard. "It lies six days' ride to the south. Hard country full of bandits and war parties. You had no escort to defend you from them, and Lahar hadn't the strength to live that long."

"Six days' ride . . ." Her breath caught in her throat. "You . . . know exactly where it is?"

He nodded. "I've been there."

Forgetting her anger, caught in the memory of all

her hopes, she seized his shoulders. "You've *been* there? Oh, please, tell me! If I take his body there and offer all I have to the gods, can they breathe life back into him?"

"Sirara . . ."

"No one dies or grows old there. It is a paradise!" Her voice broke as she begged him to give her hope again.

His eyes held the same pity she had seen in them the first time she told him she was taking Lahar to Dilmun. "Sirara . . ." He sighed. "It's only an ordinary city. They . . . grow dates there. They trade copper." He shook his head. "It is no paradise, and no gods live there."

"*No!*" she cried fiercely, shaking him. "No! No one ever dies there!"

"Sirara, my own . . ." He shook off her hands and turned away. "People die there, Sirara. Every day. A woman I once took as my own died there."

She stared at him in blank, horrified shock. "You're lying," she whispered, knowing he was not.

He met her eyes again, and the pity was fading, replaced by impatience. "Even had the boy lived to reach Dilmun, he would have died there."

"No. . . ." It felt as if her own heart had stopped beating.

'Yes, Sirara," he insisted. "He would have died there, just as surely as he died here."

There was a long, deadly silence in the tent. Finally, in a voice she scarcely recognized as her own, she said, "And yet you convinced me to help you destroy Ur by promising to let me go to Dilmun when you won the battle."

His expression was impassive. "I offered what you wanted in exchange for what I wanted."

Her eyes clouded with bitter tears. "But what I offered was real, and you offered only a foolish dream."

He nodded. "True."

"You could have told me. . . ."

"You wouldn't have believed me. You wouldn't have wanted to, and, besides . . ." He shrugged. "We were enemies."

"We still are." She glared at him and swore, "More so now than ever before, Elamite."

He hesitated, then nodded again and rose to his feet. Looking down at her, he said, "We will bury your son before sunset. In the morning, I will give you back your two mules, and enough gold to go wherever you want."

She looked up at him. "It doesn't matter what of mine you keep, barbarian. I am one with the goddess, and I will make you pay."

"And when you make me pay, will thousands of others pay, too, as they did for Ibbi-Sin's crime against you?" he asked quietly.

His words echoed inside the tent long after he left.

She had seen visions that night would fall upon Ur and darkness would cover the land. But she had not understood Inanna's promise. Was this disaster her fault? Had her prayers to Inanna asked for too much blood? Or had this been the goddess' plan all along? Had Sirara been sent into the desert to be seized by Chedor's men, all so this would happen?

Calling to the goddess, she asked, "Is this my doing or yours?" Grief chilled her as a new thought struck her like cold water. "Did you send the demon to take Lahar's life so that I would leave Ur and come here?"

What now? Chedor was confident enough of his power to let her go now that he had taken Ur; should she try to destroy him? Should she *join* him? No; the Elamites would bring their own gods and priests to ruined Ur now. There would be no place for her there.

Having contemplated her destiny throughout the

night, she had only one wish in her heart when dawn finally painted the sky. She wanted to join Lahar, to protect her son in the Land of No Return. For how could she let her little boy, so young and so weak, sojourn there alone?

With one final ritual, she asked the goddess, whom she had always served as well as she knew how, to entrance the Elamite who guarded her tent. Then, just as she heard the men in camp begin to stir, she crept out of her tent and took the insensible guard's short sword from his limp grasp.

Breathing hard and listening to the pounding of her own blood, she turned the point of the sword against her belly as she chanted the proper blessing for a sacrifice to Inanna.

"Sirara! *No!*"

She looked up in time to see Chedor running toward her, his eyes wide, his face contorted. She met his gaze and saw that, in this final act, she would have her revenge after all.

Then, with one brief, hard thrust, she offered herself to the goddess and sought her son in the netherworld.

EYE OF FLAME
by Pamela Sargent

This next author brings us an engaging story of magic set in twelfth-century Mongolia. She makes this little-known society live again for the modern reader. Her commitment to research and accuracy show in her superb writing as she brings a distant people, place, and time alive for the modern reader. One of the supporting players in this tale is the young Temujin who later becomes Genghis Khan.

Pam Sargent has published thirteen novels and two short story collections which range from science fiction to historicals for both adults and young adults. In 1992 she won the Nebula for the novelette "Danny Goes to Mars." She had edited several anthologies, including *Nebula Awards 29, Women of Wonder, the Classic Years,* and *Women of Wonder, the Contemporary Years.* Her historical novel about Genghis Khan, *Ruler of the Sky,* was published in 1993 and is now being translated into Russian. She tells me the Russian publisher not only paid her in dollars, but did so promptly!

1

Old Khokakhchin listened as the other women gossiped. They had been going on about Jali-gulug all day, and were still murmuring to one another about the afflicted boy as they herded sheep back to camp. Jali-gulug had fled sometime during the night, unseen by the men on guard. His father Dobon had ridden out that morning and found his son wandering the steppe on foot.

The women spoke of evil spirits and possession. This was not the first time Jali-gulug had wandered off in a trance. He saw visions, fell into fits, and sometimes babbled meaningless chants. The spirits tormented him often. Khokakhchin dropped behind the other women, wondering how long it would take these people to see what the boy was.

She had sensed for some time that young Jali-gulug was destined to follow the shaman's path. Bughu should have seen that by now, and done something about it, but Bughu was not much of a shaman. He knew chants and spells and how to banish evil spirits from those who were ailing; he read the bones for Yesugei Bahadur, who was chief in this camp, as he had for Yesugei's father. But Bughu was not a shaman who could ride to Heaven or command the most powerful of the spirits. Khokakhchin suspected that Jali-gulug had much more power in him.

Koko Mongke Tengri, the Eternal Blue Sky that covered all of Earth, had granted them a warm and windless day, although the late summer weather could change suddenly. The stream that had watered the sheep was a slender blue ribbon that wound in sharp loops over the endless grassland. Hoelun Ujin, Khokakhchin's young mistress, nudged a straying lamb back toward the flock with her juniper stick. With her golden-brown eyes and smooth light brown skin, Hoelun was still a beautiful woman; it was easy to see why her husband Yesugei prized her.

Khasar, Hoelun's two-year-old son, rode toward Khokakhchin on a ewe, clinging to the short shorn wool with both hands. The ewe bleated; Khasar fell from her back. His older brother Temujin quickly pushed his way through the sheep milling around the ewe, grabbed one sleeve of Khasar's short brown

tunic, and dragged him to safety. The four-year-old
Temujin had his father's odd pale eyes of green and
gold mixed with brown, and his straight dark hair had
a coppery sheen. He could sit a horse by himself and
already showed skill in handling his small bow. Khokakhchin felt a pang of sorrow, remembering the son
she had lost when he was no older than Temujin.

Temujin helped Khasar climb back onto the ewe,
then led him toward their mother. Hoelun Ujin rested
her hands on her swollen belly and smiled at her sons.
The Ujin's third child would come soon. Khokakhchin
would be with Hoelun during her labor, as she had
been when Temujin and Khasar were born.

Knowing how to aid in bringing new life into the
world had helped Khokakhchin save her own life. She
thought of the first time she had seen Yesugei Bahadur, sitting on his horse with his sword in hand, yurts
burning behind him as he shouted orders to his men;
he had terrified her. Later, as she huddled with the
other prisoners, waiting to learn if they would be put
to the sword or taken away as slaves, she had heard
the Bahadur speak to one of his comrades of the child
his first wife would soon give him.

Khokakhchin had seen her chance and seized it. "I
have some of an idughan's lore," she had called out
to the man whose Mongol warriors had brought such
ruin to the Tatar camp. "I know of birthing." Yesugei
Bahadur had ridden toward her; she had forced herself
to meet his pale greenish eyes, so unlike any eyes she
had ever seen. "These Tatars attacked my people
years ago," she continued, "and killed those I loved,
and my life among them has been a hard one. I would
more willingly serve you."

The Mongol studied her for a while without speaking. "My first wife may need your skill," Yesugei said
at last. "You'll be taken to my camp. If all goes well,
you'll be her servant, but if any harm comes to her or

to my child, you will die, and painfully—I promise you that." He had then sent her on a hard ride back to his camp with his brother Nekun-taisi and another man.

The spirits had favored Khokakhchin. Hoelun had suffered in labor, but her son was born whole and healthy and clutching a clot of blood in his fist, a sign that he would be a great leader. Yesugei had named the boy Temujin, after the Tatar chief he had just defeated and killed.

Ahead of the women herding the sheep lay the wagons and black felt yurts of Yesugei's camping circle. Yesugei and his brothers were milking the mares tethered with their foals outside the Bahadur's tent. Khokakhchin caught up with two of the younger women, found that they were still talking about Jali-gulug, and fell behind them once more. She did not want to hear talk of Jali-gulug and spirits and magic. She had dealt in magic once, long ago, and had sworn never to do so again.

"Dobon's son has the makings of a shaman," Hoelun said to Sochigil, Yesugei's second wife. Khokakhchin fed more fuel to the fire burning in the metal hearth. She had come to respect Hoelun's wisdom during her years as the young woman's servant, and was pleased the Ujin finally understood what Jali-gulug was.

"Do you think so?" Sochigil set a platter of dried curds and strips of cooked lamb on the low table in the back of the tent. "I saw Bughu riding to Dobon's yurt from the tent of Orbey Khatun. I thought she might have sent him there to drive the evil spirits from Jali-gulug."

"Bughu ought to be teaching the boy some of the shaman's arts," Hoelun said as she took her place next to her husband.

"Perhaps he will," Yesugei Bahadur muttered. "Let

us hope Jali-gulug has the shaman's calling. He's not good for much else."

Yesugei was sitting on a felt cushion at the north of the tent, with his four sons on his right and his two wives at his left. He was a handsome, broad-shouldered man with sharp cheekbones, long mustaches, and black braids coiled behind the ears of his shaven head. Belgutei, Sochigil's three-year-old son, jostled against Khasar at the low table. Khokakhchin settled on her cushion and shot a warning glance at Bekter, Sochigil's older son, who got into fights with his half brother Temujin far too often. Hoelun handed her husband a cup of kumiss. Yesugei dipped his fingers into the mare's milk and scattered the drops while whispering a blessing.

The Bahadur seemed contented tonight. The herds of sheep, cattle, and horses had found good grazing this summer. There had been no raids on his camp during this season, and none of the sudden fierce and deadly storms that even summer could bring, while his scouts had reported that Yesugei's Tatar enemies were now camped farther to the east and south, away from these lands. This autumn, Yesugei and his men would make a foray against the Merkits, who camped in the northern lands. They would be richly rewarded for that effort by Toghril, the wealthy Khan of the Kereits, who hated the Merkit tribes as much as Yesugei did. Even Jali-gulug's afflictions and wanderings could be seen as a good omen; Yesugei might eventually have a powerful shaman in his service.

Such contentment, Khokakhchin knew, might endure for an evening, a moon, a season, but rarely for longer than that. Yesugei needed accord among his people if they were to stand against their enemies, but the unity he had brought about could easily fracture, as it had before among the Mongol clans. Sooner or later, the Bahadur would again be arguing with his

younger brother Daritai over such matters as when
and where to move camp and which men were to herd
the horses to their new grazing lands. Orbey Khatun
still believed that her grandson Targhutai should be
chief in this camp instead of Yesugei, even if she no
longer said so openly. Orbey, the widow of Ambaghai
Khan, was consumed by two ambitions; wreaking vengeance on the Tatars who had sent her husband to his
death, and having a leader in this camp whom she
could control.

Khokakhchin listened to Yesugei and his wives as
they talked of Orbey and Bughu and Jali-gulug, but
said nothing. She was used to keeping her thoughts to
herself, knowing that the safest course for a servant
or slave was to be useful, trusted, and silent. She
would follow the ways of the marmot, burrowing into
her hole, keeping her ear to the ground, surviving.

The dream came to her again. The spirits always
sent the same dream to her after she had come to
believe herself free of it forever. She was running for
the horses, hearing her husband's voice calling to her
above the curses and screams of the others. The
steppe was a plain of fire, the flames a wall moving
closer to the camp. People were fleeing the flames on
horseback, in wagons, on foot. She cried her husband's
name and saw him in the doorway of a burning yurt,
the tent collapsing around him. In the distance, she
heard the war drums and the shouts of the enemies
who had sent the flames against them.

Khokakhchin woke with a start. The dream did not
tell all of the truth, only a part of it. A fire had consumed her camp long ago, when she was still a young
woman. Her husband Bujur had died in the flames.
Tatar warriors riding against her people had used the
fire as their shield in attacking the camp; Khokakhchin
and others who had survived the attack had been

taken into captivity. But the Tatars had not sent the flames against them.

The only sound inside the yurt was the deep, steady breathing of sleepers. Temujin and Khasar lay on beds of felt cushions on the western side of the tent; Hoelun was asleep in the bed in the back. Yesugei had gone to Sochigil's tent for the night. It was good for him to divide his attentions as equally as possible between his wives, and Hoelun was too heavy with child now to take much pleasure from her husband, but Khokakhchin knew that the Bahadur preferred Hoelun's bed to Sochigil's.

Khokakhchin lay under her hide, wondering why her old dream had come to her that night, then got up, covered her head with a scarf, and crept from her bed toward the hearth. The argal burning in the six-legged metal hearth under the cauldron glowed dimly. Fire was sacred; without it, people could not have cooked their food, could not have been purified by passing between two fires before entering a camp, could not have found warmth when the winter winds swept across the steppe, could not have lighted their way through moonless and cloudy nights. She could not imagine the world without fire. But fire was also something to be feared.

Khokakhchin knelt by the fire and stretched her gnarled hands toward the heat. Her thoughts often wandered to the past, especially at night. Sometimes what she recalled was so clear that she almost felt that her spirit had been carried back to her old life, to live through it again. Now she thought of the man who had shown her the eye of fire so long ago.

He had come to her camp with a caravan not long after her marriage to Bujur. The traders in the caravan had gone to the northern forests to trade with the Uriangkhai, the Reindeer People, for sable pelts. Most of the caravan's goods had been traded, but there were still a few bolts of silk, some sharp knives, carved goblets, and polished mirrors to trade for sheep, wool, and hides before the strangers returned to their own Ongghut lands in the south.

One man, who had small brown eyes, a round cheerful face, and a wisp of beard on his chin, had shown Khokakhchin a mirror. She had never seen her face clearly before, having caught only an occasional glimpse of herself in a still pool of water or a polished piece of metal. She stared at her image, making faces at herself, until the women around her were laughing and demanding time to look at themselves. Bujur called her his beauty, but the mirror had shown Khokakhchin a broad face with reddish-brown cheeks and eyes that were a bit too long and narrow.

Another woman was making faces at the mirror as those near her giggled. The men, after riding out to greet the traders, rummaging through their packs of goods, leading the visitors between the fires outside the camping circles, and getting five horses in exchange for two camels the traders needed for their journey south across the desert, had left it to the women to trade for other goods. The women passed the mirror around, then got down to the serious business of trading wool for silk.

The traders laid out their goods on the ground in the center of the chief's circle of wagons and tents. Khokakhchin's yurt was in the chief's camping circle, since Bujur was his younger brother, so she had brought out her soft beaten wool and secured a trade for a bolt of blue silk by the time others were returning with their hides, rolls of wool, and pieces of felt.

"And what for the mirror?" the trader asked her.

She was tempted by the mirror, but could see well enough in a small piece of metal to braid her hair and secure the braids under her bocca, the square headdress of birch bark that sat on her head. "I need no mirror," she replied, unwilling to trade good wool for something that would only make her more vain.

The man shrugged and was about to put the mirror back into his pack when his coat fell open. Around his neck, on a thin gold chain, hung a clear disk that looked like a piece of ice encased in a round golden band.

"What is that ornament?" Khokakhchin had asked, gesturing at the disk.

"It is what the people of Khitai call a lens." The trader slipped it from his neck and held it out to her. "But the old sage who traded it to me called it a firemaker. He claimed that he could do magic with it, that by holding it in a certain way when the sun was shining, he could bring fire."

Khokakhchin shook her head. "I don't believe it."

"I saw him do it. He had other such pieces, and gave me this one for much silver. I was happy to have it at that price."

"Too much to give for such a bauble," Khokakhchin said.

More women had collected near them. The man glanced up at the cloudless blue summer sky, then said, "This is no bauble, Lady."

He asked for something that would burn easily. Two of the women sent their children for some bits of wood and dry grass. The trader directed them to stand back, then held the disk over the tinder; a point of sunlight appeared on the fuel.

The women watched for a long time in silence. Just as Khokakhchin was about to ask when magic would be made, the tinder flared up and she saw a tiny flame.

The women gasped, threw their hands over their eyes, and made signs against evil. The tiny fire quickly burned out. Khokakhchin gazed at the blackened tinder, thinking of what could happen if such a disk were left lying in a patch of dry grass away from the camp. The steppe might go up in flame. She had heard about such fires, of animals and people fleeing from them, of people moving to new grazing grounds only to find them burned away.

Lightning could bring such fires, and everyone knew that only evil deeds and grave violations of custom brought lightning to strike at the Earth. When lightning flashed across Heaven, people threw themselves to the ground in terror; to be caught out on the steppe away from camp and hear thunder was especially frightening. Lightning could strike anywhere. It came to Khokakhchin that the trader's disk had summoned a kind of lightning; she thought that she had seen a tiny bolt as thin as a thread under the disk before the tinder burned.

"Put it away," she said, waving her hands at him. "You . . . you . . ." She shook her head. "Your eye of fire will put us all under a curse."

The other women were too frightened to trade with him after that. The traders were fed that evening, given places to sleep inside the yurts in the chief's camping circle, then left the next morning, and no one spoke again of the eye of flame that could make fire and summon lightning.

Why had she thought of that trader's ornament now? Another memory came to her, of how she had fleetingly longed for the disk and its power before pushing that longing from herself. It was wrong to want such power. She would never have been able to make such a disk work its magic.

Once, she had felt the call to become a shamaness. She had heard the spirits as a child and had wandered from her camp one night to meet spirits that had torn her body apart, sent her wandering among the dead, and restored her to life once more. She had gone to Kadagen, the old shamaness who lived among her father's people, to learn of herbs and spells and chants and how to beat on a small drum to summon spirits.

The training was not wasted. Khokakhchin learned ways to banish some of the evil spirits that brought illness and how to ease women in childbirth. But after a year, Kadagen had told her that she would teach her no more. "You are not an idughan, Khokakhchin." She could still recall the old woman's words. "I don't know what it is that you are. There is power in you, and to have you nearby seems to aid my spells, but I sense that you are not a true shamaness. You cannot use whatever lies inside you."

A dream had come to Kadagen, telling her that Khokakhchin should not follow the shaman's path. The spirits had told her that Khokakhchin had much power, but that to use it would only bring evil. For her to learn any more from Kadagen would only tempt her to use powers that she could not control, powers that should have been given to only the most powerful of shamans. Hers might be a power that others could draw upon for good, yet if she summoned it herself, she risked losing it and bringing ruin to those she loved.

Kadagen did not know why the spirits would give a girl a great gift that she could not make use of herself, but it was not for her to know their purpose. The gift of great beauty could sometimes make a girl no more than a prize to be fought over by men, a captive with a succession of masters. The prize of great strength could be wasted by men in violent, drunken, pointless displays that ended in injury, death, and blood feuds. Gifts were not always the blessings they seemed to be.

Kadagen had been right. Khokakhchin's gift had brought only suffering and death. She supposed that was why she had so easily accepted her captivity among the Tatars; it had been no more than she deserved.

A dog barked outside, once, then was silent. Khokakhchin listened, then got up and moved to the doorway. Hoelun had left the flap partly rolled up. Yesugei's tugh, the pole adorned with nine horsetails that was his standard, stood in the ground just outside the entrance. The Bahadur's big black dog was stretched out under the tugh, head on his front paws, whimpering softly at Jali-gulug.

Khokakhchin tensed, surprised. The dog would snarl and bark at anyone approaching Yesugei's dwellings, howling until his master hushed him. Temujin, brave child that he was, went out of his way to avoid the animal. No one else could do anything with the creature, yet he was cringing before Dobon's son.

Jali-gulug motioned to Khokakhchin. She slipped outside, seeming to feel the pull of invisible cords. When she was closer to the boy, he said, "Something in you called to me."

In the moonlight, she could make out his features. His hollow-cheeked face was calm, his dark eyes focused on her. She thought of all the times she had seen him prattling gibberish and the other times when he had rolled on the ground outside his father's tent, his body shaking and twitching.

He beckoned to her again. She followed him to one of the wagons at the edge of the circle. He sank to the ground and motioned to her to sit.

Khokakhchin knelt, then sat back on her heels. The night was almost too quiet. The sheep resting near the yurts were still, the dogs chained near other yurts as silent as Yesugei's.

"What do you want from me?" she asked.

"Why are you not a shamaness?" Jali-gulug said.

"Once, I thought the spirits had called to me," Khokakhchin replied, "but I was wrong. The spirits decreed that I turn away from the idughan's path."

"There's more power in you than in Bughu." His

voice usually shook, breaking when he pitched it too high, and often his tongue tripped over his words, but now Jali-gulug sounded like a man. "Bughu is a poor shaman. I might have learned more from you."

"I know only a little of a shamaness' lore. Whatever you may think of Bughu, he has more such learning than I do—he'll teach you much of what you need to know. After that, you may have the power to learn more by yourself."

"Your dream called to me," Jali-gulug whispered. "I saw a wall of fire. I heard the cries of people."

Did he have the power to touch thoughts and enter dreams? She thrust out her hand and made a sign. "If you can sense that much," she said, "then you must know why I can't use whatever power I have."

"I know only that you somehow summoned the fire I saw in your dream."

Khokakhchin bowed her head and pulled her scarf closer around her face. "I thought that I could help my people. Instead, I brought them terror and death."

"Tell me of what you did."

Jali-gulug seemed to be drawing the words from her. "I've always had sharp ears," Khokakhchin murmured. "Those in my camp used to say that they couldn't keep their secrets from me even if they whispered them." She rested her hands against her knees. "It was late summer, a night much like this one. We had made camp to the west of Lake Kolen and the lands the Onggirats wander, hoping to find better grazing, because there had been so little rain that summer that even the watering holes were drying up. I woke while it was still dark. The air was too still, as if a storm was coming, and I thought I heard distant thunder, but the patch of sky above my smokehole was clear and black and filled with stars." She found herself unable to speak for a moment.

"Go on," Jali-gulug murmured.

"My children were asleep, my husband Bujur resting at my side. I left my bed without waking him,
without even troubling to put on my boots, and went
outside. I still sensed thunder, but the sound seemed
to be coming from below instead of above me. I
dropped to my knees and put my ear to the ground.
Then I knew the sound for what it was, the sound of
horses galloping in our direction."

She paused to take a breath, remembering how fear
had welled up inside her. "The Tatars were riding
against us. It couldn't be anyone else. The Merkits
camped to the north of our pastures were on the move
toward Lake Baikal, and the Onggirats and our people
were at peace." Her voice shook; she swallowed.
"There had to be hundreds of them. The sound I
heard was that of an army. We couldn't fight them—
our only chance was to get away."

As she spoke, she saw herself back in her camp,
outside her yurt on that last night. She had cried out
to Bujur; in moments, everyone was awake. By then
the wind was rising, blowing from the northwest to
the southeast, toward the enemy. She ran into her
yurt, pulled on her pants under her shift, and told
her two daughters and young son to bring only their
weapons and what food they could carry. She was running for the horses when she saw a spark leap from
the watch fire just outside the camp to the grass.

"That flame died quickly," Khokakhchin went on.
"The men on guard by the fire put it out and mounted
their horses. We still couldn't see any Tatars, but others had put their ears to the ground and heard the
enemy approaching." She was silent for a bit. "The
sight of that flame leaping into the dry grass had made
me long desperately for another way to defend ourselves. The Kerulen River lay to the south of us. A
few of the men could cross and set fire to the grass.
The wind was blowing toward the Tatars—it would

carry the fire toward them. We would have time to get safely away while the fire held them back."

Jali-gulug recoiled.

"It was madness," she continued, "the wish of a moment, the words of a malign spirit whispering inside me. To misuse fire is one of the gravest of sins." She made a sign to ward off evil. "But my wish had roused the spirits. They granted my wish. Almost at once, lightning flashed from the sky and struck the ground to the south."

Convinced that she had summoned the lightning, she fell to the ground and covered her face, terrified and yet fascinated by the power now flaring inside her. Flames danced where the lightning had struck. Her skin prickled. She looked up as another bolt hit the ground and knew that she had called it to Earth.

"People were flinging themselves to the ground, trying to hide from the lightning," Khokakhchin said. "Thunder came, and more lightning flashed across Heaven, but no rain fell. The wind grew stronger, and the flames spread over the grass until a wall of fire was moving south."

She had forced herself to her feet, crying out to the others. A few people stood up, then ran toward the pen where some of their horses were kept. Lightning was no longer flashing overhead, and the wind was dying. The fire spreading across the steppe on the other side of the river would hold off their enemies until they could escape.

Then the wind rose once more and shifted, shrieking past Khokakhchin as it blew north. She watched in horror as sparks flew across the narrow stream of the Kerulen and flared up in the grass along the river's northern bank. She ran for her yurt, screaming for her children. Her son scurried through the doorway, clutching his child's bow; she swept him up in her arms. The fire was upon the camp by the time Khokakhchin reached the horses; by then, she was praying, calling upon the spirits to forgive her for calling down the lightning.

She looked back. Her daughters were running toward her, their masses of long black braids whipping in the wind. She saw Bujur dart back inside their yurt for a moment, perhaps to get his bow or his sword. The wagon next to the yurt was beginning to burn; the wind quickly carried the flames to the tent's felt panels, and then a curtain of fire hid the dwelling from view.

"A few people got away," Khokakhchin murmured. "Others died in the flames. Tengri showed the land some mercy then by sending rain to douse the fire. By then, the Tatars were in sight. They killed most of the men they captured and raped the women and girls. I think no more than forty of us survived—our camp was small, much smaller than the Bahadur's here. My daughters were taken away by one band of warriors, and I never saw them again. My son was put to the sword. He was only a child, no more than four, but the Tatars had sworn to kill all the men and boys of our chief's family, and my husband was brother to our chief."

"I weep with you, old woman," Jali-gulug said. "I pity you."

"One of the men who raped me took me under his tent as a wife, but he fell in battle before I could give him a son. His first wife made a slave of me." Khokakhchin sighed. "I brought our fate upon us by wishing down the lightning, by treating fire so carelessly. I earned my suffering." She covered her eyes for a moment. She could weep for all of them, her dead son and her husband and her lost daughters, even after all these years. "And that is more than I have said to anyone about this ever since that evil night."

"I will not tell this tale to others."

"I'm grateful for that."

"You have suffered enough, Old Woman Khokakh-chin. You don't have to suffer more by hearing your story retold. It would also do no good to have others here know of your powers."

She had heard the coldness in his voice even while he was speaking kindly to her. His concern was not for her, but for whatever abilities she might still possess. The shamaness Kadagen had told her that others might draw upon them for good. Perhaps a powerful shaman, the kind of shaman this boy might become, could use them to protect Yesugei's people.

No, she told herself. She would not allow a moment's arrogance to bring more ruin upon others.

Jali-gulug said, "The spirits will use us as they wish. What we want doesn't matter."

Khokakhchin got to her feet. "You have much power, young one. I saw that sooner than anyone here. Take care that you don't make my mistake."

2

Hoelun Ujin gave birth to her third son, Khachigun, in early autumn, just after Yesugei and his men rode off to raid their Merkit enemies. The birth went more quickly and easily than had those of Temujin and Khasar. Khokakhchin stayed with her mistress during her labor, summoned Bughu to bless the child, and nursed Hoelun during the days when the Ujin was confined to her tent with the infant.

Yesugei returned with little loot and tales of having to pursue Merkits into pine-covered hills and losing their trail there; someone had warned the enemy and given the Merkits time to escape. Hearing of his new son soon cheered him, and there was still the prospect of Toghril Khan's reward for the foray against the Merkits. The Bahadur's followers broke camp and moved south, to the Senggur River valley. From there, Yesugei, his two brothers, and his close comrade Charakha rode west to meet with Toghril and his Kereits and claim their payment.

The Bahadur came back from the Kereit Khan's court with only a couple of gold goblets, a few trinkets, some goats, and three breeding mares past their prime. Toghril might be Yesugei's sworn brother, bound to him by an anda oath, but he was apparently unwilling to give away any more of his great wealth until the Mongols had killed more Merkits.

By then, it was time for Yesugei to meet with the leaders of clans and tribes that often joined him for the annual great hunt. Jarchiudai, an Uriangkhai chief and comrade of Yesugei's, arrived with his men and announced that he would join the Bahadur for the hunt before returning to his lands north of the Kentei Mountains. A Jajirat chief rode there soon afterward, and Seche Beki brought men of his Jurkin clan, but Khokakhchin saw that fewer men would be hunting with Yesugei this year. Men unwilling to hunt with him this season might later refuse to fight under his command.

The men gathered to make a sacrifice for luck during the hunt and began arguing almost immediately. Orbey Khatun's grandson Targhutai openly demanded command over more men of his Taychiut clan, and Daritai took Targhutai's side. Yesugei and Daritai nearly came to blows before Nekun-taisi interceded, begging his two brothers not to fight. Bughu then read the bones of a sacrificed sheep and predicted a hard winter.

The men left the camp to fan out in two wings and gradually encircle their prey; the women took down the tents again and followed with the children in their carts. By the time they had caught up with the men and had finished skinning the carcasses of the deer that littered the ground, a snowstorm struck. The women dried as much of the meat as they could, cutting it into strips and hanging it up to dry before the howling winds and the sharp lashing of the snow forced them to stay inside their yurts and huddle by their hearth fires.

They made their winter camp near the southern slopes of the Gurelgu Mountains, not far from the Senggur River. The mountain cliffs offered protection from the fiercest winds, but Khokakhchin knew that this winter would be harder than many; the rivers had hardened into ice early. Bughu, whatever his failings in other respects, had read the bones correctly.

More snow came, a thick blanket that covered the ground. The women and children had to uncover the snow with brooms and sticks so that the sheep and cattle could graze, while the smaller lambs had to be fed by hand. Soon, even Orbey Khatun, who usually left the harder work to her servants, was leaving her tent with Sokhatai Khatun, Ambaghai Khan's other widow, to help with the sheep and goats.

In spite of these efforts, too many animals died. The women butchered the carcasses and dressed the hides with salted milk, fearing that not enough lambs would be born that spring and summer to make up for the losses. Yesugei and his brothers, who were often away from the camp either to hunt or to guard the horses grazing near the mountains, returned with stories of wolf packs attacking stray horses and of tiger tracks in the snow.

A tiger soon struck near the camp, killing a stray lamb. Three nights later, the tiger came near Daritai's yurt, killed a dog, and dragged off another lamb. Esugei, Daritai's wife, had heard the bleating of frightened sheep, the howls of other dogs, and the snarling of the tiger, but had not dared to go outside.

Yesugei returned to the camp with Daritai, then sent for Bughu. The shaman arrived with his apprentice Jali-gulug. Khokakhchin poured broth for the visitors while Hoelun set out jugs of kumiss, then sat down next to her husband, Khachigun's cradle at her side. Temujin and Khasar sprawled by the hearth, playing knucklebone dice; Khokakhchin sat with them, close enough to hear what would be said in the back of the tent.

"Is that tiger only a tiger," Yesugei was saying, "or is it a spirit in the guise of a cat?"

"It isn't a ghost," Bughu replied in his high soft voice. "I'm sure of that. If we set out a poisoned carcass, we'll rid ourselves of the beast. I'll prepare the poison tonight."

Jali-gulug said, "This tiger won't take the poison."

Khokakhchin lifted her head. Hoelun was staring at the young man, eyes wide with surprise; Yesugei frowned. Bughu's dark eyes had narrowed into slits.

"Can you be so certain?" Yesugei said. "Bughu served my father as a shaman. You've only begun to learn what he knows."

"That is so." Jali-gulug's voice was firm. "But I think setting out a carcass filled with poison will only waste good meat. This tiger killed one of Daritai's dogs and carried off a lamb without the other dogs attacking it. I don't think it will be foolish enough to eat poison."

Bughu was struggling to restrain himself. His mustache twitched; Khokakhchin saw his left hand tremble. She was suddenly relieved that Sochigil was in her own tent with her sons. Had Yesugei's second wife witnessed this, talk of the apprentice's challenge to his master would have flown around the camp, shaming Bughu. Yesugei and Hoelun would at least have the wit to keep silent, knowing that even a weak shaman could be a dangerous enemy.

"And how do you mean to rid us of the tiger?" Bughu pointed his chin at Jali-gulug. "By hunting it? I've never seen you bring down anything larger than a hare."

Khokakhchin tensed. Young Temujin glanced up from his dice, clearly aware of the shaman's anger.

Yesugei held up a hand. "Enough. Bughu has served me well for some time. We'll do as he advises, and set out the carcass." He turned to Jali-gulug. "If the tiger doesn't take the bait, you'll get your chance at it. Until then, you'll follow Bughu's instructions."

Khokakhchin did not look at Bughu and Jali-gulug as they left. Jali-gulug should have known better than to disagree with the shaman in front of their chief; better to have taken Bughu aside later and spoken to him alone. But Jali-gulug was barely more than a boy, still learning, Bughu, old enough to have learned some forbearance, had only made matters worse by insulting him in Yesugei's presence. She wondered if the shaman was still blind to Jali-gulug's growing abilities.

The shaman set out the poisoned carcass of a lamb. Sochigil claimed to have heard that Bughu had mixed the poison alone, refusing to show Jali-gulug how to prepare it.

For four nights, the carcass lay just outside the camp, untouched. On the fifth night, the tiger killed an ewe outside Charakha's tent. Charakha's son Munglik had awakened to the sound of howling dogs, and left his tent to find a large white cat feeding on the dead animal. He had never seen such a tiger before, white and without stripes. He had not dared to move, afraid the tiger might leap at his throat, and had waited until the beast slipped away over the snow.

Charakha rode with his son to Yesugei's camping

circle. The Bahadur listened to Munglik's tale, then sent Charakha and Munglik to fetch Bughu and his apprentice. Jali-gulug arrived alone, but Bughu was accompanied by Targhutai. Khokakhchin saw the Bahadur scowl as Bughu explained that Targhutai had come here to volunteer to hunt the tiger. She did not believe it. Targhutai was here so that he could later tell his grandmother Orbey Khatun what had been said.

Khokakhchin served jugs of kumiss, then seated herself with Hoelun and the children on Yesugei's left. "Munglik," Yesugei said, "have you told the shaman your story?"

Munglik nodded. "Never have I been so frightened." He was a good-looking, sturdily built lad of thirteen, not the sort to admit easily to being afraid. "Even our dogs were cowering." Munglik drew his brows together. "The more I think about that tiger, the more I wonder if it was a tiger at all."

"Maybe it was a shape-changer," Charakha muttered, making a sign against evil.

"If it's a tiger, it can be brought down," Targhutai said. "I'm willing to lead the hunt. If it isn't a tiger, but something else, then it means a curse may lie upon us here. Perhaps the spirits don't want us grazing these lands."

Khokakhchin studied Targhutai's chubby, petulant face. How obvious the young Taychiut man was. If by some miracle he captured the tiger, more of the men would view him as a possible new chief, and Yesugei's position would be weakened. If the tiger escaped him, but continued to prey on their flocks and herds, more would come to believe that this land was under a curse. Yesugei would be blamed for that, since he had chosen the site. Some of his men might even desert him for another chief.

"There will be no tiger hunt," Yesugei said. "I

won't put men at such risk until we've tried everything else. You know how dangerous and treacherous a tiger can be."

Jali-gulug leaned forward. "Bahadur," he said softly, "I ask for my chance at this tiger."

Bughu shot him a glance. Yesugei stroked his long mustaches, looking thoughtful. "I'll need Bughu's help," Jali-gulug continued. "He will have to cast a spell to protect the camp from evil spirits and ghosts. I will go outside the camp and wait for the tiger there." Bughu looked relieved that his apprentice had acknowledged needing his aid.

Targhutai snorted. "Wait for the tiger? Do you think it'll just walk up to you so you'll have an easy shot?"

"That is my plan. I can say no more about it."

"Very well," Yesugei said. "Bughu will cast his spell, and you'll wait for the tiger. If you have no luck, Targhutai can lead his hunt."

Targhutai's cheeks grew even rounder as he grinned. The men talked for a while, finished their kumiss, then made their farewells. Khokakhchin went to the entrance to roll up the flap for the men. Charakha and Munglik were to ride out and relieve some of the men guarding the horses, and Targhutai would probably ride directly to his grandmother's yurt.

"I will cast a powerful spell," Bughu said as he got to his feet. "Perhaps my spell alone will be enough to rid us of that tiger."

Jali-gulug stood up slowly. "I have one more request, Bahadur."

"And what is that?" Yesugei asked.

"Someone else must wait for the tiger with me. A dream has told me this. The one called Old Woman Khokakhchin must come with me."

Startled, Khokakhchin let go of the rope, letting the flap at the entrance fall. Bughu, in the middle of pulling on his long sable coat, turned toward his apprentice. "That old woman? Of what use can she be?"

"A dream came to me," Jali-gulug replied, "and you know well that the spirits speak through dreams. A dream told me that Khokakhchin must wait with me if I am to succeed."

"I have something to say about this," Hoelun said. "Khokakhchin is my servant, a good woman who has helped me in childbirth, done her work without complaint, looked out for my sons, and earned my trust. We would all grieve if any harm came to her." Khokakhchin warmed at her mistress' words, pleased and surprised that Hoelun thought so much of her.

"I can't promise that she won't be harmed," Jali-gulug said. "I can only swear to do what I can to protect her. She must come with me—my dream said it."

"This is madness," Bughu muttered. "Yesugei, are you going to listen to—"

"Silence!" Yesugei raised a hand; his pale eyes glittered, as they always did when he was about to lose his temper. "You had your chance. I promised the boy he would have his." He rested his hands on his knees. "You'll cast your spell, Bughu. Jali-gulug will take Khokakhchin and go where he must to await the tiger." Hoelun seemed about to protest, but one angry look from her husband kept her silent.

"I will come here tomorrow for the old woman," Jali-gulug said. "I'll need two horses, a boiled lamb, a small tent for shelter, and a cart. The rest I can provide for myself."

"If this works," Yesugei said, "you'll both be richly rewarded, you for your efforts and Bughu for his spell."

Bughu looked mollified as he left. If Jali-gulug failed, the shaman could not be blamed; if the young man succeeded, Bughu was likely to claim part of the credit. Khokakhchin lowered the flap after Jali-gulug went outside, tied it shut, then moved toward the hearth. "If this works," Hoelun said to Yesugei, "Khokakhchin will deserve a reward as well. I insist upon that."

Someone tugged at Khokakhchin's sleeve. She looked down into Temujin's small face. "You'll be brave," the boy said. "I know you will."

She knelt to embrace the child, fearing for herself.

Jali-gulug came for her just after dawn, as she was sipping her morning broth. Hoelun helped her load the felt panels and willow framework of a small yurt into the two-wheeled cart, then handed her two oxhide jugs of kumiss. "Take care," Hoelun whispered through the woolen scarf that covered most of her face. "I'll pray for you, old woman."

Jali-gulug mounted his horse and began to trot north. Another of Yesugei's horses had been hitched to the cart. Khokakhchin climbed up to the seat and picked up the reins.

The air was cold, dry, and still; the wind that had been howling through their camp for days had died. Khokakhchin followed Jali-gulug across the icy white plain toward the cliffs looming in the distance. To the west, the horses grazing away from the camp were small dark specks against the whiteness.

They rode until they came to a finger of rock that pointed out from the nearest cliff, then halted. Khokakhchin raised the yurt, tying the felt panels to the frame, while Jali-gulug unsaddled the horses and set out some of the boiled lamb. It was cold inside the small yurt; in winter, at least three layers of felt were needed against the cold, and this tent had only one. Khokakhchin longed for a fire, but the flames would keep the tiger away.

It was growing dark when Jali-gulug came inside the

tent and sat down at her right to face the entrance.
"How long will we have to wait here?" she asked.

"As long as we must."

He was so calm. Did he lack the wit to be as frightened as he should be?

"I am afraid," he said then, as if hearing her thoughts, "but it will do no good to give in to my fear." He handed her a piece of lamb.

"I thought," she said, "that this food was for the tiger."

"It's for us as well. That tiger would come even without the meat I set out. It isn't a tiger, you see."

"What is it?"

"A ghost. Bughu should have seen that for himself from the start, when Daritai's dogs wouldn't fight it."

Khokakhchin made a sign. "Why did you bring me here? What good can I do you? I swore that I would never meddle in magic again after what I brought upon my people."

"You have power I can use, Old Woman Khokakhchin. But that isn't the only reason you're here. My dream told me that the tiger is seeking you."

She forced herself to eat the piece of lamb, nearly choking on the food. "You aren't a shaman yet," she said. "You're still learning how to be one. How do you know—"

"Be quiet, old woman. The tiger is not far away."

She listened, but heard nothing. Jali-gulug was staring at the entrance. He had not even brought a small drum to beat upon, to aid him in calling upon the spirits. She wondered how many chants he had mastered, how many spells he had learned to cast.

The smokeholes of Tengri glittered in the night sky. The plain outside glowed blue; there were no clouds to hide the full moon. Jali-gulug set his weapons at his side; he had brought along his bow, a quiver of arrows, and a sword, for all the good they would do him. No man would willingly hunt a tiger. Everyone knew how dangerous the creatures were. This boy was setting her out to lure the cat just as he had done with the meat.

Jali-gulug tensed. A pale blue creature was slinking across the snow toward them. Khokakhchin squinted, thinking the light might be playing tricks on her, and then the form became that of a tiger.

"The ghost knows you're here," Jali-gulug said softly. "We must go outside to meet it."

She was an old woman. She had lived her life and there had been times when she had longed for death. If this tiger was to carry death to her, she would meet it bravely and hope that the creature tore out her throat quickly without making her suffer too long. Khokakhchin got to her feet and felt her knees tremble; her breath came in short, sharp gasps.

Jali-gulug ducked through the entrance; she crouched down and followed him outside. The horses, still tied to the cart, had their ears flat against their heads and their nostrils distended in fear, but made no sound. The meat had been set out several paces from the cart. The tiger crept toward the food, lowered its head, and began to feed.

"Aaaah," Jali-gulug cried. His arms were suddenly flailing about him like whips; he threw himself to the ground, writhing and twisting.

Why did the boy have to fall into one of his fits now? Khokakhchin watched his thrashings helplessly, afraid to move, expecting the tiger to leap upon him at any moment. The tiger lifted its head from the meat and stared directly at her. She wondered if she would have enough time to go for the weapons inside the yurt.

Jali-gulug let out a wail, then stiffened. At that moment, the tiger howled, then fell to the ground as if dead. Khokakhchin stepped back, terrified, as Jali-gulug sat up slowly, his face twisted into a grimace.

"Khokakhchin," he said in a voice much deeper than his own, a voice she had never thought to hear again in this life. "Khokakhchin, am I to have no rest? Am I to roam in this world, hearing the blood of our son cry out for vengeance?"

"Bujur," she whispered, making a sign, "my dear lost husband. I still ache for you and our children, I've never forgiven myself for what I did. Are you here to punish me for daring to call down the lightning?"

"You have suffered enough for that already," her husband said from Jali-gulug's mouth. "You endured the loss of all those you loved and suffered a hard life among our murderers. The spirits must have ended your captivity and brought you to live among these people for a reason. I cannot see their intentions clearly, but it may be that the power you possess will be used for good. It may be that I and all the ghosts of your people will have the revenge we seek."

"My power is useless." Khokakhchin covered her eyes briefly, afraid she would weep and that the tears would freeze on her face. "I swore never to call upon it again."

"Listen to me. I have wandered the steppe in the body of a wolf, searching for you. I came down from the mountains as a tiger, waiting for you to see me and know what I was. You swore not to use your power, but that does not mean refusing to let others draw upon it."

"Are you telling me that Jali-gulug—"

The boy let out a shriek. His body was writhing again, and then he leaped to his feet. The tiger was watching him. She sensed that the ghost of her husband had fled, that the cat housed only a tiger's spirit now. She wondered which of them the cat would go for first.

"Khokakhchin." Jali-gulug was now speaking in his own voice, but so softly that she could barely hear him. "Fetch my bow and one arrow. Move very slowly, and keep facing the tiger as you move. It's under my spell now, but I don't know how much longer I can hold it."

She backed toward the tent as slowly as she could. The weapons should be just inside the entrance. She bent low and backed inside, still keeping her eyes on the cat. The tiger snarled and got to its feet. She knelt and moved her hand over the ground; her fingers brushed against the sword, then touched the quiver. She drew out an arrow and found the bow.

Holding the bow and arrow close at her side, she crept outside. One arrow, she thought. Would he shoot that accurately, even at close range? It did not matter. He would not get a second chance.

The tiger snarled again, showing its sharp teeth, then went into a crouch. She thrust the bow and arrow into Jali-gulug's hands. He fitted the shaft, drew the bow, and slowly took aim.

The tiger leaped toward them. Khokakhchin stumbled back, throwing up her arms. Jali-gulug's arrow flew from his bow, but the great cat struck the young man, knocking him onto his back. Khokakhchin reached under her coat, found her knife, and pulled it from her belt, even while knowing that her weapon would be useless against this creature.

The tiger was very still. Then the beast moved, but she saw that Jali-gulug was pushing the cat from himself. He sat up, his hand still around his bow.

"It's dead," she murmured.

"Help me up." She pulled him to his feet, then peered at the carcass. The arrow had pierced the roof of the tiger's mouth. A lucky shot, she thought; not many men could have made it. Perhaps the spirits had guided his aim. Jali-gulug stared at the animal that had carried Bujur's ghost to them, then knelt and cut its throat, spilling blood over the silvery snow.

Khokakhchin took down the yurt, hitched her horse to the cart, and rode with Jali-gulug to the camp. The dead cat lay in the back of her cart. Jali-gulug's horse had been too skittish to carry it, whinnying and pawing at the ground as if still fearing that the cat harbored a ghost.

The sky was still dark, but growing gray in the east, as they approached the camp. Three men were on guard near the two fires to the north of Yesugei's circle of yurts and wagons. Jali-gulug dismounted and walked between the fires, followed by Khokakhchin. One of the sentries spotted the tiger; the others moved toward the cart to stare at the body of the white cat.

Jali-gulug did not speak. She saw how the men looked at him, eyes wide with awe and a little fear.

"Is that the tiger that was killing our sheep?" one man said at last.

"It is," Khokakhchin replied.

The guard gaped at her, then turned to order one of the others to ride to Yesugei's tent with the news.

3

In a day, the story of Jali-gulug and the white tiger had flown to the farthest circles of Yesugei's camp. The young man had spoken to a ghost, driven it from the tiger, and killed the beast with one arrow. The ghost, it was said, had been someone known to Hoelun Ujin's servant Old Woman Khokakhchin, but that spirit was at peace now and would trouble them no more.

Yesugei gave Jali-gulug a man's bow made by old Baghaji, the best bowmaker in the camp, and also one of his prized white mares. He was careful to reward Bughu for his spell with three soft-wooled black-headed sheep and a jade goblet. Khokakhchin was given a long tunic of green silk, despite her protests that such a garment was much too fine for her.

Jali-gulug spoke of his deed only once, when reporting it to Yesugei. Khokakhchin told the story to Hoelun and Sochigil, then to other women in the camp. By the end of winter, the tale had grown in the telling until many believed that Jali-gulug had vanquished the ghost and killed the great cat only after several nights of battling evil spirits. Khokakhchin soon disappeared from the story, and by spring people had nearly forgotten that Jali-gulug had taken her with him to meet the tiger.

This was just as well with her. The white tiger pelt Jali-gulug wore over his coat was a constant reminder of his deed; she had occasionally glimpsed the envy and hatred in Bughu's eyes when he glanced at his apprentice. Bughu would be thinking of the rewards he might lose to Jali-gulug, of the influence he might no longer have. Khokakhchin was content not to have any of his hatred and resentment directed at her.

In spring, they moved north, toward the Onon River, and made camp within sight of the Kentei massif and the mountain of Burkhan Khaldun. The mountain harbored a powerful spirit, and Yesugei was soon riding there with his shaman and his close comrades to make an offering and to pray.

They returned to the camp without Jali-gulug. Some said that the spirit of the mountain had kept him there, even that the young man had been given the power to ride to Heaven from Burkhan Khaldun. Others, noting Bughu's easier mood during the absence of his apprentice, whispered that Bughu had told Jali-gulug to remain there in the hope that the spirits, or the rigors of spending days alone on the tree-covered slopes, would send the lad to dwell among the dead for good.

Hoelun heard the whispers, and repeated her suspicions to Khokakhchin while preparing to join the other women for the spring sacrifice to the ancestors. "Bughu thinks only of himself," Hoelun murmured as she adjusted a square birch headdress adorned with feathers on her head, then pushed her thick black braids under its cap. "He knows that Jali-gulug might someday be a great shaman, perhaps even one who could strike fear into my husband's enemies. He should have stayed with the lad on the mountain to guide him."

"Bughu had to return to set the time for the sacrifice," Khokakhchin reminded her mistress.

"He could have done that before he left." Hoelun stamped her booted feet and smoothed her long pleated tunic down over her trousers. "Instead of training Jali-gulug, he avoids him whenever he can. Instead of using his magic to help us, he curries favor with Orbey Khatun in case her grandson ever decides to challenge my husband."

Her mistress, Khokakhchin realized, was irritated not only by the shaman, but also by the prospect of spending the day with the old Khatun. Orbey and Sokhatai, as the widows of Ambaghai Khan and the oldest women in Yesugei's camp, always presided over the spring sacrifice. They would be picking at Hoelun as they dined on their sacrificed sheep, trying to affront her while being careful not to openly insult her, resenting her because she was Yesugei's wife.

"When Jali-gulug knows more magic," Hoelun went on, "I'll advise Yesugei to consult him more often. Maybe by then—" She fell silent. Sochigil was calling to her from outside. Hoelun tightened the sash around her waist, secured her knife, slipped on a coat, then left the tent.

Khachigun crawled to her over the carpet. Khokakhchin picked up Hoelun's youngest son and went outside. Blue and white flowers dotted the land; women were riding toward the yurt Orbey had raised beyond the camp. The wives of Yesugei's brothers and his close comrades would honor the ancestors today, and Hoelun would no doubt be hoping that the two old Taychiut Khatuns would soon join those forebears.

Temujin and Bekter were watching the sheep. The scowls on their faces as they glanced at each other told Khokakhchin that the two half brothers were working themselves up to a fight. Khasar and Belgutei stood to one side, their eyes on the two older boys.

"Bekter!" Khokakhchin shouted as she approached. "You and Belgutei will go to your mother's tent, fetch baskets, and gather argal for the hearth. Make sure you bring only the driest of the dung back. Temujin, you and I will look out for the sheep. Khasar, you'll watch Khachigun."

Bekter glared at her with eyes as black as kara stones. "Why do I have to—"

"Silence!" Khokakhchin raised a hand. "Temujin and Khasar will gather fuel later, while you watch the sheep. Any more from you, and I'll tell your father you've been disobedient and deserve a good beating."

Bekter hurried off with his brother. Khokakhchin moved toward the sheep. Yesugei's camping circle was near the Onon, and a few sheep had wandered toward the river to drink. One black-headed ewe would drop her lamb soon, perhaps today. They would need many lambs to replace the ones lost over the winter.

"Khokakhchin," Temujin called out. He was gazing northwest, toward Burkhan Khaldun. She turned and saw the tiny form of a man on horseback riding over the snow-strewn land below the massif. Jali-gulug was returning from the mountain. Her eyes were still sharp; even at this distance, she saw that he was slumped over his horse, barely staying in his saddle. She was suddenly afraid.

"What's wrong with him?" Temujin asked. "Even I can ride better than that."

"Watch the sheep," she said.

Bekter and Belgutei had returned with dry dung, and Temujin had gone to gather more fuel with Khasar, by the time Jali-gulug neared the camp. By then, the men near the horse pen and the men churning kumiss behind Daritai's tent had paused in their work to stare at him. Temujin, usually quick about doing his chores, had stopped picking up dung and was watching with the men. Jali-gulug's face was thinner, his cheeks hollow, and his dark eyes had the entranced look of one who had communed with spirits.

He rode toward Yesugei's circle, stopped by the horse pen, said something to the men there, then continued toward her. Temujin ran after him, Khasar at his heels. Jali-gulug's bay horse was moving at a walk; by the time he reached Khokakhchin, the boys had caught up with him. Khachigun whimpered and pulled at the hem of her coat; she handed him a small skin of kumiss to keep him quiet. Bekter, standing near one of the dogs, made a sign against evil.

Jali-gulug reined in his horse. His braids had come undone; his matted hair hung down from under his wide-brimmed fur hat. "Old woman," he muttered, "one can see much from a mountain." His voice was so low that she could hardly hear him. "The spirits have spoken to me. They warned me . . . they . . ." He toppled from the horse; his body writhed against the ground, then stiffened.

She ran to his side and knelt. His body was as rigid as a board; his eyes were half-open, with only the whites showing. Two of the pouches hanging from his belt had spilled their contents. Khokakhchin carefully picked up the small bones used in casting spells and the large round jada stones that were used to make rain and slipped them back inside the pouches.

Khasar reached for Khachigun, holding his younger brother's hand tightly. "I'll fetch Bughu," Temujin said, and ran off before Khokakhchin could stop him.

She managed to drag Jali-gulug into Hoelun's tent and stretch him out on a felt carpet. His body was cold; she covered him with a blanket and moved him closer to the hearth. Too late, she thought of how the yurt and everything in it would have to be purified if he died here. If she was at his side when his spirit left him, she would be forced to stay outside the camp and under a ban for months.

Bughu soon arrived, and spent several moments prodding and poking the inert young man. "He won't die," the shaman said at last as he stood up.

She wondered if she could believe him. Bughu knew something of healing, even if he lacked the gifts of a great shaman. But he also resented his apprentice. He might be thinking of how to use his knowledge to rid himself of Jali-gulug.

The young man moaned. Khokakhchin sat back on her heels, determined not to leave him alone with the shaman. The sky above the smokehole was growing dark; she heard the voices of men outside the tent. Yesugei suddenly came through the entrance, drawing himself up as he caught sight of Jali-gulug lying by the hearth.

"Bahadur," Jali-gulug gasped.

"A spirit is inside him," Bughu said. "It must have seized him on the mountain. Pitch a tent for him outside the camp and I'll do what I can to drive the spirit from him."

Jali-gulug was trying to sit up. Khokakhchin slipped

a pillow under his shoulders. "No spirit is in me now," he whispered. "I need no help. Bahadur, listen to me. On the mountainside, I dreamed, and in my dream I flew east until I saw black birds hovering over your camp. Your tent was below me, Bahadur, its frame broken and its household spirits desecrated. I saw no people in your camp, only a great bull standing by your tent with a yoke around its neck." Jali-gulug closed his eyes for a moment. His sallow face had grown even paler; Khokakhchin saw how weak he was. "This was the only dream that was sent to me on Burkhan Khaldun. It was a warning—you must not go east when we break camp."

Bughu snorted. "I read the bones on the mountain. I saw no such omen in the cracks."

"I tell you—"

Bughu stood up and faced Yesugei. "I served your father," he said in his soft high voice. "I've read the bones for you ever since you were chosen as chief. I have told you what the stars decree for your sons. Does this boy know more than I do?"

Yesugei's mouth worked. "He rid us of the ghost-tiger." He gestured at the furry white pelt that covered Jali-gulug's shoulders.

"And my spell protected your camp while he was going to meet that tiger." There was a coldness in the shaman's eyes, an empty look as he gazed at Yesugei, the kind of look a man might have after his spirit had flown from him.

"If we're not to go east," Yesugei said, "exactly where would you have us go?"

"I'm not certain." Jali-gulug sounded hoarse.

"He doesn't think we should go there," Bughu said, "yet he can't tell us where else to go."

"West," Jali-gulug murmured. "We could camp near the Tula River."

"Those lands are Kereit pastures," Bughu said.

"Toghril Khan would surely let us graze our herds there, but you would have to offer him some tribute in return. I don't know how much we have to give him after the winter just past."

Khokakhchin knew what Yesugei would decide; he had little choice. He would heed Bughu because he could not afford to slight him. If he did, the shaman would turn to Orbey Khatun, who would grasp at any reason to cast doubt on the Bahadur's ability to lead. The men would also wonder how much Yesugei's oath of brotherhood with the Kereit Khan meant if they had to lose even more of their depleted flocks and herds in exchange for grazing on Toghril's land. Jali-gulug might have met and overcome a ghost and a tiger, but he was still young, still learning; he could be wrong. They would go east, whatever Jali-gulug's dream had told him.

"Are you well enough to move?" Yesugei said to Jali-gulug. The young man nodded, sat up, and slowly got to his feet. "Good. Old woman, give him some kumiss and send him on his way." The Bahadur motioned to Bughu. "Come with me while I finish milking my mares. The women will soon return from their spring sacrifice. I'll want to know what the bones told Orbey Khatun."

The two men left the tent. Khokakhchin rose and went to the eastern side of the tent, where jars of kumiss hung from goat's horns set in the yurt's wicker frame. She took down a jar and brought it to Jali-gulug.

"Here," she said as she sat down. He knelt and whispered a blessing as he poured out a few drops. "I must be rude and beg you to drink it quickly, so that I can fetch the Bahadur's sons, settle the sheep, and prepare supper."

"You must tell Yesugei Bahadur not to go east."

"Oh, yes." She shifted her weight on her felt cushion. "I, a servant and an old woman without sons, will tell a chief, a man with Khans among his ancestors, what to do."

"You could tell his chief wife. He listens to her."

"I'll tell no one. Hoelun Ujin would say only that it's not something for me to meddle in."

"It's something you don't want to meddle in. You think your life ended for you on the night you called down the lightning. You've lived in your body like a ghost ever since. Hoelun Ujin cares for you, her children seem to have affection for you, and Yesugei Bahadur probably holds some fondness for you, even if he won't admit it. But you'll do nothing to try to shield them from harm."

"Stop it," she said, knowing he had struck close to the truth.

"I didn't think you were a coward. I thought you were more than that. After we faced the tiger together, after you spoke to the spirit of your husband, I thought you'd see how your power might be used for good, how you might make up for the suffering you brought to your people. I could draw on the force inside you, Khokakhchin. Tell the Bahadur and Hoelun Ujin what they must do, and I'll draw on your power to cast my spell. They'll listen—"

"They will not listen!" She looked into his eyes and saw only the glazed stare of a madman. "Leave me alone. I want nothing to do with your magic. Bughu hates you already, and I don't want him seeing me as another enemy. He's more dangerous than you know."

"I know what Bughu is." Jali-gulug set down the jug. "He has no true power, and no great gift, because he doesn't believe in the spirits. No voices sing to him in the wind, and no spirits speak to him in his dreams. He wouldn't know them even if they did, for he doesn't think they exist."

Khokakhchin was too shocked to speak.

"His spells are meaningless," the young man went on, "his chants empty gestures. I've seen it for some time, while he was teaching me, I heard it in the way he spoke. The world to him is a soulless place. That's what makes him so dangerous, Khokakhchin. He has knowledge, but will not use it to serve the spirits, to honor Etugen, the Earth, or to bow to the will of Heaven, but only for his own ends."

She had glimpsed the emptiness inside Bughu without knowing what it was. The horror of what lay inside him nearly made her choke. That had to be why he had been so blind to Jali-gulug in the beginning, and refused to see his talents even now.

"He has some skill," Jali-gulug continued. "He can cast a few spells. It wouldn't be hard for him to make the Bahadur see you as merely a useless old woman and me as no more than an afflicted boy."

"That's why we must keep out of his way," Khokakhchin murmured.

"It is also what gives us a chance to stand against him, because that is all he sees." He leaned toward her. "Say only that you'll lend me your power if I need it."

"I promise nothing." She stood up. "I am going to get the Bahadur's children. Please be gone from this tent before I return." She moved toward the doorway, whispering a prayer.

The bones were saying different things. Bughu had seen no evil omens in the bones he had read on Burkhan Khaldun, but Orbey Khatun, at the spring sacrifice, had burned a clavicle that refused to crack at all. Yesugei demanded another sacrifice, with an exact question to be put to the spirits: should they appeal to the Kereit Khan for the use of his lands, or go east?

Bughu killed three sheep and burned their bones.

All three of the clavicles split down the middle. The omen was clear.

Yesugei's followers took down their tents and moved east. Yesugei rode in front of the procession with most of the younger men and the horses, the women followed in their ox-drawn carts with the sheep and cattle, while the boys and older men brought up the rear. They went at a slow pace, so that their animals would not lose fat.

Yesugei had sent scouts ahead of his main force with orders to treat with the Onggirats for the use of the lands bordering their pastures. His scouts returned to him with disturbing news, while the Bahadur's people were still far from Lake Kolen, in land bordering a mountain ridge and foothills. The Onggirats were camped along the Urchun River and near Lake Buyur, farther south than they usually were in late spring. A large encampment of Tatars led by Ghunan Bahadur was traveling north of the Yellow Steppe and the Kerulen River to the lands the Mongols had hoped to graze.

Yesugei cursed when his scouts brought him this report, but Khokakhchin noticed the half-smile on his face after the men had left his tent. The Tatars would pay for encroaching on lands that bordered Mongol pastures. War would come now, and Yesugei welcomed the prospect of fighting the Tatar chief Ghunan. This was too good an opportunity to be missed. The Tatars might be prepared for one of Yesugei's raids, but not for a larger Mongol force.

Yesugei sent out messengers, summoning his allies to a kuriltai. Other chiefs were soon riding to his camp for the war council. Seche Beki and his brother Taichu came with a few of their Jurkin retainers, Yesugei's cousin Altan swore to lead his men into battle under the Bahadur's command, and the Arulat chieftain Nakhu Bayan was willing to fight at his side. The horses tethered outside Yesugei's yurt grew so numerous that one might have thought a Khan dwelled in this camp.

The men practiced their archery, raced their horses, honed weapons, dined in Yesugei's tent, went hunting with their falcons, got drunk and recited stories, and spent the rest of their time talking of war and planning their tactics. They would strike at Ghunan in summer, when he would not expect an attack, and exterminate his people.

Khokakhchin thought of Jali-gulug's prediction as she moved among the men, helping her mistress and the other women serve boiled lamb and airagh, the stronger fermented mare's milk offered on special occasions. Yesugei had ignored Jali-gulug's advice, and now more Mongols would join him in punishing the Tatars. At the agreed time, each force would advance east before converging on Ghunan's camp. With a victory, they would destroy one of the most powerful Tatar chiefs and strike terror into the other Tatar leaders. More people were saying that the Mongols, who had lacked a Khan since the death of Yesugei's uncle Khutula, might soon have a Khan again, that the chiefs would elect Yesugei. Even Orbey Khatun would soften toward Yesugei if he took Ghunan's head.

Khokakhchin listened to the loud drunken voices of the Mongol chiefs as they sang their songs and told herself that she was wrong to worry. Temujin, who was learning about his ancestors, recited the tale of Bortei Chino and Maral Khohai, the Blue-Gray Wolf and the Tawny Doe who were the forebears of all Mongols, and won high praise from the men for both his performance and his memory. The warriors complimented Yesugei on the beauty and the cooking of his wives, the strength and swiftness of his horses, the soundness of his strategy. The omens were favorable, the early summer weather was warm, wildflowers were blooming on the steppe, and there was every reason to think that the war against Ghunan's Tatars would go well.

Yet Khokakhchin could not keep her darker thoughts at bay. Bughu had told Jali-gulug that he would no longer instruct him, that he had shown himself unworthy to be a shaman. When she glimpsed Jali-gulug taking his turn at archery practice with the younger men, or riding in one of the races across the steppe, she saw how poor his aim was and how awkwardly he held himself in the saddle. The young man belonged in the rear guard, casting his spells and protecting his comrades from harm with his magic, not in the midst of battle. If one of his fits came upon him during the fighting, he would not survive.

The kuriltai was over. Khokakhchin circled Hoelun's tent, seeing that the sheep at the back of the yurt were settled for the night. The other Mongol chiefs had left Yesugei's camp. They would ride against the Tatars after the twenty-first day of the summer's first moon; Bughu had chosen the time.

The camp seemed more quiet than usual, after the past nights of hearing men singing and shouting tales of past battles. She remembered how Yesugei had danced the night before, when everyone had gathered outside for a last feast to celebrate the end of the kuriltai. His booted feet had pounded the ground with such force that he had made ruts in the grass. His shaven head had gleamed with sweat, the braids looped behind his ears had come undone and slapped against his back like whips. He had looked like a Khan.

Two men rode past her, on their way to join the night guard just outside this camping circle. Daritai's wife Esugei left her yurt to throw a few bones to her dogs, then went back inside. To the northwest, above the sparsely wooded foothills bordering the steppe, a high black mountain ridge thrust toward the stars, reaching for Tengri. Khokakhchin was near the entrance to Hoelun's tent when she saw another man ride out from a circle of tents and wagons to the south.

He was riding in her direction, slouched in his saddle; she recognized Jali-gulug. He had tied a band of cloth around his head and wore his tattered dark wool tunic under his pale tiger skin. People were quickly forgetting the courage he had shown in meeting the ghost-tiger. Even she could think of that night and wonder if only luck had guided his arrow, if an evil spirit rather than her husband had spoken to her through Jali-gulug. She watched him ride toward her, pitying him.

Fifty paces beyond Yesugei's circle, he reined in his horse, then beckoned to her. Khokakhchin refused to move until he motioned to her more vehemently. Cursing under her breath, she went to meet him.

"What is it?" she muttered.

He dismounted. A bowcase and quiver hung from his belt, next to his sword, but no man could have seemed less of a warrior. He still wore the pouches that contained his small bones, amulets, jada stones, and other tools of magic, even though he would never become a shaman. A faint mustache had begun to sprout on his upper lip, but his face was still that of a sickly, hollow-cheeked boy.

"I came to tell you—" His voice stumbled over the words; his stammer had grown worse. "I've been sent to join the men grazing the horses."

Khokakhchin sighed. "You made me walk all the way out here to tell me that?" She spoke softly; even a feeble voice could carry far on a nearly windless summer night.

"M—my father—my father s—said—" He shook his

head and wiped his mouth with one hand. "He ordered me to look after his spare horses when we ride against the enemy," he said in steadier tones. "He wants me in the rear, you see."

"Your father's wise," she said, relieved. "That's the best place for someone who hasn't done much fighting to be."

"Young men my age, even many of the older boys, know more of fighting than I ever shall." She heard the despair in his voice. "I'm not going to guard the horses, Old Woman Khokakhchin, or ride with my father to war. I came to say farewell, to tell you that I'm leaving this camp."

She drew in her breath sharply. "I can't believe it. There's nothing lower than a coward, nothing worse than a man who would desert his comrades. Are you the same man who faced a ghost and killed a tiger?"

"The spirits are tearing at me again." He looked up at the sky. "They're driving me from this camp. I'm useless here. I can do nothing."

"You can fight with our chief against his enemies. You can—"

"The same dream still troubles me. The enemy will trample on the threshold of Yesugei's tent. The great bull will wear a yoke."

He was mad, she told herself. Bughu's shaming of him and his own fear of battle had driven him mad. "I ought to do my duty," she whispered, "by going to the Bahadur now and telling him that you're deserting us. Bughu would be happy to see you punished for your cowardice and your head lying on the ground."

"I must go, old woman. The spirits tear at me. Perhaps they'll show me what to do now, how to—" His chest heaved. He turned away and mounted his horse. "Farewell."

"The Bahadur will send men after you, you cursed boy." She shook her fist. "Or you'll die out there all alone, without shelter, without—'' But he was already riding away.

The men grazing the horses would not miss him for a while. Two or three days might pass before Dobon found out that his son had not ridden there. His trail could be followed, but by then everyone would be preparing for war, and Yesugei would not change his plans to search for Jali-gulug.

She had once sensed power in him. Maybe his madness had touched her, making her see what was not there. She tucked her hands into her sleeves and walked back to Hoelun's tent.

The men sharpened and oiled their curved lances and knives, polished their lacquered leather breastplates, fletched arrows, and selected the horses they would use in the campaign. On the day before they were to ride out, another sheep was sacrificed, and Bughu predicted victory. Yesugei took off his belt, hung it around his shoulders, and poured out some kumiss as an offering to his sulde, the protective spirit that lived in his nine-tailed standard.

No one spoke of Jali-gulug's desertion. Yesugei had gone into a rage when Daritai suggested going after the coward. Even Dobon seemed content to regard his son as dead. They would have their war, and then Jali-gulug, if he still lived, would be punished.

The men rode out on a day when the blue sky was so clear that it hurt Khokakhchin's eyes to look toward Heaven. The nine horsetails of Yesugei's tugh, carried by Nekun-taisi, danced in the wind. Women and boys on horseback galloped after the men, shouting their farewells. Hoelun was astride one white horse, calling out to her husband.

Khokakhchin gazed after the men, her fingers around Khachigun's small hand, thinking of the times she had sent her husband Bujur off to war. If Yesugei had his victory, they would have the better grazing land they needed for their herds. There would be loot in Ghunan's camp, riches given to his people by the rulers of Khitai so that the Tatars would not attack the villages outside Khitai's Great Wall. Yesugei would win the respect of other chiefs and clan leaders and a measure of vengeance for all the Mongols who had died fighting the Tatars; he might even be raised on the felt and proclaimed Khan.

But eventually the Tatars would find a way to strike back at him. The fighting would go on, Khokakhchin thought; there would never be an end to it. She tried to shake off the darker spirits that had entered her thoughts. She had suffered among the Tatars; Yesugei would be avenging her.

Temujin was riding back to her, his brother Khasar on the saddle in front of him. Temujin sat his horse well for one so young. "Khokakhchin," he shouted, "I want to go to war. When will I ride with Father?"

"When you're older," she said.

"Father told me he'd bring me a Tatar sword." His horse danced under him. "I wish I could ride into battle now."

"Don't be so impatient." She let go of Khachigun; he sat down and stretched his arms toward his brothers. "You'll have your chance. There will always be wars, Temujin."

Khokakhchin sat with Hoelun near a cart, making rope from horsehair and wool. She had been beating wool with Hoelun for most of the morning, while Sochigil and the children looked after their sheep. Hoelun was making a shirt from a hide for Khasar. Esugei was working near them, separating the softer wool from the coarser fleece in the cart. Most of the sheep had been sheared, and they had less of the coarser wool they needed for making felt this summer than last.

The oldest men and the boys under fourteen were still in the camp; all of the others, except the few left to guard the grazing horses, had gone to fight the Tatars. By now, Khokakhchin thought, the Mongols would have met the enemy in battle. Maybe Yesugei was already celebrating a victory.

"Hoelun." Esugei was looking east; she let the wool drop from her hands and stood up slowly. "Someone's riding here." She narrowed her eyes. "It's my husband."

Khokakhchin set down her rope and looked up, shading her eyes. The tiny black form was so small against the horizon that it was a few more moments before she recognized Daritai. His mount was raising dust, pounding the dirt into clouds that hid his horse's legs. He would not have been riding like that, without a spare horse and risking death to his mount, to tell them of victory.

Hoelun got to her feet, still holding her hide. As Daritai came closer, Khokakhchin saw more riders appear behind him.

By the time Daritai was clearly visible, Hoelun had sounded the warning. The women and boys with the sheep quickly herded them back to the camp; others were saddling the horses in the pen near Yesugei's circle. Daritai's chest heaved as he galloped toward them; his face was caked with dirt and dust. His horse gleamed with sweat; specks of foam flew from the animal's mouth. Khokakhchin wondered that he had not ridden the horse to death already.

"Yesugei sent me," Daritai shouted. "Take what you can carry! Leave everything else behind! Head for the foothills and make a stand there—the enemy's after us!"

*   *   *

More of the men retreating with Daritai soon reached the camp. By the time the sun was setting, people were fleeing in carts, wagons, and on horseback toward the foothills and the wooded mountain ridge in the northwest. They took food, weapons, skins for water and jugs of kumiss, and little else. The sheep and cattle were driven off, to fend for themselves until they could be rounded up once more. Most of the yurts were left behind, along with much of the new wool, the newly dressed skins, and most of the household goods.

Khokakhchin rode in an ox-drawn cart with Belgutei, Khasar, and Khachigun sitting behind her. Hoelun and Sochigil had ridden ahead on two horses, carrying Temujin and Bekter in the saddles with them; there had not been enough horses for them all. Khokakhchin lashed at the ox, willing it to move at a quicker pace.

Night was upon them, and the Golden Stake, the star at the center of Heaven, was high in the sky when they reached the foothills. They rode on until they came to the lower slopes of the mountain ridge, then unhitched the horses and oxen. The wagons and carts would become barricades; they might have a chance against the Tatars on higher ground.

Hoelun was rallying the women, riding from one group to another on her horse. She would be telling them to be brave, to hold together, to fight with their husbands and sons. Khokakhchin sat with Sochigil and the children by their cart, listening as one of the men who had retreated with Daritai told Nekun-taisi's wife what had happened.

As Yesugei's forces had converged, the Tatars had flanked them. Near Ghunan's camp, another force, led by the Tatar chief Gogun, had struck from the south. Yesugei had not known that Gogun and Ghunan had joined forces, but the Tatar chiefs were prepared for the Mongol attack. They had begun to close around them in a pincer movement. Yesugei had ordered a retreat, telling the chiefs with him to scatter and draw off the enemy. Instead, the main force of the Tatars was pursuing Yesugei while letting the other Mongol commanders escape.

"They mean to put an end to Yesugei," Khokakhchin heard the man say. "He's the one they want. All we can do is hold out here and hope the other chiefs come to our defense."

"They won't," another man said. "They'll get ready to defend their own. Yesugei would tell them to lie low for now and fight the enemy another day. And some of them may already be blaming the Bahadur for this rout. They'll wait before they fight again."

"It's almost as if the enemy knew our plans," the first man said. "Someone might have told them. That son of Dobon's, the false shaman—maybe that's why he disappeared. He wouldn't have lasted long in battle, and Bughu wanted nothing more to do with him. What did he have to lose? Maybe he rode to the Tatars thinking he'd get a reward."

Khokakhchin did not believe it, but others would. The story would spread; people would be ready to believe that an outcast and coward who had often seemed mad was also a traitor. It was an easy way to explain defeat.

The children slept soundly, curled up under the cart, their heads on packs. Sochigil tossed restlessly at Khokakhchin's side. Khokakhchin could not sleep. The sky was growing gray in the east when Hoelun rode back to them. Munglik, Charakha's son, was with her.

"Our people are united," the Ujin said in a weary voice as she dismounted. One of her braids had come loose, trailing down from under her scarf; Hoelun fingered the thick plait absently. "Even Orbey Khatun is offering me support instead of complaints." She took a breath, then knelt by Khokakhchin. "I must ask something of you, old woman. I want you to take the children to higher ground and find a place for them to hide."

Khokakhchin nodded; she had expected such a request.

"Munglik will go with you." Hoelun motioned at the boy, who was still seated on his horse. "He'll help you look out for the boys."

"No," a child's voice said. Temujin crawled out from under the cart. "I won't go. I'll fight with you, Mother."

"You'll go with your brothers," Hoelun said.

"Why?"

"Because you and your brothers are Yesugei's sons. You're the first ones they'll kill if we're captured." Hoelun put her hands on Temujin's shoulders and drew the boy to her. "You are your father's heir, Temujin. You may have to avenge him if—"

"He'll win," Temujin said.

Hoelun turned to Khokakhchin. "Take a little food with you. If—" Hoelun fell silent, clearly not wanting to say aloud that her husband might fall in battle. "If what I most fear happens, make your way to the camp of Charakha's uncle, where the Kerulen River meets the Senggur. His Khongkhotats will give you refuge. From there, send a message to Toghril Khan, begging him to take the sons of his anda and sworn brother into his household."

"I'm honored," Khokakhchin said, "that you would trust me with your sons, Ujin."

"Go, before it's light." Hoelun crawled under the cart to wake the other children.

They went up the slope on foot. The underbrush grew thicker as they climbed, and the tangled roots of the pines that covered the ridge's southeastern face would have made passage on horseback difficult.

Hoelun had strapped Khachigun to a board and tied him to Khokakhchin's back. Barely a year old, he was the least likely of the children to survive. She would do what she could to save him, but not at the risk of losing the others. She refused to think of how slight the chances of survival were for all of them.

A creek, barely more than a trickle, ran down one patch of the slope before disappearing under rocks. Khokakhchin told Temujin and Bekter to fill the empty skins Hoelun had given to them. They had some dried meat, dried curds, and their weapons— knives, bows, and arrows. She hoped that they would not have to use them; the smaller bows of the boys would not offer much of a defense against those of men.

It was dark under the trees. They came to stonier ground where the trees grew more sparsely and Khokakhchin saw that it was growing light. She continued to climb, ignoring the weight of Khachigun on her back. A great rock blocked their path, and they were forced to go around it.

They went on until Khokakhchin looked up to see a small rocky ledge jutting out from the slope. The mountainside had grown steeper. They had to move away from the ledge, making their way slowly up the slope, then double back to reach it.

Khokakhchin untied the straps binding Khachigun to her, then sat down under the trees bordering the ledge. The children settled around her, panting for breath. From here, she could see the plain and the barricades lining the bottom of the ridge.

"Listen to me," she said to the boys. "Stay under these trees, not out on the ledge where you might be seen from below. Temujin and Bekter, you'll look out for your younger brothers. Munglik, you'll help me make a shelter. If all goes well, we'll be able to come out of hiding before too long." She wondered if the Tatars hated Yesugei enough to search the ridge for his sons.

Khokakhchin and Munglik made a makeshift shelter of branches and dead tree limbs, then sat down to rest. The younger three children were soon asleep under the shelter on a bed of pine needles. Temujin and Bekter were silent as they gazed out at the land below.

The sun was high when Khokakhchin saw three dust clouds on the horizon to the southeast. Soon she could make out the forms of the men and horses amid the dust. The army in the center was Yesugei's; his tugh was in the middle of a forest of curved lances. On either side of his force, two wings of the Tatar light cavalry were firing on his men, the archers turning in their saddles to shoot at the Mongols. Gorge rose in Khokakhchin's throat as arrows arched through the air and fell toward Yesugei's men. The Tatars were driving the Mongols toward the mountain, the two wings closing around them as if they were game.

Khokakhchin trembled with fear. Temujin said, "I see Father."

Khokakhchin narrowed her eyes and spotted the Bahadur's leather helmet with its metal ornaments and white horsetail. Yesugei's men were massed around him. The Tatar forces were allowing them a retreat, but in the distance, another dust cloud had appeared against the sky. That would be the enemy's heavy cavalry. When Yesugei's men reached the foothills and the people barricaded there, they would have to turn and fight.

"We're outnumbered," Munglik muttered.

"Father's worth ten of their men," Temujin said.

More arrows flew toward Yesugei's men. The Mongols fired back. An enemy archer rose closer to the Mongols; Dobon's curved lance swept out and un-horsed him.

"If the Bahadur can hold them off until dark," Munglik said, "he and his commanders might be able to escape. Maybe we should try to get away then. I could sneak down to steal us some horses, and—"

Temujin glared at the older boy. "Father won't leave his men, and I won't run away until I have to."

"We're staying here for now," Khokakhchin said. "The Bahadur isn't beaten yet." She tried to sound confident. "Pray for him, young ones. Perhaps the spirits will listen."

Yesugei's forces reached the foothills before dusk. Arrows flew toward the enemy from the wagons lining the ridge. The Tatar forces fell back, out of range of the people behind the barricades, but were soon massing in the distance. Khokakhchin had been watching the fighting all day. Yesugei had held off the enemy for now, but the Tatars would attack again in the morning.

Khasar crawled out from under the shelter. "I'm hungry," he said.

"Munglik will be back with food soon," Khokakhchin replied, wondering why the boy was taking so long. She had sent him to gather ripening berries from some bushes she had spied farther up the slope. The little food they had might have to last for some time.

On the plain, the Tatars were lighting their fires, getting ready for the night. She shivered, longing for a fire; the air was turning sharply colder and the wind moving the trees overhead was now blowing from the north.

She heard footsteps behind her and turned to see Munglik descending the slope. He had found enough berries to fill his fur hat. He knelt by the shelter and divided them among the boys, then gave Khokakhchin a small handful.

"You eat them," she said. "I can do without food for one night."

"Take them. I ate some off the bushes." He got up and tugged at her arm. "There's something I must tell you." He drew her aside. "By the bushes, I found broken branches and trampled underbrush and the droppings of a horse," he said softly. "I followed the trail and it led me to a small spring. A horse was there, still with its saddle and reins, drinking from the spring. It looked almost as thin as a horse in spring, as if it hadn't grazed well in some time." He lowered his voice still more. "It was Jali-gulug's horse."

Khokakhchin caught her breath. "Are you certain?"

He nodded. "It was his saddle, and I've seen him on that bay gelding of his father's many times."

"Then he must be on this mountain, too." Jali-gulug had spoken of spirits tearing at him on the night he left Yesugei's camp; perhaps they had driven him to this ridge. That he was here proved he was no traitor, that he had not gone to the Tatars with Yesugei's battle plan.

"Yesugei will kill him," Munglik said.

"The Bahadur would first have to admit that Jali-gulug's prophecy was truer than Bughu's," Khokakhchin said angrily. "You'll say nothing of this to the boys. In the morning, you will take me to where you found the horse. If Jali-gulug still lives—"

"What are you going to do?"

"Ask no more questions, Munglik. You're not to speak of this—do you understand?"

He nodded. They walked back to the shelter. Jali-gulug had asked her to lend him her power if he ever needed it. She hoped that she had not waited too long to offer it to him.

*   *   *

The plain below was as dotted with tiny fires as the night sky overhead. From the number of fires, she guessed that the Tatars outnumbered the Mongol forces four times over. Khokakhchin kept watch for a while, then woke Munglik to take his turn on guard.

She dreamed as she lay under the shelter, and fire burned in her dream. She was holding a small transparent disk, an eye of flame like the one a trader had shown her so long ago. As she lifted it to the sky, a bolt of lightning flashed toward her, passed through the disk, and struck near her. Flames leaped from the ground; she had called down the lightning, yet felt no fear.

She woke, knowing what she would have to do. Temujin stirred next to her; she gently nudged him awake. They crawled out from under the twigs and branches toward Munglik and the ledge.

The sky was gray. A strong wind was blowing across the plain from the north, making waves in the grass and whipping at the yak tails of the Tatar standards. "Munglik," Khokakhchin said, "you and I will gather more berries. Temujin, you keep watch."

Munglik went ahead of her, leading her up the slope. When they came to the berry bushes, he pointed out the flattened underbrush of the trail he had found.

"Gather some berries and go back," Khokakhchin said. "I'll follow this trail."

"By yourself? But—"

"I remind you that Jali-gulug took me with him when he hunted the ghost-tiger," she said. "I'm not afraid to meet him now."

Munglik shook back his long black hair. "He may be dead, after so many days alone."

"Then I will say a prayer for him." She made a sign. "Keep the Bahadur's children safe. Don't let them wander from the shelter. I'll return as soon as I can."

She left him and followed the trail to the clearing. Jali-gulug's horse, the same one he had been riding when she had last seen him, was drinking from the spring. The gelding's bay coat was dull and marked by scratches; it lifted its head and whinnied as she approached. She circled the clearing and soon found more underbrush with broken branches; Jali-gulug had not troubled to hide his tracks.

The trail led her higher, to another clearing. Above her, Jali-gulug sat on an outcropping, eyes closed, back against the fallen trunk of a tree. She climbed up to him, clinging to the bushes and branches as she ascended the steep hillside.

Jali-gulug's face had the tight dry skin of a corpse; the hands resting on his folded legs were claws. His shaven head was uncovered, his braids hanging over his chest. At first she was sure that he was dead, and then he opened his eyes.

"Khokakhchin."

She sat down next to him on the rocky outcropping. Over the tops of the pines below them, she saw the battlefield. The Tatars had put out their fires; the men of their heavy cavalry were mounting their horses. Near the man bearing Ghunan's tugh, the Tatar war drummer was astride his horse, his drums hanging at his mount's sides. The warriors looked so small from here, waiting for Yesugei to ride across the empty expanse to meet them. This had to be how Tengri saw men, as tiny creatures that could be swept away in an instant.

"Do you have water?" he asked.

"Yes." She slipped her waterskin from her belt and lifted it to his lips. He drank only a few drops, then feebly pushed the skin from himself.

"You found me," he said. "The spirits sent you to me."

"My mistress sent me up the mountain with her children. Your trail led me here." But he had spoken the truth. Her dream that night had sent her to his side.

"I know now why the spirits led me here," he said. "I can save our people, but I must draw on what's inside you to do it."

"What are you going to do?" she asked.

"You must help me, Khokakhchin. I need a basin, a cup, anything that can hold water."

"I didn't bring such things with me."

"Then give me your waterskin."

She handed it to him. He leaned forward; seeing how weak he was, she slipped an arm around him to support him. He poured some water into a small cavity in the rocky ground, then fumbled at his waist.

He drew out one of his pouches and opened it, his fingers fumbling at the leather ties, and shook several large round white stones as smooth as jade into his hand. Khokakhchin tensed, realizing what he intended to do.

"Your jada stones," she whispered. "You mean to call down rain."

"I mean to call down a storm."

"You mustn't," she cried, drawing away from him. "A storm might turn on us."

"Khokakhchin." His voice had changed. "You still deny me my vengeance against the Tatars. You deny rest to the ghosts of your people." Her husband was speaking through Jali-gulug once more. "You must consent to this," the young man continued in his own voice, "or I cannot call down the storm."

"Do what you must," she said, bowing her head, knowing she was now no more than an eye of fire in Jali-gulug's hand.

He put his jada stones in the small cavity of water, then poured more water over them as he chanted. She did not know the words he spoke, and wondered where he had learned the spell. Bughu might have taught him the words, or perhaps a spirit had whispered the spell to him.

The wind rose. She heard the wind shriek above them, crying out as it swept toward the plain. She felt it rise inside herself and knew that Jali-gulug was drawing on her strength. Khokakhchin screamed; the wind howled back at her, wailing through the trees.

Jali-gulug kept chanting. The wind was coming over the mountain ridge, gusting to the southeast. If the wind did not change, Yesugei's people, behind their barricades at the bottom of the ridge, would escape the brunt of the storm. The wind would not shift; she would aim it at the enemy. She screamed again, feeling her soul feed the storm.

Thunder rolled over the ridge, bringing thick clouds as black as felt. The dark clouds billowed over the sky above the plain; lightning slashed through the darkness. The Tatars milled around on the plain, their battle plan forgotten in their terror of storms and lightning. Horses reared, throwing their riders. Men threw themselves to the ground as a bolt of lightning flashed from Heaven and struck the Earth.

The trees below bowed in the wind. Khokakhchin's skin prickled; her face flamed as more lightning forked and struck the plain. Lightning severed a mass of dark clouds. A gust tore Ghunan's standard from the hand of the Tatar warrior holding it. A bolt shot down from the sky, stabbing into the midst of a knot of Tatar warriors on horseback. Some of the enemy rear forces were already in retreat, streaming east.

The rain came in sheets, hiding the battlefield from Khokakhchin. She called out to the spirits and another bolt pierced the plain. Thunder beat against her ears

with the sound of a war drum. Jali-gulug was taking
all her power. The air grew sharply colder, and soon
the rain had turned to ice.

Sleet lashed her face; ice glittered on Jali-gulug's
coat. Shielded as they were on this side of the ridge,
they could not escape the storm altogether. Khokakhchin huddled against the tree trunk and covered her
face with her arms, feeling her power ebb from her.
There was a hollowness inside her; the strength given
to her by the spirits had been spent. She would die
here, she supposed. It did not matter. Yesugei's people
would survive, and her mistress' children would be
safe. Her husband's spirit would be at peace; she
would join him at last.

The wind was dying. Khokakhchin lay still, waiting
until the spirits among the trees were speaking only in
sighs. She sat up slowly, marveling that she still lived.

Tatar bodies littered the plain. Panic had probably
killed as many of the enemy as the storm. The enemy
was retreating. Two wings of Yesugei's force were already in pursuit, fanning out as they galloped after
the Tatars. They would pick off more of the enemy,
then close around them like talons. Both the Tatars
and Yesugei's allies would tell stories of how Heaven
had come to the Bahadur's aid.

"Jali-gulug," Khokakhchin said, "you are the greatest of shamans. Even Bughu would admit that now."

He did not reply.

"He will of course claim that his prophecy of victory
turned out to be true after all."

Jali-gulug was silent. She turned to him. He lay
against the tree trunk, his legs folded, his bony hands
resting against his thighs. His lips were drawn back
from his teeth; his dark eyes stared sightlessly at
Heaven. His chest did not move, he made no sound,
and she saw that his spirit had left him.

Yesugei's people would never know of his greatness.

They would not believe an old woman who was the only witness to his power, and who had lost what power she had in aiding him. She bowed her head and let her tears fall, mourning Jali-gulug and the honor he should have been granted but would never have, then wiped her face.

Some of the Mongol men and boys were moving among the enemy dead, stripping the bodies. She reached for Jali-gulug's jada stones, put them into his pouch, then slipped the pouch under his shirt. She would make a shelter of tree limbs to house his body before she left him.

She stood up and began searching the ground near the outcropping for dead branches. Munglik would be waiting with Yesugei's children, perhaps fearing that she had been lost, and Hoelun Ujin would be worrying about her sons. She could tell Munglik truthfully that she had found Jali-gulug and that he had died on the mountainside. She would have to pay her respects to the young shaman quickly. She would pray for him later, when Yesugei and his people celebrated their victory.

PHAISTIDES
by Lois Tilton

After having received about half the volume of stories for this anthology it seemed as if many of the pieces were upbeat. This struck me as unusual because war is, after all, a very dark business—for every winner there is a loser. Where were those other stories? Then about the time the oppressive summer heat chased most everyone inside during the summer of '95, the darker stories starting arriving. This next story is full of dark matter, but it will also sweep you away with the author's skill at recreating a Greek tragedy and the wonder of that ancient time.

Lois Tilton has several novel and short story publications. She tends to write more fantasy than science fiction, and is very fond of writing dark stories, really dark ones. She uses mythology in many of her stories, with Greek and Norse myths being her favorite sources. Her novel *Darkness on the Ice* is a World War II vampire thriller.

War, man-slaying war, waged on this blood-soaked plain
Where bright-helmed Trojans fight Achaians armed in bronze—
Warriors bred for battle, Ares' favorite sons—
Where brazen sword blades clash, and the hooves of horses
Yoked to chariots churn up clouds of choking dust.
This is war, where men contend, men grown strong
To take the shield upon their arms, to hurl the spear,
Warriors formed for battle, trained in weapons-work
Since they were boys. The hands that grip the ash-wood shafts
And hilts of swords are callused; their arms are muscled hard,

Their shoulders broad beneath the weight of polished bronze.
War: domain of men. No place for women here,
For wives or white-armed daughters, robed in fine-spun wool,
Their hands too soft, their arms too weak to bear a shield,
To wield a sword. The maenads, with their bloodied hands,
Ran dressed in fawn-skins, bare of breast, not armed
In heavy bronze. What reason brings a woman, then,
Parted from her loom, from her familiar hearth,
Onto this plain of war? What urgency compels her
To contend with men, to buckle on the heavy greaves
And breastplate of a warrior, to hide her gentle face
Beneath a gleaming helmet with its fearsome crest?
What calls a woman to the battlefield of Troy?

As soon as she saw the messenger enter the room, Phaiste knew what news he had brought them, but she did her duty, rising from her loom to properly welcome a guest to her father's house, offering refreshments: wine, fresh fruit, a cushioned seat in the place of honor, fitting for a guest.

He accepted the wine, taking the level of the cup down halfway in a single deep swallow. It was obvious from the sweat-caked dust on his face that he was thirsty and weary from the long, hot road, and obvious what news must have sent him here with such urgent haste. Sharp grief speared her heart foreknowing what he would say, but she maintained the decorum proper for the mistress of the household and told him, "I've sent for my brother. He's out in the pasture with the yearling colts. While you wait for him, I can have the servants prepare a bath and a proper meal."

But the messenger put down his cup. "Lady, you are gracious, but I can't accept your hospitality without telling you first: your father, the noble Phaistos, is dead."

With the words spoken openly now, she was free to express her grief, to wail and keen for her father's

death, to tear her hair and her robe. The messenger
would respect her grief, her need to mourn. But first
she had to know the worst. "How? Tell me."

"Idomeneus killed him—the Cretan prince, Deucali-
on's son. We had all thought there would be a truce,
but suddenly both armies were at each other's throats.
It was the hand of Ares, or some other god—they
love this war too much to let men make peace.
Phaistos had dismounted his chariot to fight, and he
was reaching for his reins when the Cretan spearman
cut him down. The javelin's blade stabbed him from
behind, hit him below the shoulder, and he fell back
from his chariot, dropping the reins, coughing up his
deathblood."

She was surprised at how calmly she could reply,
how steady her voice was. But it was not so bad a
death as it might have been, at the hand of such a
prince. Yet the most important question remained
unanswered: "And his body? Are you bringing him
home to be buried?"

But now the messenger lowered his eyes to the
floor. "The Cretan's henchmen stripped his armor,
piled it into his own chariot, drove it back to the
Achaian lines as spoils of war. It was impossible to
recover the body."

Now, knowing the worst, she could let her grief
have its way, and she cried aloud, tearing her robe,
scoring her face with her nails. She let the servants
lead her away, into her own room, where she cut off
her hair in mourning and poured the ashes from the
hearth over her head. Her father was dead, but now
she would have to endure the disgrace of knowing his
body lay naked and abandoned on Troy's battlefield,
trampled by the heedless Argive warriors and their
chariots, carrion for the dogs and vultures, no better
than any nameless slave. If only someone had been
able to recover his body and bear it home! Phaistos

could have had the tomb that his honor deserved, an altar, and proper sacrifice for a captain of the Meionians.

He had been a good and dutiful man, Phaistos Boros' son. His father and his father before him had held these lands in Tarne, near Gyge Lake in the shadow of Mount Tmolos, south of Troy. They were famous charioteers and breeders of long-maned horses, Meionia's best stock. He had two young motherless children when Mesthles and Antiphos, Talaimenes' sons, summoned him to the defense of Troy, but he never hesitated, he harnessed his best team to his chariot and led his men to war to fulfill the ancient pledges of alliance made between his forebears and the line of Priam, generations past. An honorable man, an honorable death—why had the gods been so cruel as to deny him an honorable tomb?

So she wept, and only left her room to attend the funeral feast, but every mouthful of food choked her, and she couldn't even swallow the wine, pouring her portion out instead in his name. After it was done, she refused the servants when they tried to bring her food and drink. But when her brother sent word that he wanted to speak to her, she went to him at once, for she supposed he would be leaving for the war and would want her to take over the governing of the farm in addition to the household, as was her duty.

The first thing she noticed was that he was in their father's seat, where only the master of the house should sit, or the most honored guests. His hair was cut short and his garments were torn and stained with ashes for mourning, but there were no visible signs of grief or tears on his face. She took her usual low seat and waited to hear what he had to say.

He came bluntly to the point, but his words were not what she expected, what she had looked to hear from a son whose father lay unburied on the battle-

field of Troy. "It's past time that you were married,
Sister. Antiphos has three sons, and I know that either
of the two younger would be glad to have a wife with
your reputation. I know no maiden of good family
who is considered more virtuous, more skilled in all a
woman's arts."

Shocked, she said nothing as he went on, "You've
kept this house for our father long enough, and done
it well. But I mean to marry Mesthles' daughter, and
she won't want another woman in her house, ordering
the servants. And you deserve better than a life as an
aging maiden in your brother's house."

She stood to face him, then, swaying with hunger
and grief. "But what of our father? Have you forgotten he lies dead in Troy, killed by Argive hands? How
can you think of marrying with his body stripped, his
armor and his chariot in Idomeneus' tent, his corpse
left to rot on the battlefield, his soul sent down to
Haides' realm with no sacrifice laid at his bier, de-
prived of all the solemn honors owed the dead? You
are a man, our father's only son, and your duty now
is clear: Phaistos lies dead and unavenged, his slayer
lives, his place among the Meionian ranks remains un-
filled. Only his son can fill it now, only Phaistides can
take a righteous vengeance on the one who brought
him down."

But her brother was unmoved, he who called himself Phaistos' son. Bitterly, he replied, "And if I die
on that battlefield, if my corpse lies rotting there while
my killer drives off to his tent with my armor as his
spoils—who will be my avenger then? Who will cut
his hair and burn it at my tomb? I have no son. Our
father left us nine years ago when we were children,
left us to be raised by servants. He never found me a
wife, or you a husband."

She objected, "How long will you wait, then, until
you have a son to carry on your name? How long

does our father's ghost have to languish unavenged
before you go to seek out his killer on the battlefield?
Do you expect Idomeneus to wait for you that long?
Do you expect this war to last another nine years?"

Coldly, he answered her, "Idomeneus can wait until
he dies of old age, but he will never have the pleasure
of spitting Phaistides on his spear, as he did Phaistos."

"You mean to do nothing?"

"I mean to see my own son grow to manhood, if
the gods allow. I mean to see our pasture filled with
long-maned horses, as it was before they were all
driven away to war. Why must I be killed, just because
my father was? Why should I add my death to so
many others who've fallen before the walls of Troy?
When will it all end? The gods have all gone mad
over this war, spending men's lives to settle their own
quarrels. Let Menelaus and Paris meet in single combat to settle which lucky man gets to keep their prize
harlot Helen. Let other men tend to their own lands
in peace. I mean to tend to mine."

"And our father's honor? How will you sleep at
night, knowing his soul is weeping outside the gate of
Haides' mansion, refused entry as an unburied man?"

But he burst out, "I've done what I can do! You
know the sacrifices I've made for him—a fine bull, a
flawlesss ram for his funeral feast! A pair of our best
horses! I've cut off my hair and burned it in the sacri-
ficial flames. I've poured our best wine out onto the
ground in his name. I gave a bronze tripod as a prize
in the chariot race to honor him. What more could I
have done? If they'd brought his body home to me, I
swear, I would have set his pyre blazing with the fat
flayed from the beasts of sacrifice, I would have
quenched the flames in wine and laid his bones in a
painted urn, I would have given him the finest tomb
in all Meionia and wreathed it in myrtle!

"But his body is lost! The battle swept over the

place where he lay fallen, fierce Diomedes drove the
Trojan forces from the field, and it was impossible to
recover his remains. You heard the messenger yourself, you know the truth! There is nothing more I can
do—except to follow him into the darkness of Haides'
realm—and that alone I refuse."

"Are you another Achilles, then?" she demanded
with bitter scorn. "Have the gods foretold your death
if you venture onto the battlefield?"

"It takes no oracle to foresee my death if I face
Idomeneus in battle, Sister. This Cretan is a famous
warrior, one of the most deadly spearmen on the
Achaian side. All I know of war is what my trainer
taught me when I was a boy. How can I stand against
such a man with any hope? And what if some god did
take pity on me and guided my spear straight to his
heart? Then doesn't Idomeneus have a son? Wouldn't
he seek me out in vengeance for his father's death?

"I ask you again: where will it end? Will I leave my
son unborn for you to raise and seek vengeance for
my death, and his son after him? No, I'm no Achilles,
but if I had been, I tell you I would have chosen the
other path: the life that is long and dull and empty of
glory. I would have rather grown up at my father's
side than have him gone to war all the years I was
a boy."

So he spoke, and would not be persuaded otherwise.
Then Phaistos' daughter retired back into her own
room, to mourn her father's death again, and the un-
dutiful behavior of his only son. For a long time she
wept, tore what remained of her hair, and scored her
face until it bled. Finally, exhausted, she fell in a faint
to the floor.

But there the ghost of Phaistos came to her in a
dream, lamenting his fate. Her father's image was
gray, stained with his own dried blood and the dust
of the battlefield, and his hair and beard were streaked

with gray, more than she remembered. But the eidolon was insubstantial, as if it might dissipate like fog at sunrise.

"Daughter, named for me," he moaned, "why do you neglect my funeral rites? I languish in darkness here outside the gates of Haides' house in the company of the damned—parricides, oathbreakers, and exiles. Specters bar my way. I cannot pass through into the domain of the honored dead."

"Father!" she cried. "Oh, never believe that you are forgotten! Your funeral feast was rich, and all the proper sacrifices were offered in your name! See how my hair is cut, my robe is torn and stained in mourning for you! But they could not recover your body from the battlefield. The Argives overran your lines and it was lost. We couldn't bury you, but never believe that your rites were neglected! As far as it was possible, everything proper was done."

But the ghost would not be appeased. "My son and daughter feast in my name while the kites and the dogs tear at my flesh, denied the cleansing flames. My death goes unavenged. O, I am a man accursed, that I have no heirs to care for my honor!"

Then Phaiste woke to see that the gray hour before dawn had come. She went straightaway and opened up a chest of fragrant wood, bound with gleaming copper bands, in which were stored her finest robes. She took them up, wool thrice-combed to softness, whitened by the sun, woven and embroidered by her own skilled hands in colored threads: designs of cranes and waterfowl on the borders, so finely stitched they seemed to fly.

She brought them to the altar, these well-woven robes, and prayed aloud to the goddess: "O maiden huntress Artemis, accept my gift, these robes I wove with my hands, and hear my prayer. My father lies unburied on the plain of Troy, his death is unavenged, his ghost reproaches me in dreams. His only son refuses to take up arms to seek his slayer out among the Argive host and face him on the field of war. And what the son will not, the daughter must, who bears his name.

"So, goddess, I pray you, accept my vow that I will never marry or lie with any man. As a maiden I will take up the cause of avenging Phaistos' death, even if I die in the attempt. Grant me then strength to wear the armor of a man, to bend a bow, an archer's skill to send my arrows straight and true to strike the Cretan's heart. And grant me also the strength to look on War, to stand there on the plain of Troy face-to-face with death in Argive guise and not give shameful way to fear. Let me not disgrace my father's noble name in bearing it upon the bloody field of war."

So she prayed, and Artemis the goddess heard her prayer, Artemis the huntress with her deadly bow, who loved the Trojan cause, doomed as it might be by Hera's spite. The goddess gave her arms, a gleaming panoply of bronze: high-crested helmet, polished breastplate, forged to fit a woman's shape, greaves of tin, and best of all a shield which bore the image of a stag, in leaping flight from a maiden huntress with her curved bow bent, her arrow nocked to fly straight to its noble heart.

"Wear this armor in my name, maiden warrior, and I will grant you the strength to bear it well. Even more, I will cast a semblance over you so that all men will see Phaistos' son and not his daughter when you drive onto the battlefield."

So Phaiste yoked her favorite pair of horses to the chariot, long-maned bays with flashing eyes, and drove them to the field of war, into the camp where the Meionian forces mustered—men she had known as a child, and their sons, who had followed them to war. There was Antiphos, the Meionian captain, and his sons, these young men she might have married if she hadn't made her vow to the maiden goddess Artemis.

But they greeted her in her brother's name and welcomed her to the war, offering condolences on her father's death. Many other men had died since that day, princes of Troy, Priam's sons, and noble captains of the allied lands, but the camp was all heady with the scent of victory, for the gods had finally favored the Trojan cause. Their forces, led by the incomparable hero Hector, first among Priam's sons, had routed the Achaians, sent them fleeing in terror back to the shelter of their black-hulled ships.

As Antiphos related, "Even when Patroclos came out to rally their warriors, wearing the armor of Achilles, the Achaians could not prevail. Hector met him in the middle of the battlefield, directly beneath the walls of Troy. They both dismounted from their chariots and fought each other, spear to spear, but it was Patroclos who fell with Hector's shaft through his belly. Never have I seen such fierce fighting as was waged over his body then!"

But this tale of heroism only reminded Phaiste of the way her father's remains had been lost. "What of Idomeneus," she asked. "What of the man whose spear took Phaistos' life? Is he still living? Can I hope to meet him on the battlefield?"

"He lives," Antiphos told her. "He was one of those who fought over Patroclos' body, in the center of it all. And you were almost robbed of your revenge, Phaistides, for Hector was inspired in battle like a god, and when Idomeneus cast his spear at him, it broke and left the Cretan weaponless, on foot among his enemies, and he barely escaped with his life. Some god must have been saving him for you, for when Coiranos had taken him up in his chariot, Hector cast his own spear at him, but he missed and killed Coiranos instead—I saw it—his blade went under his ear, out through the other jaw—broken teeth everywhere! Then Idomeneus fled the field, the Argives all fled, like a flock of jackdaws when the falcon stoops on them. You should have seen them, throwing away their shields and weapons as they ran!''

So the veteran warrior laughed, exulting in victory, but Phaiste's heart quailed to hear him describe the carnage of the battle, the many deaths, the terrible wounds. Nothing in her life had prepared her for this. How could she venture out onto such a battlefield, with its blood-soaked earth and the stench of unburied corpses that filled her gorge?

But the goddess Artemis had not deserted her, and strengthened her resolve. "Remember that your brother knew nothing of war, but it was still his duty to take his place among the Meionians. Each man here once had to endure his own first day of battle, his first companion killed, his first enemy slain. Remember that death waits in the end for every woman as well as every man, but this is the important thing: to face it with courage and honor, and not disgrace your name."

So Phaiste took heart, and in the morning she girded herself in the armor that was the goddess' gift. Beneath the gleaming helmet her face had the seeming of a man's, and the thick oxhide shield was light upon her arm. She took up the reins of her team, from Meionia's best stock, and drove into battle, determined to prove herself worthy of the goddess' gifts.

But only defeat and grief were to meet the Trojan forces on the field that day, for Achilles had rejoined the war at last, spurred by the lust to take vengeance for Patroclos' death. Then Zeus, the ruler of men and gods, lifted his hand from his scales and no longer was victory withheld from the Achaians by his will, no longer were the bitter enmity of Hera and Athene restrained, nor the wrath of Poseidon. Hephaistos

himself had forged Achilles a new panoply to replace
the armor Hector had stripped from Patroclos' dead
flesh, and Athene had wrapped him in a cloak of
victory.

Achilles charged the Trojan lines like the incarna-
tion of wrath, and the first man he killed was of Meionian blood: Iphition, son of Otrynteus who lived in
the shadow of Mount Tmolos. Achilles split his skull,
spilling his brains, and crushed his body beneath the
wheels of his chariot, leaving him for the dogs. Others
followed him into death at the avenger's hands—De-
moleon, Hippodamus, and Priam's favorite child,
young Polydoros. His sword blade and spear were red
and dripping with their blood, his chariot wheels were
splashed with it. There was no mercy in him, no appeal could move him to pity. No man could stand
against him and live.

Panic and Rout were among the Trojans now, lashing them with fear, and they fled Achilles as men run
to escape a wildfire driven by high winds. Phaiste was
among them, unable to stand and face the sight of
him bearing down on the Trojan lines, terrible in his
killing rage, slaughtering one man after another. Even
the courage of Artemis was not enough to stay her
flight, for the gods were in this battle, and vengeful
Athene was at Achilles' side, until Ares himself fell
before her wrath. So Phaiste fled, and Achilles drove
the Trojans ahead of his chariot, slaying as he went,
until he had them pinned against the steep banks of
the river Scamandros, whom the gods called Xanthos.

There, seeing that there was no way to escape, one
or two of the Trojans took courage again and turned
to face the dreadful son of Peleus, and Asteropaios
wounded him before he was himself killed. But a moment later Phaiste found herself suddenly thrown from
her chariot over the front rail, for a cast from Achilles'
javelin had passed through the spokes and jammed

them. Instantly the terrible slayer was looming over
her, sword in his hand, and the lifeblood of men had
poured down the blade onto his arm, staining it red.

Artemis! she cried, *Goddess, help me!*

The Huntress appeared in a fog which wrapped
them both, as if they were no longer on the bloody
riverbanks, surrounded by the clash of weapons and
the screams of dying men. "Maiden warrior, I can help
you," the goddess answered, "but you must choose. I
can take you from this battlefield, wrapped in fog, and
carry you back to Meionia, to your loom. But you will
never return here to the war, and the armor I gave
you will be gone. Antiphos and his sons will not remember you, and to all the Meionians, to all the warriors in the Trojan ranks, it will be as if no son of
Phaistos had ever come to avenge his father's death.

"Or I can grant you the courage you prayed from
me: to face death in the form of Achilles and not to
disgrace your father's name, even if you die. For I will
tell you this: it was fated if Phaistides came to Troy
to avenge his father's death, that he would die, here
on this river's banks. Now you stand here in his place.
So choose, child of Phaistos."

At that very moment the fog surrounding them disappeared, and Phaiste found herself facing Achilles in
all his wrath, but at the same time she was standing
before the altar in her brother's house, making her
vow to the goddess that she would avenge her father's
death or die in the attempt. And next to her on the
ground was the shaft of her spear, but on the altar
was the shuttle from her loom.

Choose, came the echo of the goddess' voice, and
Phaiste reached for the spear. Then suddenly she was
on her feet, her spear poised to fight, facing the
bloody-handed son of Peleus, whose fierce expression
suddenly changed to startlement. "Who are you who

leaps so quickly to your feet to meet my sword? Whose son is so eager to die?"

"My father was Phaistos," she declared proudly, "Boros' son, from Tarne in Meionia. Idomeneus killed him, but if I am denied the Cretan's death in payment, yours will do as well, Peleides."

Achilles laughed, a grimly fearsome sound. "The blood you see on my hands came from other men, Phaistides, but my sword will be glad to shed yours as well. For I have a thirst for Trojan blood that is not so easily quenched." As he spoke, his bronze blade flashed out to sever her head, but instead it struck off her helmet with a glancing blow. That gleaming bronze helmet, the gift of Artemis, deflected the sword, and she fell to her knees, head ringing from the force of it.

And Achilles, poised to strike again, suddenly held his blow, for without the helmet Phaiste no longer had the seeming of a man. "What is this?" he demanded. "A woman? A girl—here on the battlefield, in armor like a man?"

"I am who I said I was," she replied. "Phaistos was my father, and I came to this war to take vengeance for his death."

But Achilles shook his head, making the high crest of his helmet wave fiercely. "Phaistos had no sons? No one else to care for his honor?"

"My brother refused to go to the war. He claimed he preferred long life with no glory to an honorable death. And my father's ghost came to me in dreams, crying out that his heirs refused to honor him. What else could I do?"

Peleus' son said bitterly, "Do not curse your brother. There are many times when I wish I was still on Scyros, before the crafty Odysseus found me there and brought me to this man-slaying war where I know I'm doomed to die. Many times I wish I had chosen that long life, with my loyal Patroclos alive at my side. And I tell you this: even a slave has more joy in his miserable life than the most noble prince when he is sent down to Haides' realm.

"I had no mercy on the Trojan boys who begged me for their lives, but I can spare a woman this one time, even on the battlefield. Come, my men will take you back to my tent and you will join the other captive Trojan girls in slavery—a bitter fate, I know, but not so bleak as death."

"I beg no mercy," she answered him, still on her knees. "I do not ask you for my life. I swore a solemn vow, Peleides, a vow to Maiden Artemis, that I would not marry or lie with any man if she would give me strength to bear weapons in this war and seek repayment for my father's death. I know the fate of captives in wartime, I know the lusts of men. I would never remain a maiden in the tents of your Myrmidons.

"But if you are inclined to be merciful, then I would ask this much: when you kill me, do not strip the armor from my body. Replace my helmet on my head, for it was the gift of Artemis. Then men will all say that it was Phaistides who died here, as he was fated, attempting to avenge his father and restore the honor to his name. That is all I ask."

"Take it, then," he said, letting her pick up the helmet from the ground. "Take it and die, if that is what you will."

Her life flowed out like blood, then hateful darkness took her,
Darkness dragged her shade far down to Haides' realm,
That joyless place, where neither light nor life can thrive.
Now she felt the pain of all she left behind:
Youth and love and hope—of husband, daughters, sons—
Exchanged for death. For fleeting glory, fading there
To pale gray dust. For honor, for an honored name
As long as men remember it on earth—so short

A time they live, compared to an eternity in death.
But on the battlefield of Troy they found her corpse,
They knew it by its arms and by the famous shield
Of Huntress Artemis, still lying at her side.
Her gleaming armor was not stripped from her dead flesh,
Untouched, which still retained the semblance of a man.
They gave her honor, gave her body to the flames
And all the sacred rites and duties owed the dead,
To Phaistides, who died in vain, but, dying, paid
Full honor to her father and her father's name.

A WOLF UPON THE WIND
by Jennifer Roberson

A warrior's honor! In so many tales this is held before us as a shining banner to be respected by all; almost as if it is a holy object. But fighting and death are seldom confined to the plains of battle and the warriors. This next story is very short, and very dark, but within these few lines the author manages to capture so much of war's aftermath, especially that of Norse warfare.

Jennifer Roberson is an accomplished storyteller with numerous published short stories and novels, including her fantasy series, *The Chronicles of the Cheysuli* and the *Sword-Dancer* novels, and the historicals *Lady of the Forest* and *Lady of the Glen*. She also has a fantasy collaboration with Melanie Rawn and Kate Elliott, *The Golden Key*. She edited *Return to Avalon*, a tribute anthology celebrating Marion Zimmer Bradley. I think you'll find that few writers can tell a short-short story with as much punch as Jennifer manages to include in her writings.

"*—bitch-begotten whore—*"

She had bitten him, bitten him hard, catching his bottom lip within her teeth; and now blood painted his chin, was channeled by saffron-hued beard into crimson ribbons that streamed against soiled tunic. He spat more ribbons, more blood aside, then smiled grimly and spat it also into her face.

She did not know why a man was honored for defending his life, while she was called names as she defended hers. Or why a man was granted a clean death, a warrior's death, taken up to Odin's Valhalla, while a woman, equally victim, was degraded. Abused. And killed without honor; or died of *dis*honor, because the body gave up hope.

She would not, and did not—and so he was forced to take it from her: her body, and thus her life.

Bitch-begotten whore, he said—because she was *not* a whore, and therefore fought to preserve that which another honored: virginity, modesty, a quiet demeanor. But he took all from her, this man, this warrior; raped her soul as well as her body, and the demeanor others honored was now vilified because she sought to change it, to preserve what had been hers, was *meant* to be hers, until she chose otherwise.

First with himself. Then with his ax-hilt.

"Bitch-begotten whore."

What did he think she should do? Let him do as he would without protest?

Permit him to do such as *this?*

He bore wounds of her now, though she doubted any would scar. Bitten lip, clawed face, before the nails broke, before her fingers were crushed. Before teeth and jaw were shattered with a single great blow of his hand.

So much broken, now. Inside and out.

He used her again, slick now with her blood as much as spilled seed. And complained of her, that she no longer fit. But that was his fault, too; the ax-handle had torn her.

Little time left. No glory, she thought; no battlefield song of a warrior's honorable death. Just—*death.* Without glory, honor, song. A woman, apparently, merited none.

No Valhalla for *her.* No Valkyrie come down from the heavens to carry her from the field. There was no provision for slain women in the honor of Odin's hall.

No hope either, now, for reparation. Revenge.

She gave nothing. He took it. Took it all, including her life.

"Bitch-begotten whore."

The last words she heard.

Vision was a red haze of sunset, of blood. He squinted, blinked, twitched his head in a tiny, wayward motion meant to rid his eyes of the veil so he might see again. There was much to see, he knew: the battle was ended. There was a victor, and also a vanquished.

He was uncertain which he was.

By the hand of Tyr, god of war, had he lost? Had he won? *Was* he lost?

To either side, he might be lost. Might be dead. How they counted him, lost or won, was wholly dependent on which side was victor. He did not know himself.

Wind howled down the field, whipping a frenzy among the dead, for what rode upon the wind was a vanguard of beasts and steeds come down to collect the souls. The living saw nothing save the remains of the battle, the aftermath of war.

He felt it then, felt the wind, heard its song, saw the vanguard stoop out of the darkening sky, riding friezes of lowering clouds. A Brisingamen of beasts strung like monstrous ornaments torn from Freya's throat, adornment for the dead.

Ah. He *was* dead, then. Or dying.

His old name was as dead. He bore a new one, now: *einheriar*. A warrior dead in battle, bound for Valhalla.

He felt no pain, neither of body nor soul. There was glory in life, glory in battle, glory in death. He would go to Valhalla, bow to Odin, eat of the great boar, Saehrimnir, roasted by Andhrimnir, Odin's own cook; and drink of the mead from out of Heidrun's teats, Odin's sacred goat—and he would never be alone, never lack a woman. Never truly be dead within the hall of Odin.

A red haze, a smear against his eyes, bloodying the world. It obscured his vision of those who came to claim him, to gather up fallen heroes. He heard them still, fleet steeds and panting beasts; felt it still, wild wind wailing down the field. And welcomed them all, for he knew what rode them.

Valhalla, and Valkyrie.

She came down then, upon a storm-gray wolf. Was it Freki? Geri? Was it one of Odin's pets come to honor him? He saw its amber eyes, slitted as if it laughed; saw its perfect teeth in a snarl that was also leer. And the woman upon it.

Flags of wheat-gold hair whipped back in the haste of her journey. She was made of the songs they sang over mead, the glories told of *Valkyrien* over roasted boar. A woman for each of them, claimed the warriors; as many as could be had by an inexhaustible man, for what was Valhalla but perfection in a male, and reward for an *einheriar*'s valor? Warm hall, fresh mead, well-tended boar, and women for every warrior.

Oh, by one-eyed Odin, death was no distress. Not when it promised *this*.

He would have stood for her, but the ax-blow had shattered a leg. Would have sat for her, save ribs were splintered to fragments. Would have bowed his head to her, but for the hole where his throat had been.

None of it mattered, now. She was as he had been promised, as they each of them had been promised, and his foretold future was infinitely preferable to his painful present.

Fierce maiden, fierce smile, baring perfect teeth in a leer that matched the wolf's. Hair settled now from her ride, whipped no more by the wild wind. She wore a cloak of it; as she bent to him it spilled down over shoulders to drift across his face, to mingle with his beard. He feared his blood would sully it.

She saw it in his eyes: distress that he would soil her. And laughed. Nothing of him could soil her, nothing of blood, of viscera, of the produce of battle. She was one of Tyr's blessed maidens, and thus inviolable.

"Einheriar," she said, "will you come with me?"

At her voice, the wind rose. The wolf—Freki? Geri?—shook storm-hued pelt, and panted.

When he spoke, no voice issued; he had nothing left of his throat save a sliver of bloodied bone. But she heard him. Knew the words: *indeed, come,* and *gladly.*

"Then come," she said, and put out her slim, strong hand.

His body trembled. Fingertips barely touched. Behind her, the wolf growled.

"Come," she said, impatient. "Are you not worthy of Valhalla?"

How *dared* she question it?

Fingertips touched. Clawed. With effort, he gripped her hand. With no effort, she gripped his.

"What are you?" she asked. "Hero?"

Einheriar! Had he not died in Tyr's name? How could he be other?

His turn for impatience. Still the wolf growled.

"More," she said. "Oh, indeed, more than hero— or less. I think you are not worthy to be hosted in Odin's hall."

Fury kindled. —*bitch-begotten whore*—

The Valkyrie bared perfect teeth. Lightnings were in her eyes, and thunder in her laughter. "This is what I am. Now see what I *was,* when you were done with me."

And there was nothing of beauty in her, nothing at all save the truth he had made himself in the woman he had killed: flattened nose, shattered teeth, broken jaw unhinged. And ax-born blood flowing down her thighs to mingle with his own.

He knew her then, *knew* her, and wept with fear.

She bent to his torn ear. "You gave me to Tyr," she said. "Now I send you to Hel."

THE LADY OF THE MERCIANS
by Mary Frances Zambreno

This next story is set in England at a time when Europe seemed forever immersed in war and is about a truly great woman, Aethelflaed of Mercia. When Aethelflaed's husband, Aethelred, was incapacitated by illness in 903 A.D., she took over effective rule of Mercia in his name. From the time of his death in 911 until her own death in 918 she ruled Mercia in her own right. This brave woman was no stranger to war and its bloody effects and earned the right to rule her land and helped unify Christian England.

Mary Frances Zambreno has a background in medieval history, with several young adult fantasy novels published and one young adult science fiction novel (under the name Robyn Tallis). Her short stories have appeared in such places as *Marion Zimmer Bradley's Fantasy Magazine* and several anthologies, including *Ancient Enchantresses* and *Temporary Walls*.

Aethelflaed, Lady of the Mercians, clenched her frozen hands tightly in her pony's mane and wished for a heavier cloak. Beneath her, the beast shifted unhappily; late autumn was no time of year to be wandering, he seemed to feel. On the whole, she thought she agreed with him. It looked like another night sleeping on the ground, with cold food and no fire for fear of attracting the enemy.

They were on their way from Tamworth to Eddisbury, to reinforce the garrison there. A few paces ahead, Earl Eadric, her war leader, conferred with Rhodri the Welshman, chief of scouts. Her nephew Aelstan hovered anxiously at the fringes of the group. Aethelflaed smiled fondly at her brother Edward's eldest son: not quite fifteen and riding with his first war band, Aelstan was as eager for glory as a boy his age could be. *Please, Sweet Jesus, let his first battle not happen soon,* she thought, tucking a few gold strands of hair escaped from her braid back under her hood. *Not on this journey, at least. Time enough next spring . . . what* are *those men talking about? Ah, they've finished.*

Eadric reined his horse around impatiently to where she waited; his face was dark.

"What's wrong?" she asked, before he had a chance to speak.

"There's an army between us and Eddisbury, Lady," the earl said, not looking at her. "A full war band, the scouts say. Of all the luck—if we'd gone by Lichfield, this wouldn't have happened."

"No help for it now." Aethelflaed suppressed a prickle of annoyance; it had been his idea to take the northern route, not hers. She would have preferred the longer, safer way, but he had insisted that they had no time. "Will we have to fight?"

"I hope not," Eadric said, scowling. "There's a man—an Alban named Oittir—who says he can guide us around."

Aethelflaed frowned. "An Alban—you mean a Pict. Can we trust him?"

"Perhaps." He shrugged his broad shoulders. "The Picts have as much to fear from these Irish Norse as we do—time will show. I've told Rhodri to ride at his back, with a spear ready."

"A good thought," Aethelflaed said, ignoring his assumption that she would agree. She did, after all. This time. "And tell Rhodri to keep his scouts riding, but not so far out that we lose touch. I will *not* be delayed.''

During her husband's long illness, she wouldn't have needed to be so emphatic; his death had changed things. Aethelred had been the loyal supporter of Alfred of Wessex, ealdorman rather than king, but he had been Lord of the Mercians for all that, and Aethelflaed their acknowledged lady. Now that she was no longer relaying her husband's commands ... well. *They don't trust my judgment,* she reflected, thinking back to the day before they'd started this perilous journey. *Don't trust me, for all that my father was that same king of Wessex whom Aethelred served. If only I were more certain that they should. ...*

On the day news of Corbridge arrived, she had been in the hall at Tamworth, conferring with Eadric over accounts. The autumn had been chill but clear; the harvest as rich as any the Mercian fields had yielded in years. It would be a good winter, providing the Danes stayed home. Of course, if the Danes ever stayed home, they would not be Danes.

Eadric had seen no reason to be optimistic.

"And word from the north is disheartening," he said gloomily, when she'd finally laid aside the last household roll. "The Norse in Ireland will be giving us trouble yet."

"Norse or Dane, we have to face it," Aethelflaed said, sighing. "Please God, we'll be ready for them when they come. Have the emissaries from my brother of Wessex left yet?"

"This morning." A note of disapproval entered Eadric's voice. He did not trust Edward of Wessex, whom he believed to have ambitions toward the vacant throne of Mercia.

Well, and so Edward does, after a fashion, Aethelflaed told herself with a slightly bitter humor. *That is*

*why Aelstan is being fostered in Mercia, after all, so
that he will be acceptable to the fyrd one day. It's working, too—even Eadric sees Aelstan as a promising lad.*
Not that her brother truly wanted another throne, for
himself or for his son; Wessex was enough for him, as
it had been for their father. But if the Great Alfred
could not hold Wessex without a friendly and coopera-
tive Mercia, then no one could, and Edward meant to
be sure that Mercia stayed friendly. *As well he does.
Mercia without allies would last no longer than in Ceol-
wulf's time, when we had Danish rule as far south as
London.*

The struggle against the invaders had been going on
since her father was a boy. Now both husband and
father were gone, and enemies still came with every
tide. Aethelred's death was her chance to escape, she
knew that. She could retire to a convent, if she wished,
leaving the rest of this long war to men like Eadric.
But should she? If she and Aethelred had had a son
of their own, or if her daughter Elfwynn were of a
mind to marry ... but there, Elfwynn was a scholar
and destined for the church, and might-have-beens
were not answers.

There was a noise at the door. Pushing her useless
thoughts aside, she looked up to see Aelstan dashing
into the room, his fair face flushed becomingly with
haste.

"Lady!" he blurted, and gasped for air. Her nephew
and heir of Wessex he might be, but Aelstan knew
the manners that were due the Lady of the Mercians.
"Lady Aethelflaed, the Norsemen—"

"Norsemen?" Eadric asked sharply. "Not Danes?
Surely—calm yourself, boy, you can't speak if you're
fighting for breath."

"Norse out of Ireland," Aelstan managed, almost
choking in his rush to speak. "It's said—there's been

a battle at Corbridge, on the Tyne. Ragnald, Ivar's grandson, has won a great victory."

"Ragnald of Dumlane." Aethelflaed stood up, her heart suddenly cold. "How many men? Has Rhodri been told?"

Eadric was no less anxious; Corbridge was entirely too close for comfort. "Who fought? What were the names there? Did Ragnald come by ship or on foot?"

"Both ship and foot," Aelstan said. "One of Rhodri's scouts brought the news, I just chanced to be at the gate—I don't know the names of those who fought."

"He fought Britons, mostly," Rhodri said from the door. There were those who called Aethelflaed a fool for keeping a Welshman in her service, but she and Aethelred had always taken good men wherever they could find them, and Rhodri was the best chief of scouts she'd ever had. "A mixed band. My man didn't linger for specifics, but he says that the Norsemen hold the field as far west as Thelwall and nearly as far east as Lastingham."

Eadric almost snarled. "Where was the war band? Was there no one guarding the river?"

"It seems not," Rhodri told him somberly. "Or not well enough. They say Ragnald has magicians in his pay . . . Lady, I brought the map."

"Good." Trying not to think of pagan Norse magic, Aethelflaed moved to the table. With one heave, she pushed the household rolls off of it and onto the floor. "Spread it out here."

Quickly, Rhodri did as she ordered. For a long moment, no one spoke.

"Eddisbury," Aethelflaed said then, tracing the probable line of invasion with one finger. "They must be after the fortress at Eddisbury—here. If they can take that, they can hold the way south open all winter, call up more men and invade in the spring."

"You're right," Eadric said, studying the map in his turn. *Does he have to sound so surprised about it?* She would have been annoyed, if the situation weren't so serious. "How goes the fortress at Eddisbury?"

"It's only half-finished," she said, answering for herself though she knew he'd been speaking to Rhodri. "There are men there, but I meant to garrison it fully over the winter. Now we dare not wait. We ride tomorrow. I'll take—Gerda, I think. No other women. Eadric, gather the fyrd."

"It's almost winter," he protested, startled. "Only a madman goes to war in winter."

Or a woman, his tone implied. "If we're quick, it won't come to that," she said crisply. "But I won't let my enemies sit snug in my own fortress until the weather turns warm again. You heard me, Eadric. Give the order."

Her voice was hard, allowing no disagreement short of open rebellion. "As you will, Lady," he said, though he still sounded doubtful. "Young Aelstan, with me. Rhodri, see to your scouts. We'll want intelligence as we ride."

The three left, leaving Aethelflaed alone with the map. She sat down on the stool, trying not to tremble. Norsemen, at Corbridge. If Ragnald came in force, they would be badly outnumbered, and it would be a long, hard winter for Mercia. Should she send to Edward? No, he would be busy in the south, too far away to do her any good. And Eadric wouldn't like it.

Ah, God, I am sick unto death of this war. I faced it, ruling in Aethelred's name, but I did not know that I would be so alone without him. I'm neither crowned queen nor king's wife, and there is no one of mine to rule after me in Mercia—why can't I lay this burden down? No one would blame me . . . many would honor me for it.

Eadric would certainly honor me for it.
Eddisbury. Eddisbury was the key.

And now, two days later, it all depended on a strange Pict finding his way around an army. Eyes narrowed, Aethelflaed watched him as they went. A sallow, shifty little man, this Oittir, with a pointed nose looming over a scraggly mustache. As he trotted on foot next to Eadric's horse, he kept nodding his head ingratiatingly. She liked neither his looks nor his demeanor, she decided, but it mattered little so long as he knew he was dead if he didn't keep faith.

The horses stopped, so suddenly that her pony jostled Eadric's mount.

"What is it?" she asked. "Why have we stopped?"

He craned his neck upward. "We should be at that ford the Alban promised. Yes, I can see the river."

Rhodri rode back to them, from the vanguard. "The water is higher than it should be, Lady," he reported.

"At this time of year?" Aethelflaed glanced down at the Pict sharply. "If you've led us into a trap—"

"Oh, no great one," the man said, bowing over clasped hands. "Oittir is honest. Oittir would not deceive so great a lady. The river is always a little high, but there is a shallow place in the middle. If you cross all at once, so that each may help the other through the deep, all will be well."

"All at once." She exchanged a long look with Eadric, who shrugged.

"If we stay here, we're as likely to be pinned against the river as swept into it," he pointed out. "The other shore isn't far."

"Very well, then, we cross," she said. "But not all at once. You, Oittir, will cross first. Rhodri, your horse is strong enough to carry two. Take the Pict up before you, and ride with your knife out. Just in case."

"Yes, Lady," the Welshman said, grinning. "I'll be ready."

The Pict's face was sour, as if he wanted to protest but didn't dare. He took the hand which Rhodri offered him and unenthusiastically pulled himself over the saddlebow to perch on the horse's withers. The double-laden beast snorted at the riverbank, but waded in obediently. As they entered the water, the Pict leaned forward toward dark waves, but Rhodri kept a firm arm around his waist with the hand that held the knife.

Eadric scanned the opposite shore. "I dislike this, Lady," he said. "I know this river. Water so high at this season is unnatural."

"Perhaps." Aethelflaed had her eyes fixed on the swimming horse. "Do you know this ford?"

"No, but—"

Rhodri needed both hands on the reins now. Water lapped his thighs, and he had the knife turned so that the hilt pointed toward him and gave him more freedom; she could see the blade gleam when the sunlight touched it.

"Easy, easy," Eadric muttered, as though the scout-chieftain could hear him. "You've a good horse under you ... mind the Pict! Rhodri!"

Oittir laughed, a high, squealing sound that made Aethelflaed's hair stand on end. Suddenly, there was no man in front of Rhodri but an otter, its furry brown form twisting like a mad thing. It bit Rhodri in his knife hand, and he cried out.

"Magic!" Eadric gasped, his face gone ashen. "A shape-changer!"

"Ambush!" Aethelflaed cried, her voice soaring effortlessly over the shouts of the men. "Into the river, all of you! We've got to get across!"

Urging her pony toward the water, she cursed herself for her inattention. *Where were your wits, girl?*

*"Oittir" the man said his name was—that's close
enough to the English "otter" for you to guess he was
no Pict! And for a shape-changer to give a name so
close to his other form—oh, he must be laughing at us
all! You with your scholar's training that your father
was so proud of—how could you miss such a clue?*

Rhodri's scouts had ridden in close; their battle
called mixed with the shouts of the fyrd. Horses milled
and whickered in the mud, as their riders toppled,
spear shot. But the pikemen were not taken by surprise, she saw with fierce pleasure; they had formed
the shieldwall, and they were giving as good as they
got. The water was crowded with horses and men,
bumping into each other. Aethelflaed's skirts were
quickly sodden, threatening to pull her down into the
flood; beside her, a man surfaced, face white over a
red tunic—no. That was blood and torn flesh. She
retched, wildly kicking out at the body with her foot,
and hung on grimly.

*Blood and death. I didn't want it to come to this,
not yet, not ever, we weren't ready. . . .*

Her pony's hooves found firm footing. There was
dry ground in front of her; she rode for it. The little
beast scrambled up on the bank, making much of an
incline that the larger horses had no trouble with, and
a hand appeared out of nowhere to seize his bridle
and pull him forward.

A bleeding hand, with a ragged bite-wound on it.
"Rhodri," she gasped. "You're alive, then. Good
man."

"Yes, Lady," he said, but his face was grim. "And
sorry that I didn't gut the little bastard, but he was
too fast for me."

"Not your fault," she told him, meaning it. *The fault
is mine, if anyone's. I sent him out there.* "Just praise
God you made it through. What now?"

"Ride for high ground, under the trees. We'll be sheltered there."

Willingly, she followed him. When they reached high ground, Eadric was waiting. An excited Aelstan was with him, Aethelflaed saw with relief. *Not dead in this skirmish, at least. Thank you, Lord.*

"Magic." The earl's voice was disgusted. "Filthy, heathen magic."

"No time for that now," Aethelflaed interrupted crisply. "We've work to do. Rhodri, your men?"

"Battered, but whole, Lady," the Welshman said. "And wondering. Do we fight or run?"

"That depends on what your scouts find," she said. "Run, if we can. Fight, if they are between us and Eddisbury."

He nodded his understanding. "I go to bring you news, then. Young Aelstan, I could use your keen eyes."

Alone with Eadric under the trees, Aethelflaed dismounted from her pony. She looked up at her war leader, who was scanning the horizon intently.

"Lady, they are on this side of the river, too," he said.

"You can't possibly see so far," she began sharply, then paused. Eadric was a seasoned soldier; he wouldn't say such a thing for no reason. With an effort, she softened her tone. "How do you know?"

He shrugged. "Logic. The plan would have been for that Oittir to get us into the river before we were attacked. It would make sense for them to hit us on both sides, as soon as he signaled. He must have had to signal the attack too soon, the way it happened, before those ahead of us were in position. But they'll be there, when Rhodri's scouts look for them."

She sighed, leaning wearily in her pony's flank. "Then they'll be between us and Eddisbury, and we'll have to fight."

"Even against sorcery?" he asked, his words dubious.

She had been trying to avoid that, but there was only one answer to the question. "Against all the powers of darkness, if need be."

Eadric did not look satisfied. *Did I expect him to be?* she thought, but her usual irritation was muted. No sane man or woman relished the thought of magic.

It was almost sunset by the time the scouts came back, and Aethelflaed sat by her tent, warming herself in front of a fire—no need to hide from the enemy now—while Gerda clucked over her damp, muddied skirts in the background.

"Good news, Lady!" Rhodri hailed her from the edge of the clearing. "It isn't Ragnald's main force we're facing."

"That may be good news," Aethelflaed said mildly. "Or it may not be. Eadric?"

"According to Rhodri, here, the banners are of one Sihtric, Colm's son," the earl said, avoiding the issue. "They're camped ahead of us, in a copse on a small hill. We're outnumbered, but not badly."

"Some good news, then," she said. "But since they're ahead of us, they're between us and Eddisbury, and we will have to fight." *And so young Aelstan will have his first taste of real battle,* she thought unhappily. *Sweet Jesus, defend him.* "Rhodri, do you know this Sihtric?"

"I've heard of him," the Welshman said. "He's an ally of Ragnald's, with a none-too-savory reputation."

Aethelflaed grimaced. "A well-earned reputation, I'd say. Still, if Sihtric is Ragnald's ally, he might be expecting reinforcements. We'll have to win this one quickly, then. Prepare for a dawn attack."

For once, Eadric did not argue with her at all. Perhaps he simply agreed that they had no choice. When he had left, Rhodri lingered briefly.

"Lady, I have been thinking," he began hesitantly. "You are ruler of this land in your husband's right, but you are also of the royal blood of Merçia. Through your mother, who was Eadburh's daughter."

"True," she said, frowning impatiently. "What of it?" It was fact, but not particularly important; she was no more than one-quarter Mercian.

He traced one toe through the dirt, as if writing in it.

"I am no sorcerer," he said at last. "But among my people are those who know things. Shape-shifting such as Oittir did today is earth-magic, Lady—and Oittir is a foreigner. In dire need, the land will choose to protect its own."

"I see. . . ." She thought she did. It was not unlike what she knew of magic from her own studies. "Would Oittir know this?"

"He should, if he has any skill at all."

She considered the matter, wondering what—if anything—could be made of it. *If Oittir knows, then he might be prepared for me to do something. That's no help. Still, Oittir cannot know everything.*

"Thank you, Rhodri."

Nodding slightly, he left her alone to her fire and her thoughts.

The morning dawned clear and bitterly chill; dry leaves rustled underfoot, and Aethelflaed sent Gerda—and her tent—to the relative safety of the baggage cart as soon as the sun was up. When she joined Eadric and the others, the fyrd was already gathered. Long rows of pikemen and axmen stood facing away from the sunlight, westward.

"The line looks well in order," she observed, her stomach taut and sour with tension. Her voice held steady; she was proud of that. "Rhodri, the scouts?"

"Ready, Lady."

"Let's move out, then," she said, making the order hers. "Aelstan, uncover my banner."

It was his place and honor, as her blood-kin. His eyes were bright but serious as he shook the cloth free of its covering. Unfurled, the dragon of Wessex and the cross of Mercia gleamed gold in the morning sun. The fyrd followed it like a living beast, all the parts working together to make an unwieldy whole. Aethelflaed sat as tall as she could on her pony, her uncovered head shining as gold as her banner, so that the men might see her. *So every man knows that the Lady of the Mercians rides with him.*

The ground was beginning to slope upward beneath them when Rhodri suddenly raised a hand.

"What is it?" Aethelflaed said, riding forward.

"Spears," he told her, pointing. "Look."

"They're waiting at the outer edge of the forest," Eadric said. "No cover. We'll have the advantage if we can catch them out in the open like that."

"I wonder..." Aethelflaed said. "Surely Sihtric wouldn't choose his ground so badly? The man who organized the ambush at the ford should know better than that."

Rhodri shrugged. "One of my spies said this morning that Sihtric is ill. Oittir the sorcerer is in charge now."

"Still—Oittir was at the ford, too." She hesitated, then nodded. "One charge. Let's find out if this is a trap, and if it is, what sort."

Eadric frowned. "We'll lose our advantage."

"If it is an advantage," she pointed out. "Hold the main body of the fyrd in reserve until I say otherwise."

She stared at him until he nodded stiffly: she was right in this, and he knew it. Aethelred would have done the same. But it was at his order that the noise started, running up the line—battle cries, weapons clashing, horns blowing. Beside her, Rhodri called out in Welsh. The line quivered and surged forward, with Aelstan and her banner leading the way.

"Why aren't the Danes coming to meet us?" she shouted, struggling to keep her terrified pony under control.

"I don't know," Rhodri shouted back. "They have to answer this charge or we'll run right over them!"

The first tier of men reached the enemy line—and halted. An arm's length from the smallest trees, a shimmering, translucent circle appeared in the air; every man who touched it began to *change*. Before Aethelflaed's unbelieving gaze, arms grew into sides, legs grew together—a tall, leafy crown sprouted, with branches reaching for the sky.

"They're—they're trees!" she cried, her appalled eyes clinging to what had once been a young man, and her brother's son. The banner he had carried so proudly twisted free in the wind as if seeking release from such an unnatural grasp. "Oittir is turning them into trees!"

"Back!" Eadric shouted. "Back to the line!"

Terrified men scrambled away from their own comrades, tripping themselves in their haste. Now, at last, Sihtric's men reacted, and spears rained down on the fleeing and demoralized Mercians. Screams of horses and men mingled with strange battle cries and shouts of triumph.

"Eadric, get us out of spear range!" Aethelflaed said, jerking her reins free from his grasp. "Hold the line, I say!"

The earl was shouting at his men, ordering them to stand fast.

"It's a transformation spell," Rhodri said numbly, from her pony's flank. He was unhorsed, and his eyes were wild. "I've heard of such things. Earth-magic—"

"Never mind what kind of magic it is," Aethelflaed told him. "Do you know how we can stop it?"

"I—I don't—you must—royal blood of Mercia—"

He stopped, mouth hanging open. Aethelflaed almost hit him. "My nephew bears royal blood of Mercia, too, and it didn't help him!"

"It must be shed!" he cried. "Blood falling will awaken the land—"

"So. That way, is it?" She bit her lip, thinking as quickly and as savagely as she ever had in her life. Perhaps—but even if she could get herself across the circle, what then?

She had it. She thought. Almost, she quailed at her own conception. *I can't do that! Dear God, don't ask it of me—I can't order such a thing.* But she was the only one who had any chance ... "Eadric!"

"The fyrd is holding," the earl gasped, coming alongside her. "But not for long. The Norsemen are hiding among—among the trees. We cannot go forward—"

"We retreat no farther," Aethelflaed said through her teeth. "The enemy has the advantage only so long as we let him. If we can get through those trees, he loses it. Tell the men to stand in a line, axmen in front and pikemen just behind."

"The circle of magic—"

"I'll get them through the damned circle. Isn't that right, Rhodri? If I spill some of that royal blood of Mercia, I'll be protected. All I have to do is stay alive long enough to get across—and I don't think Oittir wants me dead." Would he understand? Part of it, perhaps. He looked sick.

"Lady Aethelflaed, the trees—are not truly trees. If you cut them, they, too, will bleed."

"I want the axmen in front," she said again, harshly.

Her words had reached Earl Eadric at last; he was horrified. "You mean to use axes on—but they're kin! We can't kill our own—"

"I ask no man to do what I will not do myself," she said. "Bring me an ax. When I give the signal—

the first stroke of the ax—they will do what must be done."

"Lady—you wouldn't—"

"Bring me an ax, or I'll use my dagger!"

The first ax they offered her was an ornate battle weapon; far too heavy. Aethelflaed sent it back. "Find me something I can lift—a hand ax, such as women use when chopping wood."

When it came, it was as ordinary as a hearthfire: a triangular blade fastened with leather thongs to a rough wooden haft. There were chips in the edge of the metal, and one of the thongs was loose. Swinging down from her pony to take the humble weapon, Aethelflaed hefted it in her right hand. "Yes, that will do. Stay here, all of you. Wait for my signal."

Turning, she walked away from them, out into the ensorcelled field. The first stroke of the ax—would they understand? She could only pray. *Lord God of Hosts, be with me now. Oittir* does *make mistakes. He was trapped into starting the attack early, at the ford. I can take him. If this works.*

As she took her first steps, the line quieted, even the raucous taunts of the enemy fading away. Behind her, she could sense her men shifting into the formation she had ordered, but she never looked back. She had to concentrate on where she was walking, not to stumble over the slain.

She was halfway across the field when the first spear came out of the forest at her; it went wide. She stopped briefly, raised the hand with the ax in it as if in salute, and kept walking. Things seemed unnaturally clear, as if the air had been new-washed by rain; wherever she looked, she saw the vivid browns and oranges of autumn.

The second spear was the one she had been hoping for; it caught her in the shoulder, so that she gasped and bent over the pain. *Flesh wound. Not bad, but the outer barb is stuck.* It would do. Steeling herself, she pulled the thing loose and tossed it aside with one motion. Blood dripped down the white of her tunic, staining the skirts. *Oittir will be expecting me to bleed as if my life depended on it. It does. Let's not disappoint him.*

She came to the circle of magic; paused. It glowed in front of her, wavering and evanescent as smoke. Drawing in a deep breath, she took one long stride across—to where the first of the transformed trees stood waiting for her, a sapling tangled in the banner of Mercia and Wessex.

The air shivered around her; beneath her feet the earth trembled and held still. Royal blood of Mercia dripped down her arm onto the rich loam of the battlefield. Grain would grow here, someday, she knew. Men would live in peace. . . .

Another step, and she was through, unchanged. Rhodri was right, it seemed—the land protected the blood of Mercia. For what it was worth. Behind her, the circle still stood, but a low moan lifted from among the trees, from where the Norsemen stood sheltering behind the transformed bodies of her own warriors. They had not believed she could cross, evidently. Now they knew better. The men of Mercia stirred all along the line, waiting, waiting . . . the trees rustled dryly in the autumn wind. She swallowed bile, thinking of them. *So far, so good. If only Oittir—*

The third spear came out of the shadows of the trees, and this one had her heart's blood on it. She knew as soon as she saw the shaft that she was dead—and then a flash of lightning engulfed the spear with fire, and it fell, ashes at her feet.

A voice rang out: Oittir's. "Stop, you fools! Don't kill her!"

She stopped, swaying slightly where she stood. *Ah. Good timing, Oittir.*

The sorcerer stepped out from under the trees, his eyes furious.

"Well, magician?" she said softly, *Talk to him. Don't let him think.* "Aren't you going to change me into something? Or, better yet, kill me? That would truly take the heart out of my men."

"You'd like that, wouldn't you," he said, contemptuously. "If I killed you, the earth itself would rise up against me and mine. That would break the spell, but a mere wounding will not. And since your foolish Christianity will not permit you to take your own life ... I saw your axmen moving forward, but they'll never cut *this* wood."

"So I assumed," Aethelflaed said. With her bloodied hand, she reached out to the sapling and steadied herself. One chance—she would only have one chance. "But you see, you're wrong. I never meant to die. I only meant to get close enough to do—this!"

She whirled, and threw the ax. It caught Oittir in the throat, his hands half raised in front of him. Blood spewed forth.

"Attack!" Aethelflaed, Lady of the Mercians, shouted, her voice ringing across the field. "Men of Mercia, defend your homes!"

In front of her, magicked trees were shaking as if in a strong wind, bending before it—crying out as they turned again into men. It was as she'd remembered, as she'd hoped—kill the magician, and you kill the magic, too. The Danes hiding among them gibbered with terror as they suddenly found themselves in the middle of an enemy army.

Sweet Jesus, thank you. Swaying, Aethelflaed closed her eyes to the confusion and slaughter, allowed herself to feel the pain in her wounded arm. *Blessed Lord ... defend ... the right. ...*

Knowing that she was doing something very foolish

even as she did it, she opened her arms to the blackness and slipped into a blessed unconsciousness.

She woke in her tent, in darkness. It was night—very late, long past sunset. Eadric sat by the tent flap, tending the fire.

She whispered: "Eadric . . ."

At once he was by her side. "Lady Aethelflaed, your woman has gone for more water. She said you would sleep—"

She didn't care where Gerda was, or what she was doing. "The battle?"

"The Norsemen are fled. Rhodri has set pickets around the camp, but there is no real need."

She closed her eyes, savoring the relief of it. "Did the trees—"

"All changed back and well, including your nephew. We will start for Eddisbury as soon as you are strong enough to travel."

"That will be tomorrow," she said faintly.

"I—yes. So I thought you would say." He paused, as if searching for the right words, but she already knew what he was about to ask her. And what she would say in response. "Lady, what would you have done if it hadn't worked? If Oittir hadn't come out to face you?"

"I would have ordered the trees cut down," the Lady of the Mercians said, feeling the grief of her words as far worse than the pain in her shoulder. *I would have ordered the slaughter of my own men, helpless and ensorcelled.* She opened her eyes, turned her head to face him. "Eddisbury must be reinforced, or Mercia will have no peace this year."

His eyes met hers gravely. "I could not have done that."

"It was not your place to do it," she told him, with a calm she did not—quite—feel. "It was mine."

There was a long moment of silence. Then he nodded, accepting it. Accepting her. "So be it," he said, and she knew that from now on he would follow her into Hell itself without question. "We'll leave at first light, then, or at your will. I'll tell the men."

Alone in the dark tent, she faced her final burden unafraid: Mercia was her land, and she would defend it. She could do it, she knew now, however hard and long the road; the men would follow her, if she was willing to lead. Nor would any other be able to lead them so well as she could. Edward might, eventually, or Aelstan if he lived to grow up—but for now, she was needed.

"Lady of the Mercians I am, and Lady of the Mercians I will be," she whispered, her words a promise to the future—to her dead husband and father, to her absent brother. To herself. *For as long as my life shall last.*

SUMMONING THE RIVER
by Deborah Wheeler

The Indus Valley, now Pakistan, enjoyed a peaceful society from about 4000 B.C.E. to about 1500 B.C.E. This long tradition of peace allowed these people to flourish, technically and socially, creating wondrous feats of engineering such as the Great Bath. This is in sharp contrast to so many other cultures where we see rapid technological advances only as a result of war pressures. The decline of the Indus Valley culture may have been caused by invading Aryan tribes or natural pressures, science had yet to fully determine what brought about their demise.

Deborah Wheeler's short fantasy has delighted DAW anthology readers for years with her many appearances in the *Sword and Sorceress* series, as well as in the *Darkover* anthologies. She has stories in *Witch Fantastic* and *Star Wars: Tales From Jabba's Palace*. Her fiction can also be found in various magazines such as *Fantasy and Science Fiction, Marion Zimmer Bradley's Fantasy Magazine,* and *Realms of Fantasy*. She also has two science fiction novels published, *Jaydium* and *Northlight*. Her third novel, *Collaborators,* is due out soon.

Despite the early hour, crowds surged through the lower city of Moenjo-Daro. Traders rubbed shoulders with weavers, camel drovers, and bronze-smiths. Sellers of incense, fish, and carved stone amulets called out their wares. The smells of sweet almond oil and spices mingled with steam arising from cauldrous of boiled rice to hang like a fragrant vapor in the air. An elephant, its harness decked with bells and its hide painted with spiral chalk patterns, shuffled through the crowd.

As she climbed the hill to the upper city, Amris of Banhara ran one hand over her face, leaving a smear of sweat and dirt, rust against her honey-dark skin. Sweat dampened her skirt of undyed cotton and made wet crescents under her bare breasts.

Amris' servant, Parva, trudged beside her, trying not to stare. Parva had never been this far from Banhara's hills before and she was a little nervous in so large a city. A half step back, their two bodyguards carried caskets of cinnamon bark and peppercorns.

Amris paused at the top of the hill to catch her breath. At the edges of the city, row after row of what had once been two-story houses now showed only the outlines of the top walls. Beyond them, the Indus River, source of Moenjo-Daro's richness, stretched flat and sullen.

"Perhaps such a big river always looks fat and lazy like that," Parva said in an uncertain voice.

Amris shivered in the morning heat. Her mother, the Priestess, had often told her, "All things end in their proper time, my inquisitive daughter. Animals, crops, people, even the most skillfully constructed buildings. But the River . . . *the River is a Mother who never dies.*"

Did she look now upon a dying River?

A Mother who never dies. . . .

Just a few days before Amris left for Moenjo-Daro, a fever had come upon her mother, bringing weakness and a strange brightening of the eyes. All the long miles from Banhara, Amris tried to make herself believe her mother would be all right and had almost succeeded. Until now . . .

They passed through the neat grid of the residential

areas, the shops and secondary bathhouses. Guards
stood at intersections, on watch against pickpockets.
Amris noticed the masons chipping bricks from the
walls of older houses to build new ones. The bricks
must have been wonderfully smooth and hard when
they were first fired, but uncounted seasons had rough-
ened their edges, giving them a moth-eaten look.

Moenjo-Daro, Jewel of the Indus Valley, might be
the center of the civilized world, but it was dying now,
drowning in mud and scavenging its own wreckage. If
Amris could not find the answers she sought here,
where else was there to turn?

After sending Parva and the bodyguards to pur-
chase goods for the return trip, precise weights for
measuring spices and gold, toys for the palace children, and indigo for dyeing cloth, Amris went on to
the hall of records and water engineering. A servant
escorted her to a room where three men, one of them
almost hairless with age, bent over a huge fired-clay
map of the city.

Amris offered her gifts to them and they sat beside
a window overlooking the central courtyard. The
chairs, inlaid with delicate designs in bone and shell,
were sought after from as far away as Sumer. Amris'
mother possessed one such chair.

After the traditional refreshments, barley-beer and
dates, Amris explained Banhara's problem. The Hakra
River, a minor tributary of the Indus, had changed
over the last decade, fallen so that only during the
seasonal floods did the water rise high enough to fill
the irrigation ditches. They'd tried digging deeper or
scooping water by hand. Even with the use of a
counterweighted bucket system, they couldn't dip
enough to keep their crops through the dry season.

One of the younger water-engineers suggested raising the water level by means of a dam. This had al-

ready been tried, but it had been swept away during the next rainy season. They discussed various methods of dam construction and what materials were locally available. Amris wondered if her sister Istara might not be right after all and the problem was not one which could be solved by any human efforts.

Istara was truly their mother's daughter and followed the ways of the Mother Goddess. Amris had never been able to give herself over so completely, which was why she abandoned her Priestess training for a post with the King's water-engineers. Even as a child, she was always asking questions. *Why do people die? Why is the white bull sacred? Why does it rain here and not there?* Too often, she felt as if she continually straddled two worlds, the spiritual and earthly, belonging truly to neither.

"In Banhara, we have too little water," she said thoughtfully, "and here you have too much."

"It's a matter of simple mechanical principles," the younger man said.

"Mechanics alone can't explain why the river has gone up in one place and down in another," said Amris. "They only tell us what to do to remedy the situation. They say nothing of where to turn when such attempts fail."

"The ancient records tell us," the elder said, "that in the days of our ancestors, we lived in loving harmony with the Mother of All Things. Our earthly Mother, the Priestess, sang to the River as to her beloved. And the River would rise or fall at her command. Perhaps, as we came to depend so much on the labor of our hands and minds, the old powers were lost, forgotten because they were no longer needed."

If they ever existed. . . . Amris thought.

A sultry breeze gusted through the open window. Sweat beaded Amris' upper lip. She wished, for the hundredth time, that she could believe as Istara did.

A young boy servant, bare to the waist and breathing heavily, appeared in the doorway. He wore a stone seal carved with the sigil of Moenjo-Daro's King.

"I bear a message for the Lady Amris," he said, between gulps of air. "It was given to me by a runner who arrived at the city gates just a few minutes ago. The watch captain bid me come at once."

Amris rose.

The boy straightened his shoulders and recited, "Lady Amris, you are to return to Banhara as soon as possible. Your mother lies gravely ill."

Amris felt the blood rush to her feet. She put out one hand to catch her balance against the chair. Parva uttered a soft cry.

The River is a Mother who never dies. . . .

"I will leave at once," someone said with her voice.

Amris and her retinue returned as they had come, in a light cart drawn by a single ox, young and strong. They left the Indus River Valley with its flooded rice paddies and stretches of swampy grasslands where the sharp-horned rhinoceros grazed. The land rose and grew drier. One night, they heard lions coughing in the distance, but they saw no trace of them the next day. All the while, Amris thought of her mother as she had last seen her, sitting in her inlaid chair beside the window, her graceful hands limp in her lap.

One afternoon, they met a handful of families coming south. The people spoke strangely and looked haggard. Their oxen were footsore, ribs pressing against lusterless coats. They made camp together and Amris shared out an extra portion of grain for the animals.

As they ate, the refugees told their story. They came from a village in the hills to the northwest. For some years now, traders across the mountain passes had brought word of a warlike tribe beyond the mountain passes. They rode in flimsy carts pulled by small, swift horses, or sometimes on the backs of the beasts themselves, shooting arrows into every living thing they passed.

"They came at midday, when we were working in the fields," the elder woman said. "They killed everyone who stood against them, burned our huts, slaughtered half our cattle. We are all of our village that survive."

"How can such a thing be?" said Amris. The Chariot People sounded so outlandish, so stupidly brutal, she would have thought them a tale to frighten disobedient children, except for the haunted eyes of the refugees.

The bodyguards clutched their spears and looked nervous. The worst dangers they knew on the road were bands of poorly armed thieves.

The next morning, before they parted ways, Amris took a few of the smaller toys and gave them to the hill people. The children's eyes brightened. They were tough, resilient. They would scavenge the mud-drowned houses of Moenjo-Daro for building bricks, work the fields, merge into the city. They would survive.

They climbed farther into the hills. Amris pushed the ox harder each day until it bellowed its complaints against the pace.

To distract herself from worry about her mother, Amris pondered what might be done to defend Banhara, should the Chariot People come. The valley cities had thick walls as protection against invasion from the sea, but not against a land attack. Sister cities had never, not in five centuries and more, made war upon one another. Banhara did not even have walls, for it was far enough upriver that pirates had never been a threat.

It might be possible to erect some sort of earth-

works. Amris would have to submit the matter to the
King, but she did not think anything they could raise
would do more than slow a determined assault. The
only barrier from the northwest was the Hakra.

Finally they reached the Hakra River. Amris shuddered to see how the water level had fallen even further. On the other side, the citadel of Banhara
gleamed like a pink pearl in the afternoon sun.

A picture flashed across Amris' mind—riders forcing their horses across the river, the water beaten to
a froth under galloping hooves, spears upraised, voices
roaring out the cries of hunting beasts, faces contorted
with ferocity.

She blinked and the image was gone, leaving a sick,
metallic taste in her mouth.

Sentries stood on either side of the ford, one man
and one woman. They carried spears tipped with finely
forged bronze. Men were stronger, but women had
subtlety and wisdom. So it was said, although Amris
had often remarked the presence of both strong
women and intelligent men.

"How fares my mother?" Amris asked the guard
on the near side.

"She still lives and asks for you every hour," the
woman said.

"While she was able, she sat at her window, watching this road," the man said.

Amris left Parva and the bodyguards to ease the ox
and cart across the ford. She went straight to the high
town, hurried through the central courtyard, and raced
up the stairs to the sleeping quarters. Her sandals
slapped on the fired-brick paving. The attendants
stepped back to let her pass. Amris' older sister, Istara, came forward. She was tall and strong as a dancer
from her years of training in the Priestess rites. She
wore a low-waisted skirt decorated with tiny shells and

bronze beads. Seeing the expression on her sister's face, Amris hesitated.

"The Goddess calls her more strongly every hour," Istara said.

The room was light and airy, cooled by the breezes from the hills. As a child, it had been Amris' favorite place. She remembered it as filled with things much more fascinating than her pottery toys, and the smells of sandalwood and cloves. Now what struck her was the sense of emptiness, as if no one had lived in the room for a long while. Her mother's chair had been drawn up next to the window and her bed moved into the far corner, deep in the shadows. The old woman who had been her mother's servant for as long as Amris could remember sat on the floor. Seeing Amris, she scrambled to her feet.

Amris fell on her knees beside the bed. The woman lying there seemed no more than a husk, bones arching beneath the dark, shriveled skin. Amris trembled. Behind her, Istara murmured a prayer.

Amris wondered if she'd come too late, perhaps only by a moment. She reached out, surprised at how soft the skin felt.

Eyes opened, moist and dark between the reddened lids. For a moment they stared, unfocused, then came to rest on her.

"Amris ..."

"Yes, Amma." Using the childhood name for her mother, Amris caught the hand which stirred on the covers and held it to her own cheek, touched it with her lips.

"... in time ..."

A sob welled in Amris' chest, but she held it in tight. "I'm here," she whispered. "I'm here."

The legends said that at certain times during a woman's life—when her own mother brought her into the world, when she first lay with a man in holy joy, when she stood on the brink of her own death—then she might see the world with the Goddess' own wisdom.

"Banhara is in danger!" Amris cried. "The river falls, parching our land and leaving us open to the invaders from beyond the mountains. What can save us?"

But a film had already passed over the luminous dark eyes. The lids, like dried flower petals, closed. The hand in Amris' grew dense as clay. The rib cage with its shrunken breasts shivered.

"The river ... Summon ... the river ..."

Confusion, hot and pungent, shot through Amris. *Summon the river? What does that mean? Stand on the bank and shout its name? Beseech the Goddess to send more rain? Build the proposed dam?*

Istara reached out and drew the hand from Amris', then carefully arranged it over the other. Amris rocked back on her heels. The room turned gray and chill.

For a moment, Amris dared not speak. Her breath caught in a sob. She felt as if she stood on the brink of an abyss, that the slightest misstep would send her and all Banhara plunging into darkness. Her belly tightened around a core of ice. When she stood up, her eyes were dry.

Through the next days, Amris moved through the city as if in a dream. Dutifully, she reported the suggestions of the Moenjo-Daro engineers to the King and told him of the refugees on the road. The King listened gravely, as was his way, asked her advice about the dam, and granted her leave from her water duties to mourn her mother.

Of the funeral itself, Amris remembered very little. It was as if a stranger had taken her place, walked in her sandals. Someone else's voice sang the prayers to the Heavenly Mother to welcome her servant.

Amris saw little of her sister during those first days. Istara was busy with the funeral details and ceremonial rites, then with her own new responsibilities. Even as life returned to its normal rhythms, Istara's Priestesshood set them apart. They might discuss the dam project or the management of the family enclave, but in the end, part of Istara had been sealed to the Goddess and Her mysteries. She had been called. And Amris could not follow her.

Something had frozen within Amris. She felt it keenly at first, an unbleeding wound. Then, as the days melted by and the pain endured, it became part of her.

As for the mysterious words of her dying mother . . .

She discussed them briefly with Istara one evening as they sat on the roof, watching the sun grow red and swollen as it neared the western horizon. Tonight, no twilight breeze blew from the north, sweetening the passage to darkness. A blanket of hot, stale air pressed down on Banhara.

"Summon the river?" Istara looked thoughtful, drawing her brows into a single straight line. "Perhaps, so close to the Mother of All Things, she was already wandering in time, back to the ages when Priestess-queens had that gift."

Amris had clung to those last moments, turning them over in her memory as if they were precious gems, peering into their incomprehensible depths. "If only I could ask her what she meant!"

"Ask the dead?" Istara made the sign of the sacred bull, whose strength stood between darkness and life.

"No, no, of course not," Amris said quickly. Too quickly. It was the heat and the still, heavy air that put such thoughts into her mind, nothing more.

Days wore on into weeks. Banhara settled into a new routine. A site for the dam was selected. At the

King's command, ordinary citizens now drilled with the city guards in the park where couples had once strolled and children played games with hoops and balls.

In the mornings, Amris took a shallow-bottomed boat downriver to inspect the progress on the dam. Little remained of the once-lush rice fields. They had given way to wheat and barley, which could survive with less water.

Far across the hills, on the other side of the headwaters of the Indus itself and through the mountain passes, she felt a new wind rising, slicing through the stagnant heat of the valley cities.

If her mother's dying words had not been ravings born of a fever, if she had known something of those old, secret powers. . . .

Her mother no longer dwelt in the house of the living. What if . . . what if it were possible to seek her in the house of the dead?

A caravan of traders from the northwest hills, leading gaunt, heavily laden camels, arrived in Banhara, bringing word of new raids by the Chariot People. With them rode a seer, reputed to have mystical abilities.

Amris summoned the seer to a private audience in her own rooms. His beard lay in a mat over breasts like flaps of leather and he wore a kilt of trail-strained wool, layered like overlapping petals. He claimed to come from Sumer, from the ancient city of Ur, said that he knew many things, how to make a man fall into a sleep like death, how to tell the coming of a storm, or the number of bees in a swarm. Most of these, Amris suspected, were either bragging or bits of simple lore the seer had gathered from his travels.

Amris poured barley-beer, according to the custom of hospitality, and offered the seer dates dusted with powdered almonds. The man ate greedily, his bright eyes fixed on her.

"I know the answer you seek, Holy One," the seer said.

"Do not call me Holy One. I am not a Priestess of the Mother."

"In Sumer, we pray to different gods."

Amris had heard tales of how the Sumerian god Enlil destroyed an entire city, trampling mighty Agade into dust. "And do these gods know many things?"

"So it is said." Black eyes glittered like the crushed wings of a beetle. "Even how to visit the house of the dead."

After the seer left, Amris sat with her face in her hands. A heaviness of heart filled her, a sickness like the aftertaste of her vision of the invading horde. That, and the lump in her breast, the eyes dry with unshed tears.

Suddenly she became aware of a movement at the top of the ladder. She looked up. Istara peered down at her. The rooftop had always been Istara's favorite place to hide when she was a child.

Istara climbed down the ladder. Amris caught the gleam of tear runnels down her sister's cheeks.

"Amris—Amris, you must not do it!"

"Why not?" A sudden wild mood swept over Amris, hot and dangerous. She could say anything, do anything, *be* anything. "Has the Mother forbidden it?"

"No, there is no mention of it in Her teachings." Istara drew herself up to her full height. Her breasts shone like polished bronze in the torchlight. "But who has traveled to the house of the dead and come back to tell of it?"

"Someone must have . . ." Now Amris was less certain. ". . . Or the old man would not have known of it."

"Superstition! Tales told to amuse the simple!" Istara took a step, gesturing emphatically. "Amris, you have always been so sensible. How can you ever consider such a thing? More than likely, there is poison in the seer's draught, so that you will never return to accuse him!"

Amris got to her feet. "Do you speak now as Priestess ... or as sister?"

"I am a Priestess of the Mother and I say, in Her name, you must not do this thing." Istara's cheeks went dusky in the flickering orange light. Her breasts rose and fell. "And I say also as a sister, I would not lose you, too."

Amris' throat clenched. The room blurred. Once she would have gone to her sister and found comfort in her arms, as when they were children together. Now she could only say stiffly, "I will think on what you have said."

Amris made her way down the corridor to the room which had been her mother's and was now Istara's. The room seemed a world unto itself, mysterious and silent. Istara was absent, perhaps on some official Priestess duty, perhaps beseeching the Goddess to grant her younger sister wisdom. The old attendant snored gently on her pallet.

Amris moved toward her mother's bed. . . .

And for a moment saw a shape there, rounded silver in the moonlight streaming through the roof opening. Not the sunken body she had last seen, the withered thread barely holding spirit to flesh, but the curves of hip and breast, moving now, the ribs arching upward, the shoulder, so strong and graceful, the masses of braided ebony hair. The face turned toward hers, the eyes, so full of light, the dark lips parting in a smile of delight as they so often had, every line imprinted on her child's heart. . . .

Amma!

Amris rushed forward just as the light shifted, a cloud across the moon perhaps. The image vanished.

She flung herself down beside the bed, fingers twisting in the pillow-cloth, searching for the faded scent, lungs gulping air, chest aching, splitting, something inside her tearing open. . . .

No!

Bitterness filled Amris like ashes. She sat up and rubbed her aching eyes. Istara could sit alone beneath the stars and weep. Those first few weeks, Amris had tried and found no comfort there. Her heart was a desert, barren of tears.

Nor would she find her mother in the land of the dark Sumerian gods. The seer's promise was nothing but poisoned smoke, a momentary hope. She could not make herself believe in it. But she still might take a small measure of comfort from the talisman he described.

Soundlessly, she crept across the room to the heavy wooden chest. It had been her mother's, and her mother's mother's before her. The air inside held the lingering fragrance of the cedarwood, carried on the backs of camels from the lands beyond Babylon. She pushed aside the skirts and ceremonial cape and took out a steatite box. Inside were her mother's favorite pieces of jewelry, beads of lapis, ivory ornaments carved in the shape of elephants, bronze rings and bracelets. A leather thong held her mother's personal seal of fine-grained chert, a rhinoceros at the sacred trough. Several long white hairs tangled in the loop.

Amris pulled one of the hairs free, then yanked another from her own head. In the moonlight, one glimmered like fine silver, the other like onyx. She twisted them together and knotted them around the seal she wore around her own neck. The idea that

some part of her mother now entwined with some part
of herself gave her a curious, fluttery feeling.

She replaced the clothing in the chest and went to
the bed, but could not sleep. The seal weighed on her
chest, heavier with every breath, and yet she dared
not take it off. Rather than risk disturbing the attendant, she went outside.

The street was quiet and almost empty, except for
the night watch. An acolyte met her at the entrance
and went to light fresh incense. Amris went into the
private room reserved for her family and disrobed.
Alone, she approached the Great Bath. The pool of
water stretched before her like a mirror. Amris had
never seen it so still, almost expectant. The glassy surface reflected everything.

She waded in, descending the steps. The fired-brick
tiles felt slick under her feet. Somewhere in the re-
cessed shadows, the acolyte began intoning the opening chant of the cleansing ritual.

*Purify my spirit with your wisdom, O Compassionate
Mother. Lift this sickness from my heart. Lend me the
strength to do what I must. . . .*

She moved deeper into the pool. It swirled around
her knees, her thighs and belly. She shivered, although
the water was warm from the day's heat. When she
reached the last step, the water reached her collar-
bones. She grasped the seal in both hands, lest the
entwined hairs slip free. She closed her eyes and
continued.

Incense wafted through the air. Other smells arose
from the water itself, asphalt and gypsum mortar. As
she went on, Amris became aware of another, deeper
fragrance. It surrounded her, penetrated her, heady
and dizzying. The knot of pain in her chest throbbed.

Lift this sickness from my heart. . . .

Something hot and sharp shot through her as if
she'd been stung. Her eyes jerked open. She looked

out on the Hakra River, the shallow ford. Banharans
clustered on the near shore, some carrying spears and
knives. Others held bows and arrows. Their eyes
looked bruised, lost. On the other side, dust churned
up in billows, pierced by pennants bearing strange
emblems.

In eerie silence, a mass of men spurred their horses
forward, a wall of spears and flashing helmets. She
could not see their faces, but their battle fever raced
along her nerves. Wild-eyed and laced with lather, the
horses plunged into the river.

Rise, rise, O river!

But the river did not rise. Sluggish with silt, the
water scattered under the horses' hooves.

The first riders scrambled onto the far bank. Banhara's people rushed forward to meet them. A guard
drew back his spear and took aim at a rider's chest
an instant before he was struck down. His body disappeared beneath a horse's spinning hooves. Amris
screamed, but no sound came from her lungs.

All around her, white-garbed Banharans struggled
and fell, cut down by arrows or impaled on spears.
The mud turned dark with their blood. Horses reared
and wheeled, riders slashed with long bronze knives,
all in the same heart-numbing silence. Amris snatched
up a fallen spear and spun around. A horseman spotted her and clapped his heels against his mount's red-
streaked side. His helmet made him look more demon
than human. Below the curving metal, his eyes flashed
crimson. He lowered his spear.

Amris braced herself and took aim. She hurled her
spear with all her strength. The next instant, something huge knocked her off her feet. She fell, her legs
crushed under the body of a falling horse. The horse
thrashed, throwing its head, and lashed out with its
legs. She struggled to roll free. The horse shuddered

and she saw that its belly had been ripped open. Her body went shivering cold.

She glanced up, a moment before a second rider's spear pierced her chest.

She opened her eyes to blackness. Not the wondrous, living dark of the night sky, but an utter absence of light and form. Slowly the rage and terror of the battle seeped away. She felt warmer. Her knotted muscles relaxed. She felt as if she were a child once more, curled in her mother's lap, her cheek pressed against the softness of her mother's body. Gentle fingers stroked her hair. She heard a voice, distorted and breathy but unmistakable. Her eyes focused on a filmy wisp hovering in the darkness, seeking the lines of the familiar face, now softened and radiant.

"Amris my baby, Amris my treasure, Amris my daughter. . . ."

"Amma?"

Amris reached out with one hand. There was nothing to touch, only the faintest suggestion of light in a shape that might have been her mother's.

"Amris . . ." The ghostly face steadied and Amris could see her eyes clearly. Closer and closer they came, until Amris felt the silken whisper of her mother's lips on her brow.

Then Amris stood once more in the pool of the Great Bath, clutching the seal with its intertwined hairs. The acolyte droned on, finishing the chant. Amris licked her lips and tasted salt. The next moment her feet found the stairs at the far end and she climbed out of the water. Numbly, she allowed the acolyte to wrap her skirt around her. She hardly saw the streets as she passed through the sleeping town.

Amris sat up, heart suddenly pounding. Daylight streamed through the window. Her sleep had been

deep and dreamless. She wore the same rumpled skirt
from last night. The seal, still damp, hung between
her breasts.

She scrambled from her bed, grabbed a cotton square,
and knotted it around her breasts. Parva stood outside
the door with a cluster of household servants, who
looked dazed and grim.

"The Chariot People! They've come!"

Amris paused at the edge of the hill to scan the
land beyond the river. Broad and flat, the Hakra shimmered in the dawning light. Lazy ripples broke the
reflections into swirls of pearl and apricot light. Even
the muddy banks took on a glow, as if brushed with
gold.

There, to the northwest, she spotted a vast, boiling
blackness.

So many . . . Compassionate Mother preserve us!

Istara and her acolytes would be in the temple of
the Great Bath, chanting for divine protection for
Banhara. In the beating of her heart, Amris felt their
frenzied prayers. But sacred words alone would not
stop the oncoming horde. Istara would die in her temple and Amris in the river mud, all the same.

The lower city churned with confusion, people scur-
rying in every direction, calling out, babies crying,
dogs yipping. Guard captains shouted for order. A
bright metallic smell rose along with the dust.

The King's commanders organized the archers into
groups, placed to shoot over the spearmen. Amris,
scanning the forces, noticed the gray heads scattered
in the crowd and the awkward way many held their
weapons.

The King himself, surrounded by the finest of his
guards, strode to the forefront. He held a spear bound
with rings of gold. His beard and hair shone like
curled silver. The clatter and tumult died and a silence
blanketed the shore. Amris caught the sound of gal-

loping horses. It grew to a roar, pierced by shrill, ulu-
lating cries. The next instant, the dark mass came
clearly into view. Spear points glittered in its smoky
heart like gems. The sky turned from brassy to clear.

The invaders slowed at the riverbank. Mounted riders surged ahead of brightly painted carts. Horses
reared and whinnied as the riders spurred them forward, splashing into the shallows.

"Hold steady!" The King's voice rose above the din.
"Wait for them to come in range! And may the Goddess guide your arrows!"

Amris took a step forward, as if the river itself
pulled her. A guard made as if to stop her.

O Mother! O River of Life! Help us now!

The shallows barely reached her calves. The mud
yielded under her weight as if it no longer cared who
stepped on it. She searched the depths and saw only
swirled green-brown water, heavy with silt. She didn't
know what she expected—an oracular voice ringing
within her mind? Some mystical symbol written on
the waters?

But there was nothing.

The first riders were well into the river now. Their
headdresses and saddle ornaments shone bright red
and blue in the sunlight. The horses scrambled
through the deepest, chest-high portion and began
the charge.

There was very little time left now. The first chariots
began the crossing. Their archers had drawn their
bows. Soon Amris would truly join her mother in the
house of the dead.

Amris felt the imprint of her mother's last kiss on
her brow. The memory of her vision filled her. She
remembered the strength of her mother's arms around
her, the softness of the breasts where she had suckled,
the intimacy of her mother's scent.

No comfort came to her as she stood ankle-deep in

the river. Her vision blurred. Pain brimmed up in her heart until it could hold no more. Something burst open, swept through her, each wave rising higher, tearing her, flooding all her heart and being.

She gave herself over to the hot bright pain, to every moment of her mother's love that would never come again. Gone now, gone forever, leaving a wound which could never be healed. All her questions vanished, flecks of ash on the torrent of her grief. Not until this moment did she truly feel what she had lost.

Her body rocked with sobs. Tears coursed down her cheeks, unchecked. She did not care if the Chariot People saw them. She had lost everything—mother, sister, city—she who could summon only salt tears against their spears and arrows.

Tears streamed down her face and soaked the cotton knotted over her heart. More and more came, falling unchecked into the river.

Another presence, immense and powerful, filled her. It grew until she towered over the river plain, until Banhara and the northern invaders shrank to the size of children's toys. She mourned the dying, silt-choked cities, drowning in the River which had once brought them life, the haunted eyes of the refugee children, the withered fields.

Ah! Moenjo-Daro and her fair daughters! Pearl of the River, gone forever!

Woman and Goddess, mother and daughter, she wept for the world's pain, for the passing of an era, as surely she wept for her own.

Something splashed against Amris' knees. Startled, she looked down.

The river, which had pooled sluggishly around her ankles, was rising in waves, surging upward, as if to meet her tears. It was no longer placid and green, but silver-bright, laced with foam. Now it swirled around her thighs, every moment reaching higher.

As she wept, mingling salt water with fresh, she reached out one hand and gathered the river's power. Just as she had opened the doors to her own grief, now she opened the floodgates of the river.

Waves crashed toward the invaders, leaping higher than the points of their spears. A wall of water hit the first riders. Horses screamed and reared as the waves rolled over them. Some fell over backward, to disappear instantly.

Beyond her control now, the water surged higher and higher, engulfing the chariots on the far bank. The river roared. Men screamed. Those at the rear of the horde tried to turn their panic-stricken horses. The waters swept them away.

When there was no more weeping in her, the flood subsided. She stood alone in the shallows. Behind her, she heard murmurs of awe. The few remaining invaders wheeled their chariots and fled. But in that moment, Amris saw the Chariot People as they truly were, not demon-crazed monsters but men who lived and bled and died.

The river plain sparkled, cleansed. She felt emptied and full, exhausted and powerful beyond imagining. And charged with a vision beyond the moment. Even without the invasion of the Chariot People, the Indus Valley cities and all their glory had passed. She knew that now, felt it in the very texture of her bones. As great Moenjo-Daro sank into the mud, so would tiny Banhara fade and be forgotten. A new wind had come sweeping down from the mountain passes.

Amris looked at the clear river water and something deep inside grew clear also. A vision spread out like a river before her, mothers suckling their babies and children splashing in the shallows, lovers embracing, women singing as they stooped to plant rice seedlings, a holy man dipping his hands in a stream. . . .

Rivers would rise and cities crumble, giving way to

the fierce barbarian energy, but Banhara's people, like the resilient hill farmers, would find a way to survive.

Only the outer form changes, Amris thought with her mother's voice. Istara, with all her knowledge and her blind devotion to the Priestess' mysteries, could never have seen that truth or opened herself to its power.

Amris curled her fingers around her seal and felt the tight, intertwined hairs. Mother and daughter ... life and death. The death of people and of cities, but never of the magic of the heart.

This, this shall endure forever.

FANTASY ANTHOLOGIES

☐ **ALIEN PREGNANT BY ELVIS**　　　　　　　　　UE2610—$4.9☐
　　Esther M. Friesner & Martin H. Greenberg, editors

Imagination-grabbing tales that could have come straight out of the supermark☐ tabloid headlines. It's all the "news" that's not fit to print!

☐ **ANCIENT ENCHANTRESSES**　　　　　　　　　UE2677—$5.5☐
　　Kathleen M. Massie-Ferch, Martin H. Greenberg, & Richard Gilliam, editor☐

Here are timeless works about those most fascinating and dangerous women—Ancient Enchantresses.

☐ **CASTLE FANTASTIC**　　　　　　　　　　　　UE2686—$5.9☐
　　John DeChancie & Martin H. Greenberg, editors

Fifteen of fantasy's finest lead us on some of the most unforgettable of cast☐ adventures.

☐ **HEAVEN SENT**　　　　　　　　　　　　　　UE2656—$5.5☐
　　Peter Crowther, editor

Enjoy eighteen unforgettable encounters with those guardians of the mort☐ realm—the angels.

☐ **WARRIOR ENCHANTRESSES**　　　　　　　　UE2690—$5.5☐
　　Kathleen M. Massie-Ferch & Martin H. Greenberg, editors

Some of fantasy's top writers present stories of women gifted—for good or ill☐ with powers of both sword and spell.

☐ **WEIRD TALES FROM SHAKESPEARE**　　　　UE2605—$4.9☐
　　Katharine Kerr & Martin H. Greenberg, editors

Consider this the alternate Shakespeare, and explore both the life and works ☐ the Bard himself.

Melanie Rawn

EXILES
☐ **THE RUINS OF AMBRAI: Book 1**   UE2668—$5.99
☐ **THE RUINS OF AMBRAI: Book 1** (hardcover)   UE2619—$20.95

Three Mageborn sisters bound together by ties of their ancient Blood Line are forced to take their stands on opposing sides of a conflict between two powerful schools of magic. Together, the sisters will fight their own private war, and the victors will determine whether or not the Wild Magic and the Wraithen-beasts are once again loosed to wreak havoc upon their world.

THE DRAGON PRINCE NOVELS
☐ **DRAGON PRINCE : Book 1**   UE2450—$6.99
☐ **THE STAR SCROLL: Book 2**   UE2349—$6.99
☐ **SUNRUNNER'S FIRE: Book 3**   UE2403—$5.99

THE DRAGON STAR NOVELS
☐ **STRONGHOLD: Book 1**   UE2482—$5.99
☐ **STRONGHOLD: Book 1** (hardcover)   UE2440—$21.95
☐ **THE DRAGON TOKEN: Book 2**   UE2542—$5.99
☐ **SKYBOWL: Book 3**   UE2595—$6.99
☐ **SKYBOWL: Book 3** (hardcover)   UE2541—$22.00
